T0147968

PLANTANIMUS

PLANTANIMUS
Return to Mars

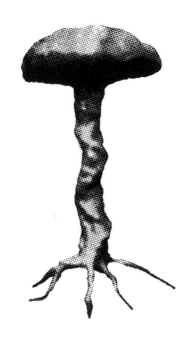

Joseph M. Armillas

iUniverse, Inc.
Bloomington

PLANTANIMUS
RETURN TO MARS

iUniverse books may be ordered through booksellers or by contacting:

iUniverse
1663 Liberty Drive
Bloomington, IN 47403
www.iuniverse.com
1-800-Authors (1-800-288-4677)

ISBN: 978-1-4759-6868-2 (sc)
ISBN: 978-1-4759-6869-9 (hc)
ISBN: 978-1-4759-6870-5 (e)

Library of Congress Control Number: 2013900777

Printed in the United States of America

iUniverse rev. date: 1/28/2013

Acknowledgements

To Barbara Markay, for her love, help and support and for the many, many hours of proof reading. To my new friend, retired Air Force officer and aerospace engineer, Dr. Jerry D. Kendrick, for his valuable contribution as a technical and scientific advisor and for all the hours of additional proofreading, excellent suggestions and ideas. To Glenda Dietz, may she rest in peace, for her recommendation to change a small but very important element of this book's plot.

"Occasionally the tree of Liberty must be watered with the blood of Patriots and Tyrants."—Thomas Jefferson

Table of Contents

*Prologue

The story of Plantanimus "Awakening" begins in the 27th century in the year 2619, four hundred and eighty six years after the "Dark Period", an environmental holocaust that nearly wipes out the entire human race on Earth in the late 21st century.

After humanity's "2nd Renaissance" in the late 23rd century, mankind resumes the course of progress and eventually colonizes the Moon and Mars.

In the year 2485 a pandemic breaks out on Mars caused by a previously unknown virus in the ground water supply. The virus, called MV Recessive, kills every single adult on the planet but spares all Martian born children under the age of sixteen. Scientists eventually develop a genetically manipulated vaccine and inoculate the entire population of the solar system.

The pandemic brings about a conflict that culminates in a revolutionary war between the mother planet and its two territorial possessions, the Moon and Mars. As had occurred with colonies of patron nations on Earth many times in the past, Mars and the Moon eventually declare independence from the mother planet in the year 2486 and secede. The Moon and Mars become independent states and Earth has no choice but to grudgingly accept their independence.

A few decades after gaining its sovereignty, Mars becomes the industrial and technical powerhouse of the solar system, a situation that

Earth resents. Unbeknownst to all, the MV Recessive vaccine causes a mutation in the DNA structure of the young Martian survivors of the pandemic. However the populations of Earth and the Moon are not similarly affected. The genetic mutation gives rise to a new generation of Martians with extraordinary abilities. From 2485 on, an unusual amount of psychically gifted children begin appearing in the Martian population. The average I.Q. of these children is unusually high.

The main character of the story is Kelem Rogeston, a member of that generation of children born after the pandemic. He is a descendant of an illustrious family of Martian scientists and explorers that were instrumental in the colonization and development of Mars dating back to the 23rd century. In 2633, at age sixteen, Kelem is a genius with an immeasurable I.Q., already working on his doctorate in Interdimensional Physics and slowly becoming aware of his psychic powers.

Since the age of thirteen, Kelem has been experiencing a bizarre and unsettling recurring dream every night. In the dream he finds himself in a strange forest populated by enormous trees that tower several hundred meters above him. The trunks of these bizarre looking trees have golden bark and emit strange vibrations that sound like music. Searching for an answer to his problem, he seeks out famed physician and psychiatrist Professor Nicolas Alfano, one of Mars' eminent medical figures.

Nicolas Alfano is the leader of a secret but humane and ethical Martian society, called The Brotherhood of the Light. The Brotherhood is a one hundred and forty four year old organization made up of Martian psychics who formed the group more than a century before to protect Mars from the Phalanx, an evil, fascist society from Earth, bent on ruling the solar system under its fanatical right wing, authoritarian dogma. The organization now controls many aspects of the Terran government and plans to take over the planet and install one of their own as leader of Earth in order to accomplish their goals. One of the organization's main goals is to repossess Mars as a colony of Earth.

When Nicolas Alfano, a skilled mind reader meets sixteen year old Kelem Rogeston, the future CEO of the Mars Mining Company, the largest most powerful corporation in the solar system, he realizes that Kelem is the most talented psychic that he's ever encountered. The boy is capable of sensing other people's emotions and can read minds at long distances.

A Martian prophet named Thorgen Kutmeier, also a member of The Brotherhood of the Light, has foretold of the coming of a new race of human beings many years before. He refers to these new humans as the Sixth Root Race. Nicolas Alfano is convinced that Kelem is the first member of that new race, the next step in the evolution of the human species. He takes Kelem under his wing to guide him and train him so that he can develop his psychic powers to their full potential.

A few months after Nicolas Alfano meets Kelem, a murder and theft is commited at the Stephen Hawking Center, a government sponsored scientific research facility on Mars that is the most advanced in the solar system. The scientists at the facility have been experimenting with a new technology called *n'time*. They have built a device designed to transport an object from a specific location in three dimensional space, into other dimensions and back again to three dimensional space, but at a different location. In theory, this interdimensional engine will allow mankind to travel a distance of several light years in mere hours, instead of centuries or even millennia.

Kelem becomes involved in the investigation by happenstance and due to his amazing intellect and psychic ability, he helps solve the murder and subsequent theft of the research data. He also prevents the destruction of a large part of Mars when he has a powerful dream in which he "sees" the Phalanx spy insert a virus in the Stephen Hawking Center's computer designed to cause the *n'time* generator to self-destruct. Kelem skillfully disables the virus and the planet is saved. Later the authorities discover that the fascist Terran group is responsible for the attempt to steal the technology.

Afterwards he is invited to join the scientists at the Stephen Hawking Center as a member of the research team. He soon becomes the leader of the project and takes over the development of the technology, advancing its progress with amazing speed. Kelem eventually perfects the technology and designs an *n'time* ship capable of interstellar travel.

Soon after turning eighteen, Kelem finds love with Carlatta Del Mar, the beautiful and exotic daughter of the Terran ambassador to Mars, Don Francisco Del Mar. Their love affair is short lived when the Phalanx interferes and kidnaps Carlatta and her whole family and imprisons them on Earth.

After Kelem travels to Earth and fails to rescue Carlatta and her family from the clutches of the Phalanx, he returns to Mars and completes the construction of the Solar Nations, the *n'time* ship that he designed. Together with a crew of one hundred, brokenhearted Kelem leaves Mars on the first voyage that will take humans beyond the confines of the solar system.

The ship meets with disaster and most of the crew perishes in a tragic accident, leaving Kelem and one of his best friends, Ndugu Nabole, stranded on Plantanimus, an Earth-like alien planet once ruled by a mighty race of humanoids, located many thousands of light years from the human solar system. On Plantanimus, he encounters the Dreamers, an ancient race of sentient plants that help Kelem expand his psychic powers and teach him the true nature of consciousness. The Dreamers are the same "trees" that Kelem has been dreaming about every night since his thirteenth birthday.

To ease his loneliness from the heartbreak of losing Carlatta Del Mar, the Dreamers create a part plant, part animal facsimile of her. At first Kelem rejects the "plantanimal" because she reminds him of the real Carlatta. But eventually Kelem accepts the facsimile who he names Anima and develops a platonic and spiritual relationship with her.

Six years after arriving on Plantanimus, an alien species (the Kren) land on Plantanimus. The Kren are an ancient and peaceful insect species who live in gigantic hive spaceships capable of faster than light travel. The Kren Queen Mother offers to return Kelem and Ndugu to Mars, their home planet.

Kelem is conflicted about leaving Plantanimus after growing so close to the Dreamers and Anima but decides to go back to Mars to bear witness for his friend Ndugu who, being a former Terran, could be blamed for the fate of the Solar Nations expedition if he returns without Kelem.

Promising to return someday, Kelem leaves Mars with a heavy heart hoping that the Kren will be able to return him to Plantanimus, the place that has become his real home.

Chapter I

The Voyage Home

September 20ᵗʰ, 2644

Kelem woke up and remembered where he was. He raised himself, swung his long legs over and sat on the edge of his bunk, his bare feet touching the deck plates of the Kren ship. He could feel the vibration of the ship's mighty engines through the soles of his feet and wished that these vibrations were instead those emitted by the bodies of the Dreamers. Behind him to the left of his bunk was a circular port window displaying a myriad of stars whizzing by in elongated strips of light. The spectacle cast a dim shadow play on the opposite bulkhead next to the pressure door of the cabin. He looked at the time display on his wrist comp lying on the metallic night table to the right of the bunk, and saw that it was 11:00 AM.

He hadn't worn a wrist comp in the last six years but soon he'd be re-entering the world of humans where time and schedules were necessary. He had slumbered for more than twelve hours, much longer than his usual sleep cycle. For the last week he had taken to sleeping unusually long hours, perhaps because he was depressed and saddened by his departure from Plantanimus. He felt listless and bored but most of all, he felt unmotivated. A kind of emotional, mental paralysis had taken over his mind and he suddenly wished that his old friend and mentor, Professor Nicholas Alfano, were there to help him out of this depressed state of mind. He realized how much he missed Anima, his soul mate, and the deep psychic connection he had with those mighty

1

sentient plants he'd come to know as the Dreamers. His decision to leave Plantanimus and return to the solar system had been made solely on behalf of his dear friend Ndugu Nabole. Other than himself, Ndugu was the only survivor of the ill-fated Solar Nations expedition. It was the first time in history that man had ventured away from his home and into the cosmos, and tragically, it had all ended in disaster. The loss of the rest of the ship's complement, ninety eight crew members in all, still weighed heavily on his mind.

The two of them had been stranded for six long years on an alien planet now known to them as Plantanimus. They had resigned themselves to spend the remainder of their lives on that world. But when the Kren, a peaceful insectoid species, fortuitously showed up on Plantanimus and offered to return them home, Kelem had to make the painful decision to accompany Ndugu back to Mars.

Ndugu was the only member of the crew that was of Terran origin, and even though he'd been granted Martian citizenship before the ship left Mars, Kelem knew that he'd likely be blamed, at least in part, for the fate of the expedition. Earth and Mars had been on the brink of war when the Solar Nations left on its maiden voyage and Kelem knew that if Ndugu returned to Mars on his own, the shadow of suspicion would fall on him. Additionally, the Phalanx had a price on his head, so returning to Earth was not an option.

By the time the Solar Nations left Mars six years before, The Phalanx had pretty much taken over Earth's government and was instrumental in creating the tension between the two planets that was leading to war. Kelem prayed and hoped that a war between the two planets never began and wondered what had taken place during the past six years.

On Plantanimus, Kelem had found the peace and tranquility that had eluded him all of his young life. His connection to the Dreamers, and especially Anima, had changed his concept of reality. Anima, who in time became his soul mate, had been the most difficult for him to leave behind. The Queen Mother, who ruled the Kren hive, had promised Kelem that Harry, the worker drone that she'd assigned to return the two of them back to Mars in a Kren ship, would wait for Kelem for six months at the edge of the solar system and then take him back to his beloved Plantanimus.

The Kren were a peaceful species but after communicating

telepathically with Kelem and thus learning about the human psyche, the Queen Mother decided, perhaps wisely, that humanity at large was not ready to meet the Kren, who were as tall as a man and whose resemblance to certain cricket/locust insect species on Earth would most likely create fear and panic in humans.

Kelem stood up and stretched his long frame and stepped into the small latrine next to his bunk. After relieving himself and washing his face with cold water he grabbed his flight suit and headed for the control room located five decks above the sleeping quarters.

On his way to the control room he stopped at the large cargo hold where one of the two landers from the Solar Nations that had survived the disaster, sat secured to the deck. He went inside and walked up to one of the six Lectrosleep chambers on the ship where Ndugu lay in suspended animation and checked on him to make sure that his vitals were normal. The small screen above the chamber displayed heartbeat, blood pressure, body chemistry and brain activity. All functions were operating according to normal parameters. Through the window Kelem could see Ndugu's wide nose dilating slowly every few seconds every time he took a breath. The African looked like he was simply asleep but Kelem knew that a series of subcutaneous nano probes were controlling his body functions and had rendered much of his brain inactive.

A human under Lectrosleep state was as close to being in a coma as was medically safe. The nanos were continuously feeding the body with concentrated nutritional enzymes that maintained muscle tone as well as eliminating urine and fecal matter and the accumulation of toxins. Upon entering Lectrosleep the probes automatically filled the stomach with an inert gel like material that prevented the organ from shrinking while under Lectrosleep. Twenty three days from now, the chamber would begin removing all artificial substances from Ndugu's body and revitalizing his organs prior to awakening. The only side effects of Lectrosleep were slight confusion and difficulty focusing the eyes for a few minutes.

Harry, the Kren drone that the Mother Queen assigned to take the two humans back to Earth, had told Kelem and Ndugu that the voyage to their solar system would take twelve months. They drew lots and Ndugu got to go under Lectrosleep first. There was plenty of air and food to last both men for the entire voyage, but considering the spare amenities of the Kren ship and the length of the trip, it was decided that each man would spend every other month in Lectrosleep. The one staying awake would monitor the other's vital functions.

Satisfied that his friend was in good shape he continued climbing the narrow stairways that led to the ship's control room. The one thing that the Kren had not considered when they refitted their ship to carry Kelem and Ndugu back to Mars, was the width of the stairways that were wide enough to fit the Kren's small narrow bodies perfectly well, but not those of humans who were physically much wider than the insectoids. Still, except for a little discomfort, both Kelem and Ndugu were able to go up and down the stairs.

When Kelem reached the control room he saw that Harry was not there and went down two decks to what he and Ndugu had dubbed the "rec-room". The large space contained several monitor stations for all the vital systems of the ship, and Kelem had discovered that Harry seemed to spend most of his time there. When the door opened, Harry, who was standing by one of the stations, turned around.

"You are awake, Kelem. Did you have a good sleep period?" the Kren asked through his voice box.

"Yes, Harry, I slept well. Actually, I slept too well. Twelve hours is too long a time for me to stay in bed."

"I can synthesize a liquid stimulant that will guarantee that you'll stay awake for hours," the Kren offered, gesturing with two of his four arms.

"No thanks, Harry, my oversleeping is due to my mental condition, not tiredness," Kelem informed him listlessly.

"As you know, we Kren do not sleep although we hibernate. Do you care to explain how a mental condition can render a human unconscious for more than twelve hours?" the Kren said looking at Kelem through his iridescent compound eyes. The insectoid was still trying to understand the concept of sleep in humans.

"Humans normally sleep eight hours or less, but when a human is emotionally distraught, depressed or saddened by circumstances, one of the effects of such condition is sometimes extended sleep periods. It's one of the ways that the human mind copes with certain types of stress."

"I am sorry, Kelem, but the concept of human emotions is still baffling to me. I have read the files on human behavior that you gave me a few days ago, and although I understand the meaning of the words, I have no way to conceptualize what an emotion is. Perhaps in time I will."

"I understand, Harry, but don't you miss your Queen? I know you told me that she changed your brain and that you no longer hear her voice in your head, so don't you feel a sense of emptiness from being separate from the hive, or being lost?" Kelem asked with curiosity.

"I do feel different, Kelem. Perhaps what I am experiencing is an emotion, but if I am, it does not seem to affect me the way that emotions appear to affect you and Ndugu. From everything that I've learned about human psychology so far, emotions are often unpleasant. Perhaps we Kren are lucky in that regard."

"Perhaps you're right, Harry. There have been many times in my life when I wished that I didn't have emotions, and right now is one of those times," Kelem replied quietly.

"You and Ndugu asked that I not hibernate during the voyage so that I can keep both of you from experiencing loneliness when each one of you is awake. Is not my company enough to keep you from experiencing strong emotional states?" the Kren asked naïvely.

"I know that this is confusing, Harry, and I apologize. Humans need companionship to keep from going insane or experiencing delusional states. However, emotions strong or otherwise, are part of the normal makeup of our personalities. Your agreeing to stay conscious during the voyage to keep each one of us company is of great help. Unfortunately humans cannot help but experience emotions."

"How can I enhance the quality of the time you spend with me?" Harry asked.

"Hmmm… Humans need entertainment and unfortunately you Kren don't seem to need that type of activity. But, we humans like to do things such as playing games and watching fictional dramas and things like that. If you're willing, I can teach you to play card games. Such things will stimulate my mind and keep me from thinking about Anima and the Dreamers. Would you be willing to learn to play some games?"

"As you know, Mother asked me to learn all I could regarding human behavior. Your request falls under the parameters of my mission. When do we begin?"

"I'll go back down to the lander and bring up a deck of cards. I'll teach you how to play poker!" Kelem said, suddenly feeling a bit of excitement.

After Kelem taught the insectoid the basics of poker and played a few games with Harry winning and losing some, the Kren appeared to become obsessed with card games. After he mastered other card games he asked Kelem to teach him new games. Kelem decided to teach him how to play chess. After two weeks of several chess games in which Harry had become an expert, Kelem decided to show him how to play video games. By the time Kelem's watch had come to an end, Harry had learned just about every game that was in the lander's database. The Kren had become a gaming junkie.

"Ndugu, watch out for Harry, he'll drive you crazy if you teach him any new games. I spent the last thirty days teaching him every possible game that I knew, as well as every video game that was in the computer's database and he's mastered everything! He seems to have a never-ending capacity to assimilate new information. So be careful what you teach him, otherwise you won't get much sleep," Kelem warned Ndugu once he'd come out of the fog of Lectrosleep.

"Really? You mean he wakes you up and doesn't let you to go back to sleep once you're up?" Ndugu asked somewhat worried.

"No, he doesn't wake me up or prevent me from going back to sleep, but whenever he sees me now, all he wants to do is play games," Kelem replied with concern. I know the Kren claim not to have any emotions, but Harry's become positively obsessive about gameplaying. It's as if a part of his brain has been activated that Kren drones normally don't use.

"Listen, man, I'm not much for card games or video games for that matter. I'll just tell him that and he'll leave me alone. I'll probably stay in my cabin reading some books and playing my keyboard. I don't need a lot of company so Harry won't see much of me during the next thirty days," Ndugu said with confidence.

"I hope so Ndugu. But I'm telling you, don't teach him anything new," Kelem warned as he lay down on his Lectrosleep chamber.

When Kelem came out of Lectrosleep during the next watch,

Ndugu surprised him by performing a Nigerian wedding dance that he had taught Harry to play on his portable keyboard. Kelem was dumbfounded as he watched Harry and Ndugu perform the dance with Harry playing the keyboard using all four of his hands while Ndugu danced. Later that day, the Kren played some piano pieces by Beethoven, Mozart and Hayden. With four hands and sixteen fingers Harry had quickly become an expert pianist.

During the next three watches Kelem became more and more amazed by the transformation in Harry's personality. Although the voice box that translated his thoughts into human speech had a monotonous mechanical sound, his conversation had definitely gained new dimensions of expression. He now was saying things like "I can't wait until I play you this next piece," the insectoid would say to Kelem regarding a new piano piece that he just learned. Or, "I had no idea that music was so interesting."

By the end of the voyage the Kren had mastered every possible game that Kelem had taught him. He had also learned all the popular music that Ndugu had taught him and the entire classical repertoire that was in the lander's database. In less than twelve months he had assimilated every bit of information that was in the lander's computers which contained several petabytes of data. Kelem wondered what would happen if Harry was let loose in one of Earth's or Mars' many libraries. Or how many degrees and doctorates he would earn if he attended Latonga City University on Mars. And although Harry still maintained that he didn't understand human emotions, Kelem was sure that he was displaying humanlike behavior.

Exactly one year from the date the ship left Plantanimus, Harry disengaged the faster than light engines and decelerated the massive ship to a relative crawl. When they reached the orbit of Pluto, Kelem began searching for a small planet or planetessimal that could hide the large Kren ship. After a while they located a misshapen lump of rock big enough to hide the huge sphere. They secured the ship in a large canyon that faced away from the interior of the solar system and then Harry shut the ship's chemical engines off.

Kelem asked Harry what he would do while he and Ndugu were gone. The Kren informed him that he would go into hibernation. Kelem could wake him up when he returned from Mars. Harry would wait for

Kelem for six months. If he didn't show up at that time, Harry would return to the hive. Kelem assured him that he'd definitely be back in less than six months. After Harry shut down all main systems, Kelem and Ndugu boarded the lander and departed for Mars. The Kren entered his cylindrical shaped hibernation chamber, wrapped his six limbs around his thorax and went into a deep state of unconsciousness.

As Kelem maneuvered the lander away from the ship and into open space, he wondered what kind of reception he and Ndugu would get when they returned home. He was sure that family and friends would be thrilled to see him and Ndugu, believing that they had perished during the voyage. He suspected that many things had changed in the six years since the Solar Nations departed. He realized that the Mars Mining Company now belonged to his childhood friend Billy Chong. Before departing on the Solar Nations mission, Kelem had made out a will leaving ownership of the company to Billy in case something went wrong. But Kelem had never cared about being the wealthiest man in the solar system, and aside from being reunited with family and friends, his main objective now was to be there when the Martian government debriefed him and Ndugu. Once he was sure that Ndugu would not be blamed or held responsible for any aspect of the solar Nations' ill-fated voyage, he planned to go back to Plantanimus with Harry.

He wondered what the current state of *n'time* technology was, now that he'd been gone for six years. He hoped that his colleagues at the Stephen Hawking Center had managed to build a new working model of the *n'time* generator and that new ships had been constructed. If not, he knew that he'd be under a tremendous amount of pressure to remain on Mars to supervise the development of a new ship.

However, nothing would deter him from going back to Plantanimus, and although many would be sad and disappointed to see him go, he knew that his destiny was with his beloved Anima. But now as he thought this, he realized he and Ndugu had a problem. How much of what had happened in the last six years should they tell the authorities?

Kelem did not want Plantanimus to become known or colonized by humans. Fortunately, the Kren lived in hive ships and were not interested in planetary settlement. But once the word got out to humans about its existence, hordes of people might descend upon the planet and surely ruin it. Perhaps he was being selfish, but he considered the

Dreamers and Anima to be sacred. In the far future, humanity might be ready to appreciate the wonders of Plantanimus and not desecrate it with war and commercialism, but certainly not now.

He and Ndugu had to tell the Martian Government something! They had to come up with a plausible explanation of where and how they had managed to survive for the last six years. The experts and the scientists would know that after the Solar Nations had been destroyed it would have been impossible for Kelem and Ndugu to have survived on one of the ship's landers for all that time. So obviously they must have managed to survive somewhere with breathable air and a source of food and water such as a planet. Another problem was to explain how he and Ndugu had made it back to the solar system without an *n'time* ship. In spite of Harry's modifications to the lander's engines, everyone would know that the ship was incapable of traveling fast enough to have covered so many light years' distance in the six years they had been gone.

Harry had made it plain that the Kren did not wish to make contact with humanity at large for the foreseeable future. He'd told Kelem that the Kren mother thought it would be unwise for the Kren to meet humans at this point in their development. Kelem knew that Harry was right.

So then, what to do?

As the lander entered the outer edge of the solar system they discussed the problem.

"Man, that is a can of worms! I really don't know what to say. You're the genius, Kelem. I think that you'll have to figure this one out by yourself. I'll go along with whatever you say," Ndugu added laughing.

"It's not funny, Ndugu. Whatever we come up with has to make sense, so we better get our story straight," Kelem said a little annoyed.

"I'm sorry man, I didn't mean to laugh. You're right, this is a serious problem! What do you suggest?" Ndugu said becoming serious.

"So far everything I've come up with sounds ludicrous, but the most plausible idea goes like this: when the Solar Nations caught fire, you and I managed to get into the lander and as the ship exploded we were thrown off with great momentum riding a 'time distortion wave' caused by the failing *n'time* generator. Fortunately for us the wave pushed us in the direction of the solar system. We managed to survive on the emergency rations that were already in the lander, and we've been taking turns in the Lectrosleep chamber a month at a time. During the voyage I modified the engines and once we entered the solar system, I brought us back to Mars."

"A time distortion wave, Kelem? Is such a thing possible?" Ndugu asked, unsure that the Martian government and the scientists at the Stephen Hawking Center would believe such a thing.

"It's theoretically possible. We have to justify somehow, having traveled so many light years' distance in such a short time," Kelem explained.

"What about everyone else on the ship, what happened to them?" Ndugu asked. "The loss of ninety eight lives is going to be the toughest thing for people to accept," he pointed out.

"When the explosion occurred, you and I happened to be in the rear of the ship inspecting the fuel tanks. We managed to get into the lander and exit the ship as the Solar Nations destroyed itself. Everyone else perished in the accident," Kelem explained.

"Well, it's a little flimsy but if we both stick to the story we should be all right," Ndugu said, somewhat uncertain.

"I know it's terrible! We'll have to face the families of all those crewmembers and it's going to be tough having to tell them lies about how their loved ones died. Particularly when it comes to Shana, Francisco, Mercedes, Chani and Briggs," Kelem said with regret.

"Their deaths were far more tragic than those of the other ninety three crewmembers. I think that, in particular, Shana's parents would feel worse if they learned how she led the other four survivors of the original accident to their untimely demise after we reached Plantanimus. It's better that they believe that their relatives died quickly as the others did," Ndugu said solemnly.

"You're right. Even though it's just another lie, at least it's a better one," Kelem agreed.

"Cripes, I hope they believe us! Otherwise, we might end up in jail. Especially if one of your mind reading Brotherhood friends discovers our web of lies," Ndugu said worriedly.

"Not to worry. The Brotherhood would never take part in exposing one of their members, particularly during a government inquiry. I do plan to tell the board of directors the complete story. No one in the organization would betray us," Kelem said with certainty.

"I hope you're right my friend," Ndugu replied, feeling uncomfortable with the idea. Even though Kelem had confessed to Ndugu that he was a mind reading psychic early on during their time on Plantanimus, and that he belonged to a secret Martian society named The Brotherhood of the Light, whose members were all powerful psychics, Ndugu still hadn't made up his mind whether the Brotherhood could be trusted to keep the true account of their adventures on Plantanimus from the rest of the world.

"Of all of our concerns, that is the one that I'm worried about the least." Kelem assured Ndugu.

"Even if nothing goes wrong, it's going to be a tough few weeks until the inquiry is over."

"We'll get through this, I promise you," Kelem said as he piloted the lander near the orbit of Neptune.

The two men fell quiet, each one dealing with his own thoughts and emotions. Through the control cabin's window the faint glow of the sun shining dimly in the distance, gave them comfort knowing that they were near home. In five or six days they'd be arriving on Mars and regardless of the situation, both were sure they'd be welcomed back. Ndugu was looking forward to some female company after six long years of bachelorhood and Kelem was hoping that both uncle Nardo and Aunt Maggie, his adoptive parents, would still be alive.

Harry's modifications to the lander's engines were working wonders. Kelem could not help but be impressed with the Kren's technical skills. They were traveling faster now than any of the passenger ships in the Martian commercial fleet that ferried people and cargo between Mars and Earth. Harry's improvements had increased the lander's engine capacity by more than five hundred percent.

As they went farther into the solar system, Kelem began to feel a sense of excitement about coming home after so many years. He planned to return to Plantanimus after spending time with his family and friends, but he had to admit that it was going to be a wonderful, heartwarming experience to be among his fellow Martians once again.

For his part, Ndugu believed that once Kelem returned to Mars and became reacquainted with friends and family, his desire to return to

Plantanimus would diminish or hopefully, disappear altogether. During the six years the two of them spent on Plantanimus, Ndugu never gave up hope of returning to human civilization, and unlike Kelem who became so psychologically and emotionally connected to the Dreamers and in particular Anima, Ndugu never felt any emotional connection to the planet or its alien inhabitants. He didn't want to lose his best friend, especially after having shared so many adventures. He was sure that he would never meet a more remarkable person than Kelem Rogeston.

CHAPTER 2

Time Out Of Time

September 23rd, 2644

Three days later, the ship was traveling faster than when they entered the solar system. So prodigious was their speed that the lander was already passing by Saturn. To their right, Titan, Saturn's biggest moon was slowly drifting by. The gravitational pull of the gas giant was giving the ship an additional slingshot assist on its way to Mars. Kelem was still amazed that the lander, which had been designed only to ferry crews from the Solar Nations to a planet under exploration, could travel so fast considering the original design of its engines.

In less than four days the ship would pass the asteroid belt and less than a day later they'd be in Mars orbit. Kelem had directed the ship's radio antenna towards Mars. Now that they had traveled several million miles, they were beginning to pick up clear audio transmissions from the two planets as well as the Moon. The first thing that came through the control cabin's speakers was a music program uninterrupted by advertising. Kelem's heart raced with excitement upon hearing the first sounds of civilization in over six years. Both men sat in their flight chairs smiling at each other anticipating their return to their homeland.

After a while, Kelem reached for the frequency selector and moved the dial to find a different station. Soon the slightly distorted dulcet voice of an announcer was heard giving the sports news for the week.

"… and in the tri-foil-wing quarterfinals for the interplanetary championships, the Terran Red Robins beat the Martian Avengers seven to three. This victory puts the Terrans in second place for the semifinals of 2659 which will be played on Terra two weeks from now. Earth is anticipating the beginning of the 320th Olympiads. And just as in the last fourteen years, Mars continues boycotting the games. These will be the most glorious games in the history of the Olympics. It's too bad that Mars refuses to participate in such an honorable tradition that dates back to the ancient Greek civilization. This is Langston Furier transmitting from Mars Colony. Thank you for listening. Stay tuned for my colleague Samuel Franklin reporting on the tennis championships in Europe...."

"Did I hear the man say something about the semifinals of 2659?" Ndugu asked confused.

"That's what I heard too but that can't be right. And another thing, he said he was transmitting from Mars colony. Mars has not been a colony for over one hundred and forty six years. We must be listening to the audio of a drama-vid," Kelem replied furrowing his brow.

"And what's this about the Olympics? As far as I know Mars has never participated in the Terran Olympics," Ndugu remarked.

"That's right! Martians could never compete against Terrans in athletics because of the difference in gravity between the two planets, and furthermore, I've never heard of Terrans participating in tri-foil games. As I said before, this transmission must be from a drama-vid."

Kelem now turned the dial and chose another station. The new program was also from Mars and it was another news broadcast. Over the next few minutes Kelem and Ndugu became more worried and confused as the announcer stated that the date was October 5th, 2659.

"Cripes Kelem! This can't possibly be another drama-vid. What the hell's going on? The year is 2644. Why is everyone saying that it's 2659?"

Kelem's mind was refusing to accept the notion that his and Ndugu's timeline was somehow out of sync with that of the solar system. "Could it be possible that twenty one years had passed since the Solar Nations departed from Mars instead of the six years that they had been stranded on Plantanimus?" Kelem thought furiously as the hair on the back of his neck stood on end at the thought. Kelem rubbed his hands nervously and stared into the cabin's instruments, his mind reeling, as he came to grips with the fact that he and Ndugu had apparently been gone for twenty one years.

"What's wrong Kelem?" Ndugu asked, noticing his friend's change of mood.

"I'm not sure Ndugu, but I think it's possible that the accident that damaged the Solar Nations caused the *n'time* generator to push the ship into the future."

"How can that be? I thought that your 'time distortion wave' phenomenon was just a theoretical excuse for our six year absence. The *n'time* generator is not a time machine! There must be an explanation for all this. The year can't possibly be 2659!"

Kelem reached for his wrist comp and began doing calculations. Ndugu sat next to him watching Kelem's fingers quickly enter data into the comp with great concentration. After several anxious minutes Kelem sat back in his chair, sighed and then closed his eyes.

"What is it?" Ndugu asked, feeling a sense of dread.

"I'm afraid that it's quite probable that we're several years out of sync with this timeline. And no, you are wrong, the *n'time* generator is actually a time machine although until now, I didn't think it was possible for the device to rematerialize the ship to a new location that much out of sync from its original timeline," Kelem concluded rubbing his chin pensively.

"I'm no Kelem Rogeston, but everything that I know about the *n'time* generator, tells me that its only purpose and ability is to push mass from our three dimensions into others and then bring it back into the three-dimensional world at a different location, but only by a few millionths of a second in the future. You once told me that the computers that run the device had multiple safeguards to prevent the atomic mass of the ship from reassembling itself out of sync with the original time signature from where it started its interdimensional jump," Ndugu argued.

"That's true, Ndugu. But as you well know, I argued mightily with President Martinez against taking that first mission so soon after its initial trial run. And now I remember that one of the main reasons for me wanting to delay the mission was the fact that I was concerned with the efficiency of the safeguards put in place to prevent exactly what has actually happened. The mathematics involved are so complicated that

I knew that Shana and I needed at least six months to figure out how to improve the software codes that controlled the _n'time_ generator's chronological actuators," Kelem replied, feeling angry with himself for not having had the courage to demand more time before obeying President Martinez' order to go on that first official mission. "The fire that destroyed the section of the ship where the _n'time_ generator was located must have caused the actuators to go out of sync with the timeline by a factor of several thousand percent."

"Shit! Twenty one years? God, everything has changed!" Ndugu said, wondering what had transpired in the last two decades. He looked at Kelem sitting next to him deep in emotional turmoil and realized that Kelem's beloved aunt and uncle were most likely dead by now. When they left Mars, Bernardo Salas and his wife Maggie were in their late seventies. He didn't feel too bad for himself since he didn't have any living relatives on Mars, and his wife and daughter had been murdered on Earth by the Phalanx a long time ago. The friends and acquaintances that he made during his short time on Mars were not close ones. Ndugu could make new friends and acquaintances. But Kelem had deep familial roots on Mars, having lived most of his adult life there. For him, the twenty one years of time difference would have a much bigger impact.

They continued listening to broadcasts, and several hours later they confirmed without doubt that the year was indeed 2659. Kelem shut the engines off and let the ship continue traveling on its own inertia. He and Ndugu had to discuss the significance of this new development. According to all the broadcasts, Mars had somehow become a colony of Earth once again. The news was very troubling and Kelem was sure that the dreaded Phalanx had obviously succeeded in subverting the Terran government and subsequently bringing about the re-conquest of Mars.

"Kelem, what a fucking mess! What are we going to do?" Ndugu said feeling depressed.

"If, as I suspect, the Phalanx is behind all this, then you and I are screwed. I'm sure that even after all these years, those bastards would like nothing better than to get their hands on us," Kelem said feeling frustrated and angry.

"Man, what a cruel twist of fate. We finally manage to return home only to find out that we're now considered criminals with a price on our heads."

"I'm sure you're right Ndugu. But for me in a way, the situation is more flexible. I'm sure that by now both Uncle Nardo and Aunt Maggie have passed away. But I wonder what has become of Nicholas, Billy and his wife Verena. Nicolas would be in his seventies by now and hopefully still alive if the Phalanx hasn't arrested or, worse, murdered him. I will miss him, Billy and Verena the most if I return to Plantanimus now." Kelem mused suddenly aware of their predicament.

"Not for me Kelem. Going back to Plantanimus is not an option, even if the Phalanx has taken over the solar system. We can turn around now and go back to the Kren ship, then you can go back to Plantanimus and I'll pilot the lander and take my chances on Mars," Ndugu said sourly.

"No Way, Ndugu. I wouldn't leave you in the lurch. I couldn't in good conscience abandon you here in the solar system wondering if you're likely to become a prisoner or worse," Kelem said with conviction.

"I appreciate your loyalty, Kelem, though misguided. I, on the other hand, would be mortified if you were arrested along with me, when you could have remained safe by returning to Plantanimus and spending the rest of your life in peace."

"Fine, so we care about each other, but we can't have it both ways. Wouldn't you prefer to live your life to a ripe old age rather than take a chance and end up in some horrible Phalanx dungeon tortured to death?" Kelem asked.

"I know it's hard for you to conceive of me refusing to go back to Plantanimus and live the rest of my life there when things look so bad here. But, Kelem, I am not like you. I think I'd rather die than have to spend the rest of my life in that place, away from civilization and, most of all, women," Ndugu said smiling. "I admire your spirituality Kelem, but you're a bit of an ascetic and I think that you would probably do well in a monastery living as a monk," Ndugu suggested with humor.

"You're probably right," Kelem admitted, laughing and recognizing that his friend wasn't too far off the mark. "Still, we're both between a rock and a hard place and we have to come up with a way to resolve our dilemma."

"There's always the chance that even though Earth has repossessed Mars, the Phalanx might not have been the main force behind the takeover. It's even possible that the Phalanx is no longer as influential in Terran politics as it was when we left," Ndugu suggested.

"I doubt it, Ndugu. The Phalanx has been in existence for over one hundred and forty six years plus twenty one, counting for the time difference," Kelem said with chagrin. "Montenegro Industries has been responsible for the election of many Terran politicians over time and has had all those politicians in their pocket for years. The Montenegro and the Voltanieu families have been planning their vendetta against Mars for over a century. I'm one hundred percent certain that the Phalanx now controls the entire solar system," Kelem said with certainty as a sense of doom enveloped his mind.

Something else was bothering Kelem. During one of the first broadcasts that he and Ndugu had listened to, he recalled that the announcer had mentioned that the tri-foil semifinals would be played on Earth two weeks from now. The Terran team, The Red Robins, had just won the championship a day or two before on Mars. But then the announcer had said that the team would be participating in the semifinals taking place on Earth within two weeks. Kelem knew that the only way the team could have scheduled the semifinals within two weeks of having won the quarterfinals on Mars, was by means of having an *n'time* vessel at their disposal. That meant that *n'time* technology was now in the hands of the Terrans. It made sense! Once the Terrans took over Mars it was logical to assume that they would have forced the Martians to construct *n'time* vessels for them. Instinctively, Kelem looked out into space expecting a Terran military spaceship to re-materialize in front of the lander at any moment.

Ndugu, noticing Kelem's intense concentration, asked him what was on his mind.

"It's too horrible to contemplate, but I'm guessing that the Terrans now have *n'time* ships."

"Damn! How can that be? The Solar Nations failed because of the fact that it was a new unproven technology. Mars would've done anything to prevent the Terrans from acquiring the technology!" Ndugu exclaimed with alarm.

"Yes. But don't forget it's been twenty one years here in the solar system. Many things could have happened to facilitate the Terrans acquiring the knowledge to build *n'time* ships," Kelem suggested.

"Crap!" Ndugu blurted out while looking out of the cabin's window, suddenly fearing the sight of a Terran vessel appearing in front of them, just as Kelem had done a few minutes before.

Both men had the same idea at the same time and Kelem reached for the ship's controls. "We are too exposed out here in open space. We've just passed Saturn. I'm going to turn around and put the lander in orbit around Titan while we figure this out," Kelem said as he restarted the ship's engines.

A few hours later they were nearing the gas giant. As Titan, Saturn's largest moon, came into view, Kelem slowed down the ship and let the moon pull the lander toward it with its gravitational force. An hour later, and with some additional thrusting, the lander was in orbit around the moon.

"We're safe for now. Out here someone would have to be specifically looking for a small ship like ours," Kelem said unstrapping himself from the pilot's flight chair as he floated in the cabin. He had shut off the gravity plating to conserve energy.

"Why don't you get some sleep, Kelem? You've been awake for over eighteen hours. I'll take the first watch and when you wake up we can discuss our next move."

"You're right, Ndugu, I'm going to get some sleep," Kelem said as he pushed himself toward the bunks at the rear of the lander.

Kelem strapped himself to a bunk and quickly fell asleep. Ndugu remained in the front of the cabin keeping an eye on things. But after only two hours his eyelids became heavy and before he knew it, he was asleep. Ndugu had also been awake for almost as many hours as Kelem and the bad news had worn him out.

While the two men slumbered in the gentle caress of zero gravity, a small blip appeared on the ship's radar screen. Over the next hour, the blip moved closer and closer to the lander's position.

Soon a large shadow darkened the control room's window.

CHAPTER 3

The Rusty Bucket

A series of loud noises startled Kelem out of a deep sleep. The lander was shaking and Kelem unstrapped himself from his bunk and pushed his body into the control room where he was met with Ndugu's panicked facial expression.

"It's the goddamn Phalanx, they've found us!" Ndugu said, as he unstrapped himself from the copilot's chair.

Kelem drifted forward and pressed his face right up to the control room's window to see what was happening outside. He twisted around until he faced upwards relative to the lander's floor and saw the outline of a large asteroid herder floating directly above the lander.

"It's an asteroid herder!" Kelem said with puzzlement. "What the hell is a herder doing this far out from the belt?"

"Did you say an asteroid herder?" Ndugu asked equally confused.

"Yes, and its attaching magnetic grappling hooks to our hull!" Kelem was bewildered. Asteroid herders had no purpose this far out from the belt.

Ndugu pushed himself towards the rear of the lander and then came back with two pulse guns.

"I don't think that two pulse handguns are going to do us any good, Ndugu," Kelem said doubtfully.

"What? Are you going to let those bastards take us without a fight?" Ndugu replied agitated.

Just as Kelem was about to answer, the lander began moving as the herder's grappling hooks began reeling the lander towards its collection basket.

"Crap! What's going on?" Ndugu said, holding onto a bulkhead.

"They are reeling us in just like they would an asteroid," Kelem answered as he strained his neck to catch a better view of the herder. As the ship entered the acre size collection basket, his heart jumped when he saw the Mars Mining Company's insignia on the side of the main bridge.

"It's an MMC Herder!" Kelem said with a mixture of relief and concern.

"That doesn't mean that they're friendly, especially if the Phalanx is running the company now," Ndugu said tightening the grip on his pulse gun.

"Well, whoever they are, they mean to board us. If the Phalanx is in control of this herder they're not going to come in here with flowers and champagne," Kelem said, putting his gun away.

"Dammit! We should have gone back to Harry's ship. This is my fault, I'm sorry Kelem!" Ndugu exclaimed apologetically.

Kelem smiled and put his hand on his friend's shoulder. "Nonsense, I could have turned the lander around and gotten back to Harry's ship without you asking me to. It's just bad luck Ndugu. We would have run into trouble eventually."

The lander's radio came alive. "To the crew inside the ship, prepare to be boarded!" a gruff voice announced, sounding none too friendly.

"MMC Herder, this is Kelem Rogeston, captain of the Solar Nations. Why are you assaulting us?" Kelem replied pushing the talkback button.

"Let us board you or we'll destroy you!" the gruff voice demanded.

Suddenly the lander came to an abrupt stop as the outer hull of the ship came in contact with the herder's giant woven metal net. As Kelem and Ndugu held their breath, they heard the sound of a boarding tube making contact with the lander's hatch. The sound of someone banging a heavy metallic object against the lander's door let them know that their captors meant business.

"Put your gun away Ndugu. These men will be armed and unless you want to die in a firefight, I suggest you stow it now," Kelem advised.

Looking miserable, Ndugu complied and Kelem threw the guns into a storage compartment. Kelem floated into the control room and pressed the button that would open the lander's hatch.

As the three sided Duraminium pressure door slid open, four dirty, bearded, disheveled men entered the lander bristling with weapons. Aside from pulse rifles and guns, they had knives, brass knuckles and clubs strapped to their bodies. They rushed in and quickly grabbed Kelem and Ndugu, tied their hands behind their backs and dragged them into the boarding tube and then brought them to the herder's cargo hold.

Kelem and Ndugu had to hold their breath as these men stunk with the kind of body odor that came from months without contact with soap and water. The interior of the vessel looked rundown and it was obvious that maintenance was not a top priority on this ship. Martian miners were a tough bunch but they always took pride in their ships and kept them in top condition. In contrast, this ship looked as if it was going to fall apart at any moment.

The tallest, meanest looking one of the bunch approached Kelem and looked at him with hatred in his eyes. Kelem read the man and was taken aback by the vitriolic, violent emotions emanating from his mind.

"Where's your mothership, you son of a bitch!" the man yelled, grabbing Kelem by the throat and choking him.

"I don't know what you're talking about," Kelem answered struggling for air.

Without warning the man's fist reared up and punched Kelem in the face. "You fucking Terran piece of crap! You're going to tell me where your mothership is or I'm going to beat you to a bloody pulp!" the man screamed, his foul breath further assaulting his senses.

Aside from the time when Kelem had nearly died in Botswana, Africa at the hands of three local thugs eight years before, Kelem had never been hit in the face or been involved in a fist fight. Kelem struggled with the wave of pain issuing from his face. Right now he was calling upon all his strength and the training he'd received from his mentors, Nicholas Alfano and Jorgen Kutmeier. These men were irate beyond measure and it was clear that they thought that he and Ndugu were Terrans. Amidst his pain and fear Kelem realized that they were not in the hands of the Phalanx, but had been taken prisoner by some sort of Martian group at odds with Earth.

Risking another assault on his face Kelem spoke again. "I know you think that we're Terrans but we're not! We are Martians! My name is Kelem Rogeston. I used to be the owner of the Mars Mining Company," Kelem said, trying to overcome a wave of nausea.

The man laughed hysterically and the other three joined him. Apparently Kelem had said something very funny. The man stopped laughing and a second later punched Kelem in the stomach bending him over in agony. "That's very funny you piece of crap! I hadn't laughed so hard in months!" the man said, looking genuinely amused. "Just for that I'm not going to kill you right away, instead I'm going to introduce you to my three friends right here," he said pointing to the others. "They're going to tenderize you a little bit," he added menacingly.

The man let go of Kelem then went over to where Ndugu was and without saying a word, began to beat him. The other three approached Kelem and pummeled him without mercy.

With his hands tied behind his back, Kelem had no way of protecting himself from the kicks and punches of his attackers. Soon he was knocked unconscious. In the zero gravity of the herder's cargo hold, Kelem and Ndugu's blood droplets floated and mixed together. Ndugu being physically much tougher than Kelem fought back, surprising the first man that had interrogated Kelem. After a few punches Ndugu hit the man on the forehead with his own head, nearly knocking him out. Surprised, the man reeled back and just as he was about to resume the beating, a voice was heard coming from the cargohold's intercom.

"That's enough! You can't interrogate a dead person, Molson!" a gruff voice commanded angrily.

"I was just having a little fun Rusty, that's all! I'll put these two in the brig and let them think about things for a bit," Molson replied, rubbing his forehead while glaring at Ndugu. The four then carried Kelem's unconscious body and dragged Ndugu into the bowels of the herder. They threw their prisoners into a small chamber with no light inside. After they slammed the pressure door closed, Ndugu moved toward Kelem as he floated near him in the zero gravity. Ndugu was in pain but he'd been in plenty of fights in his life. Now he was worried for Kelem who was still unconscious from the beating he received in the cargo hold.

A few minutes later Kelem came around, moaning in pain. "Where are we?" he asked groggily. "I can't see anything!" Kelem said in a panic, thinking that he'd been blinded.

"It's all right Kel, they've locked us up in a place without light. There's nothing wrong with your eyes. How are you feeling?"

"I've been better," Kelem replied, as he became aware of the intense pain all over his body.

"These guys are definitely not with the Phalanx," Ndugu said. "They think we're Terrans and it doesn't look like they're going to believe us no matter what we say."

Kelem fought another wave of nausea and thought that his head was about to explode. "They're definitely Martians, probably belonging to some sort of rebel group. If you think about it, you and I definitely look like Terrans. After six years under the heavier gravity of Plantanimus I certainly look like a Terran now," Kelem said tasting his own blood flowing from somewhere in his face.

"This herder smells and looks like shit! And those guys look like they haven't taken a bath in years. What do you think is going on?" Ndugu asked.

"My guess is that some of the miners working around the belt managed to escape the Terrans when they took over Mars and have been out here ever since. But that was fourteen years ago according to our reckoning! If that's the case, I'm amazed that they've lasted this long this far out from civilization."

"Well, this tub looks like it hasn't been well maintained for that long. And the gravity plating probably stopped working years ago," Ndugu surmised.

Both men fell silent, each fearing that this could be the end of the line for them. The hatred that Kelem had felt coming from these Martian rebels was so intense and they were so angry, that it made him doubt that they would ever believe that he and Ndugu were not Terrans. The first man had asked Kelem where his "mothership" was. He obviously believed that Kelem and Ndugu were part of a larger ship somewhere nearby. The Terrans were obviously still hunting these Martians even this far out from the belt.

The herder's engines came on and the ship began to move. Kelem and Ndugu were suddenly thrown against a bulkhead. Kelem moaned and complained that his head was killing him. To prevent Kelem from hurting himself Ndugu wrapped his legs around Kelem and wedged his body between two of the opposing walls inside the narrow space to keep Kelem from drifting and hitting his head again.

Hours later, the door opened and Molson appeared laughing.

"Well lookee here! These two seem to be in love with each other!" he exclaimed upon seeing Ndugu holding Kelem between his legs. "Come here you bastard!" he said as he pulled the two of them out of the tiny space.

"My friend is unconscious, he won't do you much good right now," Ndugu said still holding onto Kelem.

"Oh, don't worry! You can bring your boyfriend along, we'll help wake him up!"

Molson and the other three carried Ndugu and Kelem back to the cargo hold. This time they tied both of them to a support beam near a bulkhead. Molson was not about to let Ndugu head-butt him again. Kelem's head bobbed aimlessly in the zero gravity and Ndugu worried that he'd hit his head again.

"I was once a Terran but I became a Martian citizen a long time ago," Ndugu said, hoping to somehow convince the one named Molson that he and Kelem were not working for the Terrans. "I'm sure that by now you've looked inside our ship and noticed that the vessel is not of Terran design."

"That don't mean shit, asshole! We Martians make everything for you bastards these days. If you don't tell me where your mothership is, I'm going to beat your unconscious friend here until his brains ooze out of his head!"

Ndugu grimaced and wished that his hands were not tied. He'd show this ruffian a thing or two!

Molson smiled, then swung his arm back and punched Ndugu in the gut with great force. Ndugu coughed and threw up, blasting Molson with vomit. Enraged, Molson punched Ndugu in the face nearly knocking him out.

Risking it all Ndugu shook the pain off and yelled out. "I know that there's someone listening to what's going on in this cargo hold! Whoever you are I beg you to listen to what I'm saying. This man next to me really is Kelem Rogeston the former CEO of the MMC! You probably think, as everyone else on Mars surely believes by now, that Kelem Rogeston died twenty one years ago when the Solar Nations expedition left and never returned. You can do whatever you want with me, but I beg you to let Kelem tell you where we've been for the last two decades. Please don't hurt him! You'd be killing one of Mars' native sons!" Ndugu exclaimed emotionally, praying that whoever was on the other side of the intercom was listening.

Molson having wiped vomit from his clothes, now came at Ndugu with renewed rage and was about to resume beating him up. "Hold it! I'm coming down," the voice on the intercom said.

The other three men had to hold Molson back from striking Ndugu again. Thankfully, the man whose voice had spoken through the intercom was obviously the main authority on this herder and everyone seemed to obey him. A few seconds later, a tall red bearded man drifted into the cargo hold and moved close to Ndugu and Kelem. He stared at Ndugu with icy disdain and then moved over to where Kelem's unconscious body was. Gently, he lifted Kelem's chin and looked at his face carefully. Ndugu cringed, for if this man had ever seen an image of Kelem in his younger days he would not recognize the bloody and swollen mess that was Kelem's face after having been beaten up so savagely by his men.

"Take this one up to the infirmary and have Louie fix him up," he said pointing to Kelem. Then looking at Ndugu he added, "throw this one back in the brig," and then he left.

Relieved, Ndugu didn't mind being sent back to the tiny room where he and Kelem had been in earlier. He knew that if the red bearded man gave Kelem a chance to explain himself they both might end up keeping their lives. They took Ndugu back to his cell but before Molson opened the door to the brig, he took out his vengeance on Ndugu, now that the red bearded man couldn't hear what was going on. He beat Ndugu savagely for a while, but Ndugu took the punishment, knowing that he had to hold on until Kelem spoke to the leader of this wreck of a ship.

The hours passed and Ndugu lost all track of time. The tiny space where he was being held did not have a latrine and he was forced to urinate in his flight suit. But he held on, praying that Kelem could somehow extricate the two of them from this horrible situation. Sore, bleeding and racked with fever from the physical abuse, Ndugu's torture finally came to an end when a new group of men came and moved him to a small cabin on another deck. After untying him, they threw him inside and told him to clean himself up. To his relief, the small cabin had a latrine and after removing and washing the urine from his flight suit he managed to clean himself and then collapsed on the cabin's dirty bunk and passed out.

Kelem regained consciousness a day later and found that his arms and legs were strapped to an infirmary bed. He raised his head slowly and looked around. Here there was gravity and Kelem felt the weight of his body and the extent of his injuries. He looked down on his right arm and saw that an IV was attached to it. A bag of saline solution was slowly dripping into his vein.

His head felt like it had been run through a rock crusher at one of the MMC's processing plants. As he looked farther down he noticed that his chest was tightly wrapped with bandages. He was sure that he had some broken ribs. He called out but no one answered. Slowly he remembered where he was and wondered if Ndugu was still alive. Sometime later a redheaded skinny teenager walked into the infirmary.

"Ah, I see that you've regained consciousness, how do you feel?" the boy asked.

"Like crap. What's happened to my friend?" he croaked, barely able to speak.

"They put him in a cabin. We've never caught Terrans before here at the Rusty Bucket, you're both lucky that you're still alive," the boy said checking Kelem's bandages.

"We're not Terrans, we're Martians," Kelem replied defensively.

The boy stared at him for a few seconds. "You certainly don't look like any Martians that I've ever met!"

"The Rusty Bucket, is that the name of this herder?" Kelem asked, changing the subject.

"Yep, you're in one of the few free Martian herder's still around since the occupation," the boy said with pride.

"You look to be about twelve or thirteen years old. Where were you born?" Kelem asked.

"I was born right here on the Bucket. My mom's the ship's medic," the boy replied casually.

"I need to speak to the captain. Can you get him for me?" Kelem asked the boy.

"The captain can't see you now. We're heading out to the orbit of Neptune. One of the other ships in the rebel fleet detected a Terran cruiser near Saturn, so we're putting some distance between us and Titan," the boy informed him.

"The rebel fleet," Kelem pondered, "what fleet are you referring to?"

"The Martian rebel fleet of course," the boy answered, surprised by Kelem's question.

"What's happened to my ship?" Kelem asked, wondering what they had done with the lander.

"It's still tied securely to the herder's basket. The captain's been inspecting it trying to find out if your story makes sense. By the way, that thing is old," the boy remarked. "Where did you find that antique?" he asked with interest.

"It's a long story, I'll tell you about it sometime. Meanwhile, do you have anything for pain? I think I have some broken bones."

"Sorry, we have a limited supply of painkillers and anesthetics and we only use them in cases of life and death," the boy said apologetically.

"It's rough out here, isn't it?" Kelem asked probing for information. "How long has this herd... I mean the Rusty Bucket been out here?"

"From the very first day the Terrans began bombarding Mars," the boy answered matter of fact.

Kelem's heart sunk at the mention that Mars had actually been bombarded by Terran ships. He could only imagine the horror and the destruction. "What...what happened? How much damage did the Terrans cause during the attack?" he asked, dreading the answer.

"My mom says that they destroyed a lot of the power and communications grid but that they left the main cities intact."

Kelem sighed with relief, at least his beloved Latonga City, Mars' capital, had not been turned to rubble.

"Where were you born?" the boy asked, seeing Kelem's reaction to the news of the bombardment of Mars.

"I was born on Latonga City," Kelem said, feeling a wave of sadness.

"I've never been to Mars," the boy said with regret.

Kelem looked at the boy and saw a little bit of himself in the teenager. Tall, thin and narrow like most Martians, this kid had been born and raised in space and had never set foot on the planet that was rightfully his sovereign country. In spite of his pain Kelem was able to read the boy and saw that even though he'd been living under such harsh conditions there was a lightness of spirit and sense of hope in his mind.

"What's your name?"

"Louie, after my grandpa."

"What did your grandpa do for a living?" Kelem asked, beginning to like this young Martian.

"Just like my dad, my grandpa was a miner, and that's what I would have been if it hadn't been for the occupation," he replied. "But, I showed a talent for medicine early on and my mom trained me to be a medic. We're one of the few rebel ships that still has a medical staff, so we get a lot of business here."

"I'm sure that you're an excellent medic, Louie. I'm glad that I'm in your care," Kelem stated, feeling his head beginning to throb again. He excused himself and closed his eyes. Soon he was unconscious once again.

The next time Kelem opened his eyes he found himself in a small cabin strapped to a bunk. This part of the ship was in zero gravity conditions and after unstrapping himself from the bunk, he drifted over to the small latrine on the opposite side of the cabin. When he saw his reflection in the small dirty mirror above the toilet, he was shocked to see the condition of his face. His left eye was practically swollen shut, the right side of his face was black and blue, and his forehead had a big gash with several stitches on it. But the part of his body that hurt the most was his rib cage. His head still hurt but it was nothing in comparison to the rest. He relieved himself in the zero gravity toilet and went back to his bunk. His body was so sore that moving, even in zero gravity, was very painful.

Sometime later the cabin's pressure door opened and a crewman threw him a food container and then left. Food was not uppermost in Kelem's mind, but he knew he needed to eat to help his body heal from the beating. He reached for the enclosed mess kit floating in the middle of the cabin and opened it slowly. The only thing in it was a foul smelling gruel that looked like reconstituted emergency rations that were probably years out of date. Steeling himself, he ate the stuff with his bare hands, since his captors had not provided utensils with the food. Afterwards, he went back to his bunk and passed out again.

This went on for a while, although Kelem couldn't tell how long he'd been in this cabin. After what might have been a week or so of the same daily routine, Kelem woke up one day and felt better. His headache was gone and his face was returning to its former shape. And although his ribs were still sore, the pain was bearable.

Kelem banged on the cabin's door and yelled out asking to speak to the captain. After a few hours of him calling for the captain, the door finally opened and Molson appeared floating in the hallway outside the cabin.

"Turn around. If you want to see the captain, it'll have to be with your hands tied," the dirty disheveled Molson ordered.

Kelem complied and spun around, as Molson tied his hands so tightly that it made him wince. Two other men floated in, grabbed Kelem and dragged him toward a pressure door at the end of the hallway. When the door opened, two of the men went in first and warned Kelem that he was about to step into gravity conditions. Once on the other side of the door Kelem felt the pull of gravity and found that his legs had turned to jelly. He fell forward and just before his face hit the deck plate, the two men grabbed him by the arms and yanked him up sending a wave of pain through his rib cage.

"I see that my boys tenderized you pretty good!" Molson said with a sadistic laugh, seeing Kelem suffer.

Kelem didn't reply, wishing to avoid another beating. The two men propped him up by the armpits and led him through yet another door. They went up two decks through a set of small stairways and when they reached the bridge deck, they stopped in front of a door that read, Captain's ready Room.

Molson pressed the intercom button. "I got the prisoner here Cap'n, may we come in?"

There was no reply but the door slid open. Molson brought Kelem inside and shoved him in front of the captain who was sitting behind his desk. The man behind the metal desk was a redheaded man in his forties, sporting a large red beard and long bushy hair showing the first signs of gray. His sharp eyes studied Kelem with cold intensity as Kelem stood there fighting to keep his balance with his trembling legs. After a while the man nodded to Molson who brought a folding chair and placed it behind Kelem. Molson shoved Kelem down onto the chair making him wince in pain.

Molson retreated to the corner standing guard behind Kelem as the captain continued observing him with interest. The man, whose uniform looked a little cleaner and in better shape than those of the crew, had a definite air of authority about him, but like the rest of the crew on this herder he was unmistakably undernourished and in poor health. The dark circles under his eyes and his sallow skin spoke volumes.

Something about the herder's captain looked familiar and Kelem searched his memory trying to place this man's face. After a while, it came to him. The captain was none other than Rusty Devereaux, the bully and nemesis of his childhood!

CHAPTER 4

Back From the Dead

October 7ᵗʰ, 2659

"I don't believe it, you're Rusty Devereaux!" Kelem exclaimed, realizing why the herder was named the Rusty Bucket.

In spite of the years that had passed, the man sitting behind the desk was unmistakably the student that had intimidated and harassed Kelem and his childhood buddy, Billy Chong, when they all had attended Latonga City University more than two decades ago. The trigger for Rusty's campaign of harassment and bullying had been the friendship that Verena Müller, his then girlfriend, had developed with Kelem and Billy. Like most bullies, Rusty was insecure and felt threatened by Kelem and Billy's genius intellects. To make matters worse, Verena eventually broke up with Rusty and ended up marrying Billy a few years later. Kelem and Billy became graduate students at fourteen years of age, and Rusty, who was five years older, left Latonga City University with only a bachelor's in mining technologies and ended up working for the MMC. Kelem hadn't thought about him since then. And now he wondered if Rusty still held a grudge against him.

"Your Terran friend claims that you're Kelem Rogeston but you look nothing like him," Rusty said disdainfully.

Kelem read the man and sensed some animosity in him but also a great deal of curiosity. The fact that he and Ndugu were still alive was probably due to the fact that Rusty Devereaux was undecided as to whether Kelem and Ndugu were Terrans or not.

"Number one, Ndugu has been a Martian citizen since 2638; he got his papers just before he and I left on the Solar Nations expedition. And two, it's been a while since you've seen me. And if it hadn't been for the sadistic beating that I received from your men, you'd be able to recognize me," Kelem said with subdued anger.

Rusty exchanged glances with Molson, standing in the corner of the room. Kelem caught a slight hint of contrition in Rusty's look. Perhaps the man had mellowed and gained some wisdom in his later years.

"I have serious doubts about the claims that you and this Ndugu are making, unless you miraculously managed to come back from the dead," Rusty said with distrust. "To begin with, if you really are Kelem Rogeston, where in the hell have you, and the rest of the crew of the Solar Nations, been for the last twenty one years?" Rusty asked, unconvinced by Kelem's claims.

Kelem had to be careful with his answers regarding the disappearance of the Solar Nations. His life and that of Ndugu's hung on the balance between Rusty and his men believing their story or not. The tale that he and Ndugu had rehearsed a few days before would not work in this situation. Kelem was a Martian but he didn't really look like one anymore. Six years on Plantanimus under its heavy gravity, had widened his body and helped to bulk up his musculature. Additionally, and, unfortunately, his baby face and youthful appearance did not give credence to his chronological age of forty one in this timeline. When the Solar Nations departed Mars in 2638, Kelem had just turned twenty. Because of the time shift phenomena caused by the explosion of the solar Nation's *n'time* generator, Kelem was now only twenty six years old physically. He certainly did not look like a forty one-year-old man which would be his chronological age in 2659.

"Ndugu and I are the only survivors of the mission I'm sorry to say," Kelem stated, his mind thinking furiously about how much of what really happened he should tell Rusty to convince him that he and Ndugu were who they said they were.

"How convenient!" Rusty said, laughing sarcastically. "You and your Terran friend appear on the edge of the solar system, with you claiming to be Kelem Rogeston, saying that the rest of the crew died. Do you really expect us to believe that you made it back with that old lander that we're holding in our basket?" Rusty said, pointing to Kelem's ship, visible just outside the window behind his desk.

"We were headed to Eridanus when the *n'time* generator failed causing a fire that killed everyone except me and Ndugu. We were spared because we were in the rear of the vessel inspecting the fuel tanks at that moment. As the solar Nations began to disintegrate, Ndugu and I jumped into the lander and exited the ship unable to save the rest of the crew. When the *n'time* generator exploded, we were somehow thrown forward in time by twenty years. The accident produced a time distortion wave of unbelievable force and momentum that fortuitously threw us in the direction of the solar system at $1/10^{th}$ the speed of light. I managed to modify the engines and increase their efficiency. Additionally we each spent every other month in the ship's Lectrosleep chambers to save food and air. We were very confused when we entered the solar system and tuned in to radio broadcasts that were telling us that the date was 2659. For me and Ndugu, only a year has gone by. As far as we're concerned, the year is 2639 not 2659!

"Oh, so you're also time travelers as well I see!" Rusty said laughing sarcastically, joined by Molson in the corner of the cabin.

Kelem knew that his story sounded too fantastic, but he persisted. "After we realized to our shock, that we had traveled twenty years into the future, we learned that Mars was once again a colony. We listened to more transmissions for a few hours and then stopped the ship. Thinking that the Phalanx was surely behind the re-conquest of Mars, we needed to figure out what our next move should be. Ndugu had been a liberal political activist when he lived on Earth, and he, like me, has a Phalanx price on his head. We figured that the Terrans might have ships out here possibly looking for rebels, so we turned back and hid behind Titan. I shut our gravity plating off to conserve energy and discuss our next move. We were both exhausted and had fallen asleep, when you came along and boarded our ship."

"You know, in 2645, when the Terrans suddenly appeared over Mars with *n'time* vessels and began bombarding the planet, most people assumed that it was Kelem Rogeston who had given the Terrans the know-how to build those ships," Rusty told Kelem observing him carefully.

"Why would anyone think that?" Kelem asked confused.

"Why?" Rusty said with a bitter smile. "After the Solar Nations disappeared, everyone was saying that it would be decades before Mars could build another *n'time* ship, because the great Kelem Rogeston, the inventor of the technology was now deceased," he said, sounding resentful.

"I didn't invent the technology, I just perfected it. The scientists at the Hawking Center were the ones who originally created the first *n'time* generator. My contribution consisted mainly of reducing the bulk of the thing from the size of a small mountain to something that could fit inside the hull of a normal spaceship," Kelem countered.

Kelem was surprised and disappointed to hear that the Hawking scientists had not been able to build a new *n'time* generator, and wondered how the Terrans managed to build an entire fleet of warships in less than six years.

"There was also a rumor going around that Kelem Rogeston had traveled to Earth in early 2637, but yet there were no records of a passport or visa being issued by the Martian Government to him," Rusty commented looking at Kelem intently. "Many think that he went to Earth on a clandestine mission to help with the planning of the Martian invasion."

Kelem realized that the direction of Rusty's conversation had switched from doubting his identity, to a series of probing statements to watch his reaction. It dawned on him that the name of Kelem Rogeston had somehow been connected with the occupation by the Terrans and that he had collaborated with the Phalanx. He now intuited that Rusty believed that he was indeed Kelem Rogeston but was trying to acquire intelligence regarding his activities since he'd disappeared. Proving that he was Kelem Rogeston was suddenly not necessarily a good thing! Now Kelem had to prove to these men that he was not a turncoat who had betrayed his own nation.

"I did go to Earth in 2637 illegally. If it hadn't been for my family name and position, and the fact that the Martian government needed me to complete the assembly of the Solar Nations, I would have probably been arrested and put in jail when I returned," he admitted. "If you recall, the situation between Earth and Mars was starting to deteriorate and the Martian Government had canceled all visas to Earth. My fiancée, Carlatta Del Mar, the daughter of the Terran ambassador, had gone to Earth to settle her grandmother's estate along with her mother. But she and her mother suddenly disappeared and I knew that they'd been taken by the Phalanx. After months of trying to contact her without any response, I decided to go there and try to rescue her and her mother and bring them back to Mars."

"Yes, everyone knew that you had a Terran girlfriend," Rusty said with mistrust, addressing Kelem directly this time. Molson grunted disdainfully in the back.

Now Kelem knew that his identity was no longer in question. "Yes, she was the love of my life and she and her family were good people even though they were Terrans. Her father, Don Francisco Del Mar was the man responsible for getting Leolas Harriman elected to president of Earth.

"Huh! A lot of good it did him," Rusty retorted with sarcasm. "The Phalanx made sure that he didn't end his term by having him assassinated," he added, referring to the liberal Terran politician who became president and tried to heal the political and cultural gap between Earth and Mars.

"That's right. That's why I went to Earth when I did. Carlatta and her mother disappeared soon after Harriman's assassination. Unfortunately, I was not able to find them and I returned to Mars within a few months."

"Fascinating! Tell me something else," Rusty said with mock admiration. "Did you meet your friend Ndugu while you were on Earth?"

"Yes. My search for Carlatta led me to South Africa and while in Botswana I was attacked by street criminals and almost got killed. Ndugu came to my rescue and saved me from a certain death. I found out later that he was hiding in Botswana because he was wanted by the Phalanx. After I got to know him, I realized that he was a good honest man and so I offered to bring him to Mars. His wife and daughters had been murdered by the Phalanx and he had no living relatives on Earth. So when I offered him a chance to leave Earth, he accepted my invitation."

"Hmmm...., all very neat and tidy," Rusty said with sarcasm, looking at Molson.

"Look, until a few minutes ago I didn't know that I was considered a traitor by some people. It's obvious to me that you do believe that I am Kelem Rogeston. I am…. or rather, I was, the richest man in the solar system. The Rogeston name goes back to the very beginnings of the colonization of Mars. Why would I, with all my wealth and power, betray my nation? Can you explain that to me?" Kelem asked with sincerity.

"I don't know why you would either. But everyone believes that you betrayed us all."

"Do you believe that?" Kelem asked, sensing that Rusty had his doubts.

"It doesn't matter what I believe," Rusty answered, averting his eyes and looking down.

Kelem read Rusty's mind and found that he was under pressure from his crew to get rid of him and Ndugu. In one instant, Kelem learned that Rusty's authority on the herder had deteriorated. His word had once been law, but after so many years of running from the Terran fleet, dwindling supplies and low morale, his authority had eroded. Kelem also learned that his wife was the medical officer of the herder and that Louie, the young medic, was his son. It was only a matter of time until Molson, who was a violent psychopath, took over the leadership of the herder. Rusty was concerned for the safety of his wife and son, and he was walking a fine line between his tenuous hold on the captainship of the Rusty Bucket and Molson's influence over the crew.

Kelem realized that his and Ndugu's situation was still as precarious as when they were first taken prisoner. Rusty had somehow managed to stave off their execution, perhaps because he was looking for a way out of his own circumstance and thought that Kelem might be able to help him somehow. Kelem searched deeper into Rusty's mind and found that he feared Molson. His presence in the captain's ready room was evidence that Molson didn't trust Rusty. With this hands tied behind his back and hurt as he was, Kelem presented no risk to Rusty had the two of them been left alone in the cabin to talk. Kelem realized that for all intents and purposes, Molson was already in charge.

Kelem looked at Rusty and then purposely moved his eyes to the extreme right a few times in Molson's direction, signaling that he understood that Molson was a problem. Rusty recognized the meaning of Kelem's eye-signal, and nodded ever so slightly as if pondering something, letting Kelem know that he understood.

Now Rusty would have to make the next move. All Kelem could do for now was wait and hope that sooner rather than later, Rusty could figure out a way to meet with him in private, form an alliance and together with Ndugu find a way to neutralize Molson's power. Knowing that Louie, the ship's medic was his son, Kelem had an idea how to give Rusty and opportunity to talk to him in private.

Kelem suddenly arched his back as if having a seizure. In spite of the pain in his ribs, he threw himself on the floor faking a convulsion. Rusty came around his desk and held Kelem's head with his hands and ordered Molson to call Louie.

"I say let's throw the asshole out of an airlock now!" Molson spit out with venom in his voice.

"Not yet! This piece of crap has information that can help us," Rusty yelled back, realizing what Kelem was doing.

"What kind of information? They're Terran spies sent here to infiltrate us and get our asses killed! Why do you want to save him?" Molson shouted with anger and suspicion in his voice.

"Did you see how this guy modified the engines on that lander?" Rusty shot back as Kelem continued his supposed seizure.

"Yeah, so what?" Molson replied with indifference.

"If we can get him to tell us how he did it, we can modify our engines the same way and more than double our speed. Don't you think that kind of thing could help us next time we're trying to get away from a Terran cruiser?"

Barely convinced by Rusty's argument, Molson reached for the intercom and called Louie, ordering him to come up to the captain's ready room.

Kelem was about to pass out from the intense pain in his ribs due to his very believable performance, when Louie finally walked in and took him out of the cabin with the help of two other crew members. As soon as the two crewmen brought him to the infirmary and tied his hands and feet to the gurney, they left. Then Kelem went limp and faked unconsciousness. Louie reached for the intercom and called his mother.

"Mom, I got that Terran here in the infirmary, the Caucasian one.

He's suffered a seizure. Can you come down and help me?" the boy asked, sounding nervous.

"Okay Louie, I'll be right down," a female voice replied.

Louie checked Kelem's pulse and then inspected his pupils with a small penlight. The boy opened Kelem's mouth to see if he had swallowed his tongue. Kelem was waiting for Louie's mother to show up before he opened his eyes. A few seconds later the pressure door to the infirmary opened and he heard a woman's voice.

"Did you check his vitals?" she asked her son and then Kelem felt her hands on his shoulder.

"Mrs. Devereaux?" Kelem said, opening his eyes and startling the woman.

Mrs. Devereaux, a tall, attractive, dark-haired woman in her forties, jumped back at first, but then composed herself and looked at Kelem with suspicion. "

"What is this?" she asked, realizing that Kelem was perfectly all right.

"Mrs. Devereaux, I think your husband fears for your life and your son's as well as his own. And I'm pretty sure that he would like my help," Kelem said, hoping that his hunch was accurate.

The woman became nervous and looked around to see if anyone else was near. She stared at Kelem for a second or two and then went back to the door and locked it. She returned and studied Kelem's face, probably trying to decide whether or not to trust this stranger who looked like a Terran but claimed to be Martian. After a long pause she spoke.

"Why do you say that?" she asked cautiously.

"I figured out what's going on around here. I'm pretty sure that you and your husband have a problem on your hands regarding Mr. Molson," Kelem said with assuredness.

"Did my husband say anything to you?"

"No. But he didn't have to. Molson is going to mutiny and take over the ship anytime now. He's mentally unstable and he's likely to snap at a moment's notice," Kelem answered as he studied Louie's and his mother's reactions.

Mother and son exchanged nervous glances and it was obvious to Kelem that he had touched a nerve. He read the woman's mind and was surprised at what he found.

"I know you and your husband are worried about the immediate future, particularly now that you're carrying a new life inside," Kelem said, glancing at her still flat belly.

"Mom! You're pregnant?" Louie asked, obviously surprised.

Mrs. Devereaux was taken aback, wondering how Kelem could possibly know that she was pregnant. She had only discussed it privately with her husband a few days before.

She looked at her son with tenderness and stroked his hair with a bittersweet smile on her lips and then looked back at Kelem narrowing her eyes. "You have a very active imagination, Mr. Rogeston. But let's say that, hypothetically, I believed you. What do you expect me to do about it?"

"Okay, hypothetically, I would expect you to pass this information to your husband and then help him arrange a meeting with me away from the prying eyes of Molson and his cronies."

"What will that accomplish?" she asked with interest.

"My friend Ndugu and I are willing to back your husband and help him regain control of the ship," Kelem replied while reading the woman's emotional response.

"Go on," she said, beginning to lower her guard a little, but still feeling uncertain about Kelem's motives.

"What percentage of the crew would remain loyal to your husband in a power struggle between him and Molson?" Kelem asked, trying to judge the situation.

Mrs. Devereaux and her son looked at each other, and it was obvious to Kelem that this was a subject that Rusty, his wife and son had already discussed in depth.

Mrs. Devereaux was struggling with the decision whether to let Kelem, a complete stranger, help them get rid of the executioner's ax hanging over their heads, or take a chance and hope that Molson wouldn't take over the ship and throw her husband and son out of an airlock into space.

Kelem was sure that Molson would have no compunction in raping Rusty's wife.

"Most of them are scared and intimidated by Molson and his seven underlings. But if my husband could show that he has the upper hand with you and your friend backing him up, most of them would stand with him. I'm talking about thirty seven crew members who would side with my husband and I include me and my son in that group," she said, sharing a knowing smile with Louie who nodded at her and then at Kelem.

Kelem felt the woman's resolve and the boy's courage and his spirits rose with the prospect of staying alive. "Very well, you can depend on me and my friend completely. Please go and talk to your husband as soon as possible."

"You understand that I cannot take these restraints off you for the time being," she said politely.

"Yes of course. Would it be better for me to remain in the infirmary with your son claiming that I'm still unconscious? Or should I be sent back to my cabin?" Kelem asked, wondering which part of the ship would be more convenient for Rusty to have a private meeting with him.

"I'm not sure. It's almost time for the night shift. My husband will be coming back to our cabin pretty soon. Louie will stay with you for now, and you keep your eyes closed. Understand?"

Kelem nodded and closed his eyes. He was tired and in pain, He didn't have to try too hard to look like he'd passed out anyway.

Sometime later, Louie woke Kelem up out of a deep sleep. "Mr. Rogeston, wake-up!"

"Wha… what's going on?" Kelem asked, groggily.

"Its 02:00 AM, you're no longer unconscious so we're taking you down to your cabin," the boy said with a wink.

Soon two crewmen came in, unstrapped him from the infirmary gurney, tied his hands behind his back and brought him downstairs to a different deck of the herder. When they stepped into a hallway, Kelem once again floated in the zero gravity of that section of the ship. One crewman stood with pulse gun in hand while the other one untied his hands. As Kelem rubbed his wrists, the crewman pushed the pressure door's palm plate to a cabin, and motioned for him to go in.

When he floated in, he was pleased to see Rusty Devereaux holding on to a safety bar with one hand and a pulse gun with the other.

"I'm not sure I can trust you Rogeston, but I'll give you a few minutes to convince me otherwise," Rusty said, motioning for Kelem to get in the bunk.

Kelem obliged and strapped himself in the bunk to show Rusty that he was under no threat. Rusty relaxed and put the gun in its holster. He remained there floating on the opposite side of the small cabin with arms crossed and a stern expression on his face. Rusty, once an unusually broad and muscular Martian who had been the Adonis of the Latonga City University campus, was now a shadow of his former self. Fifteen years in exile and living in poor conditions had whittled the man down.

"We don't have much time, Rusty. If we don't work together, Molson is going to kill me and Ndugu pretty soon. Then he's going to come after you and your family. My guess is that we have to make our move tonight, because I'm sure that you, like me, suspect that he's about to mutiny and take over the ship," Kelem said with authority.

"How did you figure out that I had a problem with Molson and how in the hell did you know that my wife was pregnant?" Rusty asked warily.

"That's not important right now. What's important is that we get our asses in gear and get you back in control of this ship."

Rusty's expression showed that he realized that time was of the essence, but there was still a shred of doubt in the back of his mind. "You realize that our chances of success are fifty-fifty, don't you?" he said with apprehension.

"Whatever the odds may be Rusty, you don't have a choice. That psycho's about to pop and you know it, so let's get going while we still have the element of surprise," Kelem said with urgency.

"I have six men that are willing to help. The rest are too scared to confront Molson and his crew. Unfortunately, your friend Ndugu is being guarded by two of Molson's men, so he won't be able to help us until we take care of them. That is, if he's in any shape to fight. The last time I saw him was three days ago and he looked pretty beat up."

"I wouldn't worry too much about Ndugu. He survived several years in the Kalahari Desert in one of the toughest, most dangerous parts of Africa. I'm sure he'll be all right," Kelem said with confidence.

"The men outside this cabin are loyal to me. I have three others that are willing to help us liberate your friend and eliminate those two guards. That will leave Molson and five others. The problem is that

Molson's cabin is at the end of the hallway where your friend is being held on deck eight. Any suggestions?" Rusty asked.

"I'm pretty well acquainted with the layout of an MMC herder, but it's been a few years, so correct me if I'm wrong. Deck eight is right above the engine compartment, isn't it?"

Rusty was impressed with Kelem's knowledge of the ship and nodded.

"We need to create a diversion in the engine compartment. Something that will make some noise," Kelem said, searching for an idea.

"I think I know of a way," Rusty offered. "The wastewater is run through the purification filters periodically for drinking use and the main pump is near his cabin. I can have one of my men go down to the engine room and transfer the water to the filtering tank. The operation is noisy."

"It's 02:30 in the morning. Won't the sound of the pump wake him up and alert him?" Kelem wondered.

"It might, but there's no set schedule for the water filtration, so he'll probably go right back to sleep," Rusty replied.

"Well, it's not ideal but I suppose it's the best we can do on such short notice," Kelem said unstrapping himself from the bunk. "Ndugu and I are going to need guns. Do you have one for me now?"

Suddenly Rusty looked very uncomfortable. "Look Rogeston, my men are taking a big chance confronting Molson and his people and they're not sure that freeing you and including you and your friend in this fight is a good idea. I managed to convince them that you would be an asset, but just barely. I'm willing to give you a gun, but if I give one to your African friend, I'll lose their support."

Kelem knew he couldn't push the issue. These men had lost their freedom and had seen their nation destroyed by the Terrans. Ndugu's African accent and his Terran physique were too much for them to feel comfortable around him with a gun in his hand.

"Ndugu is good with clubs and sticks. Would you at least be willing to let him have those?"

Rusty rubbed his chin and pursed his lips looking uncertain. After a while he looked up at Kelem. "How good?" he asked.

"Deadly," Kelem assured him.

"We'll get him a couple of aluminum tubes after we free him. Will that do?"

"Yes, now let's go to break him out."

Rusty took out a small pulse gun from under his tunic and handed it to Kelem. "This is an old pulse gun, unfortunately, the power cell doesn't hold a full charge. You've got about ten shots and that's it, so don't waste them."

Kelem took the gun and followed Rusty out into the hallway where the other two crewmen were standing guard. The four of them pushed themselves along the bulkheads and then reentered gravity conditions on the next section of the ship. They were joined by three other crewmen who nodded curtly at Kelem, but with obvious reservation in their eyes. Kelem's heart was racing. He had never been in combat nor had used a gun in anger before. He hated the fact that he might kill or hurt someone but he also realized that he had no choice. In his weakened condition he was concerned about his ability to hold his own in a violent confrontation, and as the group moved throughout the ship heading down to deck eight, he took a deep breath, steeled himself and focused on the task at hand. "One thing at a time," he told himself as he struggled climbing down through several metal stairways with the rest of the men. He would feel more confident once Ndugu was freed.

When they reached deck eight, Rusty paused by the pressure door leading to the section where Ndugu was being held. He took two automatic syringes out of his pocket and handed them to two of his men. "As soon as Leonard fires up the pump downstairs, we'll hear it. Then Luke and Timothy here," he said pointing to the two men closest to him, "will go in with me. I'll distract the two guards while Luke and Timothy put them under with anesthetic. Then I'll come back and open the door. Then we can take Molson prisoner. Is that understood?" Rusty asked, looking at all of them.

Kelem nodded nervously along with the others and suddenly felt a lump in his throat. His hands felt sweaty and he worried that he might lose grip of his pulse gun if he had to use it. The seven of them waited quietly for the sound of the water filtration pump to start. After what seemed like hours, the loud whine and vibration of the pump could be felt through the deck plates coming from the engine room below.

Rusty waited a few more minutes while the pump did its work.

Then Kelem and the other three had to move away from the door as Rusty palmed the door plate and entered the corridor with Luke and Timothy following behind. Kelem could feel the tension and fear in the three men that remained behind with him as the door closed. He found himself having to fight mightily to ignore their fear while struggling to control his own. The seconds ticked by and Kelem could have sworn that time had slowed down. "How long could it possibly take for Rusty and the other two men to overpower the two guards and open the door?" Kelem asked himself, beginning to worry.

Then the unmistakable thud of a pulse gun hit the pressure door, rattling it, and Kelem snapped out of his reverie. The other three men jumped and panicked instantly and Kelem's heart sunk seeing how unprepared they were to handle any kind of fight. Without thinking, he pressed the plate and the door opened. As soon as the heavy Duraminium door cleared the frame, two pulse streams shot through the opening hitting the bulkhead near Kelem causing a shower of sparks. Kelem ducked and then stepped into the opening in a crouch and saw that the one named Timothy was down on the deck holding his left arm in pain. One of Molson's men was passed out on the floor with an automatic syringe still stuck to his neck. The other guard was staggering backwards and firing wildly as the anesthetic was beginning to take its effect. Rusty and Luke were cowering at the end of the corridor face down on the deck plate trying to avoid being hit by the erratic aim of the barely conscious guard.

Kelem threw himself down, head first, sliding forward and firing his gun at the same time. By sheer luck, he hit the guard in his right hand and the man screamed in pain as he dropped his weapon. Then his eyes rolled back, fell to his knees and crashed forward, unconscious.

Kelem jumped up on his feet ignoring the pain in his ribs, and ran to the door of the cabin where Ndugu was being held. He pressed the door plate and Ndugu came out as soon as he saw Kelem standing by the opening with a gun in his hand. Ndugu rushed out into the corridor and immediately picked up the gun that the guard had dropped after Kelem had shot him. Ndugu then surprised Kelem by grabbing him and throwing him back inside the cabin as he raised his gun and fired at someone at the other end of the corridor.

All hell broke loose and Kelem could see several pulse gun streams whizzing back and forth between the two ends of the corridor. The smell of electrical charge issuing from the guns, mixed with the acrid smoke of burning metal as pulse streams hit bulkheads, permeated the cabin.

Kelem heard a scream of agony and the sound of a body falling on the floor deck. Then everything went quiet as a cloud of blue smoke drifted by the open door of the cabin. The silence was broken by the sound of moaning from the side of the corridor where Rusty, Kelem and the others had entered. Kelem stepped out and saw Molson to his left, face down on the deck with a smoking hole in his back and a pool of blood slowly spreading under his lifeless body. To his right lay Rusty, whimpering in pain and clutching his left thigh as a stream of blood poured out. Kelem ran over to him and called out to the three men who were still cowering by the pressure door leading to the corridor.

"Get me something that I can use as a tourniquet!" he yelled out with urgency. Two of them took off, looking for something that could be used to wrap around Rusty's leg.

Ndugu came by, kneeled down, and helped Kelem put pressure on Rusty's leg to slow down the bleeding.

Kelem looked up at the third man who seemed to be frozen in shock. "Well, don't just stand there! Get on the intercom and call for Louie and Mrs. Deveraux, for god's sake!"

The man snapped out of his paralysis and went over to the intercom and called Louie.

One of the other men returned with a length of electrical cable and handed it to Kelem who took out his gun, removed the power cell and then used the barrel to make a tourniquet. Rusty moaned in pain but nodded his head with gratitude.

Once the tourniquet was secured, Kelem turned around and was saddened to see Luke, the other one of Rusty's men, slumped against the side of the corridor with a hole in his forehead, his lifeless eyes still open. Kelem went over, closed the young man's eyes and laid him down gently on the deck floor.

Rusty's wife ran in and gasped when she saw her husband lying on the floor with blood all over his leg. Louie stumbled in right after his mother and knelt next to his father. "Dad!" he said with anguish, upon seeing the seriousness of his father's wound.

"I'll live Louie, you go over to Timothy and take care of him, your mother will look after me," he said putting on a brave smile, trying to sound casual.

Ndugu collected all the weapons including his own and handed them to one of Rusty's men. Rusty saw that and knew that he had made the right choice in trusting Kelem and Ndugu. Then Ndugu walked over to where his wife was treating Rusty. "Ma'am, my name is Ndugu. I'm pretty good with serious injuries. May I help you?" he asked her politely.

"Yes, thank you. I see that you've already applied a tourniquet!" she replied with gratitude.

"My friend did that," he said pointing to Kelem. "I've seen my share of gun wounds and I can be useful," he added with a smile.

She nodded, opened her med- kit, and together they began treating Rusty's wound.

Kelem went over to Louie, already treating Timothy's arm. The boy kept looking at the other end of the corridor, worried about his father.

"Your father will be fine. Is there anything that I can help you with?" Kelem asked, kneeling next to the boy and Timothy.

"Yes, please hold his arm up so that I can finish wrapping his wound," the boy responded with a brave smile.

As Kelem assisted Louie, other members of the crew loyal to Rusty began appearing at the pressure door. One of them came into the corridor and after observing the carnage, turned to Rusty.

"Captain, me and some of the other boys have the rest of Molson's crew tied up and locked in the cargo hold. What do you want us to do with them?" he asked.

"Good to hear, how did you manage to round them all up?" Rusty inquired, slurring his words a little, as the painkiller his wife had administered was beginning to take effect.

"It was easy. Once the word got around that you and these two had taken care of Molson," the man said pointing to Kelem and Ndugu, "they gave up real easy, and told us that they didn't want any trouble."

"Good. Take those two lying on the floor," Rusty said, pointing weakly to the two unconscious guards, "and put them in the cargo hold with the others."

"Will do. Meanwhile, what do you want us to do with them?" the man asked, nodding toward Ndugu and Kelem.

"They are to be treated as honored guests," Rusty said, looking at Kelem and Ndugu with gratefulness. Then he turned to his wife. "Danielle, Mr. Ndugu needs medical care, please see to it that his wounds are treated," Rusty said, and then he passed out.

"I am fine, madam. Please see to your husband's needs and that crewman over there first," Ndugu said, pointing to Timothy.

"I will, but you will follow me to the infirmary and be treated. That's captain's orders," she said with a smile.

"Thank you ma'am, I will. I wouldn't want to disobey the captain," Ndugu replied with a grin.

Other members of the crew now came and removed Molson and Luke's bodies. Kelem and Ndugu followed Danielle Devereaux, her son and two other crew members as they took Rusty and Timothy on stretchers to the infirmary two decks above.

Kelem took a seat in the corner as Danielle and her son cleaned and closed Rusty's wound on the operating table. The shot had fortunately missed the big artery in his thigh. After they did the same with Timothy's wounds, they cleaned, sutured and bound Ndugu's cuts and bruises.

Exhausted, Kelem had dozed off with his head leaning against a bulkhead. Danielle Devereaux woke him up, gently shaking his shoulder. "Mr. Rogeston, you're still on the injured list. Please come and lie down on that gurney over there," she said, lifting him up and helping him walk to the gurney.

She removed his flight suit, changed the bandages around his ribs and gave him a mild sedative.

Louie came around and put a pillow under his head. The boy took Kelem's hand and shook it affectionately. "Thank you for helping us," he said with appreciation.

Kelem smiled and nodded to the boy. A warm sensation enveloped his body as he passed out.

CHAPTER 5

How Earth Conquered Mars

October 14th, 2659

A week had passed since Kelem and Ndugu made it possible for Rusty to regain control of his ship. While the herder's captain recuperated from his leg wound under the expert care of his wife Danielle and son Louie, Kelem and Ndugu got busy repairing and restoring many of the ship's systems. At first, the crew was leery and suspicious of their efforts, but after certain things began improving, like the quality of the air and the availability of water, the men of the asteroid herder began to see Kelem and Ndugu in a different light.

Ndugu discovered that the reason the gravity generators in several sections of the ship had stopped working was because they had been misaligned over the years. The ship had lost its systems engineer to disease, and the crew had taken to tweaking the generators on their own, eventually causing them to fail due to their lack of expertise. When the gravity on the Rusty Bucket returned to normal in all sections of the ship, Ndugu was hailed as a hero.

Rusty conducted a technical inspection of the herder and was very impressed with what Kelem and Ndugu had accomplished in less than a week while he convalesced. He realized how valuable the two of them would be as new additions to his crew.

The next morning he asked the two men to join him in the captain's ready room to discuss their becoming permanent members of the crew, but both Kelem and Ndugu refused.

"Why not? What else do you two have going for yourselves?" Rusty asked, surprised by their answer.

"I don't know what Ndugu's reasons might be," Kelem said, glancing at his friend briefly, "but as for me, I intend to go to Mars and see what I can do to get rid of the Terrans."

"Are you crazy?" Rusty exclaimed, shaking his head in disbelief. "The Phalanx has the planet sealed tighter than a gnat's ass! Besides, didn't you tell me that the Phalanx has a price on your head?"

"That's true, but I no longer look like I used to, and everyone thinks I'm dead. All I need to do is get back to Mars with a false identity. I have to find out what happened to my family and friends."

"Kelem, you really don't understand what's going on over there! There have been some developments in the past twenty one years that you should know about," Rusty said, feeling sympathy for Kelem's ignorance.

"Like what for instance?"

"I guess I should start at the beginning so that you understand what it is that you're considering doing," Rusty said, leaning back on his chair. "About three years after the Solar Nations disappeared, ex-president Solomon Vandecamp went missing. The event was big news and the Martian government, suspecting Terran involvement, demanded that Vandecamp be returned immediately. But to everyone's shock and dismay, Vandecamp sent a video communiqué from Earth through all the media channels, declaring that he was renouncing his Martian citizenship and that he would now become a Terran citizen."

"Vandecamp? Renouncing his citizenship? That's unbelievable," Kelem exclaimed, stunned.

"Exactly, that's how we all reacted. We all thought that Vandecamp was being coerced somehow. But our government asked the Martian ambassador to Earth to meet with the man, and the ambassador confirmed that Vandecamp was under no pressure or coercion by third parties, and that the decision to leave Mars had been his and no one else's. Then a few months later, the Stephen Hawking research facility was raided by a small group of Terran commandos. The media didn't say anything at the time, but later on it was revealed that the Terrans had taken the entire supply of a new element called Marsium. We didn't know it at the time of course, but as you well know, an *n'time* generator is useless without Marsium."

Kelem now understood why his colleagues at Stephen Hawking had not been able to build any more *n'time* ships. Vandecamp, who had been privy to all the security measures at the center, had apparently given the Terrans all the intelligence they needed to carry out a successful raid and steal the entire supply of the rare metal. Marsium had been discovered by the Mars Mining Company out in the belt some fifty years earlier. The newly discovered element was a liquid metal capable of releasing enormous amounts of energy when subjected to a modest electrical charge. That discovery led to the invention of the *n'time* generator. The Martians had mined several hundred kilos, but after a while they couldn't find any more of it. The MMC continued searching for more asteroids with veins of Marsium, but after a few years they realized that they had probably mined all that there was, at least within the asteroid belt. Martian scientists theorized that there might be several thousand tons of it out in the Kuiper Belt or even farther out in the Oort cloud, but it was still technically and financially impossible to send chemically powered asteroid herders that far out in space to mine asteroids and ice comets.

"Three years later, the Terran fleet suddenly appeared above Mars and began bombarding the planet," Rusty concluded sadly.

"I understand now why my name has been linked with the betrayal of Mars," Kelem said bitterly.

"That's not all, Kelem. The main reason why you were connected with the invasion was because of that son of a bitch, Billy Chong!" Rusty said, spitting the words out angrily.

"Billy? What the hell are you trying to say?" Kelem snapped back, offended than Rusty would talk that way about his best and closest childhood friend.

"I feel bad for you Kelem, but your friend Billy Chong is one of the most hated men on Mars after Soltan Voltanieu and the Phalanx Black Guards," Rusty explained.

"How...? Why would Billy betray his own nation? I've known Billy since kindergarten and I just can't believe that he became a collaborator!" Kelem said with disbelief.

"We're sure that he's the one who gave the Terrans the exact position of all of MMC's ships for the invasion! We and the rest of the rebel fleet managed to escape only because we were on the other side of the Sun on the innermost rim of the asteroid belt when the Terrans struck. Most of the MMC's fleet assets closer to Mars were captured within hours, with the exception of about fifty that were destroyed when they resisted," Rusty said with anger and bitterness in his voice.

Kelem searched Rusty's mind and found out that he was telling the truth, at least the truth as he knew it. But Kelem sensed that something was wrong. He knew his friend's heart. Something extraordinary must've happened for Billy to be known as a traitor. Kelem was sure that the Phalanx had either forced Billy to give them the coordinates of all of the MMC's ships at the time of the invasion or threatened to hurt his wife and family. Now, more than ever, he needed to go to Mars and find out what truly happened. Something had gone terribly wrong!

"I must get back to Mars now! I'm sure Billy's family was threatened or the Terrans found some way to coerce him into doing what he did," Kelem said, feeling sick in the pit of his stomach.

"I think that you're going to be sadly disappointed. Billy Chong is one of the Terrans' media stars. He's on Martian television regularly, spouting Phalanx philosophy and dogma. He wears the Phalanx insignia on his sleeve everywhere he goes. He's traveled to Earth several times on political junkets, and is often seen with best pals, Terran president for life Montenegro and Governor of Mars, Soltan Voltanieu, who, by the way is responsible for the murder of thousands of innocent Martians. I wouldn't tell anyone that you're acquainted with Billy Chong or you might come to some harm," Rusty advised.

"God damn the Phalanx and all Terran sons of bitches!" Kelem cursed, unable to hold back his anger and resentment.

"Now you sound more like a real Martian! Maybe now you'll come to understand why someone like Molson was filled with so much hate and rage and why he wanted to kill you and Ndugu so badly," Rusty said with a bitter smile.

"I only knew Billy for a couple of years, but I, like Kelem, find it impossible to believe that he has become a Phalanx collaborator!" Ndugu said, speaking for the first time.

"Later on I'll aim our main dish antenna toward Mars and I'll let you both see for yourselves how much Billy loves the Terrans," Rusty said with sarcasm.

Kelem's old hatred of the Phalanx reared its ugly head. Until a few days ago, his main concern had been that of making sure that Ndugu did not suffer any consequences because of the failed Solar Nations mission, and of returning to Plantanimus to be with his beloved Anima and the Dreamers. Now fate had conspired once again to take him away from the individuals that he loved most. Whatever happened to Billy to cause him to betray Mars was surely the work of the Phalanx.

"What about my aunt and uncle, Bernardo Salas and his wife Maggie? Do you happen to know what happened to them? They were both elderly and I know that they would be dead by now. But is there anything you can tell me about them?"

Rusty shifted uncomfortably in his chair and looked down, rubbing his hands nervously.

Kelem had a sinking feeling and knew that something terrible had happened to uncle Nardo and his beloved aunt Maggie, but he dreaded reading Rusty's mind so instead he asked. "Whatever it is Rusty, please, tell me what happened."

Rusty exhaled and looked at Kelem with a sad expression. "The Martian government, unable to put up a defense, surrendered within twenty four hours of the bombardment. The following day, two hundred and fifty thousand Terran troops landed on Mars. The first thing they did was arrest then president, Charles Gruzinsky, the vice president, the speaker of the house, the entire Senate and House of representatives and just about every important, well known Martian, and then executed the entire lot," Rusty said with tears welling in his eyes. "Your aunt and uncle were among those arrested that day".

Kelem couldn't help it and he broke down burying his face in his hands, as a deep wrenching sadness took over his heart and mind. His shoulders shook with grief as tears fell on his hands, mourning the loss of two of the dearest people that he had ever known and loved in his entire life. Though he had loved and lost Carlatta Del Mar, this pain and sadness was overwhelming. Uncle Nardo and Aunt Maggie had raised him, and although he knew that after twenty one years they'd both likely be dead from old age, to find out now, that poor Aunt Maggie and Uncle Nardo had come to such an ignominious end, hurt

Kelem in such a profound way that he couldn't help but grieve with inconsolable tears.

Rusty and Ndugu felt his pain, their hearts full of empathy for yet another victim of the evil Phalanx. Neither man could speak as Kelem sat there crying.

After a while Kelem wiped his eyes with his sleeve and composed himself. "Did you ever hear anything about a man named Nicholas Alfano, a Dr. Marla Hassett, Jasper Willis, Dimitri Kuzmenko, Susan Beaumont, Dalton Myers or Laura Finch?" Kelem asked, naming the members of the board of directors of the Brotherhood that he held most dear in his heart.

Rusty rubbed his chin and looked pensive for a few seconds. "I seem to remember that right after the Terran troops entered Latonga City, the military commander came on Martian television and offered a small fortune to anyone who could provide him with any information regarding members of a society called the Light Brotherhood or something like that," Rusty said, trying to remember the specific details.

"You mean, The Brotherhood of the Light, don't you?" Kelem corrected him as he and Ndugu exchanged a brief glance.

Rusty caught the look that Kelem and Ndugu had exchanged and furrowed his brow, realizing that certain suspicions he had regarding Kelem were well-founded. "Yes, that's it! The Brotherhood of the Light! That was the name of the organization."

"Did the man say why he was looking for these people? Kelem asked with interest.

"Yes. In typical Phalanx hate-speak, he accused the members of the organization as being corrupt practitioners of black magic, witchcraft and even devil worship. And now I remember that he was most interested about one name in particular, that of Professor Nicholas Alfano, the first name that you just mentioned a while ago."

"Did they ever catch Nicolas Alfano?" Kelem asked, dreading the answer.

"They definitely caught him. I know, because I saw a televised news conference where the Terrans paraded this poor man in front of the cameras. They had him bound and gagged claiming that he could hypnotize people with his voice and make them do evil deeds!" Rusty said, laughing at the ridiculous nature of the Terrans' claims.

Kelem swallowed hard and clenched his fists, tensing his jaw as he gritted his teeth with repressed rage.

"Later on, there was a rumor out here among us rebels, that The Brotherhood of the Light was made up of Martians with unusual abilities, like mind reading, levitating solid objects, stuff like that," Rusty added, studying Kelem's response with intense focus.

Ndugu instinctively looked at Kelem but then lowered his eyes, noticing that Rusty seemed keenly interested in the subject. Ndugu knew that Kelem was a powerful psychic and could read minds. Then he cursed himself for having been caught looking at Kelem in response to Rusty's statements. It seemed to him that Rusty knew more than he was letting on.

Kelem caught Rusty's train of thought and remembered that he had asked him how he found out that his wife was pregnant. He had put it off at that time since they were about to take down Molson and his crew. But now as he collected himself and read Rusty's mind more closely, he realized that the man suspected that he could read minds. But, he also caught a glimpse of Rusty's subconscious and found to his surprise that the man possessed a very mild form of mind reading ability.

"Tell me more about these Martians with special abilities," Kelem said, probing Rusty's knowledge on the subject.

"Oh, I think you know more about that stuff than I do, Kelem," Rusty replied, almost like a challenge.

"Oh! Why do you say that?"

"Because I think you're one of them," Rusty said with certainty.

"So you believe in this psychic stuff like reading minds, levitating and things like that?" Kelem responded, playing along.

"Yes, because my son Louie is one of you," Rusty answered, taking Kelem by surprise.

"What do you mean he's one of <u>us</u>?" Kelem said, emphasizing the word.

"Do you know why my son is the ship's medic?" Rusty asked.

Kelem shook his head but he already knew the answer from Rusty's mind. Still he continued the charade. "No, but please tell me."

Rusty laughed, knowing that Kelem was testing him, but decided to continue playing along anyway. He took a deep breath and leaned forward on his desk, fixing his eyes on Kelem. "From the age of five my son could look at a person and know what was wrong with them medically. At first we thought that he was making things up, being a child and all. Living in a ship full of miners on the run from Terran authorities, we didn't pay any attention to his claims. We were all too busy trying to stay alive. The kid was bored and we thought that he was using his imagination to entertain himself. But over time, my wife, who is a registered nurse, realized that Louie was diagnosing people accurately every single time. His ability has saved the lives of a few of my men. Until Louie came along and began displaying his abilities, I didn't believe that there was such a thing as psychics. When my wife told me that you had guessed correctly that she was pregnant, I knew that you were one of them."

Kelem smiled and looked at Ndugu briefly and then he turned his head and looked at Rusty. "You're right. I am a psychic and I do read minds. I don't do it unless it's a very serious or important occasion and in this instance both Ndugu's and my life were on the line, so I apologize for intruding into your wife's private thoughts, but I needed to know if you and your family were willing to confront Molson and his crew," Kelem said, admitting that what Rusty suspected was true.

Rusty nodded and looked like a man who had taken a weight off his shoulders. "I love my son with all my heart and soul, but I've always worried that the Phalanx might come looking for him someday. I'm paranoid that a Terran psychic might be able to find him out here using those same kinds of powers," Rusty said, with parental angst.

Kelem nodded slightly and rubbed his chin. "The phalanx has been trying to gain an upper hand in the psychic arena for a long time. But to my knowledge they've never been able to recruit any Terrans whose psychic abilities could match those of Martians. And there's a very good reason for that. You see Rusty, the Martian flu epidemic changed the course of human development on Mars."

"How so? I mean…, what does the Martian flu epidemic have to do with Martian psychics?"

"We all know how and why the epidemic occurred. What many don't know, however, and that includes most Martians, is that the MV Recessive vaccine changed the DNA of all the Martian children that survived the epidemic and were given the vaccine. I won't go into technical details, but it has been proven that the vaccine triggered the activation of a long dormant human gene in that generation of Martian children, and that change pushed our population ahead in terms of human development."

"How come the Terrans and the Lunarians weren't affected equally?" Rusty asked logically.

"The surviving children of the Martian flu epidemic had a natural immunity to the disease. It has something to do with that particular generation being exposed to Martian dust containing the inactive spores of the MV Recessive virus from early childhood. Their natural immunity, combined with the genetically manipulated vaccine, is what triggered the change. All Martians alive today carry that gene mutation. You yourself, Rusty, have that mutation in your genetic structure. However, even though we all carry that mutation, it's only one individual in every one hundred thousand, whose mutation expresses itself in the form of exceptional abilities."

"No fooling?" You mean that I passed the gene onto my son?" Rusty replied with fatherly pride.

"Yes, it could be you or your wife or both of you together," Kelem replied smiling.

"So, this Brotherhood of the Light, what is the purpose of the organization?" Rusty asked.

"The Brotherhood came into existence in response to the creation of the Phalanx over a century and a half ago. We knew back then that the Phalanx was bad news and that they were already experimenting with psychics and psychic ability after they found out about the existence of Martian psychics. And for the last century and a half we were successful in keeping the organization in check. Aside from that, the Brotherhood serves as a sort of university for psychics, helping them improve and hone their skills."

"You mean my boy can be trained by you or others like you to become better at what he does?"

"Yes. But unfortunately from what you've told me so far, it seems as though The Brotherhood has either been decimated, or is on the run, most likely hiding among the population. Perhaps some of them have joined the Martian resistance movement. I'm quite certain that the Terrans were not able to capture all the members of the Brotherhood. That's why I'm confident that if I can return to Mars and contact other members of the organization, we can begin to put together an efficient counter offensive and liberate the planet," Kelem said with certainty.

"What you've just told me does change things to a degree. But I'm doubtful as to whether you and your people can affect any significant change after fourteen years of occupation. Kelem, you don't know what it's like over there now! The planet is a virtual slave camp, manufacturing goods and technology for the Terrans. The Phalanx secret police is everywhere and they control everything. They have numerous checkpoints in every city and if you want to travel anywhere you have to get special passes from the local commanders. I don't see how you can infiltrate Mars and avoid getting arrested within the first few hours of you being there," Rusty said with concern.

"Something must be done! From the condition of your ship and crew I assume that the rest of the rebel fleet is in a similar state of affairs. How much longer do you and the others think that you'll be able to survive out here? Even if you had people with technical know-how, like me and Ndugu in every ship, fixing things up, your vessels will eventually fail. What happens then?"

Rusty lowered his head knowing that Kelem was right. After fifteen years in exile, equipment, food and morale were in short supply. Communication between the resistance on Mars and the rebel fleet was practically nonexistent. The Terrans knew that the rebel fleet was isolated and could well afford to be patient knowing that eventually they would all succumb by attrition. Rusty knew that the end was near for all those out on the edge of the solar system and Kelem was right; eventually their ships would stop working, and one by one they would all die. The rebels needed a miracle. Perhaps Kelem was that miracle.

"I wish I could clone both of you! If each ship in the fleet had two of you fixing things, we could coordinate attacks on the Terran cruisers and eventually defeat them," Rusty said wistfully.

"You're right, all the ships in the fleet need to be in top shape. But it won't do us any good if we can't coordinate things with the Martian underground. That's why I have to go to Mars so we can reconnect with the resistance. Only then can we be effective and take back our planet," Kelem asserted with confidence.

"You're a better man than me!" Rusty commented. "I guess with your mind reading ability you have an advantage, but you're still going to be risking your hide when you get there. I wish you the best. What can me and my crew do to help you?"

"Obviously I need transportation, but I can't very well arrive on Mars with a lander belonging to a Martian expedition that disappeared more than two decades ago!" Kelem said with mild sarcasm.

"You're right," Rusty agreed. "I think that there might be a way to get you back home, but it won't be fast. In cases of emergency we have a series of vessels that can eventually put you on a Terran asteroid herder headed for Mars where some in the crew are members of the resistance. The trip would take about a month or so. It's very risky and there's always the possibility that you'll get caught or killed while in transit. But it can be done."

"Fine, when can I leave?" Kelem asked, not wanting to waste any time.

"Hold on there, buckaroo!" Rusty said laughing. "It's going to take me a while to cajole and convince all the parties involved to risk their necks just to bring one person all the way from the edge of the solar system to the belt. I'm not sure how I'm going to get this done because I don't have anything to bargain or exchange with all those ship's captains. This kind of thing usually requires giving away water, food and other supplies in exchange for such a service," Rusty explained.

"What about a highly skilled technician that can fix and repair things on every ship that gets involved in transporting me?" Kelem asked.

"I'd be willing to come along and provide my services," Ndugu said, volunteering for the job.

"No can do, Ndugu! We can't go together on this one. If I get caught or killed, these folks out here need someone like you to help them. I meant me, as the highly skilled technician! I'm not a top notch systems engineer like Ndugu but I know my way around a space ship better than most folks," Kelem added.

"That's true!" Rusty conceded. "That's not a bad idea! Hey, I bet that they'll be lining up, volunteering to be part of the scheme," he said convinced that the idea would work.

"Then it's settled. As soon as you can arrange for passage to Mars, I'm out of here!" Kelem said, his spirits lifting.

"We need to celebrate!" Rusty announced, reaching for a bottle in one of his desk drawers. "I've been saving this bottle of vodka that I traded for a plasma infuser, for a special occasion. I'm sure it's nothing but rot-gut, but out here this is as precious as French champagne!" Rusty pronounced gleefully, as he produced three small tin cups and filled each one to the brim.

The men drank the vodka, which tasted like pure rocket fuel, but the effects were the same as expensive liquor.

CHAPTER 6

From Ship To Ship

October 16ᵗʰ, 2659

A week later, a Martian Navy frigate that had seen better days, docked with the Rusty Bucket. The captain, a woman named Veronica Valchek, came aboard.

When the hatch connected to the docking tunnel opened, a pale, thin, gray-haired woman in her fifties stepped through. Her Mars Space Command uniform showed its age but it was clean and neat. Her face, framed by a short hairdo was sharp and angular and her piercing gray eyes denoted the look of an individual accustomed to command.

"Rusty, it's so good to see you again, my friend!" the woman said, hugging the herder's captain who returned the hug with one arm while he leaned on his cane with his free hand.

"Allow me to introduce Kelem Rogeston," Rusty said, gesturing toward Kelem.

Captain Valchek let go of Rusty and walked straight up to Kelem and shook his hand with a gentle grip. "A pleasure to meet you Mr. Rogeston, I'm looking forward to hearing all about your experiences. Rusty has told me little about what's happened since your return, and I must say it makes for a very interesting tale," the woman said, studying his face with interest.

"I'm very glad to meet you Captain Valchek, I hope that you'll find my story entertaining," Kelem replied with a smile.

"I'm sure I will, Mr. Rogeston. Your unexpected return has created a great deal of interest within the rebel fleet."

Kelem was alarmed to find that he had already gained notoriety among the crews of other rebel ships. "Forgive me Captain, but the last thing I want or need is to have my name bandied about among the fleet's crews. My aim is to return to Mars incognito. The less everyone uses my name the better for the cause."

"I'm afraid that ship to ship gossip is one of the last forms of entertainment left for all of us out here, Mr. Rogeston. Besides, Captain Devereaux could not have arranged for your voyage back to Mars without confiding to all the ships' captains who it was that we would all be risking our lives for," Veronica Valchek informed him with a smile that bordered on mild admonishment.

Kelem nodded. "I see that there is much that I need to learn after two decades of absence."

"By the time you get to Mars you'll have your ears full of stories, complaints and requests from everyone that you'll meet throughout this voyage," the woman assured him. "And don't worry, not only have the Terrans been unable to break the encryption codes we use for ship to ship transmissions, but the codes are changed every week," she added, patting his back reassuringly.

"That's comforting to hear Captain, still I would feel better if the fleet tightened up its security protocols," Kelem added with mild criticism.

"You're right, Mr. Rogeston. I'll let the others know of your wishes."

"Thank you, ma'am. I appreciate any effort you can make in that regard."

Victoria Valchek excused herself and went over to where Rusty was waiting to help him supervise the exchange of goods between her ship and the Rusty Bucket. Her ship, the Volta, needed water for its hydroponics farm, while the Rusty Bucket was short on lubricants.

A few hours later, Kelem said his goodbyes to Ndugu, Rusty, his wife Danielle and Louie, and departed on his way to Mars.

The Volta measured thirty meters in length by ten meters wide. The old ship was a true space navy warship and had seen action several times in the last fourteen years. Its complement of ship to ship missiles had been depleted many years before after several skirmishes with Terran cruisers and destroyers. Its rail guns, however, still remained viable and were a deadly deterrent to any enemy that came within range of those powerful weapons. Like the Rusty Bucket, the Volta was in dire need of repair and spare parts. But its crew, having had military training and discipline in their earlier years had managed to maintain their ship better than the Rusty Bucket's crew, and had survived by holding on to a more professional demeanor and attitude.

When the Terrans invaded in 2645, the average age of the crew of the Volta had been twenty plus. Fifteen years later, everyone, with the exception of Captain Valchek, was now in his or her forties. Years of living on the edge of the solar system, subsisting on poor rations and almost no medical care had taken its toll on the crew. As Kelem made his way through the ship's corridors on his way to the cabin that had been assigned to him, he noticed the same pallor and low body weight among the crew members that he had witnessed on the Rusty Bucket. Their hollow eyes and protruding cheekbones together with their muted expressions spoke volumes as to their physical and mental state.

In contrast, Kelem's healthy looks, his wide-body and musculature gave rise to many curious stares as he passed from compartment to compartment. He sensed a great deal of curiosity mixed in with flashes of resentment and jealousy in the minds of some of those that he encountered. The ensign who was taking him to his assigned cabin was acting very politely, but felt angry that he had to give up his cabin to Kelem.

"Here you are, sir. This is where you'll be staying," the ensign named Jacko said with a polite bow as he pressed the palm plate to the cabin's door.

"Whose cabin is this that I'll be using?" Kelem asked.

Surprised, the ensign blushed slightly and lowered his eyes before answering. "Why, this is my cabin sir."

"I don't need a private cabin ensign. I'd be just as happy sharing a bunk in the enlisted crew's quarters. Would you please let the captain know that I don't want to be treated like a dignitary or some kind of special guest with special privileges?"

The ensign's anger disappeared and the man took an instant liking to Kelem. "You know, until you said that you didn't mind bunking with the enlisted crew just now, I was upset that I had to give up my cabin. Now I would be offended if you didn't use it," the man said with a genuine grin.

"Well, I don't want to start pissing people off on my first day on the Volta," Kelem replied laughing.

The ensign laughed in response and motioned for him to step into the cabin. "The captain requests your presence at her dinner table at 06:00 PM. Will you attend?"

"Yes, absolutely. Will you be there?"

"I'm sorry to say I won't. You'll be dining with Captain Valchek and Commander Ron Hugh, the first officer," Ensign Jacko answered.

"Very well. By the way, if you need any personal items from your cabin please don't hesitate to come by anytime," Kelem offered.

"What little personal items I have, I've taken with me so don't worry about it," the man replied.

Ensign Jacko excused himself and Kelem was left alone in the cabin. He put down his duffel bag on the floor and sat on the bunk, whose foam mattress was practically flat after so many years of use. An equally flat pillow and a wafer thin blanket were the only amenities that had been provided for his stay on the ship. Kelem tried to imagine what life must be like for these men and women, spending day after day on this military frigate, seeing the same people year after year, coming back to their meagerly appointed private quarters every evening and having to look at the same four walls night after night. In many ways these rebels were living like criminals sentenced to life imprisonment in some Terran gulag.

Kelem now understood the disengaged look in the eyes of many in the crew. After years of living in such a restricted environment, the human mind begins to shut certain pathways in the brain to avoid the emotional pain and stress of living in such poor conditions. He was sure that there was a high rate of mental illness within the rebel fleet's crews.

At 05:45 PM he took out his Solar Nations flight suit, put it on and headed for the upper decks where the captain's quarters were located. He laughed, remembering how upset he was that Mars Space Command had designed such fancy flight suits for the crew before he left on the expedition. Now he wore the uniform proudly in memory of all those who had perished during the mission.

As he made his way to the upper decks, he was surprised when many of the crew saluted him as he passed by. At first he thought it was the captain's insignia on his flight suit's shoulders that caused the response, but as he scanned a few of those he passed by, he learned that Ensign Jacko had told everyone of his willingness to bunk with enlisted crew. Apparently his request for equal treatment had endeared him to the crew.

When he reached the captain's cabin, he was greeted by a sergeant at arms standing guard by the door. The woman snapped to attention with a sharp military salute and then hit the plate on the Captain's door. Inside, Capt. Valchek rose from her chair by the cabin's dining room table and came forward to greet him.

"Welcome, Mr. Rogeston, or shall I say Capt. Rogeston?" Veronica Valchek asked, noticing his flight suit.

"I wore this flight suit out of respect for your rank, Captain Valchek, and in memory of the crew of the Solar Nations. I would appreciate it if you addressed me as Kelem. As a matter of fact I would like for your crew to address me in the same manner," Kelem said, bowing politely.

"I'll try, but it may be too late already. Your presence on the ship has already created something of a sensation. I'm afraid that your being here has served to improve the crew's morale, however temporary it may be. My people have been energized by your arrival and as I said before, every single ship that is taking part in bringing you to Mars is anxiously awaiting your arrival. You are the Lazarus returned from the dead, Capt. Rogeston!" Captain Valchek pronounced solemnly.

Kelem rubbed his forehead, dismayed by the consequences of his plan to return to Mars. The last thing he wanted was notoriety and he felt certain that this unwanted adulation by these poor rebels who had been stuck out here for years, was bad news for him. "I don't mind telling you Captain, that I'm distressed by these developments regarding my presence here," Kelem complained with concern.

Capt. Valchek smiled warily and shook her head patiently. "The fleet is hanging by a thin thread, Captain. The suicide rate among rebel crews is six percent per year and climbing. Deaths from illness and accidents have taken another ten percent in the last year alone. Six months ago, the entire crew of one of our transport ships deserted *en masse* and surrendered while at the same time, delivering the vessel to the Terrans. Not only did we lose sixty six valuable members of the fleet but also a much-needed transport ship containing food and medical supplies," the captain complained bitterly.

Kelem took a deep breath and exhaled, while at the same time feeling the pain and frustration in Veronica Valchek's mind. The woman had a strong character and powerful will, but she herself was close to a mental breakdown almost ready to give up, perhaps even taking her own life. Kelem shuddered and had to fight to push the woman's emotions away from his mind. He realized that he was in a situation where events were too powerful for him to control or prevent how everyone else saw him and what they believed he could do for them. Now more than ever he wished that he was back on Plantanimus and that he could consult Zeus and ask him what to do. Kelem's natural instincts were to shy away from fame, fortune and popularity. Yet it seemed that throughout his adult life he had been routinely placed in situations where he had to take leadership roles and have the fate of others in his hands.

"I'm afraid that you've already achieved hero status," Capt. Valchek said interrupting his thoughts.

"I can see that," Kelem replied uncomfortably. "And I assure you that no one more than I, regrets that fact."

"How does that old saying go?" Captain Valchek asked herself. "Oh yes, the saying goes: 'there are those who seek power and renown and then there are those who have power and renown thrust upon them'. I'm afraid that you're the latter," the captain of the Volta said with a bittersweet smile.

"I shall make the best with the hand that fate has dealt me, I suppose," Kelem reflected with resignation.

"I wish strongly that you would, Capt. Rogeston, for if it turns out that you're not the miracle that we've been praying for all these years, then our cause is lost and Mars will remain under the cruel yoke of the Phalanx for all time."

The door opened and in walked a thin undernourished man in his late forties, wearing long blonde hair, watery blue eyes, sporting the rank of commander on his shoulder's epaulets. "I'm sorry I'm late, Captain," the man apologized softly in a hoarse voice.

"Capt. Rogeston, this is Commander Ron Hugh, my first officer," Veronica Valchek said, motioning to the frail looking commander.

Kelem put out his hand and felt the commander's weak handshake.

"Commander Hugh is suffering from a severe case of dysentery. I asked him to remain in bed, but I'm afraid that he insisted on meeting you and welcoming you personally to the Volta," Captain Valchek said by way of introducing her first officer.

"Please commander, we can socialize any time in the next few days while I remain aboard. You didn't need to get up from your sick bed to meet me," Kelem said with sympathy.

"I wouldn't have missed it for the world, Captain Rogeston," the commander said, his face brightening with a smile.

"Commander Hugh was the one who convinced me to take this assignment, Capt. Rogeston. At first I was ambivalent about using so much of our fuel reserves to ferry you to the next ship on the list, but the commander educated me as to your previous accomplishments. The commander seems to have read a great deal about your personal history as well as that of your family. When Capt. Devereaux described your technical skills, I realized that taking you on board would be beneficial to my vessel," Veronica Valchek confessed.

"Then I am in your debt, Commander. Thank you for speaking on my behalf," Kelem declared gratefully.

"On the contrary, sir, it is we who are in your debt by gracing us with your presence and great intellect," the commander replied as he began to tremble and lose his balance.

Kelem and Captain Valchek reached for the poor man who was obviously too sick to be out of bed and helped him into a chair. Captain Valchek reached for the intercom and called the sergeant at arms standing guard outside of her quarters and ordered her to have two crewmen come and get the commander and bring him back to his quarters.

"Shouldn't the ship's medic be attending the commander?" Kelem asked concerned.

"Our ship's medic died two years ago and we haven't been able to find a replacement yet," the captain informed him. "Additionally we don't have any amoebicidal drugs or any antibiotics on board to treat the commander," she replied with frustration.

"Don't fret about me, Veronica. You know that I'll bounce back. I always do," the commander said bravely.

"I don't need you to be a hero, Ron. I just need you to get well so you can help me run the ship," Veronica Valchek chided him affectionately.

"I'm sorry Captain Rogeston, I apologize for my condition. I'll go back to my cabin, but I hope we have a chance to talk later on. I have a million questions for you," the man added with enthusiasm.

Just then, two crewmen walked in to help Commander Hugh return to his cabin.

"Please don't apologize, Commander. I'm honored by your effort to come and meet me while feeling so ill. I'll be sure to come down and visit you in your cabin tomorrow. We'll talk then," Kelem promised, patting the man's shoulder affectionately.

"I look forward to your visit, Captain. Goodbye," the commander said as he left the cabin assisted by the two crewmen.

Veronica Valchek turned her head away from Kelem to hide her tears. Kelem realized that she and the commander were in a relationship. Kelem didn't know whether to say something or go to her and comfort her. He remained where he stood, feeling uneasy.

"Please sit down, Captain Rogeston," Veronica Valchek said after a few seconds before turning around to face him.

Kelem sat down and looked down at his hands to avoid eye contact with her. He didn't want to embarrass the woman.

She sat next to Kelem, her eyes red with a trace of tears on her cheeks. "You see how desperate things are out here, Captain Rogeston? We don't even have basic medical supplies for an easily treatable condition like dysentery. Remember that transport ship that surrendered to the enemy?" she asked, Kelem nodded. "Well, that ship was the fleet's pharmacy. It was carrying a year's supply of drugs and other medical supplies. Since we lost that ship, people have started to die from infections and other preventable conditions and diseases that normally would not kill people if treated in time. We are dying out here, Captain Rogeston!" Veronica Valchek said reaching for Kelem's hand and squeezing it weakly with her thin narrow fingers.

Kelem felt the woman's pain and mental exhaustion from years of courageously maintaining her image as leader of the ship in front of her crew, while at the same time suffering from the same lack of hope and sense of defeat that everyone was struggling with. "Don't deny us hope, Mr. Rogeston! Accept the mantle of authority and leadership! Otherwise the great nation of Mars will be no more..."

Kelem was able to push away Veronica Valchek's emotions but he could not contain his own anger and pain when he thought of the ruin that the Terrans had brought to his home planet. It was at that moment that he vowed to do whatever he could to end the slow genocide against the Martian people and the tyranny of the Phalanx.

A crewman brought in two trays with food. The meal consisted of salted meats, hydroponic grown tomatoes and hard biscuits. The portions were small but Kelem realized that this meal was probably extravagant for this crew and that someone's rations had been donated in his honor. He ate the food and thanked the captain for her hospitality and then returned to his cabin.

As he lay in his bunk in the dark, he wondered what he could do to improve the lives of these hardy, tough rebels who had managed to survive for fourteen long years in conditions that would have defeated the strongest and best trained soldiers that Earth had in its military. Now more than ever, he sensed that the rebel fleet was near imminent collapse. By his own estimate, Kelem figured out that within six months the fleet would have ceased to exist due to ships breaking down beyond repair, or else by disease, desertions and suicides.

The most urgent problem that these people had was morale. Kelem realized that even if he could acquire food supplies, equipment and medicine, the situation would not really improve until people's hearts and minds could be turned around and their spirits filled with hope and dreams for the future. Kelem knew that even someone like Louie, Rusty's son, whose young mind was still open to all possibilities, would eventually crumble under the collective clinical depression from which all the rebels were suffering.

"How I wish that I was with you now, Zeus," Kelem said aloud in the dark. He longed for Plantanimus and the beautiful lake by the waterfall with its pink sandy beach next to the shack that he and Ndugu had built six years before. He missed Anima most of all, his beloved soulmate. He thought of her and her beautiful face and her sweet and gentle personality and remembered the feel of her smooth green skin in his hand and the sweet musty smell of her body. He knew that she was in Pralaya, the sleep without dreaming, but couldn't help but feel guilty that he had left her without saying goodbye.

Sleep finally came to him and he found himself lying beneath Zeus's roots.

"DEAREST KELEM, IT IS GOOD TO BE WITH YOU AGAIN," Zeus' rumbling voice said, echoing throughout the forest.

"Zeus, I can't believe it! You heard my plea and came to me in my dreams!" Kelem said with happiness and relief.

"WE DID NOT COME TO YOU, DEAR KELEM, YOU CAME TO US," Zeus replied, surprising Kelem.

"However it is that we're together, I'm glad that we are communicating. Oh Zeus! I'm in dire need of your counsel," Kelem said with anxiety. "A great burden has been placed on my shoulders and I'm at a loss as to what I should do!" Kelem said feeling overwhelmed.

"WE SENSE THE TURMOIL IN YOUR MIND, DEAR FRIEND. YOU HAVE SUFFERED MENTALLY AND PHYSICALLY SINCE WE LAST SPOKE. YOUR BODY HAS EXPERIENCED PAIN AT THE HANDS OF ANOTHER AND IT VEXES US TO LEARN OF THIS EVENT," Zeus said with great concern.

"The physical pain I suffered is not what's troubling me, Zeus. The future of my fellow countrymen, on the other hand, is. Unbeknownst to us, the explosion of the Solar Nations *n'time* generator created an accidental time shift that sent the ship fifteen years into the future. When Ndugu and I returned to our native solar system we discovered that twenty one years had passed since we had departed on our voyage. During that time, the Terrans invaded my planet and now rule Mars with the iron fist of the Phalanx!" Kelem explained.

"WE READ YOUR MEMORY OF THE EVENTS THAT YOU HAVE LIVED THROUGH SINCE WE LAST SPOKE, DEAR KELEM, AND UNDERSTAND THE SOURCE OF YOUR DISTRESS. IF YOU WERE IN ACTUAL PHYSICAL CONTACT WITH OUR BODIES, WE COULD REPAIR THE DAMAGE CAUSED BY THE BEATING THAT YOU SUFFERED. THE ONLY THING THAT WE CAN DO FOR YOU NOW IS TO HEAL YOUR MIND AND SPIRIT," Zeus commented, as his deep voice rumbled and echoed on the mountain.

"I can always use your spiritual blessing, dear Zeus, but my real concerns are the hearts and minds of my fellow Martians who are suffering greatly at the hands of their oppressors. If I could only find a way to heal their downtrodden minds and lift their spirits, then my people would have a fighting chance to regain their freedom and dream of the future once again," Kelem said, hoping for advice from Zeus and the other Dreamers.

A long silence followed. For a while, Kelem thought that he had lost his connection with Zeus and the others. But sometime after, Zeus spoke again. "DO NOT LET THE PAIN, ANGER AND HATE THAT YOUR COUNTRYMEN FEEL AFFECT YOUR MIND. INSTEAD, SURROUND YOURSELF WITH LIGHT AND JOY AND FOCUS YOUR THOUGHTS AND ENERGY ON GIVING THEM THE LOVE AND AFFECTION THAT YOU WISH FOR THEM. RADIATE THIS LOVE AND ENERGY FROM YOUR HEART AS IF YOU WERE A POWERFUL ANTENNA. ABOVE ALL, RESIST THE TEMPTATION TO DWELL IN HATE, RESENTMENT AND ANGER, FOR IT WILL SURELY CONSUME YOU AND BRING YOU DOWN A DARK PATH."

"I'm not sure that I'm capable of being so magnanimous, after witnessing the pain and sorrow that my fellow countrymen have endured for all these years. My people are dying, Zeus! I don't see how giving love and affection to my fellow Martians is going to accomplish anything without some sort of violent military action against the Terrans." Kelem replied with angst and consternation.

"WE'RE NOT SAYING THAT A COUNTER OFFENSIVE AGAINST THE TERRANS SHOULD BE AVOIDED AND THAT YOU SHOULD REFRAIN FROM GETTING INVOLVED IN THE STRUGGLE, KELEM. OUR CONCERN IS FOR THE SANCTITY OF YOUR SOUL, SO THAT YOU DON'T FALL PREY TO THE SAME EVIL TO WHICH THE TAU PRIESTS OF PLANTANIMUS FELL VICTIM MILLENNIA AGO. REMEMBER HOW THEIR HATE AND NEGATIVITY CAUSED THE END OF THE UMHAR CIVILIZATION," Zeus warned, reminding Kelem how the Umhar, the original inhabitants of Plantanimus destroyed themselves thousands of years before he and Ndugu arrived on the planet.

Kelem heard Zeus' words and thought his advice somewhat plain and simple. But as he pondered the Dreamer's words he felt a warm sensation in his heart chakra that opened his mind to what the ancient being was trying to teach him. He, Kelem Rogeston, had the power within him to heal the mental pain and anguish of others! And, like his Brotherhood of the Light mentors had taught him so many years ago, he couldn't let their suffering touch his own mind and spirit. He had to master the ability to remain free from all negative feelings and emotions that surrounded him. It was a tall order, but Kelem knew that if he relied on his early training and remembered the lessons and principles that Thor Kutmeier and Nicolas Alfano had taught him and what his other mentors and spiritual companions, the Dreamers, were trying to teach him, he would be able to help others improve their lot.

"YES, DEAR FRIEND, THIS TECHNIQUE IS A SIMPLE THING TO UNDERSTAND, BUT DIFFICULT TO EXECUTE," Zeus confirmed, having heard Kelem's thoughts. "YOUR HEART IS PURE AND YOUR MIND IS POWERFUL. ONCE YOU MASTER THIS DISCIPLINE, THE EFFECT WILL FEED UPON ITSELF AND YOU'LL FIND THAT IT BECOMES EASIER AND EASIER TO HELP OTHERS, NO MATTER HOW DIRE THE CIRCUMSTANCES THAT SURROUND THEM MAY BE."

"Thank you Zeus!" Kelem replied, realizing that he was now awake. He sat on the edge of his bunk and felt calm and at peace. The cabin's doorbell rang, and when he palmed the door plate, Ensign Jacko stuck his head in. "Good morning, Captain Rogeston. Captain Valchek requests your presence at the mess-hall for breakfast," the man announced.

He looked at his wrist comp and realized that the time was 07:00 AM. He had slept for almost ten hours! "Tell her that I'll be there presently!" Kelem responded with renewed enthusiasm as he jumped to his feet sporting a big smile. The ensign noticed Kelem's upbeat behavior and responded in kind. As he walked away, he felt good about himself and began whistling a tune as he headed back to the mess-hall.

As Kelem made his way to the ship's mess-hall, he felt different and knew that something about him had changed. Reflecting on his conversation with Zeus, he realized that the Dreamer had given him a powerful tool to fight against the Terrans. When he stepped into the mess-hall, the entire ship's company rose to their feet and saluted him. A little surprised at first, he stopped in mid-stride, then looked at everyone and said, "At ease!" Everyone had smiles on their faces as they sat down.

"Good morning, Captain Rogeston," Veronica Valchek said with a smile.

"Good morning, Captain Valchek," Kelem responded as he sat next to her.

"I would like to ask you to accept a commission as a senior commanding officer of the Martian rebel fleet and I hope you will say yes."

"I suppose this would be some sort of honorary rank?" Kelem asked, feeling a little uncomfortable with a title that he hadn't earned.

"Somewhere between honorary and official," Captain Valchek suggested. "Being the senior officer on this ship I would like the honor to appoint you to the rank of brigadier general," Veronica Valchek said observing him carefully.

Kelem knew instantly that despite his dislike for attention and popularity, this was part of what needed to be done in order to liberate Mars. "I won't have to wear some sort of ridiculous outfit with a chest full of medals, will I?" he asked, laughing nervously.

Captain Valchek laughed and patted his hand to ease his concerns. "Not at all! We'd like to remove the captain's insignia from your flight suit and replace it with a gold star on each shoulder. Will you agree?"

"Fine. I will bring you my flight suit later and you can make the changes," Kelem replied.

"Wonderful! I would like to bestow this honorary rank with a formal ceremony tomorrow morning. Is that all right with you?" she asked expectantly.

Kelem agreed.

After breakfast Kelem wasted no time finding out which ship's systems needed the most attention. The vessel's engineer, a master chief named Latimer, showed him where the biggest problems were and Kelem dove into the work. Throughout the day, members of the crew would come by wherever Kelem was at the moment, to sneak a peek at him getting his hands dirty along with the rest of the chief's crew.

The following morning Kelem was officially 'promoted' to the rank of brigadier general in a short ceremony in the ship's mess-hall.

Afterwards, every single member of the crew came by, shook his hand and congratulated him. In spite of Kelem now being an official 'senior officer' of the rebel fleet, he continued working, fixing and improving the ship's systems.

By the time he left the Volta six days later, most of the ship's systems had been refurbished to near original specs. But the most remarkable transformation had been that of the crew. Even Commander Hugh had somehow gotten over his bout with dysentery. The man's cheeks had turned rosy and Captain Valchek remarked how quickly the man had regained his vitality.

"If you could do what you did for us in just six short days, General Rogeston," Veronica Valchek observed, "I have no doubt in my mind that you will succeed in leading us in the defeat of the Terrans. You have transformed this ship physically, mentally and spiritually, and for the first time in fourteen years my crew and I are full of hope and looking forward to defeating the enemy. We wish you the best of luck, and our prayers go with you. Farewell, General, we await your return. God speed," Capt. Valchek said, embracing him warmly with tears in her eyes.

Kelem boarded the next ship that would take him on the next leg of his journey. The vessel was an old MMC ore transport with only a crew of nine. As he had done on the Volta, Kelem improved the morale of its crew and helped repair and restore much of the ship's technical equipment in a few days.

Over the next twenty eight days, Kelem traveled on five more vessels, achieving the same results with each crew and ship. Word of this 'miracle worker' had gotten around, and in two instances, other ships, whose crews wanted to meet General Rogeston, actually chased the vessels that he was traveling in and docked with those ships so they could meet Kelem.

Kelem spoke to Ndugu via encrypted audio transmission and learned that the entire fleet was abuzz with gossip about him. Ndugu had also gained his own share of notoriety. The Rusty Bucket had become a magnet for other ships that needed help with repairs. So desperate were some of these ship's captains for Ndugu's talents, that at one point, twelve of them showed up at the same time, creating a security hazard. Part of the reason why the rebel fleet had managed to survive all these years was because it was spread out all over the solar system. Twelve ships meeting at the same location in space made too tempting a target for Terran battle cruisers and destroyers.

Eventually, Rusty put his foot down and was forced to create a waiting list of ships that needed repair. The crew of the Rusty Bucket, who, but a few weeks before, had viewed Ndugu with great suspicion, had now become fiercely protective of their "star chief engineer". Other ship's captains had brazenly attempted to steal Ndugu from the Rusty Bucket. Now, whenever Ndugu boarded each ship to perform his magic, he was accompanied by either, Rusty or one of his most trusted crewmembers to make sure that Ndugu was not enticed to desert the Rusty Bucket by another ship's captain and taken away from them.

So valuable had the Rusty Bucket become because of Ndugu, that another of the surviving Martian Navy frigates had been permanently assigned to shadow the asteroid herder in case a Terran ship attacked.

One of the benefits of Ndugu being the resident star engineer was that the Rusty Bucket was now replete with food and spare equipment that had been traded with other ships for his services. In a way, Ndugu was under a benign type of house arrest.

Kelem spoke with Rusty and encouraged him to continue fixing and repairing as many ships as possible, and assured him that Ndugu would not desert the Rusty Bucket. Kelem wanted the fleet to be battle ready when he returned from Mars.

On November 30th, Kelem was transferred to a curious looking shuttle. The tiny ship had been made to look like an asteroid. The camouflage was utterly believable. The rebels had attached thousands of small space rocks to its hull, making the little vessel look exactly like a run-of-the-mill lump of rock floating aimlessly in the asteroid belt.

Kelem asked why the shuttle had been made to look that way. The captain, the only crew member of the ship, informed him that his next transport would be a Terran operated asteroid herder. Upon hearing this, Kelem became concerned, but the captain told him that aside from the herder's captain and exec officer, everyone else in the crew was a member of the resistance. Kelem now asked how in the hell was he going to board the Terran herder. The shuttle's captain explained how this was going to happen.

The captain of the fake asteroid shuttle would signal his contact on the Terran herder and that individual would then give him the position where the herder would go next to pick up asteroids to bring back to Mars for processing. The little shuttle would then travel to that exact spot on the belt, shut its engines and float along with the rest of the real asteroids waiting for the herder to show up. The shuttle would then be collected in the herder's basket along with all the other space rocks. At that point, Kelem would exit the shuttle wearing a spacesuit and then make his way to a hatch on the herder where one of the crewmembers would be waiting for him. Once inside the ship he would be taken to a hiding place and kept there until they reached Mars. Meanwhile, as Kelem knew from years of operating herder's in his youth, the ship would discard any asteroid smaller than two metric tons and only keep the larger rocks. The little shuttle would then be discarded along with all the other small asteroids. After the herder was far enough away, the captain would then fire up his engine and rejoin the rebel fleet.

The procedure was not without risk. Kelem could be easily killed if one of the huge rocks came loose from one of the magnetic grapples securing it and crush him against another asteroid. The shuttle's captain assured Kelem that the technician who operated the collection basket was highly skilled and that the risks were minimal. He told him that they had performed this trick before without anyone getting killed in the process.

In spite of the shuttle captain's assurance, Kelem had his reservations and hoped that this particular time would not be the one time when the collection basket technician made a mistake.

Twelve hours later, Kelem was exiting the little shuttle in a spacesuit, making his way slowly towards a hatch fifty meters away from the collection basket. In his gloved hand he held a small gas canister that moved him forward in small increments each time he pressed the trigger. One small mistake and he would drift past the hatch where was to enter the ship and become just one more object floating amidst the other asteroids in the belt forever, or worst, he might be seen by the captain or the first mate on one of the cameras on the bridge and be caught, arrested and then brought to Mars as a prisoner along with the crew, who would all be revealed by his presence as members of the resistance.

To his relief, Kelem reached the hatch and attached a small magnetic anchor to the ship's hull connected to his suit via a cable and waited there, tethered to the ship. After a few minutes, he began to worry, when the basket operator released the smaller asteroids and the herder's engines turned on. The magnetic anchor was not powerful enough to keep him connected to the ship once the engines fired and the herder began to move. Kelem could feel the vibrations of the massive chemical rocket engines coming to life through the cable keeping him connected to the ship. He looked toward the rear of the vessel and saw the glow of the engines. Soon the ship's momentum would dislodge him from the hull, and once he drifted into one of the engines cone exhaust, he would be instantly vaporized.

CHAPTER 7

Return to Mars

November 21st, 2659

Kelem looked for any kind of protrusion near the hatch that he could hold on to, but there were none to be seen on the hull's smooth metal surface. The ship was beginning to accelerate, and soon he'd lose his magnetic anchor. The tension on the cable that connected him to the ship grew tight and he was thrown backwards as the ship picked up speed. Kelem knew that in a few seconds he'd come loose and that would be the end of him.

The hatch suddenly opened and just as his magnetic anchor was about to dislodge from the ship's outer skin, a space suited arm reached for his hand and pulled him in. The hatch sealed and he found himself face-to-face with one of the crewmembers. The man moved his head forward until both their helmets touched.

"I'm sorry that it took so long to get you. But the exec happened to be near the airlock and I had to wait until he left the area," the man apologized, as the sound traveled acoustically through his helmet to Kelem's.

"A few more seconds and I would've been vaporized by the engines," Kelem replied loudly with relief.

"I'm sorry, we've done this before but this is the first time that we've had any trouble."

"What now?" Kelem asked.

"I'll re-pressurize the airlock then you must follow me. Your hiding place is nearby and I'm afraid that it's quite small and uncomfortable. But the good news is that we're behind schedule, so the captain is pushing the engines and we should be arriving on Mars in twenty four hours or so."

The man let go of Kelem's helmet and reached for the airlock's controls, and the chamber was re-pressurized. After opening the inner door, he looked around and motioned for Kelem to follow him. The man led him through several compartments and then stopped in front of a panel on the side of a bulkhead. He took out a small power drill from his space suit and loosened several screws, then pulled the panel open revealing a small space two and a half meters square. Inside were a portable emergency toilet, a small box full of emergency rations, two containers of water and a flashlight.

The man opened his faceplate and motioned for Kelem to do the same.

"There's air in there and just enough room for you and your spacesuit. Once you take your spacesuit off you must remain as quiet as possible. The captain and the exec never come down here but you never know. A couple of hours before we reach Mars I'll come and get you out. Then, I'll take you to the lower deck and sneak you inside one of our garbage disposal containers. After we unload the rocks to the transfer drones, another crew will come, remove the trash containers and load them onto a garbage scow. That other ship's crew is also with the resistance, but just in case they have an uninvited guest on their ship, you must remain inside the container until it reaches the sanitation department in Latonga City. Is that understood?" the man asked.

"Got it. By the way, what's your name?" Kelem asked.

"No names here. The less you and I know about each other the better, just in case one or both of us gets caught," the man replied motioning for him to get into the little space.

Kelem obeyed, knowing that these men were risking their lives by sneaking him onto the ship and bringing him to Mars. The crewman put the panel back in place and screwed it close. Kelem reached for the flashlight in the dark, found it, and removed his spacesuit.

He folded the bulky suit as best he could and sat on the floor in the dark. The deck plates were vibrating from the thrust of the engines that were pushing the huge herder at two hundred thousand kilometers per hour toward Mars. He thought of how close he'd come to dying just a few minutes before and wondered what other dangers he'd be facing in the days to come. He was curious to know how Mars and its people would appear to him after being gone for so long, now that his fellow Martians were nothing but slaves under Terran rule. He pushed all negative thoughts out of his mind and concentrated on the task at hand. He had to find a way to revitalize the resistance, both on Mars as well as in the rebel fleet spread throughout the solar system. His first move would be to contact the Brotherhood, consult with them, acquaint himself with the situation and then begin reorganizing the resistance.

The hours went by slowly as Kelem sat in his hiding place in quiet meditation. When he felt the ship turning one hundred and eighty degrees he knew that the herder was about to begin its braking maneuver as it approached the red planet. He turned the flashlight back on, and put on his spacesuit with difficulty inside the cramped space. Not long after that he heard the sound of the power drill removing the screws that held the panels closed. When the panel was removed, he saw the same crewman who put him there.

"How much air do you have in your suit's tank?" the man asked him.

Kelem looked at the wrist display on his suit's arm. "About two hours, why?"

"The garbage container you're going to be in will be exposed to the vacuum of space for about five minutes as it is towed into the cargo hold of the other ship. It's sealed but is not air tight, so you must close your faceplate and turn the air on the minute you feel the container moving."

"Will do," Kelem responded. He stepped out of the hiding place and waited until the man screwed the panel back on the bulkhead. Then he followed him down to the lower decks. They didn't run into any other crew members on the way down, yet the man was careful to look into each compartment before they stepped in. Finally, they reached the compartment where the ships garbage was compacted. Here the smell of decaying food was prevalent. The man opened a container that was half-full and helped him get in by lifting Kelem up gently.

"I know it stinks in here, but I don't recommend that you close your faceplate and breathe your suit's air in case we're thrown off schedule," the man suggested.

"I can handle it. Don't worry about me, I know what to do," Kelem answered sticking his thumb up confidently.

The man closed and secured the lid and walked away. Although the container was not airtight it was locked from the outside. If something went wrong or if his air ran out, he'd be trapped.

The smell of one month's worth of food garbage generated by a crew of forty miners was overwhelming now that the container's lid was closed. Kelem closed his eyes and imagined that he was walking in the forests of Plantanimus, taking in the sweet smell of its beautiful vegetation. Soon the herder's engines came on and he was thrown against the side of the container as the ship decelerated. He knew that the engines would come on and off for the next two hours until the herder established a stable orbit above Mars.

Almost exactly two hours later the last braking maneuver came to an end and Kelem could hear servo motors coming to life as mechanical arms grabbed the container. He slammed his faceplate closed and the suit's air came on automatically. Within seconds his suit stiffened when the garbage compartment was suddenly exposed to space. The sound of a magnetic tether hitting the side of the metal container signaled that the thing was about to be towed to the other ship. A few minutes later Kelem was jostled about as the crew of the garbage scow secured the metal box to the deck of their cargo hold.

When the floating garbage fell "down" and his suit became loose again, he knew that the cargo hold had been gravitated and re-pressurized. He opened his faceplate and heard the sound of voices near the container.

"Boy, these miners sure eat a lot! Good thing that we'll be getting rid of this stinky mess in less than an hour," a man said, speaking unusually loud. "I guess that when we reach the depot we won't have to smell the stink of this can once we roll it out of the ship, since we'll be wearing our spacesuits."

Kelem understood that the man was informing him that the ship would be landing on Mars within an hour, but also that the container would be exposed to the thin Martian atmosphere for a few minutes until it was brought into a pressurized environment.

An hour later he heard the ship's retros firing as the garbage scow entered the Martian atmosphere. Soon, he heard the landing turbines rev up, signaling that the ship was about to make contact with the ground, Kelem shut his faceplate and breathed the suit's air once again. Within seconds the cargo hold was depressurized and the container began moving. Once his suit loosened, Kelem knew that he was in a pressurized environment yet again. Nothing happened for a few minutes, then he heard a vehicle approach and the container was lifted and driven elsewhere for another five minutes. After the vehicle stopped, the container was unceremoniously dropped on the ground.

The sound of footsteps approached and then Kelem heard the container's latch being opened. A bearded man wearing a face mask stuck his head in and looked at Kelem. "Welcome to Mars, let me help you out."

Kelem, feeling stiff after sitting in a crouched position for over three hours, had a little difficulty getting up. Once out and back on his feet, he stretched and removed his helmet. The smell in this place was just as bad as the inside of the container. Now he understood why the man was wearing a face mask. "Follow me," the man said turning around heading toward a pressure door at the end of the depot. Kelem followed the man into a room that looked like an industrial shower compartment.

"Please put your helmet back on and close your faceplate. I'm going to spray you with a cleaning deodorizing agent then rinse you off," the man said, grabbing a hose with a long nozzle. Kelem obliged and the man washed the garbage stink off of his space suit. Once done, the man asked him to follow him once again. He led him to a storage room where Kelem removed his space suit and was given a Latonga City Sanitation uniform and light city pressure suit. Then the man led him several levels down into the bowels of Mars.

When they reached the entrance to a long tunnel carved out of Martian granite, the man stopped. "At the end of this tunnel is a small chamber with a cot, water and food as well as a portable toilet. You are to remain there until someone else comes along to interview you and instruct you on procedures," the man said.

"How long will it be before this person comes?" Kelem asked.

"It might be a day or two. We're under constant surveillance, and movement within the city is difficult with all the checkpoints and such," the man replied.

"I was hoping to make contact with some people I know. Is there any way that I can send out a message right now?"

"Look, whoever you are," the man said eyeballing Kelem up and down with distrust, "I don't know where you've come from or why you are here, but I can tell that you know nothing about the situation here on the ground. There's a lot that you need to know before you step out of this facility without being caught and getting others killed. Go where I told you to go, keep your mouth shut and wait until someone shows up. Got it?" the man said sternly.

Kelem nodded and continued walking to the end of the tunnel. As he walked away he read the man's mind and found that he didn't trust Kelem. But above all, the man was in fear for his life and felt that Kelem's presence was a security risk.

Kelem was surprised by the degree of paranoia and fear that he sensed on the man's mind. This was not what he expected to find once he arrived on Mars. In spite of his ability given to him by Zeus, to raise other people's spirits, he was sensing that everyone on Mars was living in abject fear every moment of their lives. Boosting people's hopes and expectations was going to be a lot tougher than he had anticipated.

Two days went by without anyone coming to see him, so Kelem stayed put not wanting to incur the ire of his keeper. Finally on the third morning of his stay in his "pseudo-cell", he heard footsteps approaching his door out in the tunnel. There was a polite knock at the door. Kelem got up from his cot and opened the door, and to his surprise, a tall pretty girl of about seventeen years old stood in the doorway, wearing a dirty pressure suit, helmet in hand.

" Good morning sir, may I come in?" the girl asked with a sweet smile.

"Please come in," Kelem said, glad to see another person at last.

The girl looked around and noticed that the only place to sit was the rickety cot on one side of the chamber. She appeared uncomfortable to be in a small room with a strange man where the only place to sit was a single cot. Kelem gestured for her to sit down and she obliged, sitting at the farthest end of the cot, obviously feeling awkward. Kelem took the hint and sat at the other end of the cot to ease her discomfort.

The girl scrutinized Kelem carefully and opened up a small pouch that she took out from inside her pressure suit with a strange look in her eyes. "I'm to begin creating your new identity profile. We were told that you look like a Terran and I see that it's true. This is going to present a bit of a problem for you," the brown haired girl said, looking concerned.

"I'm aware of my appearance, but how is the way I look problematic?" Kelem asked.

"Well sir, you look too healthy for a native. Most of us are living on meager rations and are severely underweight. You look more like one of those well fed Terran civilian workers contracted by the military to run the utilities here on Mars," she replied with unease.

Kelem looked at the girl and noticed that even under her pressure suit she looked quite thin and malnourished. In spite of the small rations he'd been eating for the last thirty four days, he was still fifteen kilos heavier than he had been when he left Mars in 2638. This was indeed a problem and Kelem realized that he had to lose weight fast!

"I'll have to lose the weight. If I go on a crash diet I can probably pass," Kelem commented.

"You'll have to do more than that sir. Your face looks like an earthman's face, all plump and tanned. I'm afraid that I'll have to get back to my people and inform them of this problem," the girl said nervously. "One thing that will be helpful is to let your beard grow. Depilatory facial gel is in short supply. Most Martian males sport beards these days."

Kelem's spirits sunk with the realization that it would be a while before he could reconnect with anyone. In spite of his disappointment, he accepted the situation.

The girl measured his height, noted the color of his eyes, hair color, body weight and measurements and then took his fingerprints. Then she took out a syringe and expertly withdrew a few milliliters of Kelem's blood into a small vial.

"I have to take your picture and blood sample for identity purposes, sir. There are those among us who don't believe that you are who you say you are," the girl said apologetically.

Kelem realized that the request for fingerprints, blood and a photo of his face made sense. The resistance had to be careful. For all they knew, he could be a Terran agent made to look like a young Kelem Rogeston. The blood taken from him and subsequent DNA test would prove his true identity. "Go ahead take a picture; I don't have a problem with that."

The girl raised her wrist comp, aimed its small lens at Kelem and captured his image.

Before the girl left, she promised him that someone would be coming by to talk to him. When he asked how many days before someone showed up, she told him it would be a day or two.

Kelem immediately curtailed his food intake and took to running back and forth in the long tunnel outside his chamber several times a day until he felt exhausted. He reduced his night's sleep to four hours and stopped using depilatory gel. The girl had said that someone would come by to talk to him within a day or two, unfortunately a week went by and still no one had come to see him. The man who had brought him down here was nowhere to be seen and even though he had reduced his food intake, he'd soon be out of food if someone didn't bring him new supplies.

Finally, ten days after the girl had visited him came a knock at the door. This time when he opened the door he recognized the person. It was Susan Beaumont, one of the Brotherhood's board members! Kelem almost gasped when he saw what the years had done to the woman. Her hair had turned white and her body looked as frail as a person with a terminal illness. She hugged him and held onto him, trembling with emotion. Kelem sensed the sadness and pain that she was carrying with her. But he pushed those feelings away and, as Zeus had instructed him, he filled his heart with love and imagined it radiating out of his body into hers.

"Kelem, dear Kelem! How is this possible? You haven't aged at all!" she remarked, pulling away and examining him from head to toe.

"Susan, it is so good to see you! I was wondering when someone would be coming by. I've been here for more than two weeks with no word from anyone. What's going on?" Kelem asked, escorting her to the little cot.

"When my colleagues and I saw the picture that my daughter Gina took of you, we could hardly believe our eyes. We long ago gave up hope of ever seeing you alive again, Kelem! There are those in my group who suspected that you were a Terran agent. But I had a feeling that it was really you and after we compared your DNA with the sample on file in the Martian data base we realized that it was really you! I had to come and see for myself," she concluded, shedding tears of joy.

"I have so much to tell you and the others, Susan. How soon can you schedule a meeting of the Brotherhood?" Kelem asked anxiously.

Susan's expression changed and she cast her eyes down, her lips pursed. "Dear Kelem, don't you know? We've lost so many of our colleagues...." she said, her voice trembling.

"I heard about Nicholas and I suspected that the Brotherhood had scattered after the invasion. How many of us are left?"

"The Terrans killed Jasper Willis, Sophia Moretti, Lars Valentine and Dimitri Kuzmenko within twenty four hours of the occupation. The rest of us, with the exception of Nicolas, managed to avoid capture by hiding and eventually assuming false identities. As far as the other members of the Board of Directors and the rest of the membership is concerned, there are very few of us left. We've all scattered to the winds trying to survive the best we can," Susan Beaumont said, almost in a whisper.

"Damn! The Brotherhood is one of the few things that can help Mars get rid of the Terrans," Kelem said, realizing that his worst fears concerning the Brotherhood had come true. "Susan, we have to reunite the membership!" he said with urgency.

"Marla Hassett is still working at the old Charmont Institute. I'm sure I can get her to meet with us and a few others, but it might be a while before we can get together. Traveling is hard in Latonga City these days. One has to get special passes to go anywhere. But we might be able to meet in another city."

"I heard about the checkpoints and the special passes one must acquire to go anywhere. But, Susan!" Kelem said, clasping his fists, "the Brotherhood is the key to get things going in our favor again. We must do everything in our power to reconvene as a group."

"I'll do my best Kelem, but I must know, what has happened to you?" she asked, looking at him with curiosity, examining his youthful face and body.

"What do you mean?" Kelem replied, wondering what she was talking about.

"How is it possible that you haven't aged in all the years that you've been away from us?"

"It's a very long story Susan, but the short version is that the Solar Nations *n'time* generator failed and when it did, it somehow brought the ship forward fifteen years into the future. Ninety three people died instantly when the ship caught fire," Kelem said, pushing away the trauma of the event. "Then, myself and six other survivors of the accident found a habitable planet by sheer luck. Unfortunately, five of them perished soon after, and then there were only two of us left, myself and my Terran friend Ndugu Nabole. We spent six years stranded on the planet and were miraculously rescued by an alien race. The aliens brought us back to the solar system. When we reached the orbit of Saturn we were shocked to discover that instead of six years away from home, we'd actually been gone twenty one years," Kelem explained, hoping that Susan wouldn't find the story hard to believe.

"Good Lord! I have no reason to doubt your story but it's going to take some time for me to digest all this and tell the others," Susan commented.

"I completely understand, Susan. Sometimes I have difficulty believing it myself. But without sounding too repetitive, I have to ask that we reconvene as soon as possible, with as many members of the Board of Directors and regular members that are still around! It's of the utmost importance Susan. I've learned a few things in my absence and I believe that with your help and that of the others, we can turn this terrible situation around."

Susan held Kelem's hands in hers and trembled with emotion. Something about Kelem had indeed changed. There was a powerful energy radiating from him that suddenly made her believe that there was hope for the future.

"I believe you, Kelem. Many of us had given up hope, but your return to Mars will change things! As we all know, there are no coincidences in life. I believe that God has heard our prayers and sent you back to free us from the Phalanx," Susan said with fervor.

"I think you're right, Susan. Thor told me a long time ago before he died, that my destiny was tightly woven with that of Mars, and that there would come a time when I'd have to make sacrifices for our nation and not shy away. I now understand what he meant. He had foreseen my role in the struggle to liberate Mars."

"Dear Kelem, for the first time in many years I feel joy in my heart! I'll go back and contact Marla and as many of the others as I can. But, please be patient because it might take a while before we can all afford to get away safely for this meeting."

"I understand, dear Susan. I look forward to seeing you and Marla and the others," Kelem replied, putting his arm around Susan's thin frame affectionately. "By the way, I'm almost out of food and if I have to wait a few more days before the meeting takes place, I'm going to need more supplies. Can you get someone to bring some food down here?"

"Oh yes! That would be Jacob, he's the one who works down here. I'll instruct him to bring you more food."

Susan kissed him and hugged him and left the chamber feeling much better than when she had arrived. Kelem stayed by the open door waving goodbye until Susan disappeared at the end of the long tunnel. He sat on the cot, took a deep breath and closed his eyes. Another two or three weeks and Kelem's beard would be fully grown. He didn't have a scale, but he knew that he'd already lost a few kilos. Soon he would be reunited with Marla Hassett and hopefully others as well. There were a lot of struggles and battles ahead, but now he knew that he was on his way.

CHAPTER 8

Breakthrough

December 20th, 2659

A few hours after Susan left, Jacob, the man who had originally met Kelem when he arrived on Mars, showed up with new boxes of food, drink and a replacement portable toilet. The one that Kelem had been using for the past few weeks had become unbearably smelly.

"I'll be gone for a few days. You won't see me until after the new year," Jacob informed him.

"That's right! I'd forgotten that Christmas is just five days away." Kelem replied, remembering past holiday celebrations with his family and friends when he'd lived on Mars so many years ago.

"Do you have any family here on Mars?" Jacob asked, showing a modicum of concern for Kelem for the first time since he'd arrived.

Sitting on his cot, Kelem's eyes lowered when the painful memory of his aunt and uncle's death by the hands of the Phalanx assailed him. "I know that my only blood relatives are dead. I pray that my closest and dearest friends are still alive," Kelem replied with hope in his heart.

"Hmmm!" Jacob uttered with sympathy. "How long have you been gone?

"More than twenty years."

Jacob paused for a long time before speaking. "You must have left when you were very young!" he observed based on Kelem's youthful appearance. The man had no idea who Kelem really was. "Look friend, I wish you the best and I hope that you succeed in finding as many of your friends as possible, but I must warn you that many Martians have been killed or starved to death by the goddamned Earthmen," he added with anger and resentment. "Be prepared to find that many of those you loved and cared for before the occupation, are now dead and gone."

Kelem looked up to the man and saw pain and suffering in his eyes and read the memory of a personal loss in his life. Within seconds Kelem knew the source of Jacob's sorrow and found that he'd lost his wife and children during a Phalanx raid of a resistance cell hideout more than ten years earlier. He now understood Jacob's gruff demeanor and sour attitude as a result of the deep trauma of losing his wife and children in such a violent manner.

"I can see that you've suffered greatly by the hands of our oppressors, Jacob," Kelem said softly, as he patted his arm gently. "But I believe that there's always hope and that we must persevere in spite of all that has been done to us. You must learn to feel joy and hope again. It's the only way that we can repel the Terrans and regain our freedom," he suggested with a smile, and let the warm glow of his heart chakra radiate outward as Zeus had taught him.

Jacob reeled back slightly, momentarily confused by the intense feeling of love and affection that he felt coming from Kelem. The emotion took him by surprise, and for a moment he almost screamed at him in anger for making him feel like a normal human being again, however briefly. After so many years of living in grief, he feared that a quick moment of joy would only serve to make the rest of his life seem worse by comparison.

"Don't fight it," Kelem said, feeling what Jacob was experiencing. "This sense of peace and joy you're feeling now can stay with you permanently and it doesn't mean that it will prevent you from continuing to fight the Terrans. It only means that you can stop suffering so deeply the loss of your wife and children and regain your humanity, because if we lose our humanity, Jacob, then the Phalanx has already won."

Jacob's eyes filled with tears and he collapsed to a sitting position on the cot.

"How?" he asked, looking at Kelem with surprise and confusion in his mind. "What did you just do to me?" he wondered in awe at how Kelem had somehow managed to instantly relieve years of pain and heartache from his mind.

"I didn't do anything Jacob," Kelem answered with a smile, hiding the fact that he'd used his newly developed skill. "You did. I only pointed the way and you opened the door and released your pain, thus freeing yourself from self-imposed suffering after so many years. It doesn't mean that you won't feel regret at having lost your family in such a tragic manner or that you'll ever forget them. But letting go of your pain will help you survive these bad times and make you a better resistance fighter."

Jacob was quiet for a while, then, he looked at Kelem and stood up.

"I was told that your presence here would bring much needed help to our struggle. But I refused to believe it. We've all been disappointed so many times when others claimed that salvation was at hand. I still don't know who you really are or how it is that you've come to us, but I now believe that you might be that someone who can really change things. For years we've all been praying for a miracle to save us from this life of bondage and slavery under the rule of the Phalanx. I think that you're capable of delivering that miracle that we've all hoped for. If you can do what you just did to me by simply talking to me, then there's hope for us all," Jacob stated with tears in his eyes. Then he pulled a tattered, faded photograph of his wife and children from his workman's coveralls, looked at it for a few seconds and then showed it to Kelem.

"I've been carrying this printed picture of my family with me for years, but I haven't been able to look at it for a long time for fear that I'd break down and sink into despair. But now I can look at it and not feel so angry and desperate that I want to take my own life. Thank you Kelem, I won't forget this."

Jacob reached out and shook Kelem's hand and then left the room.

Kelem leaned back against the wall and looked up at the ceiling feeling a sense of accomplishment even though he had only used Zeus's simple method of broadcasting a feeling of positive energy from his heart as instructed. But he had to admit that the Dreamer's teachings, though simple in principle, were quite effective in practice.

Kelem now saw real hope for the future, and whatever insecurities had been hiding in his subconscious regarding the successful eviction of the Terrans from his home planet, were now dissipating after this experience with Jacob. This new ability to raise people's spirits would go a long way to defeat the Phalanx and free Mars from Terran occupation.

He felt a great joy, and his mind began to project all sorts of positive things happening to him in the coming days. The joy turned into a sense of excitement and then a bubbling happiness that made him feel giddy. He began to laugh out loud and the laughter turned into guffaws and he practically fell on the floor from his body convulsing with hysterics as if he'd just heard the funniest joke in the world.

The feeling of warmth and love radiating from his heart had suddenly and unexpectedly ratcheted up on its own. It was expressing itself almost like physical heat and Kelem stopped laughing and jumped up on his feet feeling quite concerned, wondering what was happening to him. He looked in the little mirror by his bunk and saw that his face was beet red from the convulsive fit of laughter that he'd just experienced and he quickly realized that this was not normal.

He composed himself, sat down and thought about what had just happened and slowly came to the realization of how powerful this new skill of radiating love and warmth from within him really was. It didn't frighten him so much as it made him aware with sudden clarity that Zeus had somehow activated a part of his brain/mind/spirit that he had never used before. He sensed that some aspect of his mind that had been hidden from his consciousness behind some sort of wall or barrier had suddenly broken through and revealed itself.

On Plantanimus, when the Dreamers first made contact with Kelem through telepathy, they had spent eight days scanning his mind in an effort to understand what and who he was. Days later they brought Anima to life, the facsimile they assembled from their own bodies. She was a female form made to look like Carlatta Del Mar. The giant sentient plants created her to ease Kelem's painful memory of that event from his past after learning of Kelem's emotional pain from losing her years before arriving on the planet.

The Dreamers' powerful minds had within a few days of meeting Kelem, been able to manufacture a living breathing being. And although she was not made of flesh and blood, her body functioned just like a normal human's, except that it was made of plant matter.

At the time, Kelem had recognized what an amazing accomplishment

Anima's creation was. But after spending so much time with the sentient giants, he'd almost come to accept their abilities as normal. But now that he'd been away from Plantanimus for over year, Kelem was beginning to fully realize how powerful those giant mushroom shaped beings that he'd come to know as the Dreamers, really were.

Six years of telepathic connection with them had obviously changed Kelem in ways that he was just starting to understand. At first, Kelem and the Dreamers could only communicate when they were in physical contact with each other. But six years later, a few weeks before Kelem left Plantanimus, he found himself one night communicating with Zeus, the oldest of the Dreamers, while asleep. From that point on, Kelem didn't have to climb Mount Olympus and lie beneath Zeus' roots to commune with his alien friends.

In spite of the distance between Mars and Plantanimus, Kelem had been in contact with Zeus twice in this manner since he'd returned to the solar system. Tonight he was going to "place a call" to Zeus and discuss the ramifications of his new ability.

The Umhar of Plantanimus, the original inhabitants of the planet, had been a highly advanced race of telepathic beings with amazing mental powers. Their technology had surpassed current human development thousands of years before homo-sapiens abandoned their caves and discovered agriculture. Their history spanned fifteen millennia, but their civilization came to a catastrophic end more than ten thousand years before Kelem arrived on their world. The Umhar destroyed themselves because of their failure to control their psychic powers.

Kelem knew from experience that psychic ability could be useful and beneficial. But it could also be dangerous and downright evil.

CHAPTER 9

Stalag 47

December 21st, 2659

The tall thin man wearing a long black coat was leaning over a display console in a circular room with black walls, ceiling and floor. The ankle length garment gave him the appearance of a priest from the old Christian faith from Earth's past. The large touch-screen in front of him showed the heart rate, respiration, pulse, systolic blood pressure and electroencephalographic readings from the many contact points originating from a bizarre looking head piece on the subject's head. A visual image of the man's brain was holographically displayed above the touch screen in three dimensions.

The subject, a frail looking old man, sat strapped in a sitting position to a metal contraption in the middle of the room resembling a dentist's chair. The room was dark save for the single light hovering above the subject, who was dressed in a tattered red prison uniform. Several cables ran from the headpiece and chair to the console where the gaunt, sinister looking man was standing. The light from the screen illuminated the man's long narrow face framed by straight silver hair tied in the back of his head in a long pony tail. His cold grey eyes, long aquiline nose, high cheek bones and thin lips set over smooth pale white skin, resembled the quintessential portrait of a vampire. A pair of elongated canine teeth and a cape with an oversize collar would have completed the picture to perfection.

A person who didn't know who this man was and whose appearance was straight out of a gothic novel, would have believed him to be an actor or a carnival performer strolling the grounds of a summer county fair, handing out leaflets for the haunted house. But that person would have been wrong, deadly wrong.

Soltan Voltanieu, leader of the Phalanx, Governor of Mars, was one of the most powerful and dangerous men in the solar system. In many ways he was exactly the way he looked; a cold, cruel, heartless ghoul with a thirst for blood and the suffering of others.

Now in his seventies, the man did not look his age. Perhaps the evil inside of him was preserving his body like the character from the ancient horror classic, The Portrait of Dorian Gray. But Soltan Voltanieu's list of sadistic and murderous accomplishments made Dorian Gray seem like a misbehaving toddler by comparison. In another time and place he would have been branded a violent psychopath and a sadistic serial killer.

"Well professor, it looks like my people have finally perfected my mnemonic scanner. It won't be long before all your secrets are revealed to me," Voltanieu said in a voice that sounded more like raspy whisper.

"Go to hell, you spawn of Satan!" croaked back the old man from the center of the room in obvious discomfort.

"I must admit that once I open your subconscious like a ripe cantaloupe and extract everything from your hidden memories I will miss our little get-togethers," Voltanieu quipped with sadistic sarcasm.

"You're nothing but a second rate villain from a cheap drama-vid," the old man replied, knowing that the insult was one of the few that got under Voltanieu's cadaver-like skin.

Voltanieu's eyes flared for a moment and then he moved a virtual fader on the touch-screen. Immediately, the old man stiffened and arched his back in agony.

"Now, now professor, no need for insults. Let's keep our session civilized," Voltanieu remarked with a twisted smile of satisfaction on his thin lips.

When Soltan Voltanieu moved the fader back to its original position, the old man collapsed back on the chair and his head fell on his chest as he gasped for air. After a few seconds the old man began giggling like a child hiding in a closet, playing hide and seek.

Voltanieu stiffened his jaw and stared at the console with anger flashing in his grey eyes, though he didn't let his subject see it.

After a while, the old man spoke again, still laughing. "Do you know why I'm laughing Voltanieu?" the old man asked, raising his head and looking at his torturer.

Voltanieu ignored him and continued looking at the screen.

"Because you're nothing but a loser, Voltanieu!" the professor said, cackling hysterically. "For twelve years now, you have been trying your damnedest to get me to talk, and you're no closer now than you were when you first started interrogating me. You'll never get me to talk, even with your brand new toy over there!" the old man shouted, glaring at the machine then shaking his head with disdain.

The old man's mocking made his blood boil. Voltanieu's fingers gripped the edge of the console with fury as he fought to control his anger. He let go of the console, and with his hand shaking with rage moved his finger toward the virtual fader that would send another shock into the old man's brain, but then with his jaw clenched from frustration, he pulled back his hand at the last second and took a deep breath. He looked straight ahead and composed himself. If it had been anyone else sitting on that chair, other than Nicolas Alfano, the former leader of the Brotherhood of the Light, Voltanieu would have fried their brain without compunction. But the old man had valuable information in his head.

Nicolas Alfano knew the identity of every living member of the Brotherhood, and Voltanieu wanted those names! The Brotherhood was the last possible obstacle that stood between the utter defeat of the Martian resistance and the Phalanx's complete control of Mars.

But as much as he wanted that information, he had to stop for now. The technicians had warned Voltanieu that the scanner couldn't be used for more than a half hour on any subject, particularly a man of Nicolas Alfano's age. Though at sixty nine, the man was in surprisingly good condition considering that he'd been a prisoner here on Stalag 47 for more than twelve years, having withstood years of psychological, mental torture and now electronic brain probing.

"Mock me all you want professor, we'll continue with another session tomorrow. I have all the time in the world," Voltanieu said, sounding overly casual as he pressed a button on a bracelet on his left wrist. Within seconds, two burly Phalanx Black Guards appeared through a door. After removing the head gear and unstrapping Nicolas Alfano from the chair, they lifted him up and took him away with his feet dragging on the floor.

Soltan Voltanieu exhaled, feeling frustrated that the new scanner was not delivering as promised. If the machine didn't provide any results within the next day or two, the three technicians who designed and built it would be put to death. That would let the next group of eggheads in the technical section know that he meant business.

The chime of the audio implant in his right ear rang and Voltanieu pressed a small spot behind his ear. "Yes, what is it?" he answered, sounding annoyed.

"Sorry to disturb you, Governor," a nervous female voice said apologetically. "Your son is asking for a holoconference. He says it's very important," the operator announced, praying that she hadn't caught Soltan Voltanieu in a bad mood. In the past he'd been known to have people tortured simply for talking or interrupting him at the wrong time.

"Fine, I'll see him in my office. Have the call sent there," he responded as he ended the transmission and headed for his private suite at the top level of the massive prison complex known as Stalag 47.

Soltan Voltanieu had several personal suites and offices throughout Mars, Earth and the Moon. All of them without exception were enclosed chambers with no windows. Only two people in the universe knew or suspected that Voltanieu was an extreme agoraphobic. One was his son, Jude Voltanieu, the Commander of the Black Guard on Mars. The other was his Martian concubine, who suspected that Voltanieu was an agoraphobic, but would never dare utter a syllable of her suspicion to anyone for fear of being tortured to death. Besides those two, everyone else supposed that Voltanieu chose to live and work in windowless rooms for reasons of security.

"Hello, Father," Jude Voltanieu said, bowing slightly when the gaunt figure appeared across from him in his holo-room in Latonga City, two thousand kilometers from Stalag 47.

"Be brief, I'm in no mood to be disturbed unless it's something important," Voltanieu whispered with a blank expression.

The young man's image standing half a meter from Soltan Voltanieu, was tall and rather thin for a Terran. His light brown hair was cropped short, military style. His face was handsome almost bordering on pretty. His features were of Mediterranean and Northern European descent. In his Phalanx Black Guard officer's uniform Jude Voltanieu possessed the type of looks that made women turn around and stare. But his good looks concealed the fact that he was as cruel and vicious as his father. His deep blue eyes stared at the world like the eyes of a predator, always calculating and measuring everything with cold, relentless logic, unmoved by the pain and suffering that he witnessed every day on Mars. To him, Martian life was cheap and he never hesitated to order the death of any poor soul who broke the rules or was suspected of being a member of the resistance. Though father and son looked nothing like each other, they were identical in every other respect.

"I had a vision last night. Something has changed here on Mars and I believe that it's of a threatening nature. We should increase our patrols immediately and go over our security protocols, change passwords, encryption codes, etc."

Soltan Voltanieu pursed his lips and looked at his son with cold detachment. "What kind of threat? Can you be more specific?"

Jude Voltanieu rubbed his chin pensively and struggled to come up with an explanation that his non-psychic father could understand. Soltan Voltanieu demanded clear and precise information from all his people, but in particular from his own son. "I believe that a new person, with powerful psychic skills, has recently arrived on Mars. I'm pretty sure that it's a male and that he's come here to work with the resistance."

"Who is this man, where did he come from?" Soltan Voltanieu prodded, sounding impatient." Can't you give me any better information than a vague description? Did this man come from Earth? Is it someone from the rebel fleet? Is he a member of the Brotherhood? Specifics boy, specifics!" he added, slapping his right fist with his left hand.

"He's unlike anyone else that I've run into before, Father. This man is very different and I believe very powerful as well. Something has changed..." Jude Voltanieu reiterated, partly to himself." We must round up all suspected resistance members and undesirables and question them! We should also reach out to all our informers, collaborators and sympathizers and get some intelligence on this man, whoever he is," he added, looking concerned.

"I don't want to interrupt industrial production with another round of arrests and executions. It's bad for business," Soltan Voltanieu countered.

Arrests and executions made the population angry and caused slowdowns in all the factories that produced luxury and technology items for the people of Earth and the Moon. As powerful as Soltan Voltanieu was, his position and status was dependent on the output of Martian industry.

"Bring me some concrete evidence that your vision is based on facts, and I'll authorize a round up. You may revise our security protocols and don't neglect to call me and tell me about any further visions that you receive."

The image of Soltan Voltanieu blinked out and his son was left standing alone in the middle of his holo-chamber with the unspoken words of a response in his lips,. His father knew that Jude's psychic abilities were real, but even so, he didn't trust the world of the unseen unless it was accompanied by concrete evidence.

Frustrated, Jude Voltanieu returned to his desk and sat there wondering what the consequences would be if he had his father assassinated. He knew that his father had spies in his staff just as Jude had spies among his father's people. The old man was old, but Jude had a sense that he'd live to his nineties or beyond. This was a problem for young Colonel Jude Voltanieu, commander of the Phalanx Black Guard on Mars Colony. His ambitious timetable included taking over his father's place as leader of the Phalanx and ultimately ascending to the presidency of Earth before he turned forty.

But Jude Voltanieu didn't have enough support among the higher-ups of the Phalanx to carry out a successful take over, at least not yet. His father's ruthlessness and reputation kept everyone under him continuously second guessing themselves when it came to creating alliances or plotting any kind of *coup d'état*. The Phalanx was an organization held together by paranoia and fear.

And beyond that, Jude Voltanieu's handsome looks and angelic baby face, failed to create the same kind of dread and fear that his father's ghoulish looks generated. Soltan Voltanieu looked positively evil. His mere presence was enough for people to feel vulnerable and afraid for their lives. Jude's only advantage over his father was his psychic ability, but right now that advantage wasn't sufficient to get rid of the old man and assume his power.

Jude Voltanieu's psychic powers had helped his father root out many members of the resistance in the few short years he'd been on Mars. But so far he hadn't been able to uncover the identities of any of the surviving members of the Brotherhood of the Light. The Brotherhood's psychics, including Nicolas Alfano, were somehow able to shield their minds from Jude's powerful probing skills. And now this new threat in the form of a powerful psychic who was surely a member of the Brotherhood, was making the goal of eliminating the organization once and for all, more difficult.

The first order of business for young Jude was to find out who this new presence on Mars really was. He was sure that this individual represented a significant threat to the Phalanx and Earth. His father had ordered him not to conduct any mass arrests, but there was nothing to prevent him from taking in a few key suspects and undesirables and interrogating them personally in one of the many Phalanx dungeons throughout Latonga City.

CHAPTER 10

On The Edge of Surrender

December 21st, 2659

The guards laid Nicolas Alfano's limp body gently onto the single cot inside the small cell that had been his entire world for twelve years. Many of the prison guards had taken a liking to the plucky old man who had been able to resist Voltanieu's attempts at forcing information out of him year after year. Each time the guards took Nicolas Alfano to the 'Dragon's' interrogation room, (their nickname for Soltan Voltanieu) they made bets as to whether the old man would finally break or return to his cell without having given up his secrets.

The older guards usually won the bet. After several years of seeing how the old man could not be broken, the senior guards had come to the conclusion that Nicolas Alfano would never break and that Voltanieu would eventually have him put down. This time was no different. Most of the younger guards paid up and hoped that their luck would turn during the next interrogation session.

To date, Nicolas Alfano was the oldest and longest held prisoner at Stalag 47 since it became operational in 2647. No prisoner had managed to survive more than three years under the hellish conditions in the cell blocks of the massive complex. Becoming a prisoner at Stalag 47 was an automatic death sentence. Escape was impossible, and even if an inmate somehow succeeded in reaching the exterior of the prison, he would have the deadly atmosphere of Mars to contend with. The prison was located thousands of kilometers from the nearest settlement or town.

Even in a pressure suit with fully charged air tanks, the farthest a man could go, would be a mere fifty kilometers before he ran out of air or froze to death.

Nicolas Alfano waited until the door to his cell was shut and then allowed himself to moan in pain. He wouldn't give these bastards the pleasure of seeing him suffer as long as he could help it.

His head felt as if it was on fire. The effects of the probe played havoc with his eyes and ears. Whenever Voltanieu ratcheted up the intensity of the machine, Nicolas would begin to see a jumble of images and hear conversations and thoughts that he'd had in the past. The stream of images and sounds created a feeling of unbearable pressure inside his head that made him want to scream out loud whatever he was seeing and hearing.

This was obviously the purpose of Voltanieu's evil machine--to make someone reveal what was in their mind. And it was beginning to work. For years, Nicolas had resisted all attempts at physical torture, psychic probing, truth serums and other hellish drugs that had been administered to him at one time or another. For all that time he'd been able to resist them all. But this new wicked machine that Voltanieu had been using for the last few weeks was slowly but surely wearing down his defenses.

When he was arrested soon after the invasion, Nicolas had hypnotized himself and succeeded in burying the names of all the members of the Brotherhood somewhere in his subconscious. The strategy had worked well, for even under physical torture and even with repeated attempts by Jude Voltanieu to retrieve his secrets, he had been unable to give his torturers any information. Soltan Voltanieu had kept Nicolas alive for all these years in the hope that one day he'd find a method to extract the information that he knew was buried deep in the man's subconscious. Voltanieu's new hellish device seemed to have the ability to dig much deeper than any other method the Phalanx had used before.

The scanner had the nasty side effect of making the desire to reveal what one wanted to keep hidden, more intense after the session was over. But fortunately, Voltanieu and the technicians were unaware of this effect.

And now, the urge to start screaming the names of everyone that he'd ever known in his life was beginning to build up in his mind, like the need to vomit a really bad meal. For days, he'd been burying his face on the mattress of his bunk and proceeded to scream at the top of his lungs after each session, praying that the guards wouldn't hear him and come in to investigate and report this new behavior to Voltanieu. If the bastard learned that the urge to divulge one's secrets got stronger after the treatment, he'd hold Nicolas in the interrogation room for hours, and then Nicolas would have no choice but to give up all the names in his head.

"I must hold on, I must hold on!" Nicolas screamed inside his head, gritting his teeth and wrapping his cot's thin mattress around his head squeezing it against his face as hard as his frail hands could manage. He opened his mouth and screamed until his throat felt like it was tearing itself apart. This went on for a long time until finally, he was able to control himself and lie on his bunk quietly, his body drenched in sweat from the effort.

"Dear God, help me!" Nicolas invoked to the creator in desperation. "I won't last much longer. I can't hold on, I just can't..." he whimpered, shedding long wet tears that fell on the rough fabric of his pillow. He began to sob aloud as his weary heart and mind filled with the kind of utter despair that robs the soul of its humanity and makes one wish for death.

He fell into unconsciousness, his eyes and body twitching occasionally as if his body was being attacked by angry bees.

"Nicolas, Nicolas!" a voice called out to him.

"Who is it?" he asked, noticing that he seemed to be standing in a strange place without walls or ceiling. "Who is calling me?"

"Don't you recognize me, Nicolas?" the voice asked, this time sounding closer than before.

"You sound familiar."

"I'm glad to hear that," a young man said, as he appeared on the visible edge of this strange place and made his way to where Nicolas was standing. As the young man got closer, Nicolas' eyes opened wide in recognition of the individual now approaching him.

"Kelem! My boy! Is it really you?" he exclaimed with emotion.

"Yes, Nicolas, it's me!" Kelem said as his arms reached for his old mentor and hugged him affectionately.

"My boy, my boy!" was all that Nicolas could say, his heart filled with happiness. Then, when they separated, Nicolas held Kelem by his shoulders and looked at him with a curious expression. "Where have you been? I've missed you so. It's been so long since we've seen each oth…."

Nicolas stopped in mid-sentence and let go of Kelem. Then he stepped back and looked around nervously. "What's going on, who are you?" he asked with suspicion, suddenly aware that he was in some sort of altered state of consciousness. This place had a feeling of reality although it was clearly not a real physical place. But it felt real in a very unusual way. This 'mind space' or whatever this 'location' was, didn't feel like anything that the Phalanx had thrown at him in the past. Their attempts at this kind of stuff had always been poorly constructed, obviously fake and never as clear and well defined as this horizon-less environment where he now stood. Kelem's image looked and felt as real as anything that existed in the physical world. If this was technology, it was definitely not Phalanx.

"It's all right Nicolas, it's really me. This is not a Phalanx virtual reality-construct," Kelem assured him with a smile as if reading his mind. "I've returned to Mars and I'm going to get you out of this horrible place where you are now," he explained, then looked around as if he was actually seeing the physical cell where Nicolas was being held. "Where in hell are you exactly?" he asked.

Nicolas took a leap of faith and decided to accept this event as real. "This place is called Stalag 47. It's a huge prison for political dissidents. But, something doesn't make sense, how can you be here Kelem?" he asked, "You're supposed to be dead! The fact that you look almost exactly like the Kelem I knew is… is impossible! Help me understand," he pleaded.

"I didn't die, Nicolas," Kelem replied with a big smile. "The Solar Nations suffered a terrible accident and, save for myself and Ndugu, everyone else perished. Ndugu and I were stranded on an alien planet for six years. I can't go into many details right now, but suffice it to say that we both made it back. Unfortunately, the accident that destroyed the ship pushed us fifteen years into the future. The image that you're seeing right now, is the real me. I've only aged six chronological years since I left Mars."

Nicolas was amazed by Kelem's story, knowing in his heart of hearts that it was true. "You've certainly learned a thing or two since you left!" Nicolas said, referring to his former prodigy's ability to reach out to him in such an impressive way.

"Yes I have, Nicolas."

Kelem looked in his old mentor's eyes and saw how much pain Nicolas had endured. "You have suffered much, my old friend," he commented with sadness. Then he closed his eyes and tilted his head slightly to his left and stood still for a few seconds as if he was trying to identify a faint melody somewhere in the distance.

"This machine they're using on you is terrible!" Kelem exclaimed, suddenly aware of its effects on his frail old friend. "We must get you out of here as soon as possible!" he added with concern.

"No! Please don't come here!" Nicolas said in a panic, "for the love of God, Kelem! Leave Mars, leave right now my boy! Mars has become an evil place full of death and misery. I don't have long to live anyway. Save yourself! At least something of our culture will remain in the universe...," he concluded with sadness.

"I will do no such thing, Nicolas. Not only am I going to get you out of here but we're going to make the Terrans regret the day they invaded our beautiful planet," Kelem promised with complete confidence.

The power of Kelem's statement imbued Nicolas Alfano with a sudden feeling of confidence that took him by surprise at first, but then energized his spirit with courage and strength. "I... I believe you my boy! I don't know how or why I feel that you're telling the truth, but I do!" Nicolas remarked with amazement.

Kelem reached out and placed his hand on Nicolas' chest. Within seconds, a deep sensation of warmth began spreading from his solar plexus into the rest of his body until he was enveloped in a golden glow that was almost too wonderful to endure.

"Will I... will I remember all this?" Nicolas asked, feeling a wave of love and affection surround his entire being.

"Yes you will, my old friend. Remember this very moment and the feeling you're experiencing the next time they use that evil machine on you," Kelem said as he and the horizon-less place slowly faded away and became Nicolas' tiny cell.

Nicolas found that he was standing next to his bunk feeling as if he were weightless. A wonderful sense of peace and well-being coursed throughout his whole mind and body.

He closed his eyes and held on to the sensation that he was floating in air as a big smile spread on his face.

CHAPTER 11

The Reunification of the Brotherhood

January 4th, 2660

Kelem had finally lost enough weight to look like an average Martian, thin and gaunt. A well-developed beard was now covering his face and his continuing physical regimen of stressful exercise and low calorie intake had helped hollow out his cheeks and create dark circles under his eyes. His appearance was now that of someone who was malnourished and forced to work extremely long hours.

He had successfully communicated with Nicolas after Zeus showed him how to do it. It seemed that the Dreamer only needed to teach him a new skill once and Kelem was able to assimilate the knowledge right away.

But after Kelem had communicated with Nicolas a few times he had grown impatient with the resistance's delay in getting him out of this place, which was beginning to feel more and more like a prison every day. He had been on Mars for more than a month and hadn't accomplished any of his goals.

In spite of Kelem's ability to heal and strengthen his old friend, he was very worried for Nicolas Alfano's physical and mental health. His old friend was about to break and give up the identities of all the members of the Brotherhood that he knew prior to the invasion. Once that happened, the resistance movement would crumble and all would be lost.

He had to find a way to get Nicolas out of Stalag 47!

To his relief, Jacob showed up the following morning with two men. Jacob asked Kelem to collect his personal items and follow him, as the other two began emptying the room in which Kelem had been living in since he arrived on Mars.

"Where are we going?' Kelem asked, curious and excited to be going somewhere new after the monotony of the last five weeks.

"Something's up, so we're getting you out of Latonga City for your safety," Jacob informed him, as he opened a big heavy pressure door that led to a very long set of stairs that descended farther down into the bowels of Latonga City.

"You don't know where we're going do you?" Kelem said, after reading Jacob and finding that he didn't know.

"All I know is that the Phalanx has started to arrest and question people. That usually leads to mass arrests and interrogations. It's possible that your arrival might have something to do with it."

As he descended the long stairs following Jacob, Kelem remembered that a few days ago he had felt a new sensation in his head. It was a new uncomfortable experience that felt as if someone or something was crawling through his brain. It gave him the creeps, but at that time he dismissed it as a possible side effect caused by the use of his new skills. But now his psychic's intuition told him that that was not the case.

Someone out there, most likely a psychic working for the Phalanx, had sensed his presence! Whoever this person was, they were apparently powerful enough to reach out and touch others at a distance. Kelem knew immediately that his insight was accurate and a chill went up his spine. He suddenly became aware that he and the members of the Brotherhood were in danger. This new development was indeed serious. He had to find a way to shield himself and the others from this new menace!

After reaching the next lower level, Jacob led him through a maze of tunnels and various chambers full of water pumps and sewer processing equipment, and then stopped by an old style pressure door that probably dated back to the early days of Latonga City.

"This is as far as I go. There are people on the other side who will take you to wherever it is that you're going." Jacob said. Then he grabbed Kelem's hand, "you've changed my life somehow and I'm eternally grateful to you," he said, fighting back tears. "Good luck, Kelem, God go with you."

"Thank you, Jacob, I hope I get to see you again," Kelem replied, shaking his hand.

"I hope so too, Kelem. Be safe."

Kelem reached for the wheel on the old door, but before he could touch it, someone was already turning it and then the old door began opening slowly, its rusty hinges squealing loudly.

The door opened wide and the imposing figure of Chief Loeky, (former Chief Constable of the Latonga City Police) reached out and pulled him toward his chest, giving Kelem a bear hug that threatened to crush his ribs.

"You young pup! I never thought I'd see you again!" the big man exclaimed with tears in his eyes.

It took Kelem a few seconds to realize who this bear of a man was. The chief had finally lost whatever hair he'd had before and was now sporting a large blonde beard that gave him the appearance of an ancient Viking.

"Chief Loeky, I'm so happy to see you, I was afraid that you were no longer in the body!" Kelem said excitedly, trying to catch his breath.

"It's Major Loeky, resistance fighter now, Kelem. And no, the goddamned Terrans have tried to kill me several times but I'm too ornery to die!" he said with a laugh.

"Where are you taking me, chief...? I mean Major," Kelem asked.

"That I don't know, Kelem. We keep information compartmentalized in case any of us gets caught by the Phalanx. I'm to take you to a warehouse near a transportation depot on the edge of Latonga City where others will tell you what's next."

"Damn but it's good to see you after all these years!" Kelem declared with joy.

Major Loeky leaned back and observed Kelem for a few seconds. "They told me about your appearance, but it wasn't until now that I believe what they said about you."

"Time dilation," Kelem said cryptically, as the chief furrowed his brow. "The Solar Nations had an accident that caused the *n'time* generator to throw us into the future. That's why I haven't aged that much. I know it seems weird, but it's true."

"Well, whatever it is, your return is heaven-sent Kelem. You've given me hope that we might get out of this mess that we're in."

"About that, Major, what kind of military capability does the resistance have these days?"

"It's very limited, but you happen to be talking to the commander of the toughest, meanest group of sons o' bitches in the Martian Resistance, 'The Helter Skelters'. We're one of the few militia rebel groups that still operate on Mars. We're a special ops commando force. We're made up of former cops and Martian ex-military. We stay out of sight and only come out for special operations."

"Excellent! What do you know about Stalag 47?" Kelem asked, already planning a breakout for Nicolas Alfano.

Major Loeky's expression changed and he suddenly looked concerned. "Why are you asking?"

"We need to break Nicolas Alfano out of there. He's about to reveal the names of every single member of the Brotherhood that he knew before the invasion. The only hope we have of removing the Terrans from Mars is if the Brotherhood is able to remain free and reunite. Without their help, we'll never be a sovereign nation again," Kelem stated matter of fact.

Major Loeky leaned back against a wall and looked down at the floor, suddenly appearing weak and unsure. "Kelem," he said almost in a whisper, "you don't know what you're asking. Stalag 47 is a massive prison located in the middle of the Hellas Planitia. It's the most remote location in all of Mars. The security there is bound to be serious! It can only be accessed by air and they can see you coming for hundreds of kilometers. You would need an entire division strength force to break in there."

After hearing the description of Stalag 47, Kelem felt a sudden wave of disappointment wash over him. There had to be some way of getting Nicolas Alfano out of there. There had to be!

Loeky felt bad seeing Kelem's disappointment, and at the same time frustrated that he couldn't do anything about the situation. "We simply don't have those kinds of resources. I'm sorry to ruin your expectations," he added apologetically.

But Kelem knew that something had to be done, even if it cost the lives of resistance fighters.

"Then we'll have to do it by stealth. Can you get me as much intelligence there is about its operation, schedules for deliveries of food and supplies, work shifts etc.?"

"It would have to be a very slick operation planned by a genius," Loeky commented and then his eyes opened wide. "Hell, you're the smartest genius there is!" he said with exhilaration." If anyone can do it, it would be you, Kelem," he added, slapping his back.

"Thank you, but whatever we do, it must be done fast, because Nicolas won't be able to hold on for much longer."

"As soon as I gather all the intel, I'll have someone bring it to you," Major Loeky agreed.

"Great! Now take me to wherever it is that I'm supposed to go."

Major Loeky led Kelem through several other passageways and chambers, eventually ending up in a large sewer tunnel big enough for two men to walk through. He pulled out two flashlights from his tunic, handed one to Kelem, then picked up two face masks by the entrance of the tunnel to prevent inhaling poisonous fumes, and the two of them then walked for several kilometers, their feet splashing water with every step. Eventually they reached an access point where two other resistance fighters were waiting.

"These two gentlemen will take you up to a warehouse which is directly above us. I'll find a way to get that information you asked for and I hope that you'll consider using the Helter Skelters for the mission."

"I wouldn't have it any other way, Major. See you soon!"

"You're in safe hands, good luck," Loeky replied, referring to the two men left in his care. He turned around and disappeared down the tunnel as the echo of his splashing footsteps faded away.

The two men led Kelem up a ladder through a vertical shaft whose hatch opened to the basement of the warehouse. There he was issued an exterior pressure suit and, after going up several levels on an elevator that led to the surface of Mars, he was guided to a transport that took off as soon as he boarded the craft. It was the first time he'd seen daylight in more than five weeks.

Two hours later he was landing on another warehouse's landing pad, also on the outskirts of a city. Kelem didn't have to ask where he was. From the air he had recognized the layout of Havana Flats.

The ship was delivering food and medical supplies, and he was obliged to help unload the cargo in order to blend in with the rest of the crew should a Terran patrol be near. After the cargo was brought in and the warehouse's loading dock re-pressurized, he was told to remove his heavy outdoor suit and was given a light city suit. Then he was told to wait in a room until someone came to pick him up.

He didn't bother asking when that would be. Everyone he'd come in contact with, kept conversation short and barely looked him in the eye. The less anyone knew about anyone else, the better for the resistance at large.

Around midnight, there was a knock at the door and Susan Beaumont and her daughter Gina walked in.

As soon as they saw Kelem, the women looked surprised.

"What...? What is it?" Kelem asked concerned.

"Kelem..., your appearance! Are you ill? Susan asked.

"No, not at all, why do you ask that?"

"My dear you look so thin and malnourished. So different than when I saw you just four weeks ago!"

"Your daughter told me that I looked too different from the way most Martians look nowadays, so I let my beard grow, cut down on food and I've been exercising to lose weight."

"Perhaps you went a little too far, though I must say that no one will doubt now that you're a Martian living under years of Terran occupation."

"I feel fine, Susan. My body adapts quickly to different conditions, and I'm glad to hear that I'll be able to blend in public."

"Not quite yet, Kelem," Gina Beaumont said. "We have to take a new photo for your wrist comp ID before you can be seen in public."

"Please don't tell me that I'll have to spend more time isolated somewhere by myself. I have a bad case of cabin fever!" Kelem quipped with humor.

"Don't worry, Kelem, you'll be staying with us in my mother-in-law's warren nearby. It's small but cozy. You'll have your new ID badge in a day or two."

Kelem smiled, but a part of him suddenly realized how much he missed the open vistas of Plantanimus and the feel of the sun, the wind, the exotic vegetation and its wonderful smells and the beautiful night sky of the alien planet with its three moons.

"Susan, I don't mean to harp on the same subject over and over, but we must assemble the membership right away! There are new developments that must be addressed immediately."

"Don't worry, Kelem. we brought you to Havana Flats because the Phalanx was starting a new cycle of arrests and interrogations, but mostly because there are three Brotherhood members of the board and a few remaining regular members living here in the city. Out here, the security forces are much less stringent than in Latonga City, Olympus Mons or Amazonis and it's much easier to get around. Havana Flats has become a transport hub for all sorts of supplies. Most of us work in shipping and transportation. It helps us move around the planet and communicate with other resistance cells without having to get travel passes like most other folks."

"Excellent. How many board of directors and regular members are there, and how soon can you arrange for a meeting?" Kelem asked with eagerness.

Susan smiled patiently at Kelem's zeal and enthusiasm. She had to remember that he'd been gone from Mars for twenty one years and that he hadn't become accustomed to the slow way things happened nowadays, particularly within the resistance.

"Of the board members besides Marla Hasset and myself, there's Frank Silvera, Phillip Sontag and Dalton Myers, although he might not be able to make it. He's rather ill with pneumonia. Of the regular members, there are about twenty three depending on whether they're on a work shift or not at the time of the meeting. And as far as when the meeting can take place, I'd say probably within a day or two."

"That's it?" Kelem asked, obviously disappointed with the head count, "what happened to the rest?"

"We never learned what happened to Laura Finch. We supposed that either she died during the initial bombardment and subsequent attack of the Terran troops, or she's living somewhere on Mars under a false identity. Same thing with the rest of the regular members, of which there are one hundred and twenty eight unaccounted for."

"Damn! I was hoping for more but I guess we'll have to do the best with what we have," Kelem replied with resignation.

"Now, let us take you to our humble abode. We have a nice bowl of Martian stew waiting for you!" Susan said with a smile as she pulled Kelem by the arm leading him out of the room.

Kelem was glad to be in the company of others for a change, and even though the warren of Susan Beaumont's mother-in-law turned out to be tiny and somewhat claustrophobic, he felt comfortable.

It took three days, but finally Susan informed him that the meeting would take place that night around 03:00Am, at the same warehouse where he had arrived in Havana Flats.

By then he had received a new wrist comp with a legal Phalanx ID. Susan explained that the identity that Kelem had assumed--that of a man named Gerard Seaver who had recently passed away and who was a near perfect match for his face, body weight and dimentions-- was also an employee of the same transport company that had brought him to Havana Flats. So long as the Phalanx didn't examine his ID too closely, he'd be able to travel and move around the planet safely as an employee of the Fisher-Madjal Transport Co.

That night as he sat in one of the warehouse's storage chambers waiting nervously for the members of the Brotherhood to show up, Kelem wondered how he'd be received, particularly when he was going to ask his fellow members to risk and possibly lose their lives. He was also concerned about how his twenty one year absence and his youthful appearance would play in his request to be named leader of the Brotherhood. Kelem had complete confidence in his ability to liberate Mars. But, would the Brotherhood accept his leadership?

At 03:05 AM, Susan, Gina and Marla Hasset entered the room. Marla immediately ran to Kelem and practically jumped in his arms, hugging him and holding on to him for a long time, her body shaking with great emotion. Eventually she let go of him and then stared at him with tears in her eyes, trying to reconcile his youthful appearance with his years of absence. By now Kelem had gotten used to this reaction and waited patiently for Marla to speak.

"Oh Kelem! I know it's really you, but still, it's going to take me a little while to get over your beautiful face untouched by the years, with the exception of that beard!" she said, laughing amidst her tears. Of the old acquaintances that he'd met since he had returned to Mars, Marla Hassett was so far the only one who had held on to her original appearance in Kelem's memory. In spite of her sixty six years of age, her hair, though streaked with grey was still blonde and her face and figure had remained youthful.

"Bless you, Marla. My heart is also full of joy now that we're reunited. There was a time when I thought I'd never see any of you ever again." Kelem said, remembering how he and Ndugu had come to accept the fact that they would have to spend the rest of their lives on Plantanimus after the demise of the Solar Nations.

"Susan told me about the time dilation phenomena and the rest of your amazing story. You must tell us all in great detail the amazing adventure that you have lived through!" she exclaimed with anticipation.

"I will, dear Marla, I will. There's much that I need to tell you all but, also, to ask of you. I hope that a majority of you will agree with my requests."

"You have my vote and that of Phillip and Frank. You have Dalton's vote by proxy even though he can't attend tonight's meeting. However, I can't speak for the membership. We've all grown distant over the years, in particular the youngest among us."

"The fate of all of us rests in their hands then. Let's hope that they'll have the courage and the wisdom to choose well."

"I hope they will, Kelem."

Twenty minutes later, Kelem, Susan, Gina and Marla sat in a row of chairs flanked by Frank Silvera and Phillip Sontag. Across from them, seventeen of the twenty three possible member-attendees faced them sitting in two rows of chairs. The meeting was called to order, and after Marla introduced Kelem, he proceeded to welcome everyone and then spent the next hour telling the assembly the amazing and sometimes bizarre story of his voyage to Plantanimus, the demise of the Solar Nations and its crew, his encounter with the Dreamers, the Dreamer's creation of Anima, Kelem and Ndugu's even more amazing meeting with the Kren and ultimate rescue by them, as well as everything that had happened to him ever since he returned to the solar system.

When he finished, the group remained silent for a few seconds as they tried to digest the significance of Kelem's discoveries and adventures. For the first time in human history, mankind had found alien intelligent life in the universe. And it seemed as though telepathy and psychic ability were rather common amongst sentient species. So far, of the three alien species that Kelem had come in contact with, the Umhar, The Dreamers and the Kren Queen, all had been, or were currently, functional telepaths.

Everyone was glad to hear that the rebel fleet was still out there, though greatly diminished and in peril of fading away, and that they still had enough operational ability to be able to sneak Kelem onto Mars with relative ease. Many were under the impression that the fleet had met its end.

Once everyone recovered from their astonishment, a barrage of questions was thrown at Kelem.

Kelem raised his hands and asked for silence.

"Ladies and gentlemen, I'll be more than happy to spend as much time as necessary answering any and all questions that you may have as soon as we close this meeting officially. There are several crucial items that are of importance which affect all of us here and must be discussed immediately. Please allow me to explain."

The crowd settled down and Kelem continued. "As I told you earlier, Nicolas Alfano has been a prisoner in Stalag 47 for over twelve years. With the exception of those who joined the Brotherhood after Nicolas was arrested, the reason that most of you are alive today is that Nicolas has been able to resist all attempts at divulging the names of every single member of the Brotherhood that he knew before the Terrans took over. Unfortunately, that is no longer the case."

"We've been told that Alfano hypnotized himself and that he literally can't remember anyone's name even under torture," called out a young man in the back row.

"He's being probed with a powerful device called a mnemonic scanner that is breaking down Nicolas' will and is capable of extracting information hidden in his subconscious. The machine creates pressure in the subject's mind that compels the individual to reveal whatever he or she is hiding from the interrogator. Imagine if you will, being sick with food poisoning and trying to prevent yourself from vomiting the contents of your stomach or releasing your bowels, and you get an idea of what Nicolas is going through and the amount of sheer will power that it must be taking him to keep from revealing those names to the Phalanx."

A collective gasp from the group was followed by a murmur of concern as everyone realized the danger they were all in. Many faces turned pale.

"Where and how did you receive this information?" asked a woman who seemed unconvinced by Kelem's account.

"From Nicolas himself, I've been in telepathic communication with him for the last few days."

"You can do that?" asked another member in the group, never having heard of telepathy being possible at any distance greater than a few meters.

"Yes. Although I was able to read feelings and emotions at a distance before I left Mars, my years of communing with the Dreamers have resulted in the increase of my telepathic ability. But I have to insist on returning to the main subject which is, that we, and the rest of the resistance must attempt to liberate Nicolas from that prison very soon. Otherwise many of you will be arrested and executed within hours of Nicolas surrendering to the effects of the device."

Everyone spoke at once demanding to know how such a thing could be accomplished and suddenly the meeting appeared on the verge of falling into chaos. Then, the powerful and very loud voice of Frank Silvera, shouting, "Order, order!" brought things back to normal.

"Kelem, I think that I speak on behalf of everyone here by saying that what you're proposing is impossible," Marla Hasset interjected, aggrieved that she was contradicting her former prodigy.

"No it's not, and I'll tell you why," Kelem said with confidence. "I can and will teach all of you readers and telepaths here to communicate at any distance whatsoever. With so many of us acquiring this ability we'll be able to direct and execute clandestine operations with amazing accuracy and speed.

"But, Kelem, won't that take weeks, even months?" Susan Beaumont asked.

"No, I can literally do this in just a few hours. Additionally, I can enhance other talents and abilities in the rest of you. For example, how many here are telekinetics?

Three people raised their hands.

"How many here are 'pushers', or are able to project images or ideas into other people's minds?"

Two young men in the last row raised their hands.

"How many here have the ability to affect machines or electronic devices?"

A young teenage girl in the front row raised her hand. "I do, but it's mainly hit and miss," she confessed.

"Adriana here, is our resident computer expert, hacker and all around whizz kid," a man in his forties said pointing to her.

"In that case Adriana, you'll be my first pupil, because I have a very important job for you," Kelem said to the girl with a grin. Adriana seemed pleased and excited and couldn't help but blush.

"Listen everyone, we're under the gun here, and there's no time for subtlety or politics. I want to ask all of you to elect me leader of the Brotherhood pro-tem until such time as we've succeeded in liberating Nicolas, the true leader of the Brotherhood. Let's do it by a show of hands, and know that I won't be offended by those who vote no."

Without exception, everyone in the room raised their hands, to Kelem's relief.

"Thank you all so much. Before we conclude this meeting and I answer all the questions that I know you have, I'd like to start a new ritual at the end of our meetings. Please everyone, let us all form a big circle and hold hands together," Kelem asked, and everyone rose from their seats and formed a circle.

"The purpose of this exercise is to enhance our spirits and that of others by learning a new skill that I'm going to teach you now. Imagine your heart chakra opening up like a flower. You must release your ego and be ready to accept a feeling of love and affection that I will send to you from my heart chakra. I must warn you up front, that once you experience this effect, you will be able to give this feeling of love and affection to others. But-- and it's a big but-- this feeling can quickly turn into giddiness and even hysterical fits of laughter if you allow yourself to indulge in it too deeply or selfishly. There could be some serious consequences if you allow this to happen. So, let's do it. Close your eyes and be receptive."

Kelem brought up the feeling in his mind and soon he felt the warmth radiating from his chest then into his shoulders, arms and into his hands and out to Marla and Susan to his left and right.

Soon everyone in the room began to experience the sensation that

Kelem was emanating. As the energy traveled from one individual to another, each in turn let out a short gasp of pleasure as the effect bathed their minds and bodies, filling them with deep spiritual joy.

Kelem, careful not to overwhelm anyone, kept control of how much energy he was sending out. After a minute or so, he dialed down the effect and brought the whole procedure to a smooth end.

He let go of Marla's and Susan's hands, and then everyone let go of the hands of the person next to them. For a moment the group remained quiet trying to assimilate what had just happened.

Soon all eyes opened and turned to Kelem, some with tears of joy and relief. One woman in particular, a cleric named Sister Ornata, seemed to be overwhelmed by the experience.

The Brotherhood had made the right decision in choosing Kelem as their leader, and suddenly nothing seemed impossible.

CHAPTER 12

Intelligence Gathering

January 12th, 2660

Major Loeky entered the room where Kelem, Adriana and Marla were sitting around a large metal table crammed with computers and communication equipment. With him was T.J. Morris, a structural engineer in his late sixties who had worked on the construction of Stalag 47 thirteen years before. T.J. had intimate knowledge of the prison's layout.

It turned out that the Terrans had little experience in constructing buildings in the harsh Martian environment and therefore were forced to use experienced Martians to erect all the stalags that nowadays dotted the planet's landscape.

"Ladies and gentleman, this is T.J. Morris, the gentleman who I had talked to you about," Major Loeky announced after closing the door.

"Welcome Mr. Morris. I'm Kelem Rogeston and these are Marla Hassett and Adriana Valenti," Kelem said, pointing to the two women.

The man nodded politely at all of them, but seemed more interested in Kelem. He stared at him for an uncomfortably long time studying him with curious intensity. "When Greg here told me who it was that I was going to meet, I almost refused to come, Mr. Rogeston," the man finally said. "I'm sure that you're aware of your reputation as a traitor among many Martians. If I didn't know Greg as well as I do, I wouldn't have listened to his telling of the truth regarding your disappearance and return to Mars. Now that I see how young you've remained all these years, I'm thoroughly convinced of your story."

Kelem read the man and knew that he was being honest. "I'm certainly glad that you were persuaded to hear the truth about me as well as your willingness to lend us your knowledge and expertise."

"I hope that you don't mind my saying so, Mr. Rogeston, but I don't think that whatever information I have regarding Stalag 47 will help you break out whoever it is that you're trying to free from that place."

"Perhaps not, Mr. Morris, and please call me Kelem."

"Only if you call me T.J.," the man said smiling.

"All right T.J.," Kelem replied, pointing to a seat next to Adriana's computer station. "Adriana here has managed to hack into the stalag's data system. Amazingly enough, it wasn't that difficult for her to break their encryption codes, but then again she's a genius," Kelem said looking at the girl, who blushed slightly at his compliment. "We seem to have gained access to just about every part of the facility, including the building's schematics. I know that as foreman of one of the crews that worked on the building, you were involved in many aspects of the construction of Stalag 47. Could you tell us if these schematics match your memory of the layout?"

T.J. Morris' eyes opened wide with fear. "Are you sure that's it's safe to break into their system?" he asked, looking at everyone.

"I assure you that we're very safe from being discovered. We're behind several encryption walls of security that I established earlier. Besides, the Terran encryption systems are very primitive compared to ours," Adrian informed him with confidence.

Kelem and Marla nodded in agreement and that allayed his fear. The old construction engineer studied the three dimensional schematic of Stalag 47. The structure was shaped like an eight story octagon. T.J. asked Adriana to rotate the view and zoom in on certain sections several times and then he leaned back in his chair.

"Yep, that's exactly the way I remember it," he declared with satisfaction.

Everyone was pleased to hear the news, in particular Kelem. "Wonderful! Now, can you tell us how the building was put together, such as what materials were used, what kind of sensors were put in the floors, walls and ceilings, access points, emergency exits, etcetera?"

"I remember we had a hell of a time laying down the foundation. As you well know, Hellas Planitia is nothing but a giant dust bowl. Just about every major dust storm on Mars originates from there. But, eventually we got the foundation put down and the next step was to erect the exterior walls. The exterior walls are interlocking sections made of an artificial stone that I believe was invented by Bernardo Salas, your dearly departed uncle," T.J. said, looking at Kelem.

Kelem suddenly had a clear recollection of Uncle Nardo explaining to him how he'd come up with a way to construct solid buildings on the surface of Mars with minimum cost, when he was about six years old.

"Each section of the wall is one meter by one meter by thirty three centimeters thick and weighs approximately two hundred and fifty kilos. Each block is connected to the next one by interlocking sections, and in addition, each section is glued to the adjacent section with instant cement. The entire exterior wall and roof of the building is one giant rigid shell made of these sections and is completely air tight."

"How tough is it to penetrate this shell?" asked Kelem.

"You'd have to use a large mining drill, but a laser cutter, a 'tuber' or a 'miner's patch' would work much better," T.J. replied.

A mining drill, Kelem knew, would take hours to break through the wall, a Laser cutter, about an hour. A 'tuber', which was a mining rig as big as a truck designed to make small tunnels underground, could do it in less than ten minutes; but it was large and heavy and impractical under the circumstances. A 'miner's patch' was a circular piece of heavy fabric, imbedded with a corrosive chemical capable of creating a circular opening on Martian rock one meter deep when exposed to vacuum.

"But Kelem," T.J. said, interrupting his train of thought. "The outer shell is but one of two layers between the cell blocks and the exterior. If you were able to break through the wall you'd be faced with the next layer, the actual superstructure of the building which is made of 'I' beam frames of Carb-Plas-Steel, (CPS) enclosed with a skin of CPS sheets. This layer is a slightly smaller version of the exterior wall and roof, and is also air tight. There are no emergency exits or any type of access hatches leading to and from the outside. The only way in and out of the place is through the roof's access hatches.

"What's beyond that? " Kelem inquired, beginning to lose confidence about extracting Nicolas Alfano from the facility.

"The cell blocks occupy the lower six levels of the structure running along the edge of the exterior wall. The seventh level is administration, and the top floor has the landing pad, radar and communication antennas, missile batteries and staff quarters. Each cell block level has a service tunnel that runs around the entire building. Those tunnels are big enough for a man to walk through, and they're designed to allow the maintenance staff to service the air, plumbing and electrical modules for all the cells on each level. As a matter of fact, all the cells in the building are individual pre-fab modules attached to each other, forming blocks of one hundred cells on each side of the octagon. The middle of the octagon," he said, pointing to the spot on the schematic displayed on the computer screen, "is the general area of the prison. It contains the kitchen and mess hall on the first floor with a six story security tower in the center of the building that has a three hundred and sixty degree view of all six cell block levels."

"So, once you've broken through to the service tunnel, you now have access to the rear wall of all the cells on that level?" Kelem asked, his confidence returning.

"Yes, but only to the cells on that level. If you wanted to reach any other level in the building, you'd have to exit the service tunnel and enter the prison itself," T.J. warned.

"What are the service tunnels made of?" Kelem asked as an idea began formulating in his brain.

"Well, the service tunnels are actually part of the cell blocks. In other words, when you're in the service tunnel, you have access to the rear walls and ceilings of each cell. The other side of the tunnel is actually the inner skin of the building's superstructure."

"Hmmm, I see, and what about the cells? How big are they, what materials are they made of, and how are they attached to the building itself?"

"Each pre-fab module is two and a half by two and a half by three meters high. They're basically cubes. The floor is a flat metal box containing the connections to the sink and toilet drains, and is made of one centimeter thick steel. Each of the four walls and the ceiling are assemblies of three half-centimeter thick steel panels screwed together, from the outside of course. The middle panel facing the interior of the cell block is a heavy duty door leading to the cell block's hallway.

Each cell is screwed to the floor from the bottom plate. Air, water and electricity are fed from the ceiling."

"One more question, T.J.," Kelem asked, "how difficult would it be to remove one panel from the rear wall of the cell and how much noise would the procedure make?"

"Well, hell!" T.J. said laughing, "If you got that far, that would be the easy part! The panels are simply screwed together with either Phillips or hexagonal screws. The inside of each panel is lined with a layer of acoustic cement, so my guess is that if you're careful, the guards would be none the wiser that someone is trying break into one of the cells."

"What about security cams and vibration and pressure sensors. Where are they installed?" Kelem asked.

"We were never privy to that part of the process. Once my crews completed the installation of the cell modules, the Terrans brought in their technicians to connect the air, water and electricity to each cell block. The Stalags were designed to be escape-proof. It's possible that since these prisons were built in the middle of nowhere, the Terrans might have felt it unnecessary to make them break in-proof." T.J. surmised.

Kelem rubbed his chin pensively and leaned back on his chair deep in thought.

Major Loeky spoke, breaking the silence. "Like T.J. said, breaking into the cell is the easy part. That is, if you manage to reach the place without being detected by their air and ground radar, not to mention visually by their exterior security cams. Stalag 47 in set squarely in the middle of the Hellas Planitia, surrounded by twenty three hundred square kilometers of flat terrain. You'd have to knock out their radar, exterior cams and missile batteries to be able to reach it, which would surely alert the military base on the southern edge of the Planitia to come looking and see what was going on."

"Forgive me for adding to the list of minuses in your plan to do this, Kelem, but where are you going to acquire a ship big enough and fast enough to pull off this caper?" T.J. demanded. "No civilian transport would measure up to the challenge, not to mention that if you were to use a civilian vessel it would be traceable to its owners."

"Yes, you both have valid points, but I will still give this plan further consideration. The only other option is not to do this, and that would mean the end of the Martian resistance movement," Kelem stated gravely.

"No one individual could be that important to the resistance, could they?" T.J. asked naively. "I mean, after all, aren't we all compartmentalized? And if one or two cells become compromised, the rest of us can continue fighting."

No one in that room could explain to T.J. Morris the importance of rescuing Nicolas Alfano from the clutches of the Phalanx, nor could they divulge the existence of the Brotherhood of the Light and its importance to the resistance movement. For now, all they could do is thank him for his advice and ask him not to discuss the matter with anyone else.

"Thank you very much for coming and talking to us, T.J. We'll take your advice into consideration," Kelem said politely. "Major Loeky will see you out."

"I'll say one thing. Whoever goes on this mission has my sincere admiration, because in my opinion, it's sheer suicide to try breaking into that place," T.J. said as he stood up and shook everyone's hands.

"You're probably right. We'll most likely decide to cancel the whole idea," Kelem responded to appease the old engineer.

When the door closed behind Major Loeky and T.J., Marla Hassett turned to Kelem. "Will Jake be able to erase the memory of this meeting from his mind?" she asked, referring to one of the two Brotherhood 'pushers' that Kelem had been training for the past three days.

"Yes, after I helped him increase his range and power, he's become very proficient and accurate at memory manipulation. T.J. will remember meeting with his old friend Major Loeky, but he won't remember having come here or meeting any of us. I know it's necessary, but I don't feel good about messing with people's memories, particularly when it's a good and decent fellow Martian," Kelem reflected with uneasiness.

"Don't worry Kelem, it's only a few hours out of his whole life's memories and the erasure will not cause any brain or psychological damage." Marla assured him. "Right now we can't afford the slightest flaw in our security."

"You're right, we have to find a way to get Nicolas out of there, and I'm starting to think that we'll be able to do it."

Both Marla and Adriana looked at him and each other with surprise.

The two women thought the rescue mission impossible considering all the information that T.J. Morris had just given them.

"Adriana, didn't you tell me that there's a Terran military craft maintenance and repair facility less than five kilometers from here?" Kelem asked.

"Yes, it's on the west side of Havana Flats. You can get there by one of the small roads that runs by the warehouse's landing pad," the girl answered, puzzled by Kelem's inquiry.

"Great. How long do you think it would take you to hack into their system?"

"No more than an hour or two. It's a low security facility so it wouldn't be too hard," the girl replied, wondering what Kelem had in mind.

"Oh, and one more thing, get me the latest weather report for the entire southern hemisphere."

"Will do," Adriana answered, already beginning her hack of the military repair facility on her computer terminal.

"I'm going back to Susan's warren. I need to ask her a question. I'll see you two later," Kelem announced as he opened the door.

Marla tried to read Kelem's mind, but she'd been unable to hear his thoughts since his return. "What are you planning, Kelem?" she asked as he stepped into the hallway.

"Can't talk now, time's of the essence," he answered as the door closed behind him.

For a second Marla had a moment of doubt, feeling that Kelem was being unrealistic about the possibility of rescuing their old friend Nicolas Alfano. But then she thought about all the amazing things that he had accomplished in his young life and the incredible journey that he'd been through since he'd left Mars, and all uncertainty and reservations left her mind.

CHAPTER 13

Operation Dust Storm

January 14th, 2660

Kelem stood in front of the members of the raiding party, going over the details of the operation.

"We've sent word to the rest of the resistance that the Phalanx might retaliate within hours of our mission being completed. Whether we're successful or not, the Terrans will probably strike back in either case. It's a heavy burden we're placing on the shoulders of our fellow Martians as undoubtedly, some will suffer incarceration, torture and perhaps death," Kelem declared, agonizing over the sequence of events that would follow the attempt to free Nicolas from Stalag 47.

"That's the price of freedom, Kelem. Our countrymen will understand our decision and no blame will fall on us," Major Loeky said in support of the operation.

Kelem nodded, grateful for the emotional support. He had come up with a clever plan that required a combination of perfect timing and a healthy dose of good luck.

"Well then, I'll go over each step of the operation. If anyone has any questions, please wait until I finish describing the sequence of events.

"Step one. We'll leave here at 11:30 PM on one of Fisher-Madjal's large transports on our way to the military repair facility nearby. We'll fly under the radar and land near a group of military shuttles parked on their field. Our planet has been gracious enough to provide us with a massive dust storm that will last for days, which means that the staff there won't be able to see or hear us when we 'borrow' one of their shuttles for a few hours. Jake here, will 'push' whoever is awake there at this hour, to see a Terran shuttle instead of a civilian transport should they be crazy enough to go outside and check.

"Step two. Adriana has hacked into their system and we know which shuttle to take. The ship we're taking has been completely overhauled recently and is scheduled for pickup in a few days. That means that its tanks are full and its rail guns are charged, should we run into a problem. That's why Adam here," he said, pointing to a young man with a shaved head, member of the Helter Skelters, "will man the canons as our weapons officer. Major Loeky tells me that he's a deadshot." Adam smiled and nodded. Kelem continued. "We're bringing two large auxiliary tanks of fuel to replace whatever we burn during the operation. This way when the Terrans come to pick up their ship, there won't be any discrepancies. In addition we're bringing with us a boarding tube extension which is what we're going to use to connect to the outer wall of the structure without decompressing the building's interior. Once we retrieve Nicolas, we'll seal the extension tube, disconnect it from the shuttle, and leave it behind. If we're lucky, it'll be several hours before the guards discover that Nicolas is missing or that the outer wall has been breached.

"Step three. We take off heading toward Hellas Planitia flying below thirty meters at Mach 2, using the ship's 'map of Mars' system." At this point, everyone in the group shifted uncomfortably in their seats. In spite of the shuttle's 'map of Mars', at Mach 2, Kelem would only have fractions of a second to correct the ship's heading and altitude should the elevation of the terrain suddenly rise ahead of their course. "I know, it's very risky, but I'm an excellent pilot and should I be injured or incapacitated, Captain Sunderam here, will be my co-pilot and take over if I'm unable to fly the ship." Captain Sunderam, a dark skinned gentleman of South Asian descent, and also a member of the Helter Skelters, acknowledged Kelem's statement but was obviously nervous about flying at such speeds so low to the ground.

"Step four. Once we reach the edge of the Planitia Crater, which should be around 02:30 AM, Adriana will jam the prison's air and ground radar. Radar is very spotty during dust storms anyway, and we're confident that the operators will treat the glitch as normal. If for some unlikely reason they detect our ship, we'll activate the shuttle's transponder which will identify us as a Terran vessel. However, if that happens, we'll have to turn back and abort the mission. I pray that we won't have to abort because it's unlikely that we'll be presented with the same combination of ideal conditions anytime soon.

"Step five. About three hundred klicks from the prison, I'll decelerate and approach the building from the south. Nicolas is in Cell Block 1-S-20. Fortunately for us, he's on the ground level in the southernmost side of the octagon. I'll maneuver the ship close to the outer wall, and connect the two boarding tubes. The extension tube will be connected to the wall with instant cement. Then we'll pressurize the two connected boarding tubes. Marla will scan the upper floors of the prison and let us know if our presence has been detected. If that is the case, Jake will attempt to 'push' that individual or individuals and hopefully misdirect them to ignore our presence."

"Step six. We breach the outer wall with a miner's patch." Miners use the patch on the surface of a vertical rock wall to escape tunnel collapses. Once activated, the patch's chemicals break down any kind of rock and turn it into a soft porous material which can be torn apart by hand. The device creates a circular opening big enough for a miner to crawl through even while wearing a pressure suit. Once we breach the wall, we'll cut through the skin of the superstructure with a laser cutter and then we'll be in the service tunnel.

"Step seven. We locate Nicola's cell, unscrew the rear panel of his cell wall, take him out and put him a pressure suit. We replace the panel, seal the superstructure, bring Nicolas to the shuttle, seal the extension boarding tube, disconnect the shuttle's boarding tube and take off.

"Step eight. We fly back to the maintenance depot, land the shuttle in the same spot where we found it, refill the fuel tanks, close the hatch, board our transport ship and return to the warehouse. We should be back no later than 07:30 AM.

"Oh. One more thing, I know that all six of you have agreed to take the poison that Marla has concocted for us. But I must reiterate this in the strongest way possible. If we're discovered and are about to be taken prisoner, I will not hesitate to shoot any of you if I see that you're having doubts. Marla assures me that the stuff is instantaneous and painless. These are desperate times, people. We can't afford to get caught and be interrogated."

"What about Nicolas? What good will it do us to commit suicide if he's still alive?" Jake asked.

If we're caught before we get to him, I've assembled an explosive powerful enough to take out an entire wing of that prison. If we're compromised, while we're either inside of the building or while escaping, I'll set it off with a remote that I'm carrying with me. The blast will kill all of us and Nicolas instantaneously."

"Won't that kill a lot of other prisoners as well?" Adriana asked innocently.

Marla reached for her shoulder and patted it tenderly. Adriana looked at her and suddenly understood how dangerous and deadly this mission was, but the young girl was brave and would not avoid her duty as a Martian citizen.

"What about the military radar station at the southern end of the Planitia, won't they detect our presence? " Captain Sunderam asked, looking concerned.

"In clear weather, yes, but in the midst of a whopper of a dust storm such as the one we're having right now, no."

The answer seemed to quell the captain's concerns, but he still looked nervous.

"What about everybody who's connected to the warehouse and its operation? What happens to them if we're caught?" Jake asked, concerned for his friends and their relatives.

"Jake, haven't you noticed that the warehouse seems unusually quiet tonight? "Kelem asked with a funny smile.

"Yes, now that you mention it," he said looking around.

"Everyone involved has been temporarily relocated to an unknown location under the care of my Helter Skelters," Major Loeky announced. "Even I don't know where they are in case we get caught."

"If there are no more questions, I suggest that we board the transport and be on our way," Kelem suggested.

Everyone stood up, folded their chairs, put them away and exited the room, heading toward the top level of the warehouse on the surface of Mars.

Ten minutes later, they were on their way to the military maintenance depot.

Kelem landed the company's transport less than a meter from the shuttle they were going to borrow amidst the blinding dust storm that had enveloped the entire planet. Captain Sunderam, a very skilled pilot himself, was duly impressed with the ease and precision with which Kelem placed the unwieldy civilian transport so delicately close to the Terran Ship.

Everyone donned their pressure suits and exited the ship. After Adriana connected her wrist comp to the com port on the hull of the Terran ship, she quickly deciphered the access code and the hatch opened. Once inside, Kelem quickly and efficiently went over the ship's systems finding everything operating normally. The shuttle had room for eight passengers, and after everyone strapped themselves to their seats, Kelem fired the ship's antigrav motors. Once the craft was a few meters off the ground he fired the main engines, and within a few minutes they were traveling at 1,800 kilometers per hour, a mere thirty meters above the landscape.

This part of the mission was as dangerous as, or perhaps more perilous than, the actual breaking into the prison. Captain Sunderam soon found himself sweating profusely as he watched the surface of Mars zip by the shuttle's windows at dizzying speed. He was sure that at any moment the vessel would slam into an unexpected hill or obstruction and everyone would be instantly vaporized.

Kelem read the man's mind and made a casual comment to alleviate his fear. "Relax, Sunderam, if we hit something you won't feel a thing," he said laughing as he concentrated with all his might on the 'map of Mars' display on the shuttle's cabin window. At nearly 1,800 kilometers per hour, the ship was covering one kilometer every two seconds. By the time Kelem saw an obstruction rushing towards him through the 'map of Mars' screen, which only reached out ten kilometers ahead of the shuttle, he had only a few seconds to respond and correct to avoid disaster. The system was only designed to operate safely at 1,000 kilometers per hour or less.

The next ninety minutes were harrowing and violent as Kelem had to execute extreme maneuvers to avoid crashing into hills and other obstacles. A few of the others, including Captain Sunderam, developed severe cases of nausea.

At around 02:28 AM they had reached the edge of the Hellas Planitia crater. Suddenly, Kelem yelled out, "Adriana, now!" and the girl, who was sitting in the com officer's chair, pushed a button on a portable module that she had built and connected to the ship's antenna system and began transmitting a jamming signal. Everyone hoped it would succeed in blinding the radar tower atop Stalag 47.

A few seconds later Kelem yelled out again. "Hold on!" as the shuttle plummeted 7,120 meters in less than a minute, creating five g's of negative force. The crater was the deepest impact crater on all of Mars, and Kelem had to fly close to the ground to continue avoiding radar detection. As the minutes ticked by, Captain Sunderam kept a close eye on the ship's radar detector, praying that the monitor would remain clear of radar sweeps from the prison's radar.

The ship's 'map of Mars' system was useless in the crater. It had been designed to fly high above the surface of Mars, not thirty meters from the basin floor. In the blinding dust storm, Kelem was now flying by dead reckoning. Captain Sunderam feared that Kelem would miscalculate and fail to slow down before reaching the prison and end up crashing into it at Mach 2.

Finally, at 03:05 AM, Kelem throttled down the engines and opened the air brakes, and the ship quickly decelerated to a mere 300 kph. Then he turned south for a minute or two, and three minutes later, turned north and slowed down to 100kph.

After a few more minutes, Sunderam began to sweat again. "When are you going to turn the night vision on?"

Kelem didn't answer. He was reaching out with his mind, waiting until the very last few seconds to engage the infrared beam that would light up the terrain directly ahead of the shuttle. He didn't know if Stalag 47 had sensors that could detect infrared.

By mere instinct, Kelem decided when to cut the main engines and engaged the antigrav motors as the ship slowed down to a crawl. He flipped the night vision switch and had to slam on the retro breaks as the shuttle almost crashed against the south wall of Stalag 47. Kelem had slowed the big shuttle in time to prevent a major crash, but not enough to avoid bumping against the wall at 20 kph. Everyone's bodies slumped forward with the impact, and all held their breath fearing that the impact had alerted the guards inside the prison. The shuttle bounced back and then remained hovering a meter above the ground in front of the wall.

Kelem turned the ship left and then maneuvered it sideways so that he could connect the boarding tubes to the prison wall. He calculated when the boarding hatch would near the center of the south wall, and then slowly lowered the ship to the ground and cut the antigrav motors off.

"Marla, Jake, tell me some good news," Kelem called out, and both closed their eyes and concentrated with all their might, scanning the consciousness of the prison's staff looking for any signs of alarm or fear. After a while Marla opened her eyes. "It's all right, Kelem. No one's heard or done anything so far."

"Keep scanning, I need to know the moment that you feel the slightest change in mood from inside," Kelem stated as he unstrapped himself from the pilot's chair and went over to the boarding tube's controls on the right side of the cabin. "Everyone, put your helmets on," he announced.

"Adam, stay at your station, and fire at anything that comes within ten kilometers of us," he ordered the weapons expert.

The young man saluted with a smile, happy to still be alive after such an insane flight, and activated the ship's rail guns.

Kelem extended the flexible boarding tubes and waited until the panel's indicator read that it had made contact with the prison's wall. Then, Adriana and Jake got into the airlock with instant cement guns in hand to glue the circular edge of the outer tube against the stone wall. Kelem had trained them both on how to apply the powerful industrial adhesive. They were the youngest and thinnest of the group and both were able to fit in the tube together while wearing their suits to perform the task without getting in each other's way. They had to be careful to avoid getting the powerful adhesive on their pressure suits otherwise they'd be stuck forever.

The stuff dried in seconds and both were back in less than three minutes. Kelem waited a minute or so to make sure that the bond between the outer tube and the wall was solid and then pressurized the tubes. Once he was sure, he ordered everyone to close their helmet's face plate. From now until they brought Nicolas out of the prison and were successfully on their way, everyone would be sealed in their pressure suits. Kelem didn't want anyone identified by their fingerprints or DNA. By staying sealed in their suits, they lessened the chances of leaving any hair strands or skin flakes behind.

Kelem, Major Loeky and Jake entered the tube with all the equipment needed to break in and retrieve Nicolas, the others would stay behind. Captain Sunderam took the pilot's chair in case things went bad and they'd have to leave in a hurry, Marla continued 'reading' the prison staff and would alert the others in case they were detected. Adriana remained on electronic jamming and sensors, scanning for any signals of approaching ships or ground troops.

Kelem unsealed the miner's patch and placed it on the wall. Once it was exposed to air or vacuum, the patch quickly turned from a fabric to a gel and was immediately absorbed by the stone. Within seconds the wall began to heat and smoke. Soon a circular area of stone turned into powder and began crumbling. Kelem reached out and began tearing off chunks of the desiccated material until a perfect circular hole revealed the prison's superstructure.

Major Loeky now stepped forward and cut a circular hole on the CPS plate with a laser torch, leaving five centimeters uncut, to act as a hinge. Kelem intended to seal the CPS plate on the way out to prevent any innocent inmates from asphyxiating in case the boarding tube failed, thus preventing the cell block from decompressing after they left.

All the while, the trio's heart rate climbed high with fear and anticipation, hoping that the prison's wall didn't have any sensors or automatic alarms imbedded in it.

Marla suddenly felt a weird sensation in her head unlike anything that she'd ever experienced. The feeling made her lose her concentration and she stopped scanning. She shook it off and resumed scanning, but within seconds her head felt as if tiny insects were crawling around in the space between her skull and brain. She reacted by jumping up from her seat and unconsciously yelling out.

Kelem and Major Loeky were in the process of bending the CPS plate outwards to gain access to the service tunnel, when they heard a female voice yell in their helmet's speakers and stopped what they were doing.

"Who yelled? What's going on?" Kelem asked tensely.

Marla hesitated for a moment. "Kelem, it was me, Marla. I... I just felt a very weird sensation in my head, like... like tiny insects inside my brain!" she announced, her voice sounding nervous.

Kelem's blood froze. Major Loeky and Jake exchanged glances and wondered if they'd been detected by the prison staff.

"Did it feel like snakes crawling through your head?" he asked, remembering a similar experience a few days before.

"Yes, you could describe it that way."

Kelem knew that a very powerful Phalanx psychic on Mars had the ability to search for other psychics at great distances. This was probably that same individual, but until now no one but Kelem had felt the curious effect of that person's probing. Suddenly, Kelem felt a sense of danger and vulnerability and knew instantly that his adversary was nearby.

"Marla, stop scanning immediately and go into a meditation. Imagine your mind becoming a mirror-like sphere where no thoughts or attempts to influence you can penetrate it. Do this now!" he said with urgency. Then he looked at Jake. "Jake, whatever happens, do not use your power!" he warned.

From Kelem's tone of voice, Marla knew that she and the others were in real danger. She was scared, but being an experienced psychic she was able to slow down her breathing and followed Kelem's instructions. Soon, she had shielded her mind from the horrible energy that had afflicted her seconds earlier. Still, even though the effect had dissipated, she could still feel an evil presence hovering on the edge of her consciousness.

"We have to hurry," Kelem said to Major Loeky and Jake.

The trio picked up their tempo, quickly bent the CPS plate backwards, and rushed into the service tunnel. Once inside, they found themselves in the middle of a corridor one meter wide by three hundred meters long. Above their heads, a thin light strip ran along the length of the ceiling, providing sufficient light to illuminate the back walls of the one hundred cell modules in this section of the prison, as well as all the air, electricity and water pipes that ran along the ceiling. The cells were clearly numbered one through one hundred from right to left.

Nicolas' cell was located to their right. Kelem signaled the others to turn on their helmet's exterior microphones. They needed to listen for any alarms or the sound of approaching prison guards. As soon as they reached module # 20, Kelem and Major Loeky began loosening the screws that held the center panel of the rear wall as fast as the unwieldy gloves of their pressure suits allowed. Jake, who was carrying Nicolas' spare pressure suit on his back, stayed on the side collecting the screws from Kelem and Major Loeky.

Five minutes later they removed the panel from the rear cell wall and when Kelem stepped into the cell, his face turned pale white.

There, on a small filthy cot, lay a skeleton thin, malnourished old man wearing a dirty red prison jumpsuit. For a moment, Kelem feared that Nicolas had been transferred to another cell block and that this poor scarecrow of a man was just another victim of the Phalanx's cruel regime. But then the frail old man opened his eyes, and upon seeing Kelem's face behind his helmet's face plate, smiled.

"My boy... I knew you'd come for me..." he said with barely a whisper. Kelem's eyes filled with tears and suddenly felt a boiling rage that threatened to make him scream at the top of his lungs and bang the walls of the tiny cell. He put his index finger tenderly on Nicolas' mouth to keep him quiet and signaled for the major and Jake to come in and put the pressure suit on Nicolas.

The sight of Nicolas's withered body had stunned Kelem to such a degree that his mind had suffered a shock. Each time that he had communicated with Nicolas in the past few days, he'd seen him as he looked physically when he left Mars. And now he realized with sadness that he'd been seeing an idealized image of his old friend.

Nicolas Alfano was so weak that he couldn't stand up on his own. It took all three men more than ten minutes to put his thin frame into the suit. By then, all three were sweating from the difficult task of trying to put a limp rag doll inside a pressure suit while wearing one.

Kelem was sure that the noise of trying to put Nicolas in the suit was going to alert the guards, until he realized that he'd accidentally raised the volume of his exterior microphone. Eventually, they succeeded, and after strapping the helmet on Nicolas' suit, they turned on the air and checked the seals to make sure that the suit was tight in case of decompression.

Nicolas' limp body, in addition to the weight of the suit, required the strength of the two bigger men to carry him into the shuttle. Jake stayed behind to re-attach the panel on the back of the cell while Kelem and Loeky brought Nicolas into the shuttle. Once inside, Loeky lifted Nicolas by himself and strapped him to a chair while Kelem ran back into the service tunnel. Once Kelem and Jake finished the job, they returned to the boarding tube, and together, the two of them with Loeky's help, pushed the CPS panel back towards the building. Using an ultrasonic welder, they sealed the thin gap created by the laser cutter.

Marla suddenly screamed in pain, and everyone stopped in their tracks. Kelem ran back to the shuttle to find Marla slumped in her chair. Then, Kelem, followed by Jake and then Adriana, each felt their brains being invaded by invisible tendrils, one after the other as if an etheric octopus had encircled their brains with its tentacles.

"What is it?" Adriana and Jake asked in a panic.

Kelem yelled at Loeky to seal the outer tube and get back into the shuttle. Once inside, the major pressed the switch that disengaged the ship's tube from the outer one, and the ship was free of the building.

"Sunderam! Get us the hell out of here!" he shouted as he jumped into the co-pilot's seat. Everyone else strapped themselves in.

Sunderam didn't bother initiating the antigrav motors. He simply hit the throttle of the main engines and the ship took off with a sudden violent motion that jerked everyone back into their seats, subjecting everyone to several g's of force almost instantaneously. Nicolas, Jake and Adriana passed out immediately, while Adam, Loeky, Sunderam and Kelem fought with all their strength to maintain consciousness.

Kelem recovered first and saw that Sunderam in his panic had aimed the shuttle westwards. He switched control of the ship to the co-pilot's chair and warned the others that he was going to make a hard turn. The ship groaned and shook as Kelem held on to the controls, pushing with his diaphragm to keep the blood in his brain from migrating to his central organs. If he went into 'G-Lock' so low to the ground, he'd lose control and crash the ship. Somehow he managed to complete the turn without passing out.

With the ship heading east, Kelem turned on the 'map of Mars' system and handed the controls back to Sunderam, ordering him to keep the speed under 1,000 kph. He had lost all confidence in the man and would never use him on a mission again.

He ran back to the passenger's area and checked on Nicolas, who was still unconscious from the effects of the violent turn Kelem had executed. He wanted badly to connect with him psychically and help him regain his strength, but there was no time now. Kelem knew that his adversary was near. This psychic was very powerful and deadly, and was coming for him and the others!

Marla, Jake and Adriana had regained consciousness. Kelem went over to them. "Listen, you three, what you experienced before was the effect of a very powerful psychic probing your brains trying to get into your heads and discover who we are and what we're doing. That's the bad news. The good news is that he can only do that to us one at a time. So you, Marla and Jake must take turns enveloping this ship with a giant psychic protective shield to repel this person's energy. I need Adriana to concentrate on electronic jamming and defense, and I have to fly the ship and get us out of danger." Kelem paused and looked at all three of them, each of whom were dealing with their own fear and shock at being violated so insidiously by such a perverted, evil psychic.

"I know that right now you're scared and shook up, but I need you guys to pull it together and fight back. Otherwise, we're not getting out of this one!"

The three of them nodded and understood that they had to overcome their fears. Steeling themselves with new found courage, Jake and Marla closed their eyes and began protecting the ship, while Adriana returned her attention to the com officer's control board.

"Adam, stay sharp. I have a feeling that we're going to need your talents!" Kelem advised the young weapons officer.

Kelem ran to the front of the shuttle and took over piloting duties. He grabbed the throttle and pushed the engines to maximum and concentrated on the 'map of Mars' screen, heading east toward the rim of the Hellas Crater.

The ship's proximity alarm went off and Adriana's heart jumped. "Kelem! We have a bogie on our tail!"

CHAPTER 14

Chasing a Ghost

January 15th, 2660

Colonel Jude Voltanieu was bent forward in intense mental concentration in the co-pilot's chair of his custom made shuttle. He and his pilot were chasing a rogue ship in the Hellas Planitia in the middle of the worst dust storm in years.

Less than an hour earlier he had been reading reports at the Hellas Rim Base commandant's office, when he sensed the proximity of the man that he'd been trying to identify for several weeks. He realized that in a lucky twist of fate, the man had come to him. He was somewhere near!

And he had brought some of his friends with him!

He woke up his pilot and soon they were headed north. His psychic's intuition told him that's where the man was.

Soon after take-off, his ship's radar showed an intermittent blip heading eastwards traveling barely above the ground at an insane speed, and Jude Voltanieu knew that his mystery man was on that ship! The rogue was trying to jam their radar, but Jude Voltanieu's radar had been specially designed and was practically interference-proof. Now his pilot was pushing the engines hard, gaining steadily on the mysterious ship.

"Sir, whoever that pilot is, he's either insane or he has the reflexes of a supercomputer!" his pilot exclaimed, worried that both vessels would end up slamming against the edge of the crater any moment now.

The other ship suddenly slammed on its air brakes and Jude's ship shot past it.

Jude Voltanieu suddenly lost his link with one of the females on the rogue ship that he was just about to identify and, cursing with frustration, he took over the controls of his ship. His pilot was the best in the Terran Occupation Fleet, but Colonel Voltanieu was the best pilot in the solar system.

The other ship veered southeast heading toward the South Pole, but Jude knew it was a feint. He also turned southeast but at a narrower angle knowing that the rogue ship was going to veer north any second now. He told his pilot, now co-pilot, to aim the shuttle's rail guns directly ahead and wait for his order to fire. As soon as the other ship changed course, Jude gave the order and a long stream of ammunition traveling at several times the speed of sound issued forth from his shuttle like fire from a dragon's mouth.

But the other ship turned south again almost at the same time that his rail guns went off and the shots missed the ship by several kilometers.

"Who is this son of a bitch?" his pilot asked, impressed by the skills of the man piloting the renegade vessel.

"A ghost, a goddamned ghost!" Jude swore, gritting his teeth as he rammed the throttle to maximum and the ship jumped forward, shaking and rattling as it neared its maximum safe speed limit.

At her station's monitor, Adriana saw the other ship suddenly shoot forward in their direction. "Kelem, the other ship has caught up with us!" she yelled above the roar of the engines.

Kelem looked on his radar screen and saw the blip of the other ship coming at them at near missile speed and cursed under his breath. He didn't know if the other ship was at its maximum velocity this low to the ground or if it still had more juice in its engines. Whatever capacity his adversary's ship's engines had, the man was surely burning a lot of fuel. Kelem guessed the thing was a two-seater, fast and agile.

But once again, Kelem prepared to slam on the air brakes and let the other ship pass him. This time he alerted Adam to send a volley of rail gun fire in the direction of flight the moment he hit the brakes. His adversary would fly straight into his line of fire.

"Ready?... Now!" Kelem yelled as Adam fired all six rail guns and the shuttle decelerated and veered left, pulling almost seven g's.

Without fail, Jude Voltanieu's ship flew right into the stream of fire as several pellets of depleted uranium converted into plasma by the rail guns, slammed into the ship's fuselage. The barrage didn't hit any major mechanical parts, but now his co-pilot lay slumped forward on the instrument panel with half of his brains missing. The decompression alarm went off indicating the cabin was losing air pressure and Jude grabbed his helmet and slammed it shut.

Jude Voltanieu screamed with frustration as he also turned north firing his guns repeatedly in a blind rage.

Kelem was sure that his enemy had by now burned and crashed, until with utter surprise, he noticed the blip on his radar screen relentlessly following him as streams of rail gun fire shot past him.

He realized that he couldn't outrun this ship and that eventually it would catch up with them. Its rail guns would tear their ship apart.

Kelem turned around and called Loeky over. "Major, go grab 'the package' and put it in the air lock, and for God's sake hurry!"

Loeky raced to the back of the cabin and ran to the airlock door with the explosive that Kelem had assembled earlier. The bomb was a short stubby cylinder with rings of tubes and cables around it. He opened the inner door, put the cylinder inside and then closed the door.

"Attention everybody, please make sure that your harnesses are on tight. I'm going to be executing a very sharp maneuver and I don't want anybody coming lose and breaking their neck!" Then he called out to Jake, "Jake, make sure that Nicolas is strapped in good and tight!"

Jake left his seat, sat next to Nicolas and adjusted his harness, then strapped himself on the chair next to him with his right arm over the old man's chest for extra measure.

Jude Voltanieu was closing in on the other ship fast and was almost within firing range. He had the ship's night vision on and as he came closer to the other ship, he was surprised to see it was a medium size Terran shuttle!

"Well! Whoever this man and his friends are they're about to die!" he exclaimed jubilantly. As Jude reached for the firing button on his controls, the other ship suddenly and unexpectedly shot upwards almost vertically. Jude reacted within milliseconds and matched the bigger heavier vessel's move, knowing that the other ship couldn't climb as fast as his lighter, more agile shuttle. The other ship was actually attempting a loop! Jude laughed at the other pilot's pointless maneuver, which was draining speed and altitude from the bigger ship and would bring it into his sights within in a second or two. So concentrated on the other ship was he, that he didn't notice a small blip on his radar leaving the other ship and heading towards his.

Without warning, the other ship flipped left and dove down. Jude was about to correct when a blinding explosion went off in front of him hitting the shuttle with great force. Stunned, Jude tried to grab the controls, but the ship was falling and spinning so fast, he couldn't reach them. The windows failed and the cabin filled with swirling red-brown Martian dust. He lost consciousness and the world went black.

CHAPTER 15

Consultation with a Traitor

January 19th, 2660

Soltan Voltanieu sat in an anti-grav wheel chair across from Solomon Vandecamp's ornate antique desk on the third floor of his luxurious mansion on the outskirts of Paris. He had come to Earth seeking answers from the former president of Mars.

"I don't see how I can be of any help, Voltanieu. The last Martian citizen that I had any contact with was Ambassador Marcus a week after I renounced my citizenship," Vandecamp was explaining.

Soltan Voltanieu was in a dark mood. His most valuable intelligence asset, Jude Voltanieu, had crashed on the floor of Hellas Planitia chasing a rebel ship and was currently lying in a coma on a med-bed in the intensive care unit of Latonga City Hospital. And to add to his troubles, the most valuable prisoner held in Stalag 47, (or more accurately, in all of Mars) had been freed by the same individuals who had brought down his son's ship.

"Search your memory, Vandecamp; you must have an idea of who this new rebel leader is."

"It's been eighteen years since I left Mars. Besides, I'm an old man now. My memory doesn't serve me well these days," Vandecamp quipped humorously. He was enjoying seeing Soltan Voltanieu squirm for the first time ever. He knew that Voltanieu had ordered him killed after he renounced his Martian citizenship and gave the Terrans the information that made it possible for Earth to invade Mars. Fortunately, Terran 'President for Life', Sylvan Montenegro had countermanded the order.

"Would you be willing to submit to a brain scan?" Voltanieu asked, hiding his scorn for this Judas who had sold out his own country.

"Hell no! I don't want to spend the rest of my golden years wearing a diaper and having a nurse wipe my drool," Vandecamp replied sarcastically. Eighteen years earlier, he would have been out of his mind to speak to Soltan Voltanieu in such a manner. But Solomon Vandecamp had grown rich and powerful from the betrayal of his nation. In turn, the once feared leader of the Phalanx had fallen out of favor with President Montenegro and many of the top politicians and powerful men of Earth. Mars' industrial output had been steadily declining for several years, and many blamed it on Voltanieu's harsh treatment of the Martian population.

"Bah! You're neither senile nor forgetful. You're looking to get something in exchange for this information. What do you really want in return?"

"You're wasting your time talking to me. You could have saved your trip to Earth and reached me by video-conference. Besides, I don't need or want anything from you," Vandecamp said with a slight hint of disdain in his voice. Voltanieu must have been desperate to have decided to come to Earth just to talk to him privately in the vague hope that he could help identify this new Martian rebel leader.

"I think you're lying. You must know who this Martian is."

"What makes you think that he has to be a Martian? He could be a Terran, you know."

"Impossible! Like you, most people on Earth have grown fat, lazy and comfortable. Why would a Terran want to go to Mars to lead a rebellion against Earth?"

"But, Voltanieu, haven't you been keeping up with the news lately?" Vandecamp asked, realizing that the governor of Mars was out of touch with events here on Earth.

"Huh? What do you mean?"

"There's been a lot of political turmoil recently. Many are calling for Montenegro's resignation and for planet wide democratic elections. They're saying that at age eighty seven and after twenty years in power, Montenegro should go. But mostly, people are complaining about his expensive life style with all the fancy galas and parties that are constantly taking place and the myriad of mansions and estates that he and his cronies own throughout Earth. The truth is that their sumptuous life style is being financed by ever increasing taxes on the lower middle classes. Don't get me wrong, I love the man! His policies have helped people like me to become super rich. But, unlike the old dictators of the 20th century, he doesn't understand that he has to provide the average citizen with populist programs that appeal to the common man, like high quality entertainment and patriotic slogans to keep them distracted."

"Nonsense! I've read the reports from my Phalanx operatives in North and South America. It's just a few malcontents trying to start trouble, and I've told President Montenegro as much. He needn't worry about being deposed. This new rebel leader has to be a Martian," Voltanieu declared dismissively.

"Then, your operatives are sleeping on the job, particularly in North China and Western Russia where there's been as much trouble as in the Americas. And let's not forget Africa, where there are, at this very moment, several armed conflicts taking place among tribal leaders."

"Look, this man is definitely a Martian. For one thing, he's a very powerful psychic and is as good if not better than my own son, and you and I know that only the Brotherhood has produced such individuals. And two, he must be an incredible pilot to have bested my son in aerial combat."

Solomon Vandecamp furrowed his brow and the image of someone from his past flashed in mind, but he dismissed the possibility as unlikely.

"What?" Voltanieu asked after seeing Vandecamp's change of expression. The man had obviously thought of someone or remembered something important. "You've just thought of someone, didn't you?"

"I did, but the person I'm thinking about has been dead for years."

"Well then, who the hell is it?" Voltanieu asked with exasperation, breaking character from his usual calm and cool persona.

"The only individual that I know of, who was a member of the Brotherhood and possessed the same set of skills as your son, was Kelem Rogeston," Vandecamp replied. And as he did so, a small part of the psychic gene that all Martians are born with, suddenly kicked in and he became sure that somehow, Kelem Rogeston had survived the voyage of the Solar Nations and had returned to Mars.

Very few things frightened Soltan Voltanieu, but the name of Kelem Rogeston and the remote possibility that he had been alive all these years and had managed to return to Mars from somewhere out in space, made him tremble with fear. "It can't be," he uttered softly.

"Why not?" Vandecamp suggested. "We all assumed that the ship was lost with all hands on board. But what if they were thrown off course and ended up hundreds or thousands of light years from the solar system? It could have taken them this long to get back home," added Vandecamp, now convinced that his intuition was right.

"But an *n'time* ship can travel huge distances in a matter of seconds. How could it have taken them until now to return to Mars?" Voltanieu asked confused.

"One thing that I remember with absolute clarity was that Rogeston wanted to take his time going over the technical data from the maiden voyage before he took the ship out again. But Martian president Patricia Martinez and the senate were sure that a Terran invasion was imminent. She came to me in October of 2638 to ask my opinion of her idea to press the Solar Nations into military service which I nixed. But she didn't take my advice, and eventually forced Rogeston to take the ship out even though he warned her that it wasn't ready. My guess is that the *n'time* generator broke down and it took Rogeston and the crew all this time to fix it and get back to the solar system."

A sense of foreboding took over Voltanieu's mind. What if Rogeston and the crew did return? If the resistance had an *n'time* ship in their possession it could change the balance of power beyond the belt and eventually on Mars. The Terran Space Fleet commander had informed him that there had been some unusual rebel activity in the outer edges of the solar system. Perhaps this was a result of Rogeston's return. He had to get back to Mars and eliminate this threat!

"Don't tell anyone about this conversation," Voltanieu ordered brusquely. "I'll see my way out," he added in his raspy hiss of a voice. He pressed the controls of the anti-grav wheel chair that was supporting his body, weakened by years of living in Mars' low gravity, then turned around and exited Vandecamp's office without saying goodbye. Outside, the two Phalanx goons who had been guarding the door, followed him to the mansion's elevator.

Solomon Vandecamp left his plush office chair and walked to the window in his office that faced the front of the mansion. He leaned over and saw the two guards lift Soltan Voltanieu's stick-thin body and gently slide him into the back seat of the limousine parked on the mansion's curved driveway. As the limousine pulled away, Vandecamp grinned with pleasure at having seen Soltan Voltanieu desperate and worried about losing his skin to the Martian resistance. That pleasure however was tinted with a healthy dose of concern. If Kelem Rogeston really had returned to Mars and was mounting a new Martian resistance offensive, Vandecamp knew that he was the one individual who could successfully expel the Earthmen from his planet. As a Martian traitor and ex-president of Mars, he needed to stay ahead of the game.

If his former countrymen were about to retake their planet, Vandecamp wasn't too worried. Years before, he had put together a contingency plan in case this happened. For years, he had been feeding small bits of information to a Martian operative here on Earth under the pretense that he was still a Martian patriot. Now he would have to ramp up his efforts and begin giving the operative more substantial intel to protect his position in the future. If he saw that the Martians were likely to succeed, he would reveal really important information, thus securing his status as a faithful son of Mars.

Confident that he could play both sides of the game, Solomon Vandecamp relaxed and got ready for his afternoon massage.

CHAPTER 16

Old Friends

February 6th, 2660

It had been two weeks since Nicolas had been rescued from Stalag 47, and his health had improved dramatically thanks to Marla Hassett's medical skills, but also due to Kelem's incessant psychic ministrations. He had spent the first week of Nicolas' recovery in deep meditation, strengthening his body and spirit in the realm between reality and the place Kelem called, the Quantum Tide.

What had been done to Nicolas over the years was horrible. And the fact that he was still alive was a testament to the resiliency and strength of spirit of a man who had endured the kind of mental and physical torture that would have killed men half his age.

As soon as Nicolas was able to walk, he, Kelem, Jake and Adriana went to Laredo Heights, a small city that had once been a tiny mining prospector's outpost, one hundred kilometers from the Stephen Hawking Center in the Galle Crater Dunes.

Kelem had a specific purpose for being here, but he didn't want to tell anyone about his plans just yet. Additionally, Terran security in Laredo Heights was practically non-existent. It was a good place to lie low, away from the big cities while Nicolas recovered from his ordeal.

The quartet posed as migrant laborers looking for work in the surrounding area. The four took up residence in one of the smallest, less busy, cheap hotels on the edge of town. The town's main source of income was based on providing the Hawking Center with food and

supplies. The facility had once been the most secret scientific installation on Mars. Now, the former scientific research facility was a huge factory complex that specialized in manufacturing *n'time* generators, electronic systems for space vessels, and a host of other cutting edge technology.

Occasionally, one of the many companies that provided the center with food and drink would hire a few migrants to help deliver the supplies to the center's warehouse, and that was what Kelem was waiting for. The opportunity to get in there as Gerard Seaver (his new identity), and find the one individual who could answer many of his questions.

He had Adriana hack into the center's data base, and also the Mars Mining Company's servers on the first day they'd arrived in Laredo Heights. He asked Adriana to let him know the moment that their schedule indicated that MMC's CEO, William Chong, was going to pay a visit to the Hawking Center.

Right now, Kelem was enjoying, Nicolas' company after being separated for so many years.

"You're looking much better since we cut and dyed your hair," Kelem commented, happy to be with his mentor, who was more of a father figure than anything else.

"I almost don't recognize myself," Nicolas observed, looking at his reflection in the small mirror in the mini-bathroom of their hotel module. "All youth has left me, Kelem. Sixteen years as a prisoner of the Phalanx has worn me down. But then again, I was never one for vanity. What is important is that we're reunited once again," he said with a wide grin, reminding Kelem of the old Nicolas.

"It sure is good to be with you once again, old friend. I've lost count of how many times I thought of you and Thor while I was on Plantanimus," Kelem confessed.

"Thor was right after all," Nicolas mused, remembering that the Brotherhood's prophet, Thorgen Kutmeier had foretold that Kelem would meet an alien species someday. "I remember that at the time I made a funny comment about 'little green men from Mars'," Nicolas exclaimed, laughing heartily.

Kelem laughed with him. It was wonderful to see Nicolas in such good spirits. "Ah! I miss old Thor. I wish that he were here with us to guide us through these hard times."

"His company would be most welcome now, I agree. But Kelem,

you're not giving yourself due credit. What you have accomplished by getting me out of Stalag 47 and the amazing nature of your new skills is nothing short of a miracle. Your planning and successful execution of my rescue has revitalized the resistance. I heard from Marla that some people are talking about you with the same reverence and respect usually reserved for a deity or religious figure!"

Kelem rolled his eyes with dismay at such foolishness. "Nicolas, this is terrible! This hero worship must be avoided at all costs! People need to stop thinking of me in that way," he replied, shaking his head in disbelief.

"It already may be too late to stop people from interpreting your ability to teach people to radiate love and affection, and in turn, pass that knowledge to others, as anything other than godly or sacred."

"I never meant for members of the Brotherhood to tell anyone that they learned that from me!" Kelem protested, feeling that a religious movement based on worship of him as a messiah was a terrible idea.

"Marla, Phillip and Dalton believe that this quasi-religious notion of you performing 'miracles' will help motivate the average folks out there to get involved in the resistance movement. And I happen to agree with them. Don't forget Kelem that many Martians have given up hope of ever regaining their freedom. Your return to Mars and the things that you've accomplished in such a short time have given people hope for the first time in over two decades! The entire Martian population has been cowering and living in fear for a very long, long time. And you have changed all that," Nicolas said, pointing a finger at him. "Accept it Kelem. However it is that you're perceived, in the eyes and minds of the people of Mars, is what you must become."

Kelem shook his head with an ironic smile on his lips. "In for a penny, in for a pound I suppose."

"I'm sure that this development was the furthest thing from your mind when you said to yourself, 'I'm going to return to Mars and see if I can help free my people from the Terrans'," Nicolas joked to lighten Kelem's mood.

"You're not kidding! I'm willing to go along with this 'miracle maker' thing until we kick the Terrans from Mars. But once that happens, I'll be damned if I'm going to let people live their lives believing that I'm some sort of saint!" Kelem declared emphatically.

"I agree. Unfortunately, right now we can't afford to lose any advantage that we have over the Terrans," Nicolas added with conviction.

Kelem nodded with resignation knowing that Nicolas was right, remembering Captain Veronica Valchek's words, "There are those who seek power and renown and then there are those who have power and renown thrust upon them".

The following day, Adriana informed Kelem that CEO Billy Chong would be visiting the Hawking Center two days hence. He immediately had her hack into the Laredo Heights Grocery Company's data base and had her insert his and Jake's name atop the list of migrant workers waiting for a chance to work some part time hours for the grocer. Then, he contacted Major Loeky and had him pick up Nicolas and Adriana and move them to a new safe location. He would meet with them in a few days.

Two days later, Kelem and Jake showed up at the grocery company's depot early in the morning. When the loading dock foreman noticed their two names on the top of the list and was about to protest that something was wrong, Jake simply 'pushed' the man to believe that it was he himself who had put their names on the list. An hour later, Kelem and Jake were traveling north in the back of the company's delivery truck on the way to the Stephen Hawking Center.

"I'm certainly glad that you're with me, Jake. I couldn't pull off this particular mission without your singular talent."

"You're welcome, Kelem. And don't worry, none of the others will hear about this from me," Jake assured him.

"If I had let the others know that I was going to attempt contacting the most reviled Martian collaborator on the planet, they would have forbidden me to do it. But, aside from personal reasons, it's important for the resistance to know if Billy really is a collaborator or if he's just playing a part."

"I heard that he's constantly in the company of a Phalanx stooge named Wallace Simkus," Jake commented.

"That's right. When I heard about that, it made me think that if they really trusted Billy, they wouldn't have assigned a 'minder' to accompany him wherever he goes."

"How do you plan to get to him?" Jake asked.

"Adriana found out that Billy's secretary has scheduled a fancy dinner for him with all the top managers of the facility tonight. This truck is delivering food for that banquet along with fresh kitchen staff and waiter uniforms. I made sure Adriana included two extra sets for us. I'm hoping that we can pose as servers. If Billy recognizes me and is about to give us up to his Phalanx cohorts, I'll signal you and you can 'push' him to forget that he saw me and then we'll get out of there as best we can. If he recognizes me and doesn't give us up, that could either mean that he's Phalanx but wants to keep me from getting captured, or, that he's not a traitor, but playing along for some reason."

"If he recognizes you and doesn't give us up, what then?"

"Then we have to find a way to separate him from his Phalanx snitch so that I can talk to him in private and find out what's really going on," Kelem replied.

Later that morning, the truck was parked inside the Hawking Center's receiving dock. Kelem and Jake helped unload the merchandise, and after getting checked by security, they were allowed to go up to the kitchen area to help restock their pantry. Once inside, Kelem scanned a few staff members and learned that a man named Leonard was the dining room manager.

Kelem stayed in the kitchen area looking busy while Jake returned to the loading dock and 'pushed' the delivery foreman to forget that he and Kelem ever existed. Then he returned to the kitchen.

"What now?" he asked Kelem.

"You see that Terran over there in the corner dressed like a *maître d'*?" Kelem asked without pointing.

"You mean the one dressed like a night club entertainer?" Jake asked, never having heard the term.

"Yes, that one," Kelem answered, holding back a smile. "He's in charge of the dining room and is responsible for assigning waiters for each event. We need to get on that dinner as servers. Come with me and follow my lead. I'll clue you in on what to 'push' to him by telepathy."

Jake nodded and followed Kelem. Ever since he'd received Kelem's training he had been able to hear his thoughts telepathically.

"Leonard, where are we working tonight?" Kelem asked casually.

"Who the hell are you?" the man replied with suspicion.

Kelem signaled Jake to stand by. "Why, it's us, Merrick and Orlando.

Don't you remember us? We worked for you last December at the new year's party upstairs."

Jake 'pushed' the man. "Oh, that's right! How are you fellows?"

"We're fine. We were hoping that you can put us on that dinner tonight."

"I'm sorry but I've got all the servers I…." Leonard began saying.

Jake pushed again.

"Hold on… Why, yes! I can use you two, but you have to go see Lenny in the barbershop and have those beards trimmed. Remember, they don't like the 'prophet look' upstairs," the man informed them cheerfully.

"Sure thing, boss!" Kelem said, sporting a military salute.

Two hours later with their beards trimmed, Kelem and Jake were dressed in their fancy waiter uniforms along with the rest of the dining room staff, listening to Leonard's instructions regarding the serving order. Afterwards, Leonard gave all the servers large bibs and had them eat dinner at a large table near the kitchen. The food was the same as what they would be serving.

At seventeen, Jake had never seen or tasted most of the dishes that the occupying Earthmen enjoyed on a daily basis. It was hard for the young man, who had spent all his life under Terran rule eating bad food, to sit and enjoy such a bountiful meal, when his family and fellow countrymen were being starved to death. Kelem had to send him a lot of positive energy during the meal to keep him calm.

By 06:30 Pm, Kelem and Jake were lined up with the other servers along one of the walls of the dining room, waiting for the fifty odd guests to show up. Slowly over the next fifteen minutes, the seats began filling up with managers and executives from the factory. Most of them were Terrans and six were Martians who appeared as well fed as the others, but so far no Billy Chong and Wallace Simkus.

Kelem began to worry that Billy might not show up at all, when finally at 06:30 PM, CEO Chong entered the dining room, followed by a squat-looking bald-headed Terran and two large goons who were obviously Phalanx.

Kelem's heart was beating fast with a mixture of anticipation and fear. He was excited to see his childhood friend looking well. Billy had lost his baby fat and looked every bit the head of the largest and most powerful manufacturing enterprise in the solar system. But Kelem was not afraid of being caught, but of finding that his childhood friend had betrayed his own country.

Billy sat at the head of the table and all the guests saluted him deferentially. Wallace Simkus sat to Billy's right, and the two goons remained standing behind Billy with their backs to the wall, their eyes constantly scanning the dining room. Kelem noticed that the goons were carrying weapons judging by the large bulges under their tunics. The *maître d'* walked up to Billy, and after bowing and ingratiating himself to him, he turned around and snapped his fingers at the waiters, signaling them to begin serving the appetizers.

Kelem made sure that he and Jake had been placed close to where Billy was seated. The two of them picked up their trays filled with appetizers and approached the head of the table. Kelem went behind Billy's left and placed the appetizer in front of him and then continued on to Wallace Simkus. Jake stayed directly behind Kelem ready to 'push' whoever Kelem ordered him to. Billy didn't even look up at Kelem or Jake, being engaged in conversation with those nearest him. As Kelem continued serving others, he'd occasionally glance in Billy's direction to see if he had noticed him.

"C'mon Billy, look this way!" Kelem kept saying in his head. But Billy seemed oblivious and continued eating and talking to the others. After the appetizers came the salad, and still Billy hadn't looked at Kelem or for that matter at any of the other servers. Finally, when it was time to serve the main course, Kelem decided to take a chance.

"Are you finished with the salad, Mr. Chong?" Kelem asked, making sure that Billy heard him well enough above the din of conversations and rattle of silverware.

"Yes, go ahead, I'm done," Billy said looking up at Kelem momentarily and then turning back to his conversation with the man sitting to his left. Kelem continued picking up empty salad plates from other guests, and when he reached the opposite end of the table he saw Billy lift his eyes and stare at him with intense curiosity for a few seconds.

Then he heard Billy's thoughts.

"Good lord! That man could be Kelem's twin brother!" he heard his old friend think. Kelem's heart jumped and prayed that when Billy realized that it was really him, Kelem Rogeston in the flesh in that room, wearing a waiter's uniform, that Billy wouldn't turn around and order the two Phalanx goons to grab him.

The meal progressed normally and finally it was time to serve dessert. Kelem once again positioned himself and Jake near the head of the table and walked over to Billy to retrieve his empty plate from the main course. When he reached to retrieve the plate, Billy looked up at him.

"You look familiar, where do I know you from?" Billy asked, his eyes studying him with carefully.

"My name is Merrick, sir. I served you the last time you were here," Kelem responded politely.

"Oh yes, Merrick! Now I remember," Billy replied. "How is your wife Laura and the kids?" Billy asked, now playing along by mentioning a fictitious wife and children.

"Why, they're fine sir! Thank you for remembering me after all this time," Kelem exclaimed, realizing what Billy was doing. He had recognized him and hadn't given him away!

"Hmmm, Merrick you say?" Wallace Simkus queried, speaking up for the first time. "I don't remember you at all," he added with a hint of suspicion.

Billy was about to come to Kelem's aid and say something, when Jake 'pushed' the Phalanx snitch to remember Kelem's face and supposed conversation as a genuine memory.

"No, wait! I do remember you and Mr. Chong discussing your family. I'm sorry," the main said, genuinely embarrassed.

"No apology needed, Mr. Simkus. It's an honor to be remembered by you as well," Kelem responded with a curt smile.

"Dear God, Kelem! Is it really you?" Billy questioned in his mind with excitement, while at the same time wondering how Kelem had managed to make Simkus think that he remembered him.

Kelem nodded at Billy discreetly. Then he felt Billy's overwhelming joy and shock at seeing him, after believing that his best friend in the world had been dead all these years.

"I'm being watched by Simkus and the two guards. How can we meet?" Billy thought in his mind, hoping and praying that Kelem was reading him and could do something to separate him from Simkus and the two goons.

Kelem read Billy's thoughts and learned that Simkus stuck to him like glue day and night. The man followed him everywhere. Simkus always made sure that whenever they stayed someplace overnight, they were booked in adjoining suites. And tonight was no different. Billy was scheduled to meet with the technical staff tomorrow morning and then return to Latonga City in the afternoon. The two guards took turns at night standing watch outside their rooms wherever they stayed.

Kelem called Jake aside and formulated a plan. "Can you make someone think they're tired and have them fall asleep?"

"I can put the thought in their heads, but I don't know if they'll actually fall asleep," Jake answered hesitantly.

"Hmmm, we need to isolate Billy from Simkus and the two goons. Billy didn't give me up and I know he wants to talk to me," Kelem mused.

"Does this mean that Billy's one of us and not a traitor?"

"Yes, Jake. I need to talk to him, but he's watched by Simkus and the two guards wherever he goes."

"I used to make my little brother fall asleep when he was a little baby when he'd start crying in the middle of the night, but I don't know if I can do that to a fully grown adult. I'm willing to try however," Jake offered.

"Excellent, as soon as we serve dessert, I want you to 'push' Simkus to feel as sleepy as you can make him. Then, we'll worry about how to deal with the two guards."

"Well, if I succeed in making Simkus fall asleep, then we'll only have to worry about one of the goons later, since you said that the guards take turns watching Billy at night.

"You're right! Let's get to it," Kelem agreed, beginning to feel confident.

After dessert, the guests began to disperse. Each one would pass by Billy and engage in light conversation or just say good night and head for the center's dormitories in the upper floors of the building.

Jake 'pushed' Simkus, and soon the man began yawning repeatedly while stretching out his arms, looking every bit like a very exhausted man. Jake had succeeded in making the Phalanx snitch feel sleepy!

"I don't know what's happening to me," Simkus said mid-yawn, "but I can't seem to keep my eyes open. You must be tired as well Billy, why don't we call it a day?"

Billy realized that Kelem had something to do with his "constant shadow" suddenly wanting to go to sleep. The man always stayed up until Billy retired to his room. "Sure thing, Wallace, let's get a good night's rest," he commented, and then wondered how Kelem was going to deal with the guards.

Kelem was also wondering how he was going to get to Billy, when out of the corner of his eye he noticed that Billy was talking to Leonard the *maître d'* and pointing in his direction. The man bowed obsequiously as if he was being knighted by Billy, then turned around and approached Kelem and Jake, who were finishing clearing up the long dining table.

"You two!" he said snapping his fingers. "Come with me. Mr. Chong wants an aperitif and some pastries sent to his room. Follow me and I'll get you two trays. Remember, if he gives you a tip, I get half!"

Kelem smiled. Billy had anticipated his plan and had opened the way for them to meet. It was a good thing, because dining room staffers couldn't get into the hotel-like dormitories on the top floors without a special security badge, which Leonard was happy to provide.

Kelem had Jake 'push' Leonard to forget that they ever existed. Then, they took the elevator to the top floor of the building where Billy, Simkus and the two guards were quartered.

When the elevator door opened to the hallway, only one of the guards was present. The man was sitting at a small desk in an alcove on one side of the hallway.

"Hold on, you two!" the goon ordered gruffly, as they approached Billy's room. "I have to search you both and check your trays," he added.

Kelem and Jake handed him their trays and he put them on the desk.

"Arms up," he ordered, and the two complied. The guard padded them down, then took out a small detector from his tunic and scanned both of them with the device looking for weapons or explosives. Then, he did the same with the trays.

"All right, you can go in but don't bother Mr. Chong. Bring him the stuff and get back to the kitchen ASAP," he warned.

"By the way, would you or your partner like a coffee or something to eat?" Kelem asked very politely, trying to locate the second goon.

"Nah, he's already asleep," the man answered nodding to one of the doors at the end of the hallway. "Now, go serve Mr. Chong and get out of here," he restated.

Kelem pressed the chime button on Billy's room and the pressure door opened with a slight hiss.

As soon as the door closed, Kelem put his finger on his lips and Billy nodded, knowing to keep quiet. Then he instructed Jake telepathically to make the guard outside fall asleep. Jake complied and stood by the door with his eyes closed as he 'pushed' the guard. Kelem made gestures with his hands asking if the room was bugged for audio and Billy shook his head. Then Kelem motioned to Billy to sit down and wait in silence.

Five minutes went by without the guard coming in to see what was taking the two of them so long, and Kelem and Jake knew that the guard had fallen asleep.

"Jake, go outside and check on our friend, and then go to the end of the hallway to the last door on the right and make sure that our other friend is equally exhausted. Oh, and also check on Simkus. I don't want any surprises. Billy and I need a few minutes to ourselves," Kelem added.

"Then, what shall I do?" Jake asked looking a little nervous.

"There's another recess to the left of the elevator. Hide there with your tray and if it looks like somebody's coming to check on us, step out as if you're delivering, then push whoever it is that showed up to go away and then come and get me."

"Simkus, the guards and I are the only ones on this entire floor. No one else should be coming by tonight," Billy whispered.

Jake nodded politely at Billy, opened the door and after checking to make sure that the guard was out, left.

Kelem and Billy hugged each other with tears in their eyes. Billy began sobbing and shaking with emotion, and Kelem felt a deep sense of sadness and regret coming from his old friend's mind. Within seconds Kelem read Billy's memories and learned that he had been working with the resistance from the very beginning of the occupation.

"How… how is this possible?" Billy finally asked, dying to know how Kelem was still alive and a million other questions.

Kelem needed to ask Billy a lot of important questions so he gave Billy a condensed version of his adventures up to the current day to shorten the length of their meeting. Kelem and Jake were risking their lives being here. If they were caught, Billy would be implicated as well.

"How is Verena? And did you two have any kids?" Kelem asked of Billy's wife.

"She's fine. We have two boys. One is twenty years old and his name is Kelem, the other one is eighteen and his name is Bernardo," Billy replied, his eyes beginning to tear again.

Kelem couldn't have felt more honored to learn that his lifetime friend had not forgotten him and had named both of his children after him and his uncle.

"Billy, there's so much that I want to say to you on a personal level, but right now time is of the essence and there's much that we need to discuss."

"Kelem," Billy interrupted him. "Before you go any further, you need to know that the pilot that you defeated on the Hellas Planitia is Jude Voltanieu, son of Soltan Voltanieu, the Governor of Mars. The man is at Latonga City Hospital in a coma!"

"Hmm, so he's the powerful psychic that I'd been sensing since I returned to Mars! And now I know why I haven't felt his presence since the night that we rescued Nicolas from Stalag 47." Kelem now understood, feeling relief that he and others of the Brotherhood were safe from young Voltanieu's powerful mind probing, at least for now.

"You've done us all a favor. That bastard is responsible for the capture, torture and murder of countless Martians. And now that you've told me that he's the most powerful psychic that you've come up against, I'm doubly pleased that he's at death's door!" Billy exclaimed, with hatred in his voice.

"Thank you, Billy. I'm glad that he's out of commission for all our sakes. I hope that he remains in a coma or hopefully dies, because he's the most dangerous man on Mars, as far as I'm concerned."

"I've been hearing a lot of rumors concerning the rebel fleet, Kelem. One of the Terran admirals that I deal with regularly told me that one of their cruisers out on patrol near the orbit of Uranus was severely damaged by an old Martian Navy Frigate and nearly destroyed. They're talking about sending a ship of the line out there to investigate."

Kelem winced. The rebel fleet had obviously improved their operations most likely due to Ndugu's expertise, but they couldn't afford to deal with a dreadnaught size battleship at this time.

"Billy, the rebel fleet is in need of just about everything. Is there anything that you can do to send them food, ammunition, medical supplies?" Kelem asked, hoping that Billy could perform a miracle.

"I've wanted to send them supplies for years, Kelem, but the resistance here on Mars has almost no contact with them. We haven't been able to coordinate major operations with them for a long time. Until I heard from the Terran admiral about the frigate's attack and then from you about your dealings with them, I was sure that the fleet had ceased to exist!"

"They're doing better than they were before Ndugu and I returned, but not for long, Billy. I'm your new rebel fleet contact. What can you get for us that I can bring back to them and how soon can you arrange for shipment? It would have to be a considerable amount of cargo for it to be worth the risk that you would be taking by setting up something like that," Kelem advised him.

Billy closed his eyes in deep concentration searching for an idea that could prove viable and that could be executed relatively quickly. After a while his eyes opened and he had a half smile on his face.

"You know, I normally wouldn't dream of considering what I'm about to propose without you being involved. But if what I'm about to suggest is at all possible, you would be the person to make it work," Billy said, sounding confident about his idea. "But here it is. The Terrans had us build four large cargo ships for them, the same size as the military dreadnaughts that they're talking about sending out to the edge of the solar system. We just finished building the second one of those cargo ships, and it's due to leave for Earth in about a month, chock full of merchandise. These ships are mostly automated so the crew is made up of only a captain, first mate, navigator, *n'time* chief engineer, one assistant engineer and four cargo specialists. I can make sure that the assistant engineer and the four cargo specialists are all Martian resistance. If I can put you on that ship as one of those crewmen, do you think that you and the other four can hijack the vessel?"

"Damn Billy! If I succeed in hijacking that ship, you're going to receive a lot of attention from the Phalanx. Are you sure you can make this happen without the hijacking being traced to you directly?"

"I'm willing to take that chance. That's why I'm going to ask you to make sure that Verena and my two boys stay safe. I need to know that they can disappear at a moment's notice and be taken someplace where the Phalanx won't be able to find them."

"I'll put that in motion, Billy, I promise. Now, about that ship, what kind of merchandise will it be carrying?"

"Fully charged *n'time* generators, sub-light engines for Terran pleasure cruisers and fuel for those engines, cooling, heating and refrigeration units, industrial manufacturing machines, like lathes, heavy drills and presses, power tools and luxury items like holo projectors, household electronics and a few other miscellaneous items, and of course, the *n'time* generator powering the ship itself!"

"That's wonderful, Billy! The fleet can use just about everything that you just mentioned, but what they're sorely lacking above all is long range missiles, rail gun ammunition and lots of food and medical supplies," Kelem stated.

"Hmmm, I can't give you any missiles because if and when the rebel fleet uses them, the Terrans will know that they came from the MMC and therefore me. I'm the one who manages the manufacture and distribution of all the weapons for the Terrans. We manufacture just about everything the Terrans need these days," Billy concluded with chagrin.

"Will you be able to smuggle food and medical supplies in between the other stuff?" Kelem asked.

"It will be difficult, because in spite of everything that we make for the Terrans, most food and medical supplies come from Earth these days, and the supply chain is handled by the Terran military. But, I think that I might be able to sneak enough food and medical supplies to last the fleet for a few weeks, at least."

"That will be fine Billy. But without missiles, the fleet will never be able to engage the Terran ships. And if we can't push their fleet out of Martian territory, we can't coordinate an all-out attack here on Mars."

"Is that at all possible?" Billy asked, doubtful that Mars could face the Terrans on such scale.

"It's totally possible, so long as the rebel fleet can push its way back to Mars. The plan will work, but both the resistance and the fleet have to strike at the same moment."

"How many missiles are we talking about?" Billy asked as he considered a possibility.

Kelem calculated in his mind how many rebel ships were still out there. "Five hundred would be a start, but a thousand would be much better."

"What if I can put enough raw materials and basic parts on that ship so that the fleet can manufacture its own missiles? Are there are enough weapons technicians in the fleet to put them together?"

"I can think of two individuals right off the top of my head!" Kelem replied confidently, referring to himself and Ndugu Nabole.

"Very well, I'm sure that I can give you most of what you need. How do I contact you?" Billy wanted to know.

"Do you remember the fake identities that we set up before I went to Earth in 2637?"

"Sure, you were Bernard Clemens and I was Nolan Smith," Billy remembered clearly.

"I'll set up a net mail account under B. Clemens and you can contact me as N. Smith. We shouldn't meet again. Just send me the info regarding when and where I should meet with the other crewmen in order to plan for the takeover of the ship, and then arrange for me to gain access to the MMC's launch facility on departure day."

"What about the terrible trio out there?" Billy asked, referring to Simkus and the two goons.

"Jake is a 'pusher'. He is able to put thoughts, ideas and false memories in people's heads. By the time everyone wakes up tomorrow morning, they'll remember everything about tonight's events with the exception of Jake and me. So, as far as you're concerned, you never spoke to me, and Jake and I never came up here to bring you the aperitifs and pastries.

"What about Leonard?"

"Leonard will have never heard of Merrick and Orlando either," Kelem said pointing to himself and Jake out in the hallway.

"You have to go now, don't you, Kelem?" Billy asked already knowing the answer.

"Yes, I'm sorry to say. The longer Jake and I remain here the more likely we'll all be caught," Kelem replied looking at his old friend, aware that Billy was putting his life on the line by setting up the hijacking operation. "I know that what you're going to do for the fleet is a tremendous sacrifice, Billy, but know that you're the only one on the entire planet of Mars who can do this for the cause, that's why I had to contact you."

"I'm glad that you never had doubts about my allegiance to the resistance."

"From the moment that I heard from Rusty Deveraux that you were a turncoat, I never believed that you were a traitor, old friend. I've known you most of my life and I was sure that it was impossible that you would have done the things they accused you of."

"Bless you, Kelem, my old friend. I hope we both live to see Mars free again," Billy said, embracing Kelem.

"I'm sure we will," Kelem answered as he stood and picked up his tray. When he reached the door he turned around. "One more thing Billy, as much as it pains me, you can't tell Verena or your children that you saw me. No one must know that you and I met. I won't even tell my people that this meeting took place until after I've taken the ship out to the fleet. I hope you understand."

"I do, Kelem, I understand," Billy replied trying to hold back tears, wishing that Kelem could stay and spend more time sharing their separate experiences of the past twenty one years.

Kelem opened the door and looked out on the hallway to make sure that the guard was still asleep, then he waved goodbye and disappeared.

Billy's shoulders slumped and he allowed himself to cry for all the pain and suffering that he and his family and the rest of the Martian people had endured all these years and for all the missed opportunities to share his friendship with his childhood friend. He wondered how different things would have been if Kelem Rogeston and the crew of the Solar Nations had returned triumphantly from their exploratory mission to Eridanus in 2638.

But now was not the time to think of the past or what might have been. Kelem's return had once again influenced the future of the solar system and in turn, that of humanity at large. And as it was throughout the development of Martian society from the time it was settled by humans in the year 2279, a Rogeston would once again play a major part in the history of the red planet.

CHAPTER 17

A Crack in the Armor

March 23rd, 2660

Marla Hasset had called an emergency meeting of the Brotherhood's Board of Directors. She had been approached by a captain of the Black Guards by the name of Magrut Belichek. The man, a Terran in his late fifties claimed to be a supervising officer at Stalag 47. He told her that he knew that she was Martian resistance but that he didn't want to turn her in. Instead he wanted to give the resistance important information regarding a major event that was about to take place.

"Needless to say, I denied being resistance, but the man insisted that I pass his message to the leadership. I read the man, and what I got was that his two sons, who worked as guards, in Cell Block 1-S were executed along with all the other guards in that block the day after Nicolas escaped," Marla explained.

"Hmmm, the part about guards being executed the day after we took Nicolas out of that hell hole rings true, but the rest sounds like a Phalanx trap," Dalton Myers commented.

"Indeed, but our first problem is not whether to trust this Terran's claims or not. Marla's position has been compromised. I'd like to know how a mere captain of the Guard became privy to such information about the resistance and what else he knows!" Nicolas Alfano argued.

"Both of you may be right," Kelem interjected. "But let's look at this logically. We've been hearing a lot of chatter lately about discontent on Earth, and as we've learned recently, Soltan Voltanieu traveled to Earth a few days after his son crashed his shuttle. We've gotten intelligence reports that he went to Earth to meet with Solomon Vandecamp. It's possible that he was seeking information about what's going on here on Mars. I'm sure that he threatened Vandecamp or hooked him to one of his infernal machines to draw information from him."

"What do you think it all means?" Phillip Sontag asked.

"My guess is that Voltanieu's position and authority are in jeopardy because of the jail break from Stalag 47, and the fact that he hasn't been able to find who did it. Jude was daddy's most powerful tool because of his ability to scan people at a distance. Suddenly the Phalanx's intelligence gathering on Mars has taken a major hit with young Voltanieu being out of commission. Add to that the fact that Nicolas didn't give any of us up, and you got a very desperate Soltan Voltanieu. And it's no coincidence that, suddenly, Vandecamp has opened the floodgates of secret information to get in good terms with the resistance. Solomon Vandecamp is a shrewd and gifted Machiavellian thinker. He's always three moves ahead of everyone else. He may have seen the writing on the wall and is preparing for the day when Mars regains its independence. All this could mean that Ol' Dracul may be about to launch a major counterstrike. It's possible that this captain of the Guard, a bereaved father, has decided to take revenge on the Phalanx for having executed his two sons, by giving us intelligence." Kelem suggested, making everyone in the room quite nervous.

"That still doesn't address Marla being exposed as a resistance member," Nicolas reiterated.

"Perhaps Marla is but one of many that Captain Belichek has approached in an attempt to contact the resistance. He may be going around trying different people who he thinks might be Martian resistance, hoping that he gets lucky. And don't forget that Marla is also a mind reader and knew that this man was not trying to deceive her."

"So you think that we should contact this Belichek and take our chances?" Dalton Myers asked, sounding unconvinced by Kelem's argument.

"Let's find out if this man has tried contacting others. If he has, then he won't know which of the individuals he approached turned out to be a member of the resistance. That is, if we decide to contact him at all," Kelem proposed.

"Don't forget that we have two 'pushers' in our midst. Jake or Cameron can erase this man's memory of having been contacted by us," Marla reminded the others.

"Good point, Marla!" Nicolas declared. "But you should be ready to 'disappear' if it turns out that you've actually been tagged by the Phalanx. We must make arrangements for you and your family if it turns out to be the case."

Marla grimaced. Her position as a physician at the Charmont Institute gave her access to a lot of important information for the resistance. Having to go underground would eliminate that valuable resource.

Kelem, seeing Marla's discomfort at having to disappear from public life, offered a more measured approach to the problem. "Let's have Adriana put together a background profile for Captain Belichek. I want to know where he's from on Earth, how he and his two sons became Phalanx Black Guards, where he's been in the last few weeks, who he has contacted recently, etcetera."

"I'll contact other cells and ask if they'd heard anything about Belichek approaching others," Phillip Sontag added.

"Agreed," Kelem stated. "Let's not forget that ultimately, we can simply ignore the man's request and continue on our way."

Everyone agreed and soon the meeting came to an end.

Later that night, Kelem meditated, searching for the consciousness of Captain Magrut Belichek in the Quantum Tide. He didn't find what he was looking for. Instead, he had a vision of a piece of fabric coming apart by a thin thread that was being pulled by a hand. The piece of fabric was the Phalanx and the hand was his.

CHAPTER 18

Constitution Park

"Tell us what happened to your sons," a male voice said behind Captain Magrut Belichek.

The captain was sitting on a chair facing a blank wall in a small underground chamber somewhere in Latonga City. Behind him were two or three individuals. He couldn't tell how many because they were behind a wall of intensely bright light panels.

"I was awakened by one of my lieutenants early in the morning of January 15ᵗʰ, informing me that one of our prisoners was unaccounted for. When I went down to cell block 1-S, I found out that it was the old man we came to know as Ol' Nick."

"Go on," the same voice spoke again behind the wall of light.

"Well…." Captain Belichek started to say, his voice trembling with emotion. "Well, it turned out that you peop… I mean the resistance, had somehow broken out Ol' Nick through the outer wall. We were shocked! We'd been told that Stalag 47 was the most secure prison on the planet…." Captain Belichek then stopped and broke out in sobs, his shoulders heaving, as tears of anger and rage fell from his cheeks.

"Take your time," a female voice said, filled with compassion.

He wiped his eyes and continued. "When the 'Dragon'…, that's what we call Voltanieu, found out that Ol' Nick was gone, he went into a rage, screaming at everyone. Then he ordered every guard on cell block 1-S killed as punishment for the escape," Belichek stopped and began sobbing again and leaned forward covering his face with his hands, overwhelmed by the pain of losing his sons in such a violent manner.

No one spoke as the man continued sobbing for a long time.

"I... I begged him! Please, please don't kill my boys!" he continued amidst sobs. "They had nothing to do with the escape. They couldn't have prevented it anyway because both of them were in their bunks fast asleep! I screamed at him but the bastard didn't care! He had me restrained and locked in one of the interrogation rooms."

"Then what happened?" a new male voice asked.

"Then, one of my guards came by later and told me that both my sons had been murdered with the others execution style and then thrown outside like so much cordwood!"

Marla and Nicolas exchanged puzzled glances, never having heard the term 'cordwood'. Only Kelem who had spent time on Earth understood what the captain meant.

"We're sorry for your loss," said the female.

Belichek nodded, acknowledging the condolence. "The son of a bitch wouldn't even let me bury my boys! And then.... and then... he..., he strapped me to that hellish machine of his and tortured me for hours trying to make me confess that I was in on the plot to free Ol' Nick!" Captain Belichek roared, gritting his teeth, his mind seething with hatred for the monster who had tortured him after murdering his two sons.

Kelem didn't need to hear any more from the man. He knew with utter certainty that Belichek's loyalty to the Phalanx had ended the moment Soltan Voltanieu ordered the execution of his sons. Adriana's research had revealed that Belichek and his two boys, Anton and Janek, had been conscripted into the Phalanx Black Guard against their will. The Belichek family had been farmers in Eastern Europe since the "Recovery" on Earth in the early part of the 23rd century and had no ambition to come to Mars to work as prison guards. But Phalanx recruitment had fallen short in the last few years, and now they were resorting to forced conscription in order to fill their ranks.

"We understand your sorrow and the anger you must feel against Voltanieu. We Martians have suffered as you have in the hands of both the father and his son," Kelem said, identifying with Belichek. "But we need you to tell us about Voltanieu's plans now."

"Yes… I'm sorry. That's what I came here to do, after all," the Captain replied, sitting up straight and adjusting his tunic. "After he tortured me, I decided that I was finished with the Phalanx and the Black Guards and the whole stinking mess! I have access to the prison's data base and I began to look for ways to take my revenge on that evil bastard. I found out that he's planning some sort of mass execution of individuals who he believes to be members of the resistance. But first he's putting out a bounty on a man called Kelem Rogeston. If this Rogeston doesn't surrender to the Phalanx by a certain time, he's going to kill one person every hour until he turns himself in."

Kelem's face turned pale and he instinctively glanced at Marla, who, along with Nicolas was in utter shock at Voltanieu's knowledge that Kelem was on Mars. "Whe… when…" Kelem stuttered, clearing his throat, "when is he planning to carry out these executions?"

"Soon….., I think in the next two or three days. He's already arrested the poor souls that are to be executed. That's why I was trying to get in contact with the resistance before it's too late. I don't know what you can do to prevent the murder of so many innocent people, but there must be something that can be done!" Belichek exclaimed with sincere anguish.

Kelem's heart sunk. This was the kind of response that Major Loeky had warned him about as a consequence of liberating Nicolas Alfano. But he was totally unprepared to be the focus of Voltanieu's reprisal. The only positive aspect of what Belichek had just told them was that apparently no one from their resistance cell was on the list of people to be executed, and that included Marla Hassett, but Kelem guessed that most of those who had been arrested were unlikely to be members of the resistance.

He flashed back to his vision of the Phalanx coming apart thread by thread and realized that it was really happening! It was Voltanieu himself who was falling apart, yielding to the pressures brought about by the events of the past few weeks. Kelem was convinced that the main trigger for his poorly planned impulsive reactions was the loss of his son's ability to scan people at a distance. He was sure that Voltanieu's revenge had nothing to do with regret or sadness for his son's welfare. Jude Voltanieu was merely an important military and strategic asset to his father.

"Do you know where this public execution is to take place?" Nicolas asked.

"I'm sure it's going to take place in Constitution Park. He ordered his maintenance people and technical staff to build a large stage in the middle of the park with lights and video feeds for all of Mars."

Kelem swallowed hard and felt the hairs in the back of his neck stand on end.

"Do you know how many individuals have been arrested and condemned to die?" Marla asked this time.

"I think about fifty or so. His initial plan called for two days of continuous executions."

"Dear God!" Marla whispered.

"I'm requesting political asylum. I don't want to belong to a nation that treats people like we have. Besides, I have no close relatives left alive on Earth," Magrut Belichek told them.

"We will consider taking you in as a political refugee, but not until this crisis is resolved. If you really want to help us, we need you to stay on the inside and provide us with intelligence that can help us stop this massacre," Kelem explained.

Captain Valchek was momentarily disappointed that he couldn't get away from the Phalanx right away, but then he recovered, realizing that they were right! He could do more to thwart Voltanieu's plan by feeding the resistance as much information as he could.

"How will I contact you?" he asked.

"We will contact you and give you instructions on how to send us information," Kelem replied.

"I should have put a hole in that demon's head when he killed my boys! Maybe I should do that now and stop this thing from happening!" Belichek muttered.

"As much as we'd love to see that evil son of a bitch dead, this is not the time. Killing him will only serve to cause the Terran government to react strongly by sending a new Voltanieu along with several divisions of regular Terran troops to Mars," Kelem warned the grieving Belichek.

"You're right! What now?"

"We will blindfold you again and someone will take you back to where you were met earlier. I'm sorry that we can't reveal ourselves at this time, but I'm sure you understand that you could be found out, tortured and forced to reveal our identities," Kelem answered.

"Yes, thank you for agreeing to meet me. I hope that you can stop Voltanieu."

"So do we. Goodnight, Captain Belichek."

Belichek was taken out of the room and Marla turned off all the light panels except one.

"Pheeew! I'm out of my depth on this one!" Kelem said, exhaling and shaking his head. "What the hell are we going to do?"

"Well for one thing, you're not going to walk into downtown Phalanx headquarters and give yourself up!" Nicolas said vigorously.

"I wasn't planning to do that, but how should we deal with this situation?" Kelem asked, filled with uncertainty.

"We need to meet with the Helter Skelters. They're the resistance's military arm and there's no way that they're going to stand by and let that butcher kill innocent Martians and broadcast the massacre through the media!" Nicolas shot back, sounding untypically irate.

Marla reached out and placed her hand on Kelem's shoulder affectionately. "Kelem, I know that you feel partly responsible for this situation, but we've all discussed this before and we knew that this day was coming. You have to accept that from now on there'll be retributions every time we strike against the Phalanx. No struggle against tyranny can bring about a just resolution without the loss of innocent people."

Kelem's shoulders slumped and his head bent down as tears pooled in his eyes. Now, more than at any time since he'd returned to Mars, he wished that he'd been able to go back to Plantanimus to spend the rest of his days in Anima's loving embrace and live in deep spiritual communion with Zeus and all the Dreamers.

Nicolas' eyes also filled with tears, but they were more of a selfish nature. He read his young friend's mind and realized at that very moment that Kelem's heart belonged to Plantanimus. Once Mars was liberated, the young psychic and scientific genius that he'd met so many years ago and that he'd come to think of as a son, would leave, never to return to his place of birth.

"No time for emotion, my boy!" said Nicolas, himself struggling to keep his feelings under control. "Now is the time to fight back, and fight hard! We may lose those fifty compatriots but we must give the

Phalanx such a bloody nose that they'll think twice before they decide to do something like this again. We're at war Kelem, and it's only going to get worse from now on. Stop feeling sorry for yourself and come up with another brilliant plan like the one that you put together to free me from Stalag 47!"

Twenty four hours later, the Brotherhood's board of directors and the top officers of the Helter Skelters met to decide how the resistance was going to deal with the crisis. With typical 'Kelem ingenuity', he had devised a brilliant plan to stop the televised executions. He stayed up all night and worked out all the intricate details of the operation which was going to require the participation of more than one hundred resistance fighters. He had agreed to come up with the plan with one caveat - that he be allowed to participate in the fighting.

Major Loeky, Nicolas and the rest of the board of directors went up in an uproar when he proposed it and they threatened to bind and gag him until the operation was over. But Kelem persisted and eventually they gave in, but not without exacting some compromises from him. He could participate on the ground but he'd be surrounded by a squad of Helter Skelters commanded by Major Loeky the entire time.

Knowing that he'd pushed the envelope as far as he could, he agreed.

Voltanieu's public announcement was scheduled for the following evening at 08:00 PM. The timing had been set so that a majority of Martians were at home after the work day, watching their video screens after dinner. The Governor of Mars wanted a big audience for his horror show.

Kelem and the others would be in place by 06:00 PM. Charges had been set in several strategic places throughout the park and two other buildings. Two big explosives had been placed in one of the elevator shafts of the Phalanx Headquarters, located in the Montenegro Tower building, and several others had been placed in and around the old Terran Embassy which was now Terran Military Headquarters. Kelem's plan also included two remotely operated old style fifty-caliber sniper rifles with video scopes, placed on the upper floors of two of the business towers around Constitution Park in downtown Latonga. The rifles would be operated wirelessly by two Helter Skelter sharp-shooters. One of them was the shaven head Adam, who had served as weapons officer during Nicolas' rescue. And as before, Adriana had already hacked into several Phalanx, Terran military and media transmission stations, ready to wreak havoc on those systems once the operation began.

February 3ʳᵈ, 2660 - 06:38 PM

Kelem was sitting on a narrow ledge running along the length of a wide sewer tunnel beneath Montenegro Towers. Behind him were Major Loeky and twenty heavily armed Helter Skelters. The last five men were each carrying ten specially adapted emergency decompression helmets, with enough air for ten minutes. Captain Belichek had informed them that the condemned prisoners would be held in one of the function halls of Montenegro Tower located on the main floor of the building. The captives would be wearing nothing but red prison uniforms. Kelem's plan required that they'd be provided with 'decomp' protection.

Kelem was dealing with his own fear and nervousness and he flashed back to the time when he, Rusty Deveraux and the others, successfully eliminated Molson and his gang. He should have drawn some comfort from having had that experience, however brief it had been. But this operation was something else altogether. It involved the lives of several hundred people and was ten times more dangerous and capable of going terribly wrong. Kelem was feeling very inadequate.

Almost as if Major Loeky had read his mind the big man spoke. "Afraid?"

"Terrified!" Kelem whispered back confidentially.

"That's good!" the former chief of police answered with a laugh. "That means that you'll be careful and won't get your fool head shot off by a Phalanx pulse gun."

Kelem nodded and laughed. He powered up his wrist comp and looked at the center of Constitution Park through the video camera mounted on one of the fifty-caliber sniper rifles.

"Loeky looked at the image and pointed to a strange object in the middle of the stage that the Phalanx had erected. "What's that?"

"Kelem zoomed in on the image on his wrist comp's screen and felt sick to his stomach. "It's a guillotine…" he said with disgust.

"What's a guillotine?" asked Loeky, not being familiar with Earth's ancient history.

"It's an executioner's device that chops a person's head off with a large slanted blade."

Major Loeky's face hardened and his jaw muscles tensed and then he looked away trying to restrain himself from losing his composure.

"If everything goes right, none of the prisoners will come close to that thing," Kelem commented, hoping and praying that it would work out that way.

To Kelem, the time seemed to be passing by very slowly and he kept glancing at his wrist comp every few seconds or so. He was feeling impatient, wishing that the whole thing was already over. But time did pass and at 07:50 PM, Major Loeky gave the sign and Kelem let one of the Helter Skelters go ahead of him with a special tool that would open the sewer hatch to the sub-basement of Montenegro Tower.

From now on, they could run into Phalanx security at any moment. The lead man opened the hatch and after making sure that no one was around, gave the signal, and all twenty one crawled out of the sewer hatch and into the building's sub-basement level.

The group advanced along a narrow corridor leading to a maintenance access door that Adriana had mapped out for Kelem. She had found a full structural visual data base of the building and had hacked into their security grid without any problem.

Kelem typed on his wrist comp, "I'M DOWNSTAIRS, LET ME IN."

Within seconds, the maintenance access door opened with a heavy clunk and the men filed in. Once inside, they found themselves in a narrow circular tower with a metal rung ladder that went up several floors. In spite of Mars' light gravity, the group struggled as they climbed up the nine floors to reach the lobby level of the building carrying all the gear for battle. The lead man signaled Kelem, who was right behind him, that he had reached the main floor. Kelem wrapped his arm around one of the rungs in the ladder and typed a second message. "FORGOT MY KEYS."

The door opened outwards from the tower and once again the lead man went in first and came back after a minute or so and motioned to Kelem to climb up and enter the main floor. Once on the main floor, the group stayed put by the access door. Two Helter Skelters went ahead to make sure that the fifty prisoners were where Captain Belichek had said they would be.

After two unbearable minutes, they returned and confirmed that indeed the prisoners were in the right place and that they were being watched by only four Black Guards. Kelem looked at his wrist comp and checked the time.

"07:56," the display read. Kelem turned on the sniper rifle's screen and gasped when he saw that ten men wearing red prisoner uniforms were already lined up on the stage next to the guillotine.

"Shit! They must have moved them ahead of time!" Kelem said, cursing this turn of events.

"I thought the butcher was going to give his speech and then bring the prisoners out to the stage!" Loeky said, looking angry.

"Why waste time!" Kelem replied sarcastically. "Why not start killing right away, this way the people will know that he's not fooling around."

"We got to let the bastard make his goddamned speech, so that we can televise the attack," Loeky reminded Kelem.

The whole point of the plan was to rescue the prisoners but also to show the Martian people that the resistance was back and that it could conduct a successful attack on the Terrans.

Kelem nodded, feeling his own sweat collecting around the rubber bladder in his pressure suit's helmet.

He reached for his wrist comp and typed a message, "DINNER GUESTS ARE ALREADY SITTING AT THE TABLE. PLEASE BE READY TO SERVE APPETIZERS."

Kelem turned on his wrist comp screen and saw that both Adam and the other sharpshooter had the fifty-caliber aimed at each of the two black guards next to the guillotine.

"LEILA DOESN'T LIKE THE CENTER PIECE," Kelem typed, and then one of the rifles panned slowly to the guillotine. Kelem relaxed. Two or three shots with a fifty-caliber bullet would tear the guillotine to pieces.

"I took care of the guillotine, no heads will be chopped tonight," Kelem announced with relief.

"Kelem, it's already 07:57. What are we going to do about the ten people on the stage? When those charges go off, their heads are going to blow off anyway!" Loeky observed with alarm.

Kelem thought furiously, then typed on his wrist comp again, "DELAY MAIN COURSE, WAIT TILL I GET HOME."

Now Adriana knew to wait for Kelem's signal before she remotely detonated the charges already placed in the park. Now he had to figure out how to get those ten prisoners out of the park and into safety before the entire downtown area of Latonga City decompressed.

At exactly 08:00 PM, Kelem's wrist comp screen came to life with the Phalanx's symbol, eight black squares inside a white circle inside a red square. Soltan Voltanieu's long narrow pale face appeared. He began to speak in his raspy whispery voice.

"Citizens of Mars, I come to you tonight in the hopes that bloodshed can be avoided. A dangerous man named Kelem Rogeston is living among you. This man is wanted by the Terran Government for acts of terrorism and damage to Terran property. If you know where this man is, inform the authorities at once so that this criminal can be apprehended and brought to justice." A picture of sixteen year old Kelem from his days at Latonga university appeared next to Voltanieu's head. "If you're harboring this criminal and are discovered, you and your entire family will be arrested and incarcerated. You have one hour to report this man to the Black Guard or to the Terran military. If this man is not in the custody of the authorities within that hour, one Martian citizen will be executed every hour until Kelem Rogeston gives himself up or is brought to us with your assistance."

Soltan Voltanieu's ghoulish face blinked out and the cameras now focused on the stage in Constitution Park showing the ten prisoners next to the guillotine. An animated cartoon loop on the side of the screen showed a figure being tied to a guillotine and then having its head chopped off by the blade. This was followed by its head dropping into a bucket while the blood from the figure's neck emptied into the bucket. On the other side of the screen, a time display began running backwards from one hour, zero minutes. Voltanieu wanted to make sure that people knew how the guillotine worked.

Kelem exhaled with relief. Voltanieu was going to wait one hour before he killed the first man. He had to change his plan. Now he'd have to depend on the eighty two resistance members already assembled among the crowd around Constitution Park to rescue the ten already on the stage. Fortunately, Kelem's brilliant mind had made allowances for unseen complications. Downtown Latonga still had old decomp shelters in some of the buildings around the park. Perhaps the resistance fighters in the crowd could bring those ten prisoners to a few of those shelters after they rescued them.

He typed again," RUNNING OUT OF FOOD IN THE DINING ROOM. CALL THE OTHER GUESTS AND TELL THEM THEY HAVE TO BRING THEIR OWN."

Kelem waited two minutes to give the others in the crowd time to receive Kelem's message through Adriana's server. Then he warned Major Loeky and the others to get ready. He pressed a button on his wrist comp and a countdown began ticking, ten.. nine.. eight…

When the countdown reached zero, several things happened. First, the building shook violently as the first bomb exploded above the main elevator shaft that was connected to the roof of Montenegro Tower. Instantly the air pressure inside the building dropped and people's ears popped loudly as the near vacuum of Mars began sucking the air out of the building. The Helter Skelters burst into the function hall and killed the four Black Guards before they had time to react. The five men carrying the emergency decomp helmets rushed in behind their comrades and began handing them out to the forty condemned prisoners being held in the room. The decompression alarms went off throughout Montenegro Tower and then shut off when the auxiliary pressure door in the elevator shaft activated and the emergency system re-pressurized the building.

Loeky's men began herding the prisoners out, guiding them to the maintenance access tower. Then Kelem realized that they had a serious problem and it was something that he hadn't planned for. About a dozen of the forty prisoners in the room were as weak and wasted as Nicolas had been the day he was rescued. Three of them couldn't walk at all. It was going to be impossible for those three to descend nine stories on the metal rung ladder in the maintenance tower.

Loeky realized the situation also. "Crap and damnation!" he bellowed. "How are we gonna get these people down?" he shouted, as the security alarms suddenly went off.

Then Kelem noticed an even bigger problem. "We're going to have company any minute now!" he shouted at Major Loeky pointing to the security vid-cams on the walls of the function hall.

Loeky followed Kelem's finger and understood. "You men get back here!" he shouted to his squad, "form a firing line aimed at the front door. We have incoming Black Guards."

Kelem was about to crouch down with the rest of them when Loeky grabbed him roughly by the arm and pushed him away with a fierce expression on his face.

"Okay, young pup! This is where you obey my orders and get your ass out of here, unless you force me to manhandle you and leave my squad here one man short! Which is it going to be?"

Kelem knew that Loeky would grab him and toss him out of the room if he insisted on staying. He nodded and disappeared though the back door.

While all this was happening, Adam and the other sniper were keeping the Black Guards in Constitution Park seeking cover from the intense barrage of bullets issuing from the two large caliber guns. The guillotine lay in ruins next to a guard whose head had gone missing from the impact of a fifty- caliber bullet. The commander in charge of the execution detail was losing men one after the other as the sniper rifles kept ripping arms, legs and other body parts from those that were unlucky enough to get in the path of the rifles' accurate fire. He couldn't see where the deadly shots were coming from, being ignorant of the near invisible nature of bullets and his training didn't tell him to look up and search for the tell-tale flash of an old fashioned gunpowder weapon.

All this was continuously being broadcast to the rest of Mars, Earth and the Moon, thanks to Adriana's talents who had made sure that the media channels could not cut off the signal. She also made sure that the Terran Media also received the broadcast, with a ten minute delay, of course.

The entire area surrounding Constitution Park was in a panic with civilians, Terran military and media reporters scrambling for safety. In the confusion, the Black Guard forgot about the ten prisoners who stealthily made their way out of the center of the park and were immediately rescued by the resistance people on the ground. Then, Adriana began closing the giant pressure doors that connected downtown Latonga from the rest of the city via twenty five large tunnels.

Kelem had managed to have the three weakest prisoners lowered down the maintenance tower thanks to two of the Helter Skelters who were carrying long ropes with them. As soon as the last of the prisoners had reached the sub-basement, the sound of a large explosion rattled the building and the sound of gun fire could be heard echoing up and down the access tower.

Major Loeky and his squad were in trouble. Kelem made a decision. "You five, come with me, Major Loeky needs us!" he shouted with the best commanding voice he could come up with. The men hesitated for a moment, unsure if they should listen to Kelem.

"Are you guys stupid? Do you want to attend Loeky's funeral?"

They turned around and followed him. But one of them, a burly sergeant named Fennik who was as big as Loeky, pushed him back. You can come, but you stay in the back, understand?"

Kelem nodded and followed the others. As they approached the function room, Kelem could hear the shouts of the men mixed in with the racket of gun fire and the building's alarms. When the others ahead of him entered the room, they began firing at the Black Guards, who were behind the wall of the main entrance. Kelem dove in and was almost hit by a pulse gun stream. The room was in pieces. Someone had thrown a grenade or detonated some sort of explosive nearly destroying the room. A Black Guard lay dead just inside the room with a big grenade in his hand. The other guards were trying to retrieve it but were being prevented from taking it by the intense barrage of fire from Loeky's men.

Kelem raised his head quickly and fired repeatedly at the one guard that was the closest to reaching the grenade. He or someone else hit the man's arm and practically ripped it out of its socket. The man rolled back screaming in agony.

Kelem was about to ask why Loeky wasn't giving the order to retreat when he saw the big man lying on the floor half buried by debris from the explosion of the first grenade. He crawled over and pulled a piece of ceiling away from his body and saw that he was still alive but had a large metal splinter sticking out of his chest. Two meters away, two of his men lay dead in a pool of blood.

He went up to Fennik. "We have to retreat! We need to blow the bottom of the elevator shaft. Help me drag Loeky out of here!"

The big sergeant agreed and helped Kelem take the Major out of the room. Three other Helter Skelters appeared in the hallway having returned after sending the rescued prisoners through the sewer tunnel onto safety. "Take him out of here!" Kelem shouted. We'll hold the Black Guards here while you bring the Major down the shaft." The three men picked up Loeky and disappeared down the corridor.

"Fennik, we have to retreat back here and then close that pressure door before I blow the second charge in the elevator shaft, and the building's entrance," Kelem said, readying his wrist comp to set off the explosives, which would destroy the elevator shaft and the front pressure doors of the building's main entrance and thus decompress downtown Latonga.

Fennik dove inside to tell the others to retreat to the corridor as more Black Guards showed up and began firing into the room. Kelem stood by the door to the hallway and gave cover fire as each of the Helter Skelters crawled past him one by one until all were on the other side of the pressure door. Once Fennik was inside, he began firing into the room, and Kelem grabbed the heavy pressure door and pushed it closed, but before it shut completely, a stray pulse gun blast ricocheted off the door and hit Kelem in his right hip knocking him down, his face contorted in agony.

Kelem had never felt pain as intense as this. The wound felt like a red hot poker being pushed into his body, and the fire continued intensifying until Kelem thought he was going to pass out. Fennik flipped him around, took out a combat knife from his boot and cut open Kelem's pressure suit around the wound. One of the other men handed him a patch of liquid wound dressing, and Fennik slapped it on the hole in his side. Within seconds Kelem felt the burning subside from the topical anesthetic in the dressing. Though the pain remained, it was bearable now that the fire had been extinguished. Then Fennik took out a pressure suit emergency patch and slapped it on the place where he'd cut the suit to give Kelem first aid.

"Blow it before the bastards break through the door!" Fennik said, shaking Kelem as the door rattled from the impact of the guards' gun fire. Kelem, still in shock, reacted as fast as he could under the circumstances. He was trying to sit up but his body was not cooperating. One of the other Helter Skelters helped him up, and with a trembling hand he pushed the button on his wrist comp and the explosive went off. The building groaned like a giant mammoth in its death throes, and the Helter Skelters eyes opened wide with fear expecting the building to collapse on top of them any second.

The sound of the air rushing out of Downtown Latonga sounded like a pack of ancient gray wolves from Earth howling at the moon. The seals on the pressure door leading to the function room had weakened from the explosion and air was whistling through the gaps.

"Let's get out of here before this hallway decompresses," Fennik ordered the other men. Two grabbed Kelem while Fennik and the other four went ahead.

The Black Guards on the other side of the pressure door dropped their weapons and ran out of the function room searching for emergency pressure suits. Most didn't make it as the blood in their bodies began to boil and the air was sucked out of their lungs before they were able to get into a suit and seal it close. Meanwhile, in the park now empty of civilians, the same was happening to the Phalanx Black Guard commander and the rest of his men who had survived the sniper fire.

The image was still being broadcast to all of Mars, Earth and the Moon. The cameras were showing panicked guards grabbing their throats and collapsing as the air vented out of the giant semi spherical cupola that was downtown Latonga.

The escaping air was creating a vortex resembling a tornado from Earth. The column began lifting dirt and debris, and then plants and rocks and heavier and heavier objects as the twister became darker and darker filled with the bodies of already dead Black Guards, along with pieces of the stage that had been built for Soltan Voltanieu's execution show.

It was at this moment that Adriana placed a line of running text at the bottom of the screen.

"'YOU ARE WATCHING A LIVE BROADCAST OF AN ATTACK BY RESISTANCE FIGHTERS ON THE TERRAN INVADERS OF THE SOVEREIGN NATION OF MARS."

Before the twister sucked out all the loose objects in Constitution Park, Adriana had the cameras zoom in on the stage, and then she detonated the charges, first blowing up the stage in a glorious explosion that was right out of an action drama, followed by the cameras panning to the entrance of the former Terran embassy and detonating the charges placed on that building. Immediately, bodies and objects began flying out though the gaping hole that had once been the entrance to the building. The new supply of air, humans and debris joined the larger tornado, and for a moment grew in size until all the air was vented.

And then, a funny thing happened.

Once the air had been completely sucked out, things began to fall to the ground pulled by the planet's gravity. First, came the Black Guard vehicles crashing down and breaking apart in twisted piles of metal, plastic and glass as they hit the ground. Next, the guard's bodies and other medium size objects began to return to mother Mars. And last but not least, a gentle snowfall of dirt, leaves, pieces of paper, fabric and building material dust from the explosions.

For the first time in his life, Soltan Voltanieu sat in front of his video screen unable to react to the astonishing events that he had just witnessed. So big was his shock that he couldn't even muster any anger or hatred or any other typically negative response to the situation.

In the future, February 3rd, 2660 would become a Martian National Holiday.

CHAPTER 19

Of Recovery, Hope and Religion

February 10ᵗʰ, 2660

"WE'RE PLEASED THAT YOU SURVIVED YET ANOTHER ORDEAL, KELEM, AND WE ARE VERY CONCERNED FOR YOUR PHYSICAL FORM. WE WOULD LIKE TO BE IN YOUR COMPANY ONCE AGAIN," Zeus was saying, his deep voice echoing inside Kelem's consciousness.

"I can't stop doing what I'm doing, Zeus. If I were to stop, the resistance would collapse and everything I've done up to now would be for naught."

"CAN'T YOU LEAD THIS UPRISING WITHOUT EXPOSING YOURSELF TO SUCH RISKS?"

"I'm afraid that as the *de facto* leader it's my responsibility to contribute as the rest of my comrades do. But didn't you tell me on Plantanimus that you saw several time lines where I would return to you?" Kelem asked, trying to assure Zeus that he would come back to live with the Dreamers.

"WE ARE CONCERNED FOR YOUR WELL BEING, BOTH PHYSICALLY AND SPIRITUALLY. THERE IS MUCH CONFLICT WITHIN YOU AND THAT DISTRESSES US AS WELL," Zeus' voice boomed in the imaginary distance within the Quantum Tide.

"Ah, you're talking about my being seen as a religious figure," Kelem said, feeling uncomfortable.

"YES. YOU ARE STRUGGLING WITH THE IDEA THAT

YOU'RE HELPING TO CREATE A FALSE MYTHOLOGY BASED ON THE WORSHIP OF YOU AS A RELIGIOUS FIGURE. AND THIS IS CAUSING YOU TO FEEL THAT YOU'VE COMPROMISED YOUR MORALITY," Zeus commented.

"Yes, Zeus, I am conflicted, confused and worried that this quasi-religious phenomenon has gotten out of control. But if I were to discourage those who have been revitalized by this belief in me right now, my people will never be free. I do mean to put an end to it, but not until we've pushed the Terrans off Mars."

"BE CAREFUL, KELEM. REMEMBER WHAT HAPPENED TO THE UMHAR. THE TAU PRIESTS HAD GOOD INTENTIONS AT THE BEGINNING OF THEIR RELIGION, BUT FELL PREY TO THE LURE OF POWER AND CONTROL AND THAT CORRUPTED THEM," Zeus said, reminding Kelem of the reason why the Umhar perished.

"I do not intend to remain on Mars, anyway. Before I leave, I will make a public declaration debunking any notion that I am saintly or God-like."

"IT MAY BE TOO LATE ALREADY, KELEM. WE'VE SEEN SEVERAL TIMELINES WHERE YOUR NAME IS CONNECTED TO A RELIGIOUS MOVEMENT. WE'RE CONCERNED THAT THIS QUASI-RELIGIOUS MOVEMENT COULD BECOME A MAJOR RELIGION AND TAKE ON A LIFE OF IT'S OWN AS HAS HAPPENED IN YOUR WORLD MANY TIMES IN THE PAST," Zeus replied.

"Damn! It seems that I've opened Pandora's Box already," Kelem uttered, worried that his denial of saintliness might come too late to prevent a church from forming around his name.

"MAYBE SO, BUT AFTER PANDORA LET OUT THE CONTENTS OF HER JAR, THE ANGEL OF HOPE, ASTREA, REMAINED AT THE BOTTOM OF THE EMPTY VESSEL. THERE IS ALWAYS HOPE THAT GOOD WILL TRIUMPH OVER EVIL...."

"What were you saying just now?" Adriana asked.

"Huh?" Kelem uttered, making the transition from one reality to the other. He looked around and remembered that he was in the makeshift hospital room that Marla Hassett had set at a secret location in an abandoned aqueduct beneath Latonga City. He sat up with difficulty, feeling the stiffness in his body from the gun shot that he received during the attack on Constitution Park.

"You were talking in your sleep. You mentioned Pandora's Box and Zeus," Adriana informed him.

"Hmmm, I was dreaming I suppose. How long have you been here?"

"About an hour, I was waiting for you to wake up. I didn't want to disturb you," the girl said, her eyes unable to hide her attraction for Kelem.

"You should have awakened me instead of sitting there wasting your time."

"Oh, I don't mind! Besides, you said that you wanted to know the moment that a message from a Mr. Nolan Smith came into your mail box," the girl reminded him.

Kelem instinctively reached for his wrist comp but remembered that it had been damaged during the firefight. "What does the message say?"

Adriana opened her pad and read the message out loud.

"TO MR. BERNARD CLEMENS:
YOUR MERCHANDISE WILL BE READY FOR PICK UP ON MARCH 6TH AT APPROXIMATELY 06:30 AM AT OUR WAREHOUSE. FOUR OF OUR EMPLOYEES WILL BE THERE TO HELP YOU LOAD THE CARGO ONTO YOUR TRANSPORT. PLEASE CONTACT OUR WAREHOUSE FOREMAN, MR. ZAPPERSTEIN AT 23-6-890-888-EX, TO MAKE THE PROPER ARRANGEMENTS.

SIGNED,
NOLAN SMITH, MANUFATURING SUPERVISOR, SUNLAND TEXTILES."

Kelem remained quiet for a moment. "Write this back to Mr. Smith."

"Dear Mr. Smith:
I'm so glad to hear that my merchandise will be ready next month. I will contact Mr. Zapperstein to coordinate pick up of merchandise.

Signed,
Bernard Clemens, purchasing agent for
Bernie's Emporium"

Adriana finished typing the message with a funny expression on her face. "Are you starting a textile business, Kelem?" she asked in jest.

"Yes! I'm buying exotic fabrics for all the pretty girls I know so that they'll have beautiful gowns when we celebrate our independence," Kelem joked pointing at her.

Adriana laughed and her face blushed a little, knowing that Kelem had meant to let her know that he thought she was pretty. She was about to respond to Kelem's compliment when Nicolas entered the room.

"Ah, there you are, my boy!" Nicolas said, walking up to the med-bed and hugging Kelem lightly so as not to cause him pain. "You're looking much better and Marla says that your recovery is moving ahead of schedule. Your body seems to be able to heal itself amazingly fast!"

"Not fast enough for me!" Kelem retorted, feeling impatient and raring to get back on his feet again.

"Don't push it my boy. Your injury would have crippled most men. You're lucky that you are who you are," Nicolas replied, reminding Kelem of his Sixth Root DNA. "Marla told me that even with your healing ability you need another month of recovery before you can walk out of here."

Kelem grimaced, unhappy to hear that Marla wanted him to stay in bed for that long.

"I'll let you two talk, I'll send your reply back to Mr. Nolan," Adriana announced disappointed that she couldn't spend more time with Kelem.

"Thank you, Adriana, we'll talk later."

The girl exited the room and Nicolas sat on the chair next to the med-bed.

"What's the matter, Kelem? You look upset. Is it about you having to lie low for a while? If it is, you shouldn't worry. The operation in Constitution Park has rekindled people's hope for freedom. Just yesterday, a Phalanx ship was attacked up in the North Pole by a previously unknown resistance cell. Someone that none of us have ever heard of!" Nicolas claimed jubilantly. "And last week a group of Terran senators showed up to tour the scene of the attack. They made a big deal of condemning the 'criminals who did this' in the evening news, but I'm sure they really came here to ream Voltanieu a new ass!"

"No, Nicolas, that's not the reason why I want to get out of this bed, it's something else," Kelem replied looking concerned." I'm confident that you and the board of directors can carry on with the participation of the Helter Skelters while I recover."

Nicolas looked at Kelem and seemed unsure whether to speak his mind or not. "Look Kelem, I've tried to keep this to myself, but I have to confess that I know that you've been hiding something from me for a few weeks. Ever since Laredo Heights you've been keeping a secret, and you know that I respect you too much to intrude by reading your mind."

"I know that you've been aware of me hiding something, but I needed to keep this one to myself for a while Nicolas," Kelem admitted. "But now I can discuss it with you, however, no one else can hear of this until I say so, agreed?"

Nicolas nodded in agreement. "What is it? I'm dying to know!"

"After you left Laredo Heights, I met with Billy. And before you say anything! I know that I was taking a huge risk in doing so, but not only was I compelled emotionally and psychologically to find the truth about Billy, but tactically and strategically as well."

"I don't understand," Nicolas countered.

"Nicolas, without the rebel fleet able to face the Terran navy in space, we cannot defeat the Phalanx here on Mars. We needed a tactical advantage and I knew in my heart that if Billy was not a traitor, chances were good that he was working with the resistance. And I was right! He was one of the very first Martians to join the resistance. He is preparing a large transport for us that I'm going to take back to the rebel fleet," Kelem explained.

Nicolas now read Kelem's mind and instantly learned the details of his plan. He grimaced with a wry expression, unhappy to learn that Kelem intended to hijack the ship with only four other men in less than four weeks!

"I'm not going to try to talk you out of this because I know how stubborn you are, but at least take a few more men with you. According to Marla, you'll still be convalescing twenty four days from now. If the takeover of the ship becomes a violent affair, you'll be at a disadvantage."

"Impossible, Nicolas. Getting me into the MMC's launch site will be difficult enough for Billy to arrange. The other four resistance members are MMC employees. Besides, there's no way that more people can be added to the crew. The ship is automated and it only carries a crew complement of nine."

Nicolas smiled and shook his head. "I'm beginning to suspect that there's a hidden thrill seeking adventurer lurking in the recesses of your complicated brain!"

Kelem laughed, and even though he honestly believed that his motivations were based on logical tactical decisions, maybe Nicolas saw something in him that he was unaware of.

"Perhaps, Nicolas, but whatever the reasons, this has to be done."

"You're right. When will you tell everyone else?"

"I won't, you will," Kelem said pointing his chin at him.

Nicolas looked puzzled.

"I want you to tell everyone after I reach the orbit of Neptune. I'll communicate with you through the Quantum Tide as I did when you were in Stalag 47. This is such an important move for the resistance that I want zero chances that anything will go wrong."

"How long will you be gone?" Nicolas asked, wondering how Kelem's absence would affect the resistance here on Mars.

"You know what that ship is carrying and why I have to bring it to the fleet. It will take a few weeks for the fleet to be ready to rebuild itself, install the *n'time* generators in their ships and be ready to start fighting its way back to Mars. I'm thinking that we'll be able to defeat the Terran navy in less than three months," Kelem estimated.

"That sounds a little too optimistic, but at the same time, I hope and pray that you won't be gone longer than three months."

"I night have a secret weapon that will help defeat the Terrans. And I'm sorry that I'm hiding something else from you and the others, but believe me, when you find out what it is, you'll be impressed!" Kelem added with excitement.

"All right, I'm willing to go along with your super-hero space adventure life-style," Nicolas said jokingly. "But you have to do something for me in exchange."

Kelem nodded.

"I want you to meet with the Reverend Ornata Marchant. Actually, you already met her. She is a member of the Brotherhood. She was there during the first reunion meeting and the subsequent three days of training sessions that you conducted."

"Yes, I remember her; she is a distant cousin of mine. One of my great-great grandparents was a Marchant," Kelem recalled. "Why do you want me to meet with her?"

Nicolas steeled himself knowing that Kelem was going to balk at the idea. "Reverend Marchant is the pastor of the Church of the Universal Mind-God. Her church is responsible for the spread of your new religious status," Nicolas said, hoping that Kelem would wait before interrupting him. "You may feel confident that your absence from Mars will not affect the resistance, but I'm not. The exultation and rejoicing that you've been hearing about is only temporary. Soon, things will calm down and then people are going to be looking forward to the next 'miracle' from Kelem Rogeston. When that doesn't happen, folks here on Mars are going to need something to replace that vacuum. And my boy, if you're leaving us for three months or longer, the only thing that can compensate for your absence is religious fervor!"

Kelem looked at Nicolas and laughed internally at the irony of having had a conversation with Zeus on that very same subject, less than an hour before. Kelem sighed deeply, knowing that despite Zeus' concerns for the future of humanity's religious wellbeing, as well as his own morality, the current situation required Kelem to think in practical and concrete terms.

"Fine, what does she expect of me?" Kelem said, surprising Nicolas by his willingness to go along with his request.

"She expects you to inspire the people by speaking to them and giving them hope. You will be addressing the members of her congregation who will go out and spread your message to the rest of the planet. And Kelem, there's no government or powerful dictator that can stand against a people who have an unyielding belief and faith in an idea or a leader that inspires them in the way that I've seen you inspire others."

Kelem didn't say another word, but Nicolas knew that he'd made his point.

CHAPTER 20

The Reverend Ornata Marchant

February 21st, 2660

The large Fisher-Madjal transport was cruising above the Martian landscape on its way to Havana Flats. The only cargo aboard were Kelem and the Revered Ornata Marchant. Sister Ornata, as she was called by her congregation, was a young woman in her late twenties. She was a reasonably attractive female with the typical height and body shape of a native Martian. Her most remarkable features were her auburn hair and her striking blue eyes. She was a virgin and had pledged to remain so for her whole life. Her choice was based on her personal belief that a religious leader should be celibate in order to lead her flock. That is not to say that she was not attracted to men. When she met Kelem Rogeston she fell in love with him after she received his energetic transfer of love and affection from his heart chakra. Sister Ornata, a devout Christian, had been waiting all her life to experience divine grace, and Kelem had given her that gift.

But, Sister Ornata's love for Kelem Rogeston was not of a carnal or romantic nature and she had no desire to be wed to him or bear his children. She wanted to share the experience of divine grace that she received from him with the rest of the world. She decided that she would be Kelem's St. Peter and spread the knowledge of his gift. And she sincerely believed, and not unreasonably so, that Kelem had been sent by God Almighty to free his people from bondage just as God had chosen Moses to free his people from Egypt.

In her mind, Kelem's ability to heal people's minds and spirits was no different that Christ's healing of the sick or that of the many saints of Christendom who performed such miracles.

Now at last, this miracle of heaven named Kelem Rogeston, had agreed to address her congregation and share his blessing with her flock. To say that Sister Ornata was elated beyond words would have been an understatement.

Kelem was now able to walk with the aid of a cane but was still feeling stiff from the injury in his hip. Marla had injected several doses of nanites to rebuild muscle, sinew and bone tissue where the gun blast had put a gaping hole in his body, but the new tissue had not matured yet. His own natural healing ability had helped, but the shock to the rest of his body was still causing him pain and discomfort.

The shuttle hit turbulence, and Kelem winced a little from the motion.

"I see that you're still suffering from your injury," Sister Ornata observed, sitting opposite Kelem in the rear of the pilot's cabin.

"Only when I breathe," Kelem replied.

Sister Ornata smiled at his attempt at humor. "I want you to know that I truly appreciate your coming to speak to the congregation even though you're still recovering from your traumatic experience."

"I was joking, I'm not in constant pain."

"Still, you could have waited until you were fully recovered before you agreed to come and give us your blessing."

Kelem cringed internally at the mention of him blessing anyone, but Nicolas had been adamant that he should suspend his tendency to resist being looked upon as a source of inspiration. "You'll only have to do this once or twice," Nicolas had told him a few days ago. Kelem could only hope that this one time would be sufficient to quell the need of others to see him in person.

"The campaign to liberate Mars demands my full attention, Sister. If I don't do this now, I might not have the chance to speak to your congregation for a long time."

Sister Ornata's expression showed her disappointment upon hearing that Kelem would not be available to her congregation on a regular basis. "That is a pity, so many of our Martian brothers and sisters are in need of having their spirits raised."

"But you've already accomplished that, Sister Ornata! It's my understanding that you alone are responsible for passing on the message of hope to many others. My personal appearance couldn't possibly add that much to the raising of people's spirits," Kelem argued.

"Oh, but you're wrong, dear Kelem!" Sister Ornata exclaimed with intense passion. "You are supremely important! God has given you a gift that is rare and precious and it must be shared with others by you directly. You've taught me how to give the blessing and I am able to pass it along to others, but it is not nearly as powerful and transcendent as when you give it!"

"While that may be true, Sister, I am not a cleric nor do I have the desire to be one. If God brought me back to Mars, it is for the main purpose of liberating its people from the Terrans, and not to become a source of religious inspiration," Kelem countered, concerned by Sister Ornata's religious zeal.

"You are far above the level of a cleric like me or any other! You are the figurehead of a holy crusade, don't you see that?" Sister Ornata contended. "You can't deny God's providence, my dear Kelem. 'His will be done on Earth as it is in Heaven'," she said quoting from the Lord's Prayer.

Kelem read the woman's mind in an attempt to find any trace of subterfuge or self-aggrandizing motives and found none. Sister Ornata Marchant was a true devotee. Her faith in God and in the belief that Kelem had been delivered to the Martian people by heavenly edict was rock solid and genuine. This gave Kelem pause. His Uncle Nardo and Aunt Maggie had both been raised Catholic, and although they seldom attended church, both read the bible and believed in God. Mars had always been a nation that was mostly secular but Kelem had learned that ever since the invasion, Martians had turned to religion in great numbers. Who was he to deny his own people a way to overcome their misery and suffering? His coming back to Mars did have a preordained feeling, after all. From the moment he returned to the solar system, beginning with the rebels in the fleet, he had been put in a spiritual leadership position wherever he went. And now, Jorgen Kutmeier's prediction that Kelem's future was closely tied to the planet's destiny and that he would one day have to make sacrifices for his nation, echoed in his mind loud and clear.

The Standard Solar Dictionary described a sacrifice as; '1. The destruction or surrender of something for the sake of something else.' - and - 2. 'Giving up something of a personal nature or risking one's life for another'. By any other definition, that's what Kelem would be doing by addressing Sister Ornata's congregation. He decided then and there that he would no longer concern himself with this issue. The universe had placed him exactly where he was supposed to be.

The shuttle captain announced that they'd be landing soon. It was nighttime and the lights of Havana Flats were glittering like precious jewels on the landscape illuminating the sky above it. The weather was clear and the stars were shining brightly. Kelem felt that the beautiful view was a good omen.

After they disembarked at the Fisher-Madjal Company's landing pad, Kelem and Sister Ornata were escorted to one of the elevator shafts that led to the underground storage chambers. When they descended past the usual floor at which Kelem had been accustomed to exiting, he glanced at one of the crewmen from the transport.

"We're going to the big chamber tonight," the man said with an enigmatic smile.

"A lot of folks down there?" Kelem asked, worried that a big crowd was waiting for him.

"A few," the crewman answered.

When the elevator door opened they were greeted by Nicolas and Susan Beaumont in the corridor. Then they were led to a small chamber that was being used as an office. A crimson robe resembling a graduation gown was hanging on the wall and Sister Ornata quickly took off her pressure suit and put it on. The gown accentuated her auburn hair and blue eyes and instantly transformed her into a bonafide preacher. Kelem had to be helped out of his suit and remained in his hospital white overalls.

"Did you rehearse your speech?" Nicolas whispered in his ear.

"I did. Don't worry about me, I'm ready."

"I'm going to introduce you to the congregation and then you can step out on the stage and give the people your blessing," Sister Ornata informed him.

Kelem nodded and then one of the crewmen from the shuttle opened the door. When he did so, the sound of a large crowd inside a big space could be heard briefly until the door closed behind Sister Ornata.

"How many people are out there?"

"I didn't count Kelem, you'll see when you go out there," Nicolas replied casually.

Underground churches on Mars were usually small and typically accommodated a hundred people or so. Kelem figured that there might be two or three hundred at the most waiting for him in the warehouse judging by the noise of the crowd. When he heard Sister Ornata speak his name out loud, the crewman opened the door and Kelem walked through.

A deafening roar of applause and the sound of over two thousand people yelling his name stunned poor Kelem, who froze in mid step before reaching the podium in the middle of the large stage. Sister Ornata stood there clapping vigorously with tears in her eyes.

In a panic, Kelem looked back and saw Nicolas mouthing the words, "Go on, go on!"

Suddenly his legs felt weak and his head began to throb. For a moment he thought that he might pass out from the shock and had to force himself to remain calm. Sister Ornata seeing him hesitate, walked over to him and gently led Kelem by the arm to the podium.

The warehouse had been converted into a theatre with rows and rows of folding chairs facing a large proscenium stage. In the back of the stage facing the audience, a large printed canvas of Kelem wearing his captain's uniform, taken the day he left on the Solar Nations mission, hung majestically, waving slightly from the air currents stirred by the warehouse's ventilation system. Kelem was flabbergasted by the bizarre scene and felt as if he'd been thrown into the middle of a dramatic play to perform the part of a character whose lines he hadn't memorized.

Sister Ornata, seeing how Kelem's shock had paralyzed him, whispered in his ear, "wave to the people Kelem, wave to them…"

Kelem waved at the crowd like a robot responding to a command.

In the first few rows, women were crying and looking at him adoringly. A few of the men were also in a similar state. Kelem's mind was slowly coming to the realization that he had walked into a situation for which he was totally and dismally unprepared. Slowly, he regained his senses and turned to sister Ornata.

She leaned close to his ear once again. "Say hello and then give your speech," she recommended.

Kelem thought, "Good now I have a goal. Give my speech, thank everyone and then leave." This seemed logical and efficient until, with a sickening realization, a second wave of panic hit him when he realized that the two-sentence speech that he had prepared was woefully inadequate. His mouth and throat suddenly felt dryer than a desert dune. With a trembling hand he reached for the glass of water sitting on the podium and drank the whole thing in one big gulp.

The people were now beginning to call out to him, "Give us the word! Bless us Kelem! Save us!" and so on.

"You must forgive Brother Kelem," Sister Ornata said in a loud voice trying to be heard over the noise of the assembly. "He's still very weak from his ordeal at Constitution Park. Brothers and sisters please! Sit down and be quiet so that Kelem can address you."

The crowd obeyed and sat down, looking at Kelem with great anticipation.

Kelem closed his eyes and prayed for divine inspiration. He opened his heart and mind and imagined that the wise and gentle Zeus was guiding his words. He reached out with his mind looking for that place in his consciousness that accessed the Quantum Tide. Slowly, a feeling of peace and calm descended on him like a gentle rain and he knew what to say.

"Brothers and sisters," he began, using Sister Ornata's vernacular. "I came here tonight to give a short speech and then return to my hospital bed to continue my recovery. But I now see that I need to dismiss the words that I was going to recite to you this night and speak from the heart instead of giving a prepared statement."

"Those of you who are expecting to hear God's message from my lips, or believe that I'm an angel sent to Mars to avenge the wrongdoings of the Terrans, will be sadly disappointed. I am but a man, a fellow human of flesh and blood, full of imperfections and prone to make mistakes just like any of you."

"That providence has placed me in this time and place to contribute to the struggle to liberate our fair nation, I will not deny. Nor will I deny that I've been blessed with a powerful intellect and the ability to plan and execute a daring attack on the Terrans. That my return to Mars after an absence of twenty one years without having aged is wondrous and amazing, I will also not deny. But my youth is not a gift from God but the result of physics. The *n'time* generator on the Solar Nations malfunctioned and sent the ship fifteen years into the future. And then it took me an additional six years to return to the solar system. Were I a holy man or divine being, I would have undone these and other bad things that happened to me during the years that I was gone. So I ask you not to look upon me as anything other than a fellow Martian. To do otherwise would be unfair to individuals like Sister Ornata and other clerics who live a life of faith in service to their flock."

"If we are to praise anyone as being special, you should begin by praising yourselves individually and each other, for you are the life-blood of this planet and have the strength of spirit that has helped you survive fifteen terrible years under the yoke of the Phalanx. But now I must give you a warning and it is one that you should take to heart."

"Do not allow yourselves to become complacent, thinking that we've dealt a blow to the Terrans from which they won't be able to recover. Nothing could be further from the truth. We will suffer new retaliations from them and we'll experience more pain and tragedy in the days to come. But do not despair, Mars will be liberated and we will soon celebrate our freedom."

"Thank you for inviting me to address you tonight. I will not be able to meet with you for a few weeks as I need to recover from my injuries and attend to other matters related to our struggle. Stay true and keep your eyes on the prize. Thank you very much."

Kelem was sure that his 'common sense-realistic' speech had diminished the enthusiasm and religious zeal that he had encountered when he first walked on the stage. But he was wrong.

The crowd rose to their feet, cheering and approached the stage *en mass*. Everyone had his or her hand raised, reaching out to him and asking to be given his blessing. For a moment, it looked as though the crowd was going to rush the stage and trample Kelem and Sister Ornata in order to satisfy their demand for Kelem's blessing.

Kelem read the crowd's collective mind and felt the suffering and pain of years of slavery and the deep craving for the energy that he had given them through Sister Ornata. It was almost as if they were addicts seeking the release of endorphins that a drug is capable of creating in the human brain.

He was shocked and surprised by how much they needed to commune with him and how much it meant to them. Suddenly their desire for him generated a rush of energy that began at his root chakra, up his spinal column, onto his crown chakra and out at the top of his head like a fountain. Kelem felt lightheaded and felt as if he himself had taken a hypnotic drug. Suddenly, Zeus' image appeared semitransparently in front of his eyes with the crowd visible through his massive trunk. The juxtaposition of both visuals was utterly fascinating. Kelem then heard Zeus' booming voice in his ears. "YOU ARE NOT ALONE KELEM. WE WILL HELP YOU WITH THIS TASK."

As if in a dream, Kelem dropped his cane, kneeled down on the edge of the stage without feeling any pain or discomfort from his injury, and asked everyone to hold the hand of the person next to them. He reached for the hand closest to him at the edge of the stage as Sister Ornata grabbed his other hand and then he closed his eyes. In his mind he saw the images of all the deities and saints of humanity holding hands just like the crowd in front of him. A melody resembling the music of the Dreamers began playing in his mind, soon turning into a symphony of rarified high frequency vibrations that gave Kelem a feeling of sublime ecstasy. The beauty and intensity of the music climbed and climbed until Kelem felt as if his body was floating.

Slowly the vibrations lowered and retreated, leaving everyone in the warehouse quiet as everyone processed what had just happened. After a while, everyone opened their eyes and focused their attention on Kelem who remained kneeling with his eyes closed on the edge of the stage.

Nicolas, who had experienced the event with the crowd near the front of the stage, climbed up and gently lifted Kelem, who appeared to be in a trance.

"Brothers and sisters, let us say goodbye to Brother Kelem, who needs to return to his med-bed for a well-deserved rest," Sister Ornata announced. The crowd responded with shouts of praise for Kelem calling him a 'savior' and blessing him for his gift. Nicolas and one of the shuttle's crewmen escorted Kelem from the stage to the little office adjacent to it.

Still under the effects of his experience with the congregation,

Kelem had to be helped into his pressure suit, and after Nicolas said goodbye on Kelem's behalf to Susan Beaumont and Sister Ornata whose eyes were filled with unending tears of joy, the two of them left via elevator to the company's landing pad.

Neither one spoke on the way back to Latonga City. Nicolas sat next to his amazing young friend, feeling a mixture of awe and a little bit of jealousy. He knew that he had come in contact with Zeus' and the other Dreamers' consciousness through Kelem. Although Kelem had tried to describe to Nicolas with words what it was like to communicate with the Dreamers, until tonight, Nicolas' concept of such an event was only based on an oral description of a deep spiritual experience.

Now he understood why Kelem wanted to return to Plantanimus.

CHAPTER 21

The Argos Disappears

March 6th, 2660

The guard at the security desk of the Mars Mining Company's lobby stared at Kelem, then at the screen on his console. After comparing Kelem's face with the image on the screen, he gave the go ahead and Kelem proceeded on to the elevators. Billy had set up everything beautifully. Three days before, Kelem had met with Hiram Goldblatt, Jonas Hubert, Alonzo Stanton and Joseph Condre, the four cargo specialists who were part of the crew and also members of the resistance. Together they planned and rehearsed how they were going to take over the ship. The other four crew members were all Terran, starting with the captain, Dimitri Bravenhaus, first officer Memo Brodsky, pilot/navigator Douglas Proctor and *n'time* chief engineer Nigel Floggs.

Kelem had been assigned to the ship as a last minute replacement for the assistant engineer. Billy had seen to it that the man came down with a bad case of food poisoning the night before. The four cargo specialists had warned Kelem about Nigel Floggs, the chief engineer, who they said was a giant of a man with a nasty temper who didn't like Martians. Kelem touched his uniform's left sleeve where Marla Hassett had hidden three micro syringes filled with a knockout compound to take care of the big man when the time came to take over the ship.

The elevator brought Kelem to the thirtieth floor, one level below the surface of Mars. There he was fitted with an MMC pressure suit. Then, an employee drove him in a small electric buggy to the facility's

199

main hangar where a small shuttle was waiting to take him up to the Argos in orbit around Mars. The place had changed since Kelem had last been here twenty one years before, but it still looked familiar to him.

Twenty minutes later the shuttle was one hundred kilometers above the planet approaching the transport. The Argos was a cigar shaped vessel measuring four hundred and sixty meters by eighty seven meters. When the shuttle came within a kilometer of the ship's docking bay, Kelem realized how big the thing really was. This was the largest space vessel in existence to date and Kelem's heart was filled with excitement, realizing how much food and equipment was inside that thing and how much it would help the rebel fleet.

After the shuttle docked with the leviathan, Kelem disembarked and was met by Memo Brodsky, the first officer. "You Richard Severin?" the man asked in a not too friendly manner.

Kelem nodded, acknowledging his fake identity. After the man looked at him up and down disdainfully, he motioned to follow him through a long tubular corridor that ran along the center axis of the ship. The Argos, being an *n'time* vessel, had no gravity plating, and because trips from Mars to Earth only lasted thirty two hours, the ship also did not have any mechanically generated gravity doughnuts. The only way to move in and around the ship was by means of a motorized pulley system with metal handles that ran alongside all the connecting corridors. As Kelem and the first officer were being pulled towards the ship's command deck, he could see how much cargo this vessel could carry. The cargo was secured inside giant wheel shaped metal cages throughout the length of the ship connected to a central axle by heavy metal spokes. The cages were not designed to produce gravity, but did turn on the main axle for the purpose of loading and unloading. Kelem was astounded by how much merchandise this vessel could hold. The Argos was filled to capacity with crates of every size and description.

When they reached the command deck, the first officer introduced him to the captain. "Captain, this is Severin, the replacement."

The captain, a Germanic looking blonde man in his forties casually turned around and barely looked at Kelem. "All right, have him put his gear in the crew's quarters and then send him to Floggs right away." The navigator, the one named Proctor never even looked at him. Brodsky brought him to the crew's quarters directly below the command deck and showed Kelem where to stow his duffle bag.

"Do you know how to get to the generator from here?" he asked condescendingly as if Kelem was retarded.

"I know my way around an *n'time* vessel," Kelem replied, laughing inwardly, wondering how this prejudiced Terran would react when he found out who Kelem really was.

The *n'time* generator was separated from the rest of the ship by two bulkheads on each side in the middle of its cigar shape structure. Kelem pressed the door plate and passed into a small chamber with another pressure door at the opposite end that led to the center section, where the generator was located. When he entered the large cylinder shaped cavernous space, Kelem's jaw dropped when he saw what was in there.

To his shock and surprise the *n'time* generator on this ship was a near prefect copy of the X2 the prototype version of the generator that Kelem had designed prior to the much smaller final model for the Solar Nations.

"What's the matter, kid, haven't you ever seen a goddamned *n'time* generator?" a gruff voice said above him.

When Kelem looked up he received his second shock when he laid his eyes upon the largest human being he'd ever seen. Floating above him was a giant! Nigel Floggs was over two meters tall and had to weigh at least one hundred and thirty Kilos. This human behemoth was built like a wrestler with a head full of red hair accompanied by an equally ruddy complexion. His biceps were bigger than Kelem's thighs.

The man pushed down towards Kelem, grabbed him by his uniform's collar and unceremoniously dragged him to the center of the chamber where the generator sat anchored to the ship's hull by several support beams.

"What are those?" he said pointing to the generator.

Kelem was both angry and intimidated to be treated so disrespectfully by this ruffian. "Those are actuators," he replied trying to remain calm.

"And those?" the giant asked, pointing elsewhere with his huge index finger.

"Those are the capacitors that feed the actuators," Kelem informed him.

"Well then, what the hell were you gaping at?" the man demanded.

Kelem read the man's mind and found that he was suspicious of Kelem. Floggs hated Martians, and the last minute switch in personnel had fired up his temper and distrust of Martians.

"It's just that I've never seen such a big generator before," Kelem replied.

The large man let go of Kelem's collar and the two floated in midair as Floggs stared at him with a sour expression.

"This abomination is the work of the devil!" Floggs said pointing to the spherical device. "It does things that the laws of physics say it ain't supposed to do, yet it'll bring this big ship millions of miles from here in less than a second. I ask you, does that make any sense to you?" he challenged Kelem, his face turning redder than normal. Even though Nigel Floggs was a certified *n'time* engineer, he had a paranoid distrust of the technology, mainly because it had been invented by Martians.

"No, it doesn't make any sense to me either. I just know how to maintain this thing and keep it running so that we don't end up demolecularized in another dimension," Kelem replied, feigning ignorance of the workings of *n'time* theory.

"Hrrgh," the man grunted, sounding like a pirate from an old story. "I'll be watching ya, do you hear? If I see you trying to sabotage this generator I won't hesitate to wring yer' skinny neck with my bare hands!" he warned Kelem, who nodded, feeling totally intimidated by this bully, who reminded him a little of Rusty Deveraux in his prime.

Kelem thought it ironic that the two bullies that he'd come to know in his life were both redheads. Floggs gave Kelem a list of maintenance duties to perform, and Kelem was glad to get busy and get away from the man's intimidating presence. As the hours passed, Kelem would occasionally catch Floggs observing him from behind one of the huge girders that connected the generator to the ship's hull. Eventually the departure bell rang and both had to go to their acceleration chairs as the ship would be leaving Mars orbit using its chemical rocket motors.

The Argos would travel a million kilometers from Mars before activating the *n'time* generator.

The lumbering Argos would take more than two hours before it reached that distance.

The plan called for Kelem and the four others to strike at the same exact moment. The cargo specialists would neutralize Bravenhaus, Brodsky and Proctor up in the command deck while, Kelem would disable Floggs. Both had to happen at once, and Kelem was now worried that he might not be able to anesthetize Floggs at the right time. The man was leery of him, and getting close enough to the giant to inject the knockout drug in his neck was going to be difficult. Kelem looked at his wrist comp and noticed with alarm, that he had less than fifteen minutes before the others took action.

Time passed and Kelem's apprehension grew by the minute. He imagined that David, the future King of Israel, must have felt like he was feeling now before confronting Goliath, the Philistine's champion. David felled the giant Philistine with a small pebble thrown from his sling, a relatively small weapon compared to Goliath's spear, armor and shield. The micro syringes in his sleeve were several times smaller than David's weapon but hopefully just as effective. The only problem was that Kelem unlike David, had to get very close to his Goliath, the red haired human Orangutan, before he could defeat him.

And just like David, the future of his nation depended on winning this fight. Kelem took out two of the three syringes from his left sleeve and put them in his right hand. He gathered his courage and, unstrapping himself from the acceleration chair, walked on the wall behind him toward Flogg's chair. The wall had become the 'floor' due to the ship's acceleration. The man saw him walking towards him, and when Kelem was near him he suddenly reached for his left leg, spun him around and pulled him towards his massive chest wrapping his right arm tightly around Kelem's neck.

"Now what are ye tryin' to do?" he asked with a sinister laugh as his massive bicep encircled Kelem's throat.

"I have to go to the head, I'm nervous!" Kelem replied trying to catch his breath, and not lying about the nerves part.

Floggs had him in a choke hold and Kelem was powerless to do anything about it. It was like being squeezed by a giant anaconda.

"Let me go!" Kelem yelled trying to take a breath.

"Yer'up to sumthin'," Floggs said, noticing that Kelem was holding two small objects in his right hand. "Let's see what yer holdin', princess!" he said, pulling Kelem closer toward his left and reaching for Kelem's right hand. Flogg's choke hold was about to render Kelem unconscious, and seeing that he had no choice, he stabbed the giant's right forearm with the two syringes emptying both reservoirs of the drug below his skin.

Floggs yelled, more out of surprise than pain, and let go of Kelem, throwing him forcefully against one of the generator's support beams. Kelem hit the girder with his right thigh and a wave of pain cursed through his body. He had landed on the same spot where he'd been shot.

The giant, now irate and growling like a crazed grizzly bear, unstrapped himself from the chair and pulled the two syringes from his arm and threw them away. Then, he grabbed a large wrench from a compartment next to his chair and came at Kelem.

Kelem 'climbed' the girder in the opposite direction of the ship's thrust, in effect, going 'upwards' from the pull of gravity. Floggs being three times heavier than Kelem and beginning to feel the effects of the drug was moving slower but still gaining ground. In less than three meters, Kelem would run out of room and he'd be pinned against the spherical casing of the *n'time* generator between four beams that came together. Desperately, he looked around for an escape and realized to his horror that he was trapped. Floggs meanwhile, kept coming, though he was starting to move in slow motion now. Kelem's back was against the casing and he grabbed two of the girders closest to him and coiled his legs. When Floggs came within reach, Kelem kicked the big man in the face with both legs with all his strength. Floggs head rocked back stunning him for a moment, but then he brought his head forward, now bleeding profusely from his nose and mouth.

The red headed, bloodied, ruddy faced man looked like a nightmarish psychotic character from a horror-vid as he smiled at Kelem with a snarling grimace filled with rage and violence. He let go of the large wrench and grabbed Kelem with both of his huge beefy hands and began strangling him.

Kelem somehow managed to grab the wrench before it fell 'down' and began hitting Floggs on the ribs, to no effect. The drug had slowed the Orangutan down, but at the same time it had dulled his body to pain. In a few seconds Floggs would be crushing his larynx and then Kelem would be dead.

Kelem raised the wrench and hit Floggs in the forehead right above his left eye. The big man flinched and relaxed his grip on Kelem's throat for a second, but then recovered and resumed strangling him. Kelem hit him again in the same spot, this time the wrench made a sickening crunch as it struck, visibly denting the man's skull. The hit made Floggs body shake but somehow revived him! Floggs let go of Kelem and fell back a few centimeters and then Kelem kicked him in the gonads. This time the big man moaned and grimaced but then grabbed one of the girders and pulled himself up, head butting Kelem in the stomach throwing him against the generator's casing, the tackle knocked the wind out of Kelem and he let go of the wrench. Floggs grabbed the wrench with his right hand and swung it at Kelem with surprising speed.

Kelem instinctively raised his left arm and the wrench hit him with full force, instantly numbing his forearm. Kelem pulled his right fist back and then punched Floggs in the throat. The big man grabbed his throat and let go of the wrench. Kelem reached for it and hit Floggs in the forehead once again; this time cracking the giant's head open as blood and brain matter spilled out. The giant's eyes opened wide and his body stiffened. Then as his dead eyes stared at Kelem, he fell back all the way to the bulkhead, landing on top of his own acceleration chair with a heavy thud.

Kelem hung on to a girder, his body shaking and adrenaline pumping through his body. As his breathing normalized, a wave of nausea hit him and he vomited the contents of his stomach. Soon the numbness in his left arm gave way to intense pain followed by a throbbing ache in his right hip where he'd taken a hit when Floggs threw him against one of the generator's support beams.

The ship's engines suddenly cut off and both Kelem and Floggs' body were suddenly weightless. Kelem couldn't move his left arm and had to grab it to look at his wrist comp to see how much time had passed. The chronometer on his wrist comp read -00:58. He'd completed his part of the plan with almost a minute to spare! Now he could only hope that the others had succeeded in their part of the takeover.

Kelem pushed himself back down to the bulkhead where the acceleration chairs were and grabbed Floggs' body floating in zero G, strapping him to his own chair. The giant's eyes had remained open in death and Kelem, with disgust, reached over and closed them. Then, he found a rag and wrapped it around the man's bloody head so he wouldn't have to look at his face.

"Zero" hour had come and gone and he hadn't heard from the other four. Several minutes went by and Kelem began to worry that things had gone wrong. He tried reaching out, seeking the consciousness of the others in the vessel but his mind was in turmoil. He had never killed a man in hand to hand combat before, and especially in such a violent, bloody manner. He felt as if part of him had died with the giant, a part that he would never be able to recover. He felt ashamed for having taken another's life even though it had been in self-defense, and was sure that he had forfeited his humanity and feared that in turn he'd lost the ability to commune with Zeus and the Dreamers forever. This killing had tainted his soul and spirit and he feared that he'd been infected with the same evil energy that he despised in his enemies.

As he struggled to escape from such a negative and self-defeating mood, the intercom near his chair buzzed. "Ahoy in the engine room," the voice of Alonzo Stanton blared from the little speaker. "Come in, Floggs," Stanton added, hoping to hear Kelem's voice instead of the chief engineer's, confirming that he had succeeded in disabling the scary giant.

"Ahoy, bridge, this is Severin," Kelem responded with a shaky voice.

"Oh, thank god!" Stanton said, sounding relieved. "Are you all right?"

"I'm going to need some help. Everything go right up front?" Kelem asked.

"Hiram and Jonas are on their way to you. The captain, Proctor and Brodsky are locked in one of the storage cages in the front. You sound like you're hurt," Alonzo Stanton inquired.

"I'll be all right, nothing life threatening, I just need some first aid."

"Hiram is a medic. He'll take care of you, but what happened?" Stanton asked, curious to know how Kelem had survived a physical struggle with the huge Terran.

"Can't talk now, I have to reprogram the generator's inter-dimensional program so that we don't end up in Earth orbit," Kelem said warily.

"All right, I'll see you soon," Stanton said signing off.

Hiram Goldblatt and Jonas Hubert floated into the generator's chamber and stared in utter disbelief at the sight of Nigel Floggs dead body tethered to a chair, his head covered with a bloody rag.

"What the hell happened, did you do this?" Jonas Hubert asked Kelem, his eyes wide with surprise.

"Floggs attacked me - I barely survived. My left arm is definitely broken. I need you two to patch me up quickly so that I can reprogram the computer," Kelem said, pushing himself toward them with difficulty.

"You're all bloody!" Is that your blood or his?" Hiram asked as he retrieved the first aid kit from one of the bulkheads.

"It's his blood, not mine," Kelem answered as Jonas wiped his face and hands clean and Hiram unzipped Kelem's coveralls and looked at his left forearm, which had swollen where Floggs had struck him with the wrench. Hiram scanned Kelem's left forearm with a portable MRI and confirmed that his left ulna was definitely broken. Fortunately, it was only a hairline fracture and not a complete break.

"I'm going to give you something for the pain," Hiram announced as he prepared a pain killer.

"No, not now! Just give me a local, a small dose, enough to numb the pain. I need to be sharp when I reprogram the generator's computer," Kelem warned him.

Fifteen minutes later, Kelem was on the command deck trying to access the *n'time* generator's systems but unable to do it because Proctor had obviously locked out access to the vessel's navigation controls.

"Bring Proctor up here," Kelem ordered.

Joseph Condre and Alonzo Stanton brought the Terran pilot/ navigator onto the command deck. The man had a mocking half smile on his lips, knowing that he'd outsmarted these Martian rebels by encrypting access to the generator's systems.

Kelem tried to read the man's mind and extract the encrypted password from him, and found to his dismay that he was still too riled up to use his mind reading skill. Time was running out before the ship's computer sent the vessel to Earth! Then he thought of something that was gory and disgusting, but what the hell! He'd already killed another human being. What he was about to do was far less morally objective than killing. He asked Hiram and Jonas to meet him away from Proctor's eyes and ears and gave them instructions.

Five minutes later Kelem stood next to the handcuffed pilot/navigator as they faced the command deck's windows.

"One last chance Proctor or I'll throw you out of an air lock," Kelem menaced.

The pilot turned and spit at his face which fortunately missed its mark in the zero gravity.

Suddenly, Nigel Floggs' body hit the front windows of the command deck from the outside with a loud thud and Proctor jumped back about two meters completely startled, banging his head against the ceiling. The sight of the giant man's bloody decompressed face pressed against one of the deck's windows, rattled the man completely. He looked at Kelem in shock and horror and immediately gave up the encrypted password that he'd used to lock out access to the *n'time* generator's computers.

The man was escorted out and Kelem signaled Hiram to release Floggs body and let him drift away.

As the red headed giant's body disappeared, Kelem reprogramed the Argo's destination and the command deck's Duraminium shields closed. Soon, the hum of the *n'time* generator could be heard throughout the ship as a purple glow enveloped the vessel's hull, and in an instant, the huge transport blinked out of existence.

CHAPTER 22

A New Hope for Freedom

March 7ᵗʰ, 2660

Five months and one day after he'd returned to the solar system, Kelem Rogeston stepped into the cargo hold of the Rusty Bucket. This time he was hailed as a hero by the crew.

A cheer went up and Rusty Deveraux, his wife Danielle, son Louie and Ndugu rushed forward to embrace him, happy to see him in the flesh once again. Kelem moaned with pain as Rusty's hearty hug sent waves of pain from his broken forearm.

"Let go of the man, Dad! Can't you see you're hurting him?" complained Louie, pulling his enthusiastic father's arms away from Kelem and then shaking his hand as vigorously as his dad had hugged the returning hero.

"It's so damn good to see you Kelem!" Rusty exclaimed with tears in his eyes.

Danielle Deveraux came forward and gave Kelem a tender kiss on his cheek. Kelem patted her bulging belly and smiled.

"How's the baby?" he asked.

"Doing fine, he's kicking extra hard right now. I think he's happy that you're here!"

Ndugu put his arm around Kelem's shoulder affectionately. "Welcome back Kelem. You have accomplished what many in the fleet said was impossible!" he stated proudly, as Kelem was escorted to the mess hall for a welcome home celebration.

Kelem was exhausted and in pain but knew that if he didn't attend the party, people's feelings would be hurt. After they assembled in the mess hall, Rusty raised his glass and proposed a toast.

"To Generalissimo Kelem Rogeston, the leader of the Martian Resistance! He shouted with a big smile on his face. The group drank the vodka in one gulp and slammed their cups on the table in unison.

The alcohol felt like fire going down Kelem's throat but the results were much more pleasant. "Holy mother of God!" he exclaimed after he put his cup down. "You guys still make the worst hooch in the universe but I'm sure glad to share it with you!"

The crew laughed and yelled and hooted with excitement. Some of them were crying with happiness knowing that Kelem had brought them the means to fight back and reclaim their planet. They knew that the giant behemoth of a ship visible through the Rusty Bucket's mess hall windows was their salvation. Kelem Rogeston had revitalized the resistance on both sides of the belt, and now he had brought them enough food, weapons and supplies to send the hated Terrans back to their planet.

Kelem continued spending time with the crew of the asteroid herder until Danielle noticed how much pain Kelem was in. "All right people!" she shouted to be heard above the noise of the group. "I guess you heard from the other members of the team who brought us this amazing gift," she said pointing to the Argos, "that Kelem fought and killed a giant Terran."

The crowd cheered and yelled anew, now beginning to feel the effects of the rocket fuel they'd been drinking.

"Though he defeated his opponent, Kelem suffered broken bones during the struggle and his body has been banged up. The man is in pain people! I know that you want to celebrate his triumphant return and ask him a million questions, but right now, as the chief medical officer on this vessel, I'm ordering General Rogeston to report to the infirmary for medical treatment!"

Some in the crew grumbled, but eventually the crew accepted Danielle Deveraux's edict and the men filed past Kelem, shook his hand and wished him a speedy recovery.

"Thanks Danielle!" Kelem whispered in her ear.

Later, Kelem found himself in the same med-bed that he had spent time on when he first arrived in the solar system. Louis and Danielle removed his crewman's uniform and gave him a bonafide patient's gown. Louie put a cast on Kelem's arm and Danielle gave him a shot for his pain. Within seconds, Kelem was blissfully and peacefully unconscious.

Three days later, feeling much better but still sore from his life and death struggle with Nigel Floggs, Kelem was giving a briefing in the mess hall to a large group of rebel fleet captains who had assembled on the Rusty Bucket to hear the latest news from the man himself; General Kelem Rogeston! The group included Captain Veronica Valchek.

"We all recorded the attack on Constitution Park, but we didn't know until now that you were the one who planned and executed it. The clip is the most viewed video in the entire fleet. Some ships have it on constant replay and everyone cheers each and every time the stage blows up! I've had to order my crew to restrict playing it all the time, otherwise no work gets done!" a transport captain was saying.

"Ever since then, we've been hearing of increasing guerilla attacks on Terran facilities, transports and even kidnappings of senior Black Guards," another captain interjected with exhilaration.

"Now that we have supplies, food, and weapons we should strike the Terran Fleet and take our planet back!" an over enthusiastic captain shouted from the back.

Kelem raised his right hand and the group quieted down.

"Ladies and gentlemen, I understand your zeal and enthusiasm to go on the offensive, but the truth is that one huge _n'time_ ship and all the food and weapons in it, is no guarantee that we'll be able to defeat the Terran fleet.

"But General, if not now, when? We've been waiting fourteen years to do something and now that we have what we need, you tell us we have to wait some more?" an exasperated sounding female officer retorted near the front.

"Ladies and gentlemen, just because your bellies are full and your infirmaries are resupplied with drugs and surgical equipment, doesn't mean that you're ready to go on a full scale offensive! And although most of your ships are now running much better than they have in the last few years, all your vessels are old and many of them are obsolete. Don't forget that the Terrans have several hundred *n'time* vessels to our one, parked right outside this window," Kelem said pointing to the Argos.

"Then what should we do General?" asked another man with frustration in his voice.

"We're going to turn the Argos into a factory ship. We have enough materials to build one thousand missiles. It's not a lot but they will be effective if we use them wisely. We have several lathes and manufacturing equipment to repair and rebuild parts for many of our ships. But above all ladies and gentlemen, I have to teach the engineers on every ship how to install and operate *n'time* generators, and then train all the navigators in the fleet how to use the technology. Above all, we have to get all our crews to the point that they'll be as sharp and disciplined as Martian Navy personnel. I nominate Captain Veronica Valchek as the officer in charge of personnel training. Captain, please stand up," he asked her.

Slightly confused, Veronica Valchek stood up.

"Captain, when I first came back to the solar system you asked me, and I quote; 'to accept a commission as a senior commanding officer of the Martian Rebel Fleet.' "Then you said, 'I hope you will say yes.'"

Veronica Valchek smiled remembering the conversation.

"I accepted that commission which I'm still proud to retain. Now I return the favor to you. Being the senior officer on this ship, I would like the honor of appointing you to the rank of Admiral of the Martian Rebel fleet."

The group rose from their chairs and applauded. Kelem took out six gold braid ribbons from his pocket and placed them on Captain Valchek's tunic sleeve. "Congratulations Admiral! Kelem said shaking her hand. Admiral Valchek accepted with a smile, her heart beating wildly with gratitude to God and the universe for delivering Kelem Rogeston to the Martian people.

A week later, much of the food and medical supplies had been distributed to the fleet. Kelem had requested several mechanics and fabricators to be temporarily assigned to the Argos (which had been renamed New Hope for Freedom), to begin installing the *n'time* generators, build a thousand missiles and larger caliber rail cannons, and start manufacturing replacement parts for the ships that needed them.

The former officers of the Argos had been pressed as laborers in the effort.

Kelem had asked Rusty to meet him to discuss something very important, and now they were in Rusty's ready room.

"Rusty, what I'm about to tell you has to remain in confidence between you and me and no one else. Do you agree to keep what I'm about to say secret?"

"Of course Kelem, you know you can count on me to be discreet."

"I knew it, I just wanted to hear you say it," Kelem commented, then he leaned on Rusty's desk. "Ndugu and I did not return to the solar system on the lander. That was a lie to cover the real story which we couldn't divulge at the time."

"I knew it!" Rusty said slamming the desk with his hand with a pleased expression on his face. "You have the Solar Nations stashed somewhere out there don't you?"

"No, unfortunately, the Solar Nations was truly destroyed. But I have something better than that," Kelem added. "I have an alien ship almost as big as Mars' Charmont Space Station hidden behind a planetessimal near the orbit of Pluto."

Rusty's eyes opened wide and he leaned back in his chair completely surprised by Kelem's statement.

"Shit Rogeston! You mean to tell me that we have aliens lurking on the edge of the solar system in a ship that big?" Rusty asked with a mixture of fascination and fear.

"Not aliens, <u>an alien</u>," Kelem answered, emphasizing the words.

Kelem told Rusty the real account of his and Ndugu's adventures from the time the Solar Nations left on its mission. When he finished, Rusty was unable to speak for quite a while.

"So what is it that you want to do with this ship, and what do you hope this Kren creature will do for us?" Rusty asked after he recovered from his inability to speak.

"I'm going to ask Harry to help us develop new technology that can help the rebel fleet defeat the Terrans," Kelem stated calmly.

"Hell! At this point I'll believe whatever you say Kelem. If anyone can do it, it would be you by God!" Rusty exclaimed.

"Me and Harry you mean!" Kelem corrected him, laughing.

"So you're going to bring that alien and his ship here now?" Rusty asked, beginning to get excited.

No, Rusty, I'm going to go back to the ship and work with Harry there. Don't forget that the Kren don't want to meet humans at large just yet."

"How long will you be gone?"

"No more than two or three weeks. Harry's technical knowledge and intellect is practically immeasurable. I'm sure he will come up with something that can help us very quickly."

"You know that people are going to freak out when you go away for almost a month so soon after returning to us!" Rusty warned him.

"Kelem fidgeted feeling uncomfortable, he hated to give Rusty the bad news. "I'm taking Ndugu and five others with me," Kelem said, cringing internally, knowing how loved and appreciated Ndugu had become by many in the fleet and particularly by Rusty and the entire crew of the Rusty Bucket.

"Oh no, Kelem! Please don't do that, now that we have materials to repair everything that was wrong with our ships!" Rusty protested, dismayed by this new development.

"Don't fret Rusty, like I said it's only for two to three weeks maximum. Besides, the technology that we're probably going to bring back with us will more than make up for Ndugu's absence."

Rusty was very unhappy, but he knew that Kelem was right. "Who besides Ndugu are you going to take to this alien ship?"

"Hiram Goldblatt and Alonzo Stanton. Both are highly skilled electronics experts who were given menial jobs at MMC because the Terrans are suspicious of anyone with such skills. Then I need three fabricators, the best in the fleet. They should also be individuals who will be able to keep their mouths shut. I'm sure that Harry will cooperate with us, but only if I can assure him that he and the Kren will remain unknown by humanity at large."

"I'll put out a call to other ships for suggestions, but I'm sure Admiral Valchek will know whom to pick for this mission," Rusty assured Kelem.

"Great! Now I have one more confidence that I want to share with you," Kelem added, looking at Rusty intently. "Billy Chong is not a traitor. As a matter of fact, he was one of the first Martians to become a member of the resistance. He chose this very difficult way of serving his nation because he knew the Terrans were going to want a Martian figurehead to deal with industry and the Martian economy. He was in a perfect position to serve as a double agent. Over the years, he's the one who sent the rebel fleet supplies and weapons in the past, and he's helped thousands of Martians survive and continue the struggle against Earth. And he's the one who helped me set up the hijacking of the Argos at great risk to himself and his family. So even though you can't tell anyone about Billy until after Mars is liberated, I wanted you to know that he's a true hero and not a villain."

Rusty's eyes welled with tears for having hated Billy Chong all these years when he should have been praising him for his sacrifice on behalf of his nation.

"One more thing, from now on, I want to start a physical calisthenics regimen for all able personnel in the fleet. Beginning tomorrow, I want the gravity on all our ships to be raised incrementally over the next few weeks until all ships are operating at one Earth G."

Rusty was confused, and raised his shoulders in question. "Why do you want to do that?"

"Because, Rusty, very soon, we're going to be boarding Terran ships and we can't have our people struggling with their bodies, particularly when they might be engaged in hand to hand combat with men and women from Earth."

Rusty's eyes lit up and a big smile spread on his face.

CHAPTER 23

Harry the Kren

March 15th, 2660

Kelem was facing the five candidates that he, Rusty, Ndugu and Admiral Valchek had chosen for this mission. All had signed a non-disclosure agreement and would be subject to federal law once the Martian Government was reinstated should they reveal any facts about this mission. Aside from Hiram Goldblatt and Alonzo Stanton, three fabricators had been picked. Bea Niguchi, Lola Irigoyen and Peter Molovinsky. All five were in their early twenties and excelled in their individual fields of expertise.

"Now that we're on our way, I can tell you what this mission is all about and why you were asked to sign a non-disclosure agreement," Kelem was saying.

Hiram, Alonzo, Bea, Lola and Peter sat expectantly in the front five seats of the lander that had brought Kelem and Ndugu into the solar system. Ndugu was in the front cabin piloting the ship.

"I'm taking you to a ship that's parked behind a large planetessimal, about a million kilometers past the orbit of Pluto. That ship is an alien ship, and it belongs to a species called the Kren. The Kren are non-aggressive peaceful beings that live in gigantic colony ships the size of a small moon. However, the ship that we will be staying in, though large, is not a colony ship. In this ship is an alien of that species and you will be meeting him. This Kren responds to the name Harry. Harry's body can best be described as insect like. More specifically, his body resembles that of a cricket or locust from Earth. He is as tall as an average person, walks upright like a human and possesses two legs and four pairs of arms. He has a large head with a pair of antennae and consumes food through a mouth that contains a set of compound jaws. He has a pair of iridescent eyes the size of tea cups, two small orifices on the side of his head that work much like human ears and his body is colored medium green with mottled areas of yellow and brown. The Kren do not wear clothes, they are vegetarian and do not consume any flesh."

The five volunteers were shocked and remained silent trying to assimilate the fact that they'd just been told that they would be meeting a bonafide alien within a few days.

"Now you know why one of the questions asked on your application was, 'Are you insect phobic?' If you answered that question with a lie, it's too late and you will have to deal with the consequences. However, I have to admit that although Ndugu and I are not insect phobic, it took us a while to feel comfortable around the Kren."

"You lived among them?" asked Lola Irigoyen.

"No, but Ndugu and I visited their mothership before the Kren queen-mother offered to bring us back to the solar system."

The five volunteers had been told a modified version of Kelem and Ndugu's twenty one year absence from the solar system. Kelem had decided that the group didn't need to know about the existence of Anima and the Dreamers.

"What is the purpose of us going to this ship and meeting the alien?" Hiram Goldblatt inquired.

"You've been chosen because of your technical skills. Kren technology is more advanced than ours in some ways, and I'm hoping that Harry will agree to help us design better ways to fight the Terran fleet with some of that advanced technology."

"I thought you said that the Kren were a non-aggressive peaceful species. Why would they let us use their technology for military purposes?" asked Peter Molovinsky.

"Kren society is based on an insect hive model. The queen gives birth to all Kren in the hive. She is telepathic and is in constant contact with all the Kren in the hive. She is the only female in the hive and all the Kren under her are neuter drones. We named 'him' Harry for lack of a better word, but in essence, Harry is neither male nor female.

Harry came to the solar system to learn about humans. He is a worker drone and the queen-mother assigned him to bring us home and to learn about the human mind. The Kren have no emotions and the queen was fascinated by our intricate social history. I believe that part of his directive will allow him to help us."

"I know you said that the Kren are peaceful, but what's to prevent the Kren from coming to Mars and invading us? We're trying to get rid of the Terrans and now we might have to worry about an alien species as well?" Bea Niguchi asked, looking concerned.

"All right, here's the second reason why you were asked to sign a non-disclosure agreement. I am a mind reading psychic," Kelem announced, then paused to let the words sink in.

"No kidding! What am I thinking?" Lola challenged.

"I will tell you and the others here what you're thinking, but only if you give me permission to do so," Kelem advised.

"Go ahead," she said looking at the other four volunteers with a wink, confident that Kelem could not possibly read anyone's mind.

"Now that you heard about Harry, you're terrified to be on this mission, because you lied on your application. You had an incident with a Brown Recluse spider that bit you when you were six years old and it made you very sick. But don't worry, I won't bring disciplinary charges against you, because you're a brilliant technician and, if necessary, I will isolate you from the rest of us whenever we have to interact with the Kren."

"I'm...I'm sorry General!" Lola blurted out on the verge of tears. "I wanted to serve under you and I didn't think that one little lie would come back to haunt me like this. I never told that story to anyone, you really are a mind reader!"

"Before any of you ask me, I'd like you all to know that I don't go around invading people's private thoughts unless it's a life and death emergency or to prove a point like I did now. The reason why I've revealed to you that I have that skill is to assure you that the Kren really are who and what they say they are. I communicated with the Kren queen telepathically and learned that they truly are a non-aggressive species. Otherwise, I would have never agreed to return to the solar system with an alien species that could harm us."

"Do you communicate with Harry telepathically?" asked Alonzo.

"No, Harry does not have the ability to read or transmit thoughts, save to receive telepathic communications from his queen."

"So, he speaks like you and me? In standard solar English?" asked Peter.

"No, the Kren do not have vocal chords or anything resembling a human voice box. They communicate with each other in their own language, which to us would sound like a series of soft clicks and buzzes. After we met them, we gave the Kren the ISA kit from the Solar Nations and within a month they had built a metal box that Harry uses to talk to us. He carries it around his neck and the device translates his native speech into standard solar English. As I said before, Harry is not a telepath."

"When we took over the Argos, you had me bring Proctor over to force him to give us the encrypted password to the *n'time* computer system and he refused. How come you didn't read his mind then instead of having one of us throw Flogg's body on the command deck's window to scare him into confessing?" Hiram asked, trying to resolve in his mind the inconsistency in Kelem's behavior then and now.

"I had just killed another human being for the first time in my life in hand to hand combat. I was emotionally distraught and in severe pain from my injuries. I can't use my ability under certain circumstances. Emotional and physical trauma are some of those circumstances."

"I'm sorry, General, I didn't mean to…" Hiram began saying.

"No apologies necessary, Hiram, and to all of you, I want to say that I realize that I've just placed a heavy burden on your minds. But, unfortunately, our struggle for independence calls for desperate and extraordinary measures. The Kren do not want to meet humanity at large, and even though they're curious to learn about us, they feel that humans are too aggressive and violent, and too immature as a species to come in contact with them. However, I'm hoping that Harry will forgo that philosophy and agree to help us this one time."

Kelem also did not want to talk about the six month period that Harry had agreed to wait for Kelem's return, and that that time was almost up. He hoped that whether or not Harry agreed to help them with technological advice, he would at least be willing to wait another six months before leaving the solar system. If Harry refused to wait, Kelem would be obliged to stay behind and complete the task of liberating Mars. But that meant that he would never be able to return to Plantanimus and be with Anima and the Dreamers.

At the end of the fifth day of travel, the group had reached the planetessimal where the Kren ship had been parked, and Kelem took over the controls of the ship. As the lander approached the Kren vessel, the others gathered around the cabin's windows to catch their first glimpse of a true alien spacecraft. When Kelem maneuvered closer to the huge metallic sphere, the others let out a collective gasp when they realized how big the thing really was. Kelem broadcast the frequency to open the ship's docking bay and a large opening appeared on the shiny surface of the ships' hull. Kelem then brought the lander to a smooth touchdown on the dock's floor.

"The gravity on this planetessimal is one quarter of one Earth G. When we bring the ship out of standby mode, the gravity will increase to seven eighths of one Earth G, which is what the Kren are used to," Kelem advised the group.

The group disembarked, and the newcomers looked at everything in the docking bay with extreme interest. In many ways, the machinery and objects in the large compartment and the style of construction looked alien and strange, but in other ways some things looked eerily familiar. Kelem asked the others to follow him, and the group filed behind him as he opened a pressure door and entered a narrow stairway that led 'up', based on their sense of up and down on this small planetoid. Kelem led them to what he and Ndugu had dubbed 'the rec room'. Once there, he told everyone to wait while he climbed three other decks to reach the ship's control room. Once there, he punched in the sequence on the instrument console that Harry had instructed him to use to reboot the vessel's systems. The whine of generators and the flickering of lights told the others below that the Kren ship was coming alive. In spite of Kelem's insistence that Harry was harmless, a sense of apprehension was evident in the newcomer's faces.

Kelem returned to the rec room. "Go back to the lander and bring in your personal items. As I explained before, there are currently only two sleeping cabins on this ship. The Kren do not sleep, they hibernate so they didn't need to remodel the ship with more than two cabins to accommodate Ndugu and me. The men will double up in my cabin,

Ndugu will give up his to the two young ladies and once Harry is up we'll figure where the rest of us will bunk while we stay here."

"General, Lola and I are used to bunking with men on our ships. You needn't feel obliged to observe normal social conventions. Fourteen years of exile have changed Martian social customs," Bea Niguchi informed him.

"Fine, you can decide how to split the group into two, but I'm sure Harry will be able to provide us with more space once he's up."

Kelem announced that he was going to the 'bottom' of the ship to bring the Kren out of hibernation. He descended five decks until he reached the small chamber where he'd left Harry almost six months before. The pressure door opened and he walked up to the narrow circular opening where the Kren's large head was visible. His antennae had been tucked behind his head. The rest of his body was hidden from Kelem's view inside the cylindrical space. On a shelf to the right of the chamber, lay the Kren's voice box. Kelem entered the sequence on the numerical keypad displaying numbers in Kren language next to the opening and waited with baited breath for the Kren to stir.

A series of blips could be heard in the small space coming from a speaker somewhere in the ceiling and suddenly Harry's antennae popped up, startling Kelem, who jumped back a few centimeters. Then Harry's head moved and Kelem heard the alien's natural vocal sounds issue from his mouth. The Kren's buzzes and clicks increased in frequency and soon reached what Kelem thought to be certain urgency. Harry's head appeared to be stuck. Somehow the insectoid had gotten stuck in the tubular space that he'd been hibernating in. Alarmed, Kelem looked for any sign of a seam or switch that might open the chamber wide, but found none.

Harry now appeared to be in severe stress and his head was bulging as he attempted to free himself from the chamber. Kelem grabbed his head and carefully pulled it up, conscious not to decapitate the insectoid by pulling too hard. The Kren's neck was only ten centimeters wide. Slowly, Harry's head came loose and as soon as it was exposed, Kelem placed the talk box around Harry's neck.

"It appears that I've grown in body size since you left, Kelem. Please help me get the rest of my body out of the chamber," the Kren requested.

Kelem gingerly pulled the relatively light weight Kren out of the chamber, and as each pair of arms came loose, Harry unwrapped them from his thorax and helped pull himself out. The Kren's legs were last and as Kelem held Harry in his arms above the floor, his 'legs' slowly came away from his body and soon he was standing up on his own.

"You have grown," Kelem remarked as the insectoid straightened his posture. "When I left, the top of your head came up to my nose, now you're as tall as me."

Harry stared at Kelem, his eyes blinking in his typical non-human expressionless face. "You're right. I am a fully grown Kren and I didn't think that I could grow any further. Perhaps Mother wants me to be larger than my siblings for some reason."

"Is that unusual? Have you ever heard of any other Kren drone growing larger than normal?"

"No, all Kren are basically clones of each other," Harry answered in his monotone artificial voice.

"Well, whatever size you are now, it is certainly good to see you," Kelem remarked smiling.

"You've returned thirteen days early," the Kren said looking at the time display in the hibernation chamber. "Did you accomplish all your tasks?"

Kelem took a deep breath and proceeded to tell Harry everything that had occurred since he and Ndugu left his ship. He brought him up to the present including the reason for the presence of the additional five humans in the rec room and concluded by making his request for Harry to remain an additional six months in the solar system.

The Kren remained silent for a long time and Kelem worried that Harry would reject the presence of the five humans and refuse to remain in the solar system the additional time.

"Will these humans play games with me?" Harry asked sounding childlike.

Kelem laughed, remembering the Kren's obsession with game playing. "I'm sure they will, Harry, that is until they get over their innate fear of insects--in particular the one named Lola Irigoyen."

Harry remained silent for another minute or so. Finally he spoke. "I have an idea. Why don't you ask Ndugu to come down here, and he and I will come up with a way to introduce me to the others that will make it easy for them to accept me."

"Good, I'll send Ndugu right down."

Kelem returned to the rec room and asked Ndugu to go down and see Harry. The others, having waited a half hour were showing signs of severe apprehension mixed with curiosity.

"Is everything all right? Why did it take so long for you to return?" asked Lola, sounding very nervous.

"Harry wants to make a good impression on all of you and he's asked for Ndugu to introduce him to you. Harry is concerned that you will be afraid of him."

"We're all very nervous General. I hope that you understand that it's a normal reaction, besides the fact that we're about to meet a real alien from another world! I'm both curious and terrified at the same time. I hope that my better nature wins out!" Peter Molovinsky commented.

"Relax, people!" Kelem said lightly. "By the time we leave this ship, you'll feel toward Harry as Ndugu and I do."

The group laughed nervously and felt a little more at ease with Kelem's words that all would be well.

Ten minutes later Ndugu appeared by the pressure door that led to the lower deck where the Kren's hibernation chamber was located.

"Ladies and Gentlemen, allow me to introduce my very good friend, Harry the Kren!" Ndugu announced theatrically.

When Harry stepped through the door, the five newcomers backed off ever so slightly. The women held on to the arms of their male companions. Lola and Bea hid partially behind their male partners but were unable to take their eyes off the alien. Suddenly, Harry, who was carrying Ndugu's keyboard with a strap around his narrow neck began playing the introduction to 'It's a Miner's Life,' a song that every Martian miner knows by heart. Ndugu then began singing the first verse of the song, followed by the chorus.

The five young men and women stood in awe and fascination by the bizarre spectacle of the Kren playing the keyboard while Ndugu's raspy African accented voice performed the song for their audience. The Kren's body, bobbing up and down to the rhythm of the music as he accompanied Ndugu, only served to enhance the funny and charming quality of the performance. Slowly, the five began to relax and soon they were smiling and laughing at the astonishing event unfolding before their eyes.

When the song was over, Ndugu spoke. "Harry wants to say something. Go ahead, Harry."

"Welcome, Hiram, Lola, Peter, Bea and Alonzo," the Kren said through his mechanical voice box. "I am honored that you have decided to visit my ship. You are welcome guests and are invited to stay with me for as long as you wish. I know that my appearance is very intimidating to you, but I assure you that you have nothing to fear from me. I have watched many human fictional drama-vids that feature alien monsters from other worlds and in many cases these aliens are blood thirsty insects that crave human flesh. I don't understand the fascination that humans have for such entertainment, but we Kren are not only vegetarians, but my race is peaceful and we have never waged war against any other species."

Then Harry took off the keyboard and handed it to Ndugu. "Kelem told me that you, Lola are insect phobic," he said looking at her. "I will avoid physical contact with you and will make sure that we're never left alone in any section of the ship to ease your fear of me. For the others, I invite you to come to me and touch my body. Please be gentle with me as Kren physiology is much weaker and fragile than your human bodies."

The three men stepped forward and reached for Harry's 'hand'. As they came in contact with the Kren's soft furry limb, they were as surprised by how soft his exoskeleton was, as Kelem had been the first time that he came in physical contact with the Kren on Plantanimus. Slowly, Bea reached out from behind Hiram's shoulder and placed her small hand on Harry's forearm and gasped with a mixture of delight and fear. Lola, not to be outdone, did the same and giggled when she made contact with Harry, surprising herself and the others.

Kelem leaned back against the wall with a satisfied smile. Harry was a constant source of surprising revelations, and this moment was no different. The Kren had figured out a very ingenious and clever way to ingratiate himself to the five newcomers and put their minds at ease. It seemed to Kelem that the Kren understood human psychology better than most humans.

CHAPTER 24

The Patient in ICU Ward "C"

March 22ⁿᵈ, 2660

Doctor Kosigan's face turned pale when Soltan Voltanieu walked into Ward C at the Latonga City Hospital followed by four Phalanx goons. He'd been the attending physician for Voltanieu's son Jude for over a month, and the Governor was not happy with the results. Terran surgeons had treated Jude Voltanieu with tissue-rebuilding nanites to compensate for the young man's missing brain matter and managed to keep him alive, but in the process, Jude Voltanieu came out of his coma suffering a case of complete and permanent amnesia. The governor's son had crashed his ship into the ground at over three hundred kilometers per hour. The only thing that saved his life had been the well-designed crash harness in his flight chair. But even that safety feature could not prevent the serious brain injury the young Colonel suffered from the impact.

Jude Voltanieu could speak and understand what people said to him, and had retained full use of language and communications skills. But he had no memory of his past up to the point his shuttle went down on the Hellas Planitia Basin.

When Soltan Voltanieu found out that his son had lost his memory, he demanded that the Terran doctors fix the problem under penalty of death. When the doctors failed and then explained to him that Jude had lost the part of his brain that contained most of his life's memories,

Soltan Voltanieu blamed them for ruining his son's brain and had them executed.

Dr. Kosigan was the only Martian physician left on Mars who had advanced knowledge of nano technology in the operating room. When Soltan Voltanieu had come to him and demanded that he repair his son's memory, Kosigan explained to him that the only man on Mars who could perform such a miracle was Dr. Nicolas Alfano. Voltanieu went into a rage and threatened to kill Kosigan, but the good doctor was not intimidated. He told him that Jude's brain was in very fragile condition, and that if he killed him, his son would not survive more than a few days.

Voltanieu decided not to kill the doctor for the time being. He had been visiting his son every day for the past two weeks, and now whenever he entered Ward C, everyone on the floor was on pins and needles.

He approached Kosigan who hid his nerves and struggled to appear calm.

"Well, Kosigan, have you made any progress today?" the ghoulish looking Voltanieu demanded.

"Yes, Governor. We have stabilized a great deal of the rebuilt tissue and Colonel Voltanieu's cognitive ability has improved by ten percent," responded the doctor, hoping to appease the man known as 'The Butcher of Mars.'

"Has he regained his memory?" he asked, with restrained impatience.

"As I've already explained, Governor, the Terran doctors used the nanites willy-nilly without consulting me, and as a result they replaced the missing tissue from your son's brain without mapping its connective pathways. Your son will never regain his memory. That part of his memory and personality is gone forever. The best you can hope for is that your son can be re-educated to do the work that he had been trained to do originally," Kosigan replied, holding back his sarcasm. Jude Voltanieu had killed and tortured hundreds, perhaps thousands, of innocent Martians in the short two years that he'd been on Mars.

"My patience is running short, Doctor. There must be something you can do!" Voltanieu said threateningly.

Kosigan had spent the last fourteen years of his life terrified of the

Terran regime. But the raid on Constitution Park had given all Martians the strength to stand up against murderers and bullies like Voltanieu. Lately the doctor was becoming angrier and angrier with each new abuse heaped on him and his staff by Voltanieu.

"You and your people made sure to arrest, torture and kill most of the top Martian doctors, surgeons and top medical researchers within the first few months of the occupation. You have no one to blame for your son's condition but yourselves. Given time, your son's brain will repair itself and he will be able to function like any other normal individual his age."

"But my son was not like anyone else!" Voltanieu yelled back at Kosigan, losing his temper. "He… he's special…, he can do things that no one else is capable of doing!" the vampire railed, banging his hand on the wall.

Kosigan flinched away from Voltanieu's fist, knowing that this psychotic murderer could suddenly, without much provocation, order the entire wing of the hospital put to death. Still, he had to convince this bastard that no matter whom he tortured or killed, his son would never regain his memory and personality.

"The only other man in the solar system better qualified to treat your son is Vishnu Badnavu in India, but I understand that he's very elderly and can't travel. You son, however, is able to travel. Perhaps you can take him to Badnavu," the doctor suggested, hoping that Voltanieu would remove his son from Latonga City hospital and therefore take away the threat of imminent death from him and his staff.

"Bah!" he uttered, pushing Kosigan away with his hand in disgust. The walls were closing all around Soltan Voltanieu. Terran senators had come to see him to inform him that he would be replaced within a short time if he didn't improve the situation here on Mars. They specifically forbade him to carry on any further raids and mass arrests. They had tied his hands! And without Jude's psychic skills he had lost the ability to identify those who were plotting against him!

He burst into his son's private room.

"Oh hello sir," Jude said upon seeing him, his eyes lowered submissively. He was afraid of this man who claimed to be his father. Whenever he showed up, Jude began to feel sick to his stomach and the feeling would not go away until Voltanieu left.

"Do you remember me?' Voltanieu asked brusquely.

"Yes, sir, you're my father."

"No damn it! That's not what I meant!" yelled Voltanieu, his face turning unusually red. "I meant do you remember me like before?"

"I'm ... I'm sorry, sir, I've tried to remember the things you told me... but I just can't.. I can't remember anything! All I know is what I've learned since I woke up in this place... I mean... this hospital," Jude replied, close to tears. He was beginning to feel nauseous and his body was trembling uncontrollably.

"Governor," Kosigan said stepping in. "You won't gain anything by yelling at the boy," he argued forcefully. "As I said before, Jude should not be subjected to physical or emotional stress. His brain is very fragile and he could rupture a vessel and suffer a brain hemorrhage."

Soltan Voltanieu stared at his son with rage and frustration broiling inside of him. With his fists in knots, he turned around and stormed out of the room.

"Please, Doctor. Keep the ugly man away from me!" Jude whispered, grabbing Kosigan's sleeve.

The doctor was going to yank his arm away from Jude's hold and then say something nasty to him, but realized that the person inside Colonel Jude Voltanieu's body was no longer the same individual who was responsible for so much misery and death. He patted Jude's hand reassuringly and told him that he would try to keep the ugly man away.

For all intents and purposes, the young man lying on this med-bed had been born a month before and was as pure and innocent as a babe.

CHAPTER 25

Force Fields, _n'time_ Radar and a Surprise

March 29th, 2660

A week had passed and Kelem, Ndugu and the others had settled down and were working to come up with effective ways to improve the rebel fleet's technology. The five young miners had become used to Harry's presence and, surprisingly, Lola Irigoyen had grown close to the Kren and had become his favorite game playing partner. Lola just happened to be an avid game player, and now, whenever the workday was done, she and Harry could be found in the rec-room at all hours of the night.

The first Item that Kelem was trying to work on was defensive technology and he asked Harry what devices in his ship could be useful for that purpose. A day later the Kren called for a meeting saying he had an idea.

Harry had remodeled one of the many chambers in his ship and had converted it into a conference room with appropriate furniture. Kelem was amazed by Harry's ability to remodel interior spaces with the many fascinating and bizarre power tools that the Kren had invented for building and manufacturing.

"Kelem has asked me to suggest ideas regarding defensive capabilities for the rebel fleet," Harry was saying. "Your current weapons technology is based on high speed projectiles released from rail guns as plasma and chemically powered missiles with explosive warheads. Kelem asked me if I knew of a way to develop a shielding technology based on Kren science, and I believe that I can help you develop such a thing."

"What is it, Harry? We're dying to know," Kelem said with great interest.

"Kren ships travel through space by compressing time/space ahead of it and expanding it directly behind the ship. This allows our ships to travel faster than light. The problem with faster than light travel is that a vessel traveling at relativistic speeds gains more and more mass the closer it comes to the speed of light, eventually reaching infinite mass. The Kren solved this problem of mass increase by surrounding the ship with an antigravity field that diminishes the mass of the ship and actually makes the ship weigh less the more speed it gathers."

"Harry, what kind of energy does your ship use to provide the immense amount of power that such an antigrav field must require?" Ndugu asked with amazement.

"To put it simply, without engaging in a deep discussion of quantum mechanics, the ship uses the surplus energy of the push-pull time/space field generators to power the shield."

"So, you're saying that the greater the speed, the more power that is supplied to the shield?" Kelem asked, very impressed.

"That's correct. When the Kren developed the push/pull technology they ran into the 'infinite mass' problem but then they realized that the process produced an immense amount of surplus energy. They eventually solved the problem by recycling the energy into an antigrav shield generator."

"Fascinating," Hiram declared. "But how can the fleet use this technology? None of our ships can travel that fast or has an engine powerful enough to generate such large amounts of power."

"You don't need that kind of power if you're simply trying to repel rail gun projectiles and explosive missiles," Harry replied, his eyes blinking while his compound jaws moved incessantly.

"I think what Harry is saying is that he can help us develop a shield generator that will make a ship's hull invulnerable with very little power. Am I right?" Ndugu interjected.

"Yes, Ndugu, that's exactly what I mean."

"How much power are we talking about?" Kelem asked, his mind already engaged in mathematical calculations.

"No more than twenty megawatts."

"Hell! The old Solar Nations lander generates ten times that just for the antigrav lifters!" Ndugu commented with excitement.

"The New Hope for Freedom had several brand new high output generators, still unused when we left the Rusty Bucket," Alonzo Stanton reminded everyone.

"Yes, but we need to build one from scratch and test it here in Harry's ship before we return to the Bucket," Bea Niguchi advised.

"No need to return to your other ship. I can manufacture a generator in a few of your hours," Harry stated matter of fact.

By the following day, Harry had built the generator in an amazingly short time and connected it to the massive hull of the Kren ship which had been dubbed 'The Cricket' by the five miners in honor of its captain. Kelem and Ndugu rigged up a makeshift rail gun and mounted it on the outside of the lander. With some apprehension they exited The Cricket, and after Harry activated the generator, which created an iridescent haze around the vessel, Kelem fired a shot at the very edge of the ship's circumference to be safe, and saw the plasma projectile glance off and disappear into space. As they continued the test they fired the gun at more direct angles with the same results. No matter how close or far the rail gun fired from, the field repelled the shot with impunity. They didn't have any missiles with which to test the device with, but Kelem was sure that it would repel those as well.

Harry's generator design was very advanced and yet extremely simple in principle. Hiram and Alonzo could not believe how Harry's small generator, in comparison with equal capacity human-designed generators, was capable of producing so much power.

The group was jubilant and celebrated that night with a big party. Hiram, Bea and Peter baked a cake and Harry and Ndugu entertained the group with African folk songs, classical music and popular Martian songs.

Kelem's instincts had paid off. Not only had Harry provided the rebels with a way to defend themselves against Terran guns and missiles, but was now also collaborating with Kelem to develop a way to detect when an *n'time* ship was about to re-appear in three dimensional space. If they pulled this one off, the Terran fleet could be defeated within a month or less and Mars would be liberated soon after. Kelem could see the light at the end of the tunnel and his return to Plantanimus seemed closer every day.

"Time is like a highway and the three dimensional universe travels on that 'highway'. *N'time* ships disengage themselves from the time 'stream' and for a period of 'time' the ship appears to have ceased to exist," Harry was saying.

"That's right," Kelem replied. "In truth, the ship has not really ceased to exist, it simply has shifted its entire mass onto one of the eleven known dimensions parallel to ours. The ship follows the 'curvature' of space and for an instant, exists as a quantum state 'absurdity' within one or more of these exotic dimensions. The ship's navigational computer then sends out a signal that looks for a new logical time and space in the three dimensional world, where it can shift its mass back into three dimensional time/space. But, Harry, how can we detect when a ship is about to reappear?" Kelem asked.

"Find the exact frequency and amplitude of that signal, and you can extrapolate when and where that ship will re-appear," Harry proposed.

"By God, Harry, you're right!" Kelem exclaimed, jumping up from his chair as Harry's simple proposition caused Kelem to have a Eureka moment. "The ship's computers send out a quantum field signal to probe the exact time and space of re-assembly in three dimensional space to make sure that there's no other object in the way! All we have to do is develop an antenna that is calibrated to detect a quantum field distortion in three dimensional space and we have *n'time* radar!"

"Yes, Kelem, but one antenna can only work directionally, so we would have to solve how to make the antenna omnidirectional or build spherical arrays for each and every ship," Ndugu pointed out.

Harry and Kelem dove into solving the technical problems, and with their two amazing intellects working together, they designed an omnidirectional antenna that, theoretically, could detect incoming *n'time* ships from any direction. A week later they had built a workable model. Now all Kelem had to do was to return to the rebel fleet, test the device with an *n'time* ship, then implement all this new technology into all their ships. No small task!

"Harry, on behalf of all of us here and from all Martians, I thank you from the bottom of my heart," Kelem was saying to Harry in the rec-room which was now empty late at night. "I'm sure to return here before the end of September, six months from now. Will you go back to hibernating?" he asked.

Harry remained quiet for a while and Kelem wondered why the delay in response.

"I have grown fond of you and the others and I find myself missing the company of humans. I wish to accompany you in your effort to liberate your fellow Martians."

Kelem was dumbstruck. Harry had used the word 'fond' and 'missing' to express himself in terms that seemed to indicate that Harry was experiencing emotions. And beyond that, he was asking to come along and join the fight against the Terran fleet!

"Harry, I welcome your coming along with us, but that means that you're going to come in contact with many other humans while you're with us," Kelem warned him.

"I wouldn't have to meet any other humans if I don't allow anyone else to come onto my ship."

"You mean you want to bring your ship into the solar system and use it to engage the Terrans in battle?" Kelem asked, surprised.

"Isn't that what we've been doing all along - to prepare my ship for battle?" the Kren asked innocently.

"No, honestly I did not expect you to want to come with us. After all, the Kren are non-aggressive and Mother told you to learn from us but not make direct contact with humans at large."

"I think Mother changed me more than I thought at first. Lately, I've been formulating my own ideas and concepts as to what a Kren should and should not do. And I believe that this is what Mother wanted me to experience ultimately, to think in new ways and change the future of our species. I have become like no other Kren and I'm sure that's why Mother asked me to come with you."

"You mean Mother wanted you to be a new kind of Kren? But why? Why would she want to do that? Isn't that dangerous and wouldn't the results be unpredictable?" Kelem replied, worried that he had inflicted terrible harm to another species, by simply coming in contact with them.

"Your statement reveals that you're experiencing guilt. You think that you're responsible for this new development," Harry responded accurately.

"Harry, you're freaking me out!" Kelem replied, laughing nervously. "Yes, that's exactly what I'm thinking. I just can't help feeling that we humans have corrupted your logical Kren mind and have infected you with emotions and all the other foibles that make humans unpredictable and sometimes dangerous."

"I think Mother was concerned for the future of the Kren species. The Kren were once similar to humans in terms of behavior. Over millennia we grew too numerous to coexist peacefully in such great numbers. So at one point in our history, we took to space and decided to adopt a hive-mind culture, with each hive having a limited amount of Kren to preserve the species, but at the cost of individuality and personal expression. When Mother communicated with you through me, I now realize that she had a revelation. Until recently, I wouldn't have been able to make such a leap in logical reasoning if Mother hadn't meant for me to develop the ability to think so intuitively."

"So, I must go back to my original assumption, that by merely communicating with Mother telepathically, I have unwittingly changed the destiny of the Kren species," Kelem commented, feeling guilty once again.

"While that may be so, Kelem, it doesn't necessarily mean that the results will be bad. For all we know, the new Kren will be more advanced and beneficial to the universe at large," Harry replied.

"I hope so, Harry, but how is this new Kren generation going to come about? Doesn't it mean that you have to find a Kren female, like a queen, to start a new hive?"

"That's not necessary, Kelem. I now understand what Mother did when she changed me."

"Oh, and what is that?" Kelem asked, confused.

"Mother changed me into a female. I'm gestating the first generation of the new Kren."

CHAPTER 26

The Rebels Strike Back

April 12th, 2660

"Sir, that object has appeared again, this time ten million kilometers from its previous location," the young ensign informed the commander of the Terran Navy destroyer, the 'Hans Lüdemann'. The captain, sitting in his command chair, made a grimace and looked at the small screen attached to the end of his right armrest.

"That's impossible, ensign! No rebel ship is capable of traveling that fast. You must be looking at a comet or a large rogue asteroid.

"I'm sorry sir, but the object just returned to where it was located previously," the ensign insisted politely, trying to remain patient. Captain Brandon Meriweather was one of a new batch of commanding officers that had graduated from the ISA with the full rank of Captain only two years before. The officers who had participated in the invasion of Mars had all but retired by now, and the new captains and admirals who were now in charge of the Terran space fleet were mostly political appointees.

"Check your settings again, ensign. There must be something wrong with your equipment," the captain added, and then he turned to his first officer. "Winslow, what kind of crew is this that can't tell the difference between a comet and a man-made object?"

Commander Winslow shrugged politely and avoided the question. He disliked Meriweather who himself didn't know his ass from his elbow.

"Navigator!" the captain yelled, "plot me a solution to the last position that Ensign Narub just showed me. And be quick about it!"

The navigator plotted a destination to the coordinates that Ensign Narub had sent to his console and soon the hum of the ship's *n'time* generator began rattling the decks of the Hans Lüdemann. The Duraminium shields closed and the ship disappeared from space, instantly reassembling itself 9,574 million kilometers from its previous location in time and space.

The Terran destroyer was now further from Mars than any other Terran military ship had been in a long time. The captain was about to order the pilot to turn on the engines for maneuvering when the ship was rocked by a powerful rail gun hit on its loading dock's pressure door. The alarm claxons kicked in and the bridge lights turned red.

"What the hell was that?" the befuddled Meriweather asked, clueless that his ship had just been hit by a weapon.

"Sir! We're under attack! You know that large object that you insisted was a comet? Well sir, it's a ship. As a matter of fact, it's the biggest damned ship that I've ever seen!" Ensign Narub informed him.

The bridge's main screen came on, and floating directly above the command deck was a humongous metallic sphere surrounded by an iridescent haze that was both fascinating and frightening at the same time.

"Mother of God!" Commander Winslow said under his breath.

"Fire on that ship, Commander, immediately!" Captain Meriweather yelled in a panic.

Winslow pressed a button on his console. "Fire control, fire all guns at that ship!"

The Hans Lüdemann rocked violently, but not from the recoil of its own rail guns.

"Sir! Ensign Narub yelled again. "Two Martian frigates on our portside just took out our rail guns!"

"Martian frigates what the …?" the captain began saying when the bridge's speaker system came alive.

"Attention Terran destroyer, you are surrounded by ships of the Free Martian Space Fleet. Surrender immediately or you will be destroyed."

"Disregard!" Meriweather said, about to order missiles fired when a heavy 'clunk' was felt by all, coming from the bridge's ceiling bulkhead. "Now what?" Meriwether said with frustration.

"Terran destroyer, I just placed a one megaton atomic device on your ship's hull. Surrender now or I'll detonate the bomb," came the second warning from the large spherical monstrosity looming over the destroyer.

"Sir! That thing above us is emitting a radioactive signal! Ensign Narub announced with a shaky voice.

Captain Meriweather froze and couldn't think of a proper response to a situation for which he was totally and hopelessly unprepared. He turned around and looked at Commander Winslow, his eyes betraying his total fear and mental paralysis.

"Ensign," Commander Winslow said calmly, "inform the Martian vessel that we surrender."

"Sir?" Ensign Narub asked, hoping that he heard wrong.

Commander Winslow got up from his chair, floated over to Narub's console and pressed the com button himself. "Martian Vessel, we surrender. You can board us from our other loading dock on our starboard side," he added calmly.

"Please instruct your crew to put down all personal weapons, and to remain where they are. You will not be harmed and you will be treated fairly so long as you don't attack our boarding party," the voice from the spherical ship ordered.

"Understood, Martian Vessel. Our crew will comply."

Kelem leaned back in his chair and a cheer went up in The Cricket's command center that had been the rec-room. Hiram, Peter, Bea, Alonzo and Lola were dancing with joy at having captured a big Terran destroyer without any loss of life.

"Was this a typical battle, Kelem?" Harry asked, wondering if this was a normal way to conduct war among humans.

Kelem had decided to continue calling the Kren Harry instead of 'Harriett'. He didn't want Ndugu and the others to start worrying that little baby Kren would be crawling about any minute now. Even though 'Harriett' had informed him that she would not be giving birth for another three months, Kelem thought it best to keep the secret between the two of them.

"No, Harry, we were very lucky this time. The next encounter might not go so well," Kelem told the alien."

"What will happen to the prisoners?" the future Kren queen wanted to know.

"We will commandeer the destroyer and bring it to the New Hope for Freedom, and then the crew will be incarcerated in the former transport ship and will remain prisoners until the end of the war," Kelem informed Harry.

A few minutes later, Kelem transferred to the Volta, Admiral Valchek's frigate. The rebel command had decided that General Kelem Rogeston should be the person to accept the surrender of the first Terran ship to be captured by the rebel fleet. Besides, no one in the fleet had yet learned how to pilot an *n'time* ship.

"Well, General!" Admiral Valchek said with a big smile on her face, "you continue surpassing your previous accomplishments. Many are saying that there's nothing that you can't do."

"We've had this conversation before, Veronica, and you know how I feel about this kind of thing. For one thing, I didn't do this alone. Captain Hugh, your former exec, commands the Volta now, and it was he and his crew who fired on the destroyer. Me and my people just showed up and parked The Cricket in front of the Terrans."

"I'm sorry Kelem, it's just that I myself never thought that this day would come," she remarked. "Wherever you found that gigantic metal ball, I'm certainly glad that it's on our side."

"Damn right! Now, let's go and take possession of that ship!"

Kelem, Captain Ron Hugh and Rusty Deveraux entered the loading dock of the Hans Lüdemann and were met by Commander Jonas Winslow. The dark haired Caucasian man gave a sharp military salute. "Welcome to the Hans Lüdemann. I'm Jonas Winslow, the Hans Lüdemann's exec officer. To whom do I have the honor of addressing?" he asked, looking at Kelem who was obviously the man in charge.

"I am General Kelem Rogeston, Commander of the Free Martian Rebel Fleet. Why isn't your captain here to greet me?" Kelem demanded.

"I'm sorry, General. Captain Meriweather is indisposed. His absence is not meant as disrespect to you. The man is truly incapacitated," Winslow expressed apologetically.

Kelem read the man's mind and discovered that Brandon Meriweather was a political appointee and that Winslow was really running the ship. "Very well, Commander. In that case, I suggest that you remove Captain Meriweather from command and assume leadership of your crew."

"Yes, General, I will do that immediately," Winslow replied, sensing that this man knew a thing or two about command. "May I ask what will become of my crew?"

"Your entire crew will be transported to a large ship that will serve as your prison until the end of the war. As I mentioned before, you will be treated fairly so long as you don't attempt to escape, though I seriously doubt that any of you would be able to succeed in reaching that goal where you're going. You will be fed two meals a day and be allowed to exercise once a week. I must warn you, however, that if any of your men begin spouting Phalanx propaganda or insult any of my people by demeaning their Martian heritage, I can't be responsible for the safety of those individuals."

"You won't hear any of that trash talk from my crew, General!" Winslow replied with conviction.

Kelem read the man again and found that he was being honest. Terran Navy personnel were apparently not influenced by the Phalanx these days.

"That's to your advantage then," Kelem commented. "Captain Hugh and his men here," Kelem said pointing to the captain and the thirty rebel troops that had boarded the ship with him, "will follow you and assume command of this vessel. Please instruct your crew to assemble in this loading dock where you will remain under guard until we reach our destination."

Acting captain Winslow led Ron Hugh and his men into the ship proper. Rusty Deveraux, who had begged and pleaded to come with Kelem and who had refused to be denied the privilege, looked somewhat troubled. Kelem sensed his mood and turned to him.

"What's the matter, Rusty? What's bothering you?"

"These Terrans are not what I expected," Rusty remarked deep in thought.

"I agree," Admiral Valchek echoed. "I was expecting a bunch of rabid Phalanx goons. But these men appear to be trained professionals simply doing their jobs."

"Good observation, you two. I believe that we're going to find similar attitudes and disposition among other Terran Navy crews. But, don't let the fact that they're not Phalanx fanatics fool you into thinking that they're not going to come after us with all they've got. However, with our new technical advantage, we'll be able to subdue the Terran fleet sooner rather than later. These men are out here feeling confident in the belief that the rebel fleet is over and done with. If we move fast, the military brass on Earth won't be able to adjust their tactics quickly enough to keep us from reaching Mars in a few weeks."

"Amen to that!" Rusty agreed. Admiral Valchek began thinking about her old warren in Latonga City and how she was going to fix it up when she returned home after fifteen long years.

April 26ᵗʰ 2660

Two weeks later, Kelem and the now expanded Free Martian Rebel Fleet, had captured one of the big Terran dreadnaughts that Billy warned him about. This time the crew of the big 'ship of the line' did fight back fiercely. The disappearance of the Hans Lüdemann had alerted the Terrans that something had gone wrong. The joint chiefs decided to send the "Rupert Morau", a battleship that rivaled the Argos in size and was armed to the hilt with rail guns and missiles. The dreadnaught had come out to investigate what had happened to the missing destroyer.

The Hans Lüdemann had a crew of thirty nine with no security troops. The "Rupert Morau," however, carried a crew of one hundred and fifteen, twenty of whom were Terran Marines who refused to surrender in spite of the ship captain's order to do so.

Kelem had no choice but to order an attack on the deck where the marines were holed up. A barrage of rail gun fire from the Volta decompressed the deck where the men had barricaded themselves, and the marines died instantly.

Kelem knew that even though the rebels had been training for weeks now, they were no match for highly skilled Terran Marines in a close quarters skirmish.

The rebel fleet now consisted of The Cricket, the destroyer Firebrand, formerly known as the Hans Lüdemann, and now the dreadnaught God O' War, formerly known as the Rupert Morau. The two ships had been fitted with Harry's shields. The rest of the fleet consisted of five more Martian Navy frigates, thirty five asteroid herders, twenty transports of varying size and three hundred small shuttles.

Kelem had maintained contact with Nicolas Alfano via Quantum Tide dream state and kept getting reports from his former mentor. The Terrans were now aware that they had a problem and had sent an entire battle group from Earth to Mars. Kelem knew that they would soon come out to the edge of the solar system and engage the rebel fleet *en masse*.

Rusty Deveraux was promoted to admiral and Ndugu was given command of one of the Martian Navy frigates when its captain died unexpectedly from natural causes. He was now in charge of the Nation of Love.

April 30ᵗʰ 2660

All the commanding officers had gathered on the Man O' War to discuss strategy.

"When are they coming out here?" one of the frigate captains asked.

"My guess is that they're almost ready to depart. According to my contact, all battle group personnel on leave in Latonga City went back to their ships last night, which tells me that they'll be showing up here within a day, maybe less," Kelem explained.

"So far we've only dealt with one ship at a time, but I don't know how we're going to deal with multiple *n'time* signatures all at once," Rusty commented.

"I have an idea," Kelem suggested.

The others nodded and waited with interest. They had come to respect Kelem's military decisions. Even though he'd had no formal training, his intellect seemed capable of planning military tactics with great success.

Let's bring fifty of the fastest small shuttles in the fleet to the Man O' War and put them in the loading docks of the ship. When we get *n'time* radar hits from the incoming battle group, we'll have the pilots board the shuttles, decompress the docks and have them ready to take off at Admiral Valchek's command."

Veronica Valchek had taken charge of the dreadnaught, and the ship was now the flag ship of the rebel fleet.

"What will you do with those shuttles?" Admiral Valchek inquired.

"In the twentieth century, the Terrans fought a planet wide war called World War II. The Americans fought the Japanese in the Pacific Ocean. That war was the first war where aircraft carriers were used with great effectiveness. The Terran space navy has no small ships because they don't believe that they are effective in combat. Their tactics are based on battleship to battleship confrontations, so the giant does not know how to defend against a series of attacks by angry stinging bees," Kelem explained with a wink.

"Of course, I see!" Admiral Valchek exclaimed. "Their rail guns can't fire rapidly or accurately enough at small fast moving targets!"

"Exactly! But our stinging bees will be carrying medium size rail guns and we will put a few missiles in some of them. The Man O' War will go after their biggest ship, which I believe is the only other dreadnaught in the Terran fleet. Meanwhile, the Firebrand, The Cricket and the frigates will engage destroyers, cruisers and frigates. The fighters will support the attack on the dreadnaught and when it looks like we've disabled it or destroyed it, the fighters will switch to the destroyers, cruisers, etcetera. Meanwhile, asteroid herders will stand by in the rear and come in only to rescue damaged or incapacitated fighters."

"I've got rail guns and a few missiles in the Rusty Bucket. I can give them hell General, just give me a chance!" Rusty yelled from the back and the group laughed.

"Sorry Admiral Deveraux, a herder is just too big a target and too slow to maneuver. You'll be putting your crew and family in unnecessary danger," Kelem reminded him.

"I'll have the shuttles brought to the Man O" War," Admiral Valchek announced.

"Great, one of those shuttles will be my lander," Kelem informed the admiral.

The room burst into protest at the thought of Kelem participating as a fighter pilot in the coming battle.

"You all know that I am the best pilot in the fleet. I'm Sorry Admirals Valchek and Deveraux, but the men and women in those shuttles are going to need an expert hand out there and I'm the man to do it!"

An argument followed which Kelem ended up winning, as usual.

Sixteen hours later the fleet was ready and not a moment too soon. Hiram Goldblatt, temporarily in command of The Cricket sent out the alarm. Multiple *n'time* radar hits had appeared on his console. He sent out the probable re-appearance coordinates and the rebel fleet lined up ready to begin firing the moment the Terran ships materialized in space.

The first ship to appear was the big dreadnaught and the Man O' War began firing on it immediately. The Terrans were caught off guard and the big lumbering leviathan fired its rocket engines to get out of the Man O' War's line of fire, but it was too late. The Firebrand now positioned on the opposite side of the big ship, shot a missile into the dreadnaught's tail and disabled its engines, immobilizing the big cigar shaped vessel.

Kelem launched his lander from the Man O' War and approached the big ship from the front. The dreadnaught's rail guns were firing wildly in all directions trying to repel the attack. The lander was being hit repeatedly, but Harry's field generator kept the ship's hull from being penetrated by the plasma streams relentlessly coming at it. Kelem fired his two main rail guns and saw a portion of the of the dreadnaught's nose explode and decompress. Several bodies were thrown into space. Many of them were not wearing space suits. Kelem winced at the sight but shook his head and focused on the task at hand. He came around the side of the ship and fired a missile at the command deck, but in the confusion, a plasma stream hit his missile and it exploded before it hit the ship.

Kelem banked left and came at the command deck again. He prepped another missile and then a big impact flipped his lander over, and immediately, rail gun fire began hitting the lander's hull. He realized that he'd been hit by a Terran missile and that the explosion had fried the lander's shield generator. He decided that he was going to hit that command deck anyway and he turned toward the dreadnaught again. This time he fired the missile successfully, and the command deck vaporized in front of his eyes. Then one of the dreadnaught's big rail guns turned slowly and fired. Kelem banked to avoid the inevitable when the lander was suddenly scooped up by a herder's basket and the plasma stream hit the herder full on. Kelem felt the lander shudder violently from the impact on the herder, but fortunately, the herder's shield generator took the brunt of the hit.

"You can thank me later for saving your ass, General!" Rusty's voice said, laughing in his helmet's radio.

"Thanks, Rusty, I thought that gun was going to do me in," Kelem replied, grateful for still being alive.

"You're done for the day, Generalissimo Rogeston," Rusty informed him with mock seriousness. "You're going to stay in the rear like a good general should. You can watch the rest of the battle from my bridge drinking vodka with me."

"No argument here," Kelem replied, knowing that he couldn't return to the fight. Five minutes later Kelem was on the herder's bridge communicating with Admiral Valchek by way of video.

"The dreadnaught is out of commission, Kelem, they just surrendered. We also blew away three destroyers and it looks like several cruisers have been disabled," then she paused. "Hold on, I'm getting reports that the entire group is asking for a cease fire!" she suddenly shouted without realizing that she had done so, and then Kelem saw several bridge crew members jump up and break out in celebration on the vid screens in the Bucket's main bridge. Admiral Valchek recovered from her own shock and surprise and yelled at her staff to return to their posts. The bridge quieted down.

"Kelem! They've surrendered!" Veronica Valchek said, her voice shaking with emotion.

"You mean that they gave up, just like that?" Kelem asked, not believing his eyes and ears.

"Apparently the Terran Navy doesn't have the stomach to fight a commited group of Martians fighting for the right to return to their homeland," Veronica Valchek replied with tears in her eyes.

"Tell them to shut all their engines off and prepare to be boarded! I'll meet you on the Man O' War", Kelem said reaching for his pressure suit.

"Wait! I'm coming with you! I want to see the expression on the dreadnaught's captain's face when you walk onto his bridge," Rusty pleaded.

"Rusty, didn't you see?" Kelem said with a bitter laugh. "I blew the dreadnaught's command deck with that last missile I shot."

"You're probably right! But I want to come anyway. Hey! If that dreadnaught can be fixed, will you let me have it?" Rusty asked in jest.

"Yes, I think it's time that the esteemed Admiral Deveraux had his own battle ship," Kelem replied seriously.

Rusty laughed at Kelem's apparent joke, not realizing that tomorrow he would be in command of the damaged leviathan.

Kelem and Rusty met Admiral Valchek on the hangar deck of the disabled Terran flag ship and were surprised that it had twenty five fighters, but that they hadn't been used. After they interrogated the crew, they discovered that the captain had decided that he didn't need the fighter pilots for this mission. He was wrong. Fortunately, he would not be court martialed for his serious tactical mistake. The captain had perished along with the admiral in command of the battle group, the exec, and most of the bridge officers, when Kelem's missile hit the bridge.

The Terran Navy's command structure was apparently over bureaucratized and top heavy. Once the snake's head was cut off, the fleet fell apart not knowing how to proceed.

With one lucky missile, Kelem had brought about the defeat of an entire battle group of over three hundred ships. The Terrans only had one hundred and fifty battle ships left in their entire navy to defend Mars, the Moon and Earth. It was now the end of April and Kelem realized that the rebel fleet could reach Mars within two weeks.

CHAPTER 27

Filicide, Torture and Ruination

May 7th, 2660

Jude Voltanieu was screaming in agony from the effects of the machine that was causing him to see horrible visions of people being tortured, dismembered and killed by his own hand. His father had brought him and Dr. Kosigan from Latonga City Hospital to Stalag 47 in a last ditch attempt to restore his son's memory and psychic Powers.

Dr. Kosigan stood with his back against the rear wall of Soltan Voltanieu's interrogation chamber with tears in his eyes. He was shaking with anger and hatred for this monster that would torture his own son with such violence. He had a notion to run up to the bastard and sink a syringe with an overdose of anesthetic but the two Phalanx goons to his left and right would have stopped him. His best hope was to treat the poor boy and attempt to repair the brain damage that his father's machine was causing.

"Please…. please… no more..! " Jude Voltanieu panted out of breath, begging his father to stop. His emaciated body, from being in a hospital med-bed for so many weeks, was covered in sweat. Blood was dripping from his ears and nose, caused by the pressure the machine exerted on his head. He was on the verge of passing out.

"Think, boy! Think!" Voltanieu yelled at him, his hair and clothing disheveled, his forehead bathed in sweat. "Damn it, I know that you remember!" Voltanieu screamed, repeating the same thing over and over.

"Please… please no more!" was all that the boy could say.

Soltan Voltanieu closed his eyed and pressed the button to start the cycle again.

Jude Voltanieu arched his back and opened his jaw wide as a guttural sound came from his throat. The veins in his head puffed up and his face turned red from the strain caused by the voltage from the machine's electrodes. Now his body began to convulse and the metal chair shook violently from his uncontrolled gyrations.

Even the Phalanx goons were flinching now, themselves beginning to feel nauseated by the horrible spectacle they were witnessing. Finally, Jude Voltanieu collapsed and his body went limp.

Voltanieu shut the machine off and turned to the doctor. "Revive him, Kosigan!" he demanded.

The doctor took his med kit, leaned over the boy and surreptitiously injected him with a dose of anesthetic in his right arm away from his father's and the two goon's line of sight. "It's no good Voltanieu, he's had a seizure. I'm afraid that you've destroyed your son's brain," he announced, praying that the demon would believe him and stop tormenting his own son.

Voltanieu turned around and punched the wall with his fist and tugged at his hair. Then he began to pace the room back and forth with his eyes darting left and right muttering to himself. The goons had never seen him act like this and they were unsure as to what they should do next.

Dr. Kosigan gathered his courage. "Voltanieu!" he called out, yelling for effect. The ghoul stopped in mid stride but didn't look back at him. "If you want your son to have any chance of recovery, you have to let me take him back to Latonga City!" he pleaded.

"You can throw him out of an airlock for all I care! He's not my son anymore, he's just a piece of trash like any other goddamned Martian!"

Kosigan motioned to the two goons to help him unstrap Jude from the torture chair and get him out of Stalag 47 before Voltanieu changed his mind. The two men moved fast and rushed to help the doctor take Jude out. Even hard core Phalanx goons possessed more humanity than the wretched Soltan Voltanieu. Kosigan made it to the shuttle that had brought them to Stalag 47 from Latonga City. When the ship took off, he closed his eyes and sighed with relief.

"Doctor", the Black Guard pilot said, turning around. "Where do you want to take the Colonel?"

"Huh? What do you mean?" Kosigan asked confused. He was sure that they were heading back to Latonga City Hospital as per his request.

"I'm sure you don't want to bring this poor man to the hospital where the Dragon can get at him again, right?" the pilot said, pointing to Jude who was strapped securely in a gurney to one of the cabin's bulkheads.

Kosigan became nervous fearing that this was some sort of cruel Phalanx trick to make him admit that he was a member of the resistance.

"I'm afraid that I don't understand," he answered, trying to remain calm.

"Look, Doctor, you don't have to say anything. We're going to drop you off at Havana Flats and you can do what you want from there," the pilot told him.

Kosigan nodded and decided to wait and see what developed.

Two hours later, the Black Guard shuttle touched down on the landing pad of a commercial warehouse. The company's name, Fisher-Madjal, was displayed on the loading dock's pressure door. The big door opened and the pilot brought the shuttle in.

As soon as the dock was re-pressurized the shuttle's door opened and Marla Hassett stuck her head in. "Hello Bernard," she said as she stepped in.

"Marla?" Dr. Kosigan asked, now more confused than before.

"I'm sure that you're wondering what the hell is going on," she announced.

"You could say that!" he replied, looking nervously at the Black Guard pilot.

"Let's get the colonel out of the shuttle and then I will explain," Marla suggested.

Three warehouse employees helped unload Jude and then the Black Guard shuttle left. On the way down in the elevator the doctor finally demanded an explanation, curious to know how and why a Black

Guard pilot had deposited him and his patient in what was obviously a resistance hideout.

"All right, Marla, what the hell is going on?" he asked looking at her and the three men with suspicion.

"The pilot and a few others in Stalag 47 are working with us. Most of them were drafted into the Black Guard by forced conscription. You don't have to worry about anything connecting you to us. But we had to rescue Jude Voltanieu. Nicolas Alfano wanted him taken away from his father."

"Nicolas Alfano is alive?" Bernard Kosigan exclaimed with shock. "I thought the Phalanx had him executed several years ago!"

"No, he was a prisoner in Stalag 47 for over twelve years. We broke him out a few months ago."

"What does he want with Voltanieu's son?"

"I don't know, Bernard. All I know is that he considered his rescue of prime importance."

"Marla, you should know that this poor boy here," he said pointing to Jude Voltanieu's unconscious body, "is near death. I don't think that he will last more than a week. I doubt that even Nicolas, who invented the brain repair nanites, will be able to help him."

"I don't think that Nicolas is trying to save the boy. His main wish was to get him away from Voltanieu." Marla commented.

"There's no punishment severe or painful enough for that evil son of a bitch!" Dr. Kosigan swore under his breath.

In the dark confines of his interrogation room, Soltan Voltanieu continued pacing back and forth, his mind a chaotic jumble of conflicting emotions, mostly hate and anger, but also a sense of desperation and a gnawing fear that kept creeping up from his subconscious like a voice whispering unwelcome news. A week earlier, Marshall Heinrich Von Plame, the military commander of Terran forces on Mars, had advised him that the rebel fleet had defeated the Terran Space Navy and to expect an attack within days. The man also recommended that Voltanieu should have his own *n'time* luxury yacht fueled and ready to go.

Von Plame had withdrawn many of his troops from the planet in anticipation of a possible victory by the Martian fleet. But Soltan Voltanieu had no intention of surrendering to the rebels under any circumstances. He ordered the Phalanx Black Guards to remain on Mars under penalty of death. And as a last measure of revenge, Voltanieu had high yield atomic bombs placed all over Mars. He carried the wireless detonator under his tunic and planned to destroy the planet if the rebels won and he was forced to return to Earth.

But now he was going to enjoy himself with another round of interrogation of his new prisoner, MMC Chairman Billy Chong. The man had already confessed his involvement in the hijacking of the Argos and had revealed that indeed, Kelem Rogeston was alive and well and had returned to Mars. But now Voltanieu just wanted to see Billy Chong experience the same agony that his now ruined and worthless son had been subjected to.

Kelem Rogeston had destroyed Jude Voltanieu's psychic ability and rendered him useless, and because of him, the rebel fleet was likely to bring the Terran occupation of Mars to a swift end within days. But Voltanieu, now unable to capture, torture and murder Rogeston, was going to take his revenge on Kelem's closest and most beloved friend, Billy Chong. He planned to bring Billy to Earth and ransom him for a ridiculous amount of Kredits. Then, no matter what Kelem Rogeston offered to pay, Voltanieu would execute him publicly and make sure that Rogeston received a video copy of the execution.

The door opened and two Phalanx goons brought Billy in.

"Strap him in," Soltan Voltanieu said with a sinister grin.

CHAPTER 28

The Battle for Mars

May 15th, 2660

"It's still fascinating to me that we can meet this way," Nicolas Alfano was saying, as he stood in the middle of the featureless environment of Kelem's Quantum Tide construct.

"You can thank Zeus and the Dreamers for this development. I would have never learned of this way of communicating without them," Kelem replied.

"Hah! I'd bet that you would have found it on your own eventually. You don't give yourself enough credit for the extraordinary things that you're able to do," Nicolas argued.

"Well, credit should also be given to you, Nicolas. You're the only other human besides Jude Voltanieu who can communicate with me at a distance."

Nicolas' expression changed subtly and Kelem couldn't help but notice it. "What is it Nicolas? I sense that you're disturbed about something." Kelem inquired.

"Now is not the time my boy. Let's concentrate on the task at hand, shall we?" Nicolas said changing the subject.

Kelem could have probed his old friend's mind, but they both respected each other too much to invade the other's privacy. Yet, Kelem felt that Nicolas was carrying a heavy weight in his mind and being close to him he sensed that it was something significant and related to his own life. He was curious and felt tempted to insist that Nicolas divulge what he was keeping from him, but he decided that such matters could wait until Mars was liberated.

"Very well, Nicolas. The time now is 02:00 AM. We're going to strike at 03:00 Am, please wake up and let the others know that the attack will begin within an hour. Stay safe and I'll see you on the ground."

Kelem's image faded and Nicolas touched his right temple, a pre-arranged signal that would act as a trigger to wake him up from his dream state. He opened his eyes and saw Marla Hassett sitting next to his bunk with a smile on her face.

"Well?" she asked expectantly.

"It's on! They'll be over Mars at 03:00 Am," Nicolas said with enthusiasm.

Marla jumped up from her chair and ran from Nicolas' room to warn the others. The resistance had been ready for several days for the arrival of the rebel fleet and its attack on Mars. Kelem had kept Nicolas informed almost every night, and had warned him the day before that they would arrive the next day, early in the morning. Now the resistance shifted into action preparing to strike against the Terrans all over Mars. A significant number of non-resistance civilians who were known not to be collaborators, had also been warned. Those people in turn would alert as many of their friends and neighbors to the coming attack. The resistance knew that ever since the spectacular attack on Constitution Park, the general population was ready for a mass revolt. It wouldn't take much for Martians to rise up and fight to the death to put an end to sixteen years of Terran occupation. But Martians in general had become aware that something was going on. Five weeks before, a Terran space armada had suddenly appeared over Mars and then left within days never to return. A rumor spread that the rebel fleet had defeated the Terran Navy and that the end was near. Additionally, the Terran military had withdrawn many of their troops from Mars soon after that. It didn't take a genius to figure out that something big was about to happen.

Already, civilians had formed their own separate resistance cells and had been attacking the Terrans sporadically for weeks in different places on Mars. The resistance was counting on those new 'cells' to contribute to the fight.

Kelem and the others could only hope that the death toll would remain low. But in the back of everyone's mind lay the fear that the uprising would result in a blood bath. The Terran military had withdrawn most of their troops from the planet, but that still left the Phalanx Black Guard garrisons that numbered about two hundred thousand and were well armed. Most of them were stationed in Latonga City and Amazonis. And adding to the threat of the Black Guard were the one hundred and fifty Terran Navy ships that had arrived from Earth and were spread above the skies of Mars.

The resistance had manufactured old fashion rifles, guns, cannons and explosives with several thousand rounds of ammunition ready to be distributed to the general population once the action began. The Helter Skelters had assigned special squads to distribute these weapons to civilians and quickly teach them how to use them safely. Martian society had been crime and violence free for centuries, but that was about to change in the next few hours.

Now, Kelem was sitting next to Veronica Valchek's command chair on the bridge of the Man O' War ready to give the signal for departure. The dreadnaught had been refitted with several Kren-designed shield generators as had all the other ships in the fleet. Kelem hoped that the Terran fleet would surrender quickly, but he suspected that the crews sent to defend Mars this time, were not the same as the ones that had so easily surrendered before. The rebel fleet now numbered more than five hundred ships, but the rebels were operating captured Terran vessels that were somewhat unfamiliar to them. It was still possible that in spite of all their advantages, the Terrans could win the battle.

Admiral Rusty Deveraux had been given command of the other dreadnaught captured days earlier, now dubbed ironically 'Stalag Deveraux'. The ship had been repaired and stripped of much of its internal equipment and converted to a prison ship. Kelem knew that once the Terran fleet surrendered, the rebels would need space to put the defeated Terran crews. The New Hope for Freedom, still in the orbit of Neptune, was now replete with Terran Navy prisoners captured during the previous battles. As soon as the threat of the fleet was eliminated, the majority of the rebels would land on Mars to join their countrymen in the battle for the cities.

Unbeknownst to many of the rebels and most Martians, Earth was in turmoil. A civil war had broken out between Macro America and the Russo-Chinese territory. The defeat of the Terran fleet and loss of so many ships had triggered a revolution that had been gestating for many years. President for life, Sylvan Montenegro, declared martial law and sent troops to the Americas to quell the rebellion but his troops had been strongly opposed and huge battles were being waged in the west. The Europeans had at first remained neutral, but within a few days, the British Isles and then the territories of France, Spain, Germany and Italy joined in the fight.

The rebels knew that Soltan Voltanieu had been abandoned by the Terrans, but they also knew that the evil bastard was going to take as many Martian lives as he could before they took back their own planet. The fanatical Black Guards would fight to the death and Kelem was sure that Voltanieu had devised some sort of nasty last minute surprise as his last act of defiance. He'd gotten reports from Nicolas that the resistance suspected that high yield nuclear explosives had been placed in strategic areas of Mars. The rebels could win the battle and yet lose their planet to utter destruction.

As Kelem was preparing to launch the rebel attack, Soltan Voltanieu was boarding a shuttle to take him to his luxury yacht in preparation for the coming battle. With him was Billy Chong.

"I have a surprise for you, Mr. Chong," the ghoulish Voltanieu whispered as the shuttle rose from the roof of Stalag 47.

Billy couldn't care less. He was in bad shape after being tortured for several days by Voltanieu's mind sucking machine. But when Billy kept passing out during the last few sessions, Voltanieu changed his tactics and had him beaten by his goons in order to continue drawing pleasure from his suffering. Billy's face was bloody and swollen and his body was wrecked, but he was still as defiant as he had been when Voltanieu apprehended him and had not given up all his secrets in spite of all the torture he had endured.

"Go to hell, you evil son of a bitch," Billy shot back with venom in his voice, sitting between the two goons who had been using his body as a punching bag.

"If you think that you're angry now, wait till you witness the spectacle of your fellow Martians being destroyed," Voltanieu replied with a twisted smile.

When the shuttle reached the upper atmosphere, Voltanieu pointed to the Terran fleet above the planet. "Do you see all those ships, Mr. Chong?" They've set a trap for the rebel fleet. The Terran Navy has a few surprises for Mr. Rogeston and his band of rebels. You're about to witness the end of the Martian rebellion, Mr. Chong. I will have the pleasure of seeing Kelem Rogeston killed, and then I will go to Earth and take over the government. Once I'm declared dictator of the solar system no one will dare oppose me."

"You're delusional, Voltanieu!" Billy snorted, laughing in spite of the pain in his ribs. "The rebels outnumber your fleet seven to one."

The two Phalanx goons, who weren't very bright, agreed with Billy silently. Lately, Soltan Voltanieu had been behaving erratically and had been making outrageous statements about taking over the solar system and avenging the loss of his son.

"Am I?" Voltanieu replied, laughing with his raspy voice. "Well if I am and the Rebel Fleet defeats the Navy, then I have another surprise, Mr. Chong. And do you know what that surprise is?" he asked with a wide grin that made him look like a vampire in the semidarkness of the shuttle's cabin.

Billy ignored him and his ghoulish theatrics.

"This... this is my surprise, Mr. Chong!" Voltanieu said, holding the remote detonator that would destroy all the cities of Mars.

"What? You're going to play us videos of your early childhood?" Billy replied with sarcasm, referring to the device in Voltanieu's hand resembling a remote control for a vid-screen.

"Very funny my friend! This is a remote all right, but one that will detonate several high yield atomic devices placed in all the cities on your retched planet! If your friends somehow manage to defeat the Terran Navy, which I doubt! I will ruin Mars for thousands of years. Your beloved planet will be too radioactive to sustain human life. And finally, Earth will be rid once and for all of the disease we call Martian Society!"

Billy's spirits sank and he wished that he weren't shackled to his chair so that he could jump up and choke Soltan Voltanieu to death with his bare hands. But Billy had a surprise of his own for Soltan Voltanieu. However, now he feared that the surprise would come too late if the Spawn of Satan, sitting across from him, decided to detonate the atomics before the small device that MMC employees had placed in Voltanieu's luxury yacht's *n'time* generator, performed its job. Now that he knew what Voltanieu was planning, he prayed with all his heart and soul that no one had found the small booby trap hidden in the devil's own ship. When the shuttle arrived at Voltanieu's private vessel, Billy relaxed a little. Now it all came down to a matter of timing. The fate of Mars teetered on one man's judgment of when to press a button.

On the Man O' War, Kelem gave the com officer a signal and the young man connected him to all the ships in the fleet. "Attention, members of the Free Martian Rebel Fleet. We're about to engage the Terrans once again and this time we'll likely be facing a more professional, determined enemy. Don't let yourselves think that this engagement will be as bloodless and easy as the last one. Be alert and expect surprises. We have the advantage of numbers and our shields, but as you learned in the last battle, the shields can be defeated by missiles if they strike close enough. But, no matter what the Terrans have ready for us, we will defeat them and take our planet back. Be safe and may God be with you."

When Kelem gave the signal, the com officer played a recorded version of the Martian National Anthem. The fleet would depart at the end of the last chord of the music. When the music ended, the ships of the Free Martian Rebel fleet began to be enveloped in a purple haze. The color and size of the glowing mass of quantum sub atomic particles surrounding each ship expanded, and soon ships began disappearing, one after the other.

A billionth of a second later the Man O' War appeared in orbit around Mars. Immediately, a huge Terran dreadnaught began firing on the rebel ship. Surprised by the quick and accurate response from the Terrans, Kelem gave the order to put distance between them and the unexpected leviathan now firing on the rebel flag ship.

"Where the hell did they get another dreadnaught?" Veronica Valchek yelled.

Kelem, otherwise engaged, ordered the shield generators turned on. The rebels couldn't have the shields on while they were in *n'time* transit.

Suddenly the entire Terran Fleet glowed purple and disappeared. "What the hell?" Kelem exclaimed, taken by surprise, but then he recovered and realized what the Terrans were doing. "Quick everyone! Turn your *n'time* radar on!' he yelled, but it was too late, the Terrans re-appeared above each of the biggest rebel ships and began firing on them. Most of the rebel ships had successfully turned on their shields in time but five hadn't. Two of them exploded right away killing their crews, the other three fired back and retreated but had already sustained severe damage.

The Man O' War was shaking and rattling from the intense barrage of fire from the dreadnaught that had engaged them as soon as it rematerialized over Mars. The shields were holding but the Terrans had outfitted this particular monster with very large caliber rail guns.

Pilot, get us away from the dreadnaught before their guns break through the shield!" Kelem ordered. The Man O' War pulled away slowly but the other ship followed it, relentlessly firing with its big guns. The Man O' War was too close to fire missiles and couldn't engage the *n'time* generator so close to another ship.

"General!" the weapons officer called out to Kelem. "The Terrans must have strengthened their hulls. We're hitting them but we have to shoot in the same spot several times before we breach their new armor."

Kelem now realized that the Terrans had figured out that the rebel fleet had developed some kind of shielding technology and had compensated by reinforcing their hulls with additional layers of CarbPlasSteel. The new armor wasn't as impervious as Harry's shields but it was effective enough! Their new tactics were working. All the largest rebel ships had been matched with an equal or larger size Terran cruiser or destroyer firing at them close and personal. It was a suicidal and desperate tactic but it was working!

Suddenly, a bright flash illuminated space coming from the other side of the planet where other rebel and Terran ships were engaged in battle.

"What was that?" the weapons officer asked.

"A big explosion for sure," Kelem commented holding on to his command chair as the Man O' War shook from the impact of the dreadnaught's big guns. "Call the battle group over the Fossae Planitia and ask them what the hell that was," he ordered the com officer.

Before the com officer could call the others to inquire about the bright flash, all the Terran ships separated from their opponents and after putting a few kilometers distance from the rebel ships they began to glow purple again.

When Kelem saw what was happening he yelled to the helmsman, "Move… move now!"

The helmsman responded quickly, and Kelem was about to let out a sigh of relief when he noticed that the Terran ships had left several small objects behind. One of those objects was quickly approaching the Man O' War.

"Brace for impact!" Kelem yelled, seeing that the missile was coming right at them. The bridge crew closed the Duraminium shields on all the windows of the ship in anticipation of the missile strike in spite of the ship's electronic shield. But when it went off, the ship jerked violently, throwing people out of their station chairs as several electrical conduits and crewmen's consoles exploded in a shower of sparks. The power went down but the emergency generators took over immediately.

"Holding her broken wrist with her other hand, the Man O' War's first officer, a woman named Flannigan, turned to Kelem. "Sir, I think that was an atomic bomb!"

Get us out of here Helmsman, *n'time* solution number two, now!" Kelem yelled in desperation. The ship began to hum and soon the Man O' War reassembled a million kilometers from Mars.

"Check for radiation damage, and call the others in the fleet and tell them to do the same. I hope to God that everyone else went into *n'time* like we just did," Kelem said, hoping that all the training and practice had paid off.

The science officer called the bridge from one of the lower decks with his report. "General, I have good news and bad news! The shields apparently protected us from the radiation but they all fried soon after. It's my guess that all the other ships in the fleet also have the same problem."

Kelem knew that an atomic explosion radiated a tremendous amount of electromagnetic radiation, also known as an EM pulse. The Terrans had guessed that the rebel fleet's shields were electronic and realized that they could possibly defeat that significant advantage with an EM pulse.

"Prepare the fighters and get us back to the battle," Kelem ordered, hoping that the Terrans were still of the opinion that fighters were not of significant tactical use in open space.

"Is our *n'time* radar still working?" he asked the science officer still in communication with the bridge.

The science officer confirmed that it was.

"Good!" Call the other commanders and tell them to re-assemble in Mars orbit using *n'time* solution number seven, and make sure that everyone's *n'time* radar is on. We're going to change our tactics. From now on, we're going to shoot and scoot. The one thing the Terrans can't beat us on is the ability to know when and where we're going to be."

This time the rebels appeared over Mars and began shooting missiles at the Terrans immediately. Several ships were hit and two exploded but the rest of the Terrans went into *n'time* and disappeared again.

The crew of the Man O' War and all the other ships in the rebel fleet watched their radars carefully waiting for the Terrans to re-appear. Soon blips indicating the next appearance of the Terran ships in three dimensional space began to show up in each ship's radar screen. Kelem's crew pre-programmed a barrage of missiles and fired them timed to go off exactly the instant the big dreadnaught reassembled itself. Then the Man O' War began glowing purple and relocated its mass one million miles from Mars once again.

Above the planet, several hundred missiles found their targets almost at the same instant that the Terran ships reappeared. The Terran armada began to explode in huge balls of fire as big chunks of ship's decks, bulkheads and thousands of crewmen were ejected in all directions into the vacuum of space.

The rebels returned to Mars orbit, this time farther from the planet than before to avoid reassembling amidst all the debris and wrecked vessels burning in space. More than half of the Terran fleet had been decimated, including the big dreadnaught that had fired on the Man O' War. The Terrans regrouped and went into n'time again. But, this time they didn't return right away.

Kelem knew what they were thinking and ordered all the ships to face away from Mars. Ten minutes later *n'time* signatures began to pop up on the rebel's radars once again. Then each ship fired its missiles ahead of the re-materialization of the Terrans and then went into *n'time.*

The missiles found their targets as soon as the Terrans reappeared with the same result as before. When the rebel fleet came back, still further from the planet than before, their enemy had been vanquished. There, for thousands of kilometers all around Mars lay the remnants of the once powerful Terran Space Navy, floating in pieces above the planet that they had reigned over for sixteen years.

Messages of surrender and requests for rescue from the survivors began flooding the com boards of every rebel ship. Kelem called the Stalag Deveraux and other ships to begin picking up prisoners, but he knew that the prison ship would not be filled to capacity. Thousands of Terran bodies were floating above Mars among the litter of wrecked ships.

On the observation deck of Soltan Voltanieu's luxury yacht, Billy Chong smiled when he felt the ship begin to buzz with a slight, almost imperceptible vibration. Slowly and with difficulty, he removed a micro syringe hidden in his sleeve and with one hand he injected himself. "I have a surprise for you, Mr. Voltanieu," Billy said with a grin on his face.

"Huh?" Voltanieu answered as he watched the Terran fleet explode in pieces above Mars. "What are you talking about?" he asked, wondering what useless ploy the Martian would try to use to prevent him from destroying his planet with the flip of a switch.

"What am I talking about?" Billy said then pausing as if waiting to hear something.

A strange high frequency vibration suddenly could be felt on the observation deck's floor and Voltanieu and the goons noticed it right away. They looked at each other nervously, for this sound was different from the normal sound of an *n'time* generator revving up for interdimensional transport.

Voltanieu looked at one of the goons. "Go to the bridge and find out what's going on." Then he went over to where Billy was shackled to his chair and slapped him across the face. "Don't threaten me, you piece of shit! I'm about to destroy your goddamned planet for all time. You're gonna watch as your family and countrymen die in horrible agony!"

The vibration on the ship suddenly rose in pitch and intensity and the one goon left on the observation deck began to look around with worry.

"I don't think you're going to destroy anything, you fucking evil monster," Billy responded with a weak smile as the poison in his body began to take its deadly effect.

"What are you talking about? What have you done?" Voltanieu screamed at Billy as his life ebbed away leaving him with his eyes open and a frozen smile on his lips.

Voltanieu slapped him again and Billy's head bounced back, staring at him with dead eyes and the smile that seemed to taunt him, almost as if he was saying, "In a few seconds you'll know what I've done."

The other goon returned looking pale. "Sir, the pilot says that the *n'time* generator has turned on its own and he can't shut it off!"

Voltanieu looked at the observation window and panicked. "Then, why in the hell is he not closing the window shields?" he screamed.

"The goon swallowed hard and stared at the window with fear in his eyes. "Sir... he...he says that he can't close them!"

"What?" Voltanieu replied with alarm, heading toward the door on his way to the pilot's cabin.

As he reached for the palm plate to open the pressure door to the yacht's main hallway, the *n'time* generator began its sequence and a purple glow became visible on the big observation deck's window. Voltanieu cursed, knowing the purple quantum field was deadly to human flesh, and took out the remote from his pocket and pressed the button that would destroy Mars and its people.

But the *n'time* field had already surrounded the ship and no radio transmissions could penetrate the quantum bubble that had enveloped the ship. The effect was about to disintegrate all matter within it in a few seconds.

Voltanieu screamed with rage and ran out into the hallway, mistakenly thinking that the pressure door could hold back the effects of the interdimensional jump.

The door closed and Voltanieu smiled. He had beaten the Martians after all!

The pressure door began waving like a piece of cloth in the wind and then vaporized along with the bulkhead and the hallway itself. The glowing quantum field surrounded Soltan Voltanieu and his skin began to itch at first, then heat up slowly and then began to be consumed, a layer at a time with a pain that made him scream in agony. His body began to stretch and fold in inexplicable ways as the *n'tim*e generator attempted to convert Soltan Voltanieu's body mass into a multidimensional object. But the evil torturer and murderer of thousands of innocent people was not a ship with a metal hull, but a man of flesh and blood. No human had ever experienced the bizarre effects of quantum de-molecularization before. In the midst of this horror, his consciousness had somehow remained alive, suffering unimaginable torment even as his body disassembled bit by bit and his brain dissolved in the subatomic matter stream.

Soltan Voltanieu had entered a new mode of existence. His body had been torn apart but his mind was still aware of what was happening to him. And yet death would not come. All the pain and suffering he had caused others seemed to be bouncing back to him in never ending torture that would go on forever. He screamed and pleaded for mercy but there was no one there to save him from the universal law of karmic justice.

CHAPTER 29

The Battle for Mars (part II)

May 15ᵗʰ, 2660 - 06:34 Am

Kelem was taking a short rest in one of the officer lounges on the Man O' War before ordering the rebel fleet to descend on the planet. A young ensign came in and informed him that newly promoted General Loeky needed to speak to him. Kelem got up, zipped up his tunic and followed the ensign to the bridge.

"Hello, General, I see that you've taken care of the Terran fleet. It looks like you decimated the bastards."

"Yes, General Loeky, we blew them away, but now we're getting ready to come down and finish the job!" Kelem replied with exhilaration.

"Hold on, young pup! The Black Guards have installed hundreds of missile launchers and numerous batteries of rail guns all over Mars, the biggest I've ever seen. If your ships descend now, you'll be wiped out before you hit the atmosphere."

"Damn!" Kelem cursed quietly. "How is it going down there? How can we help?" he asked, worried that the resistance would be pushed back without the added support of rebel fleet troops.

"Don't worry about the action here on the ground, we've pushed the Terran military and the Black Guards into their rat holes and they're surrounded on all sides. However, the same can't be said for the surface of Mars. The missiles and rail guns are hidden in utility buildings and in many of the towers and spires in the industrial section above Latonga

263

City. And I'm sure that they also have them in Amazonis and Olympus Mons as well. You'll have to take them all out before you can land."

"General, if we destroy those batteries we're going to kill lots of innocent civilians!" Kelem argued with alarm, knowing that destroying the missiles and rail gun installations was going to decompress many parts of Latonga City and other cities as well.

"We all have pressure suits, General. Besides, this is war and if you don't do this, many more civilians will die as a result! You also have to worry about the civilian space port here in the city and Gambert's Landing where they've got the same setup with missiles and guns. Also, we found out last night that a huge Terran transport came in about a week ago with three hundred new Black Guards and an equal amount of small ships that look like they're designed to fly in atmosphere. We're sure that all those new guards are Terran fighter pilots."

"Do you know where those fighters are stationed?" Kelem wanted to know.

"We believe that there are about a hundred or so at Gambert's Landing. I'm sure that the rest have been stashed here at the MMC launch site and Latonga Civilian Spaceport, though there could be some at Amazonis or Olympus Mons."

"Thank you, General Loeky. Do you know how Nicolas is doing and have you heard anything about Billy Chong?" Kelem asked, anxious to know if his childhood friend had managed to avoid being captured.

"Nicolas is here with me," Loeky answered. "Let me put him on."

"Kelem! Thank god you're safe." Nicolas said with relief. "Don't worry about us down here, we're doing just fine. Loeky's right, you have to eliminate the missiles and guns."

"Have you heard anything about Billy?" Kelem asked again.

There was as slight pause before Nicolas answered, enough to let Kelem know that something had happened to Billy.

"We're not sure, but we've heard that Billy was arrested by the Phalanx a week ago. We tried locating his wife and sons but they've gone underground," Nicolas reported, keeping his voice even.

"Yes, I arranged for their disappearance."

Kelem had a bad feeling and thought of reaching out for Billy's consciousness but he was too tired and distracted to get into the right mood to use his psychic skills. "Thanks Nicolas. Tell Loeky that I'll formulate a plan and let him know what we come up with."

"Be well, my boy. Our thoughts are with you all."

Kelem leaned back in his command chair, looked at Admiral Valchek and raised his eyebrows, indicating that he wasn't sure what to do next. Valchek had more experience in air to ground tactics and he was going to rely on her advice. He was disappointed that the struggle wasn't over yet. But he himself had told the rebels to expect surprises. More fighting and dying lay ahead and he had to accept it.

"I'll call all the senior officers to the Man O' War and we'll come up with a strategy to deal with this new wrinkle," Valchek said with confidence. Kelem nodded and fell into a slight depression. He knew that Loeky and Nicolas had tried to make light of the situation on the ground and cursed the Phalanx for its evilness and vicious ways. In the back of his mind lay the suspicion that Billy had been murdered by Soltan Voltanieu.

Three hours later, sixty rebel fleet officers had gathered in one of the largest lounges in the dreadnaught to discuss strategy. Everyone listened to the dozen or so Martian Space Command officers that were still part of the rebel fleet. All agreed that the first thing they needed to do was to send all the rebel fighters to the planet to draw out the Black Guard pilots and their ships while, simultaneously, frigates and small destroyers would draw fire from the missile batteries and gun emplacements.

This time Kelem was asked to lead the rebel fighters in the ship to ship fight with the Black Guard fighters.

The fleet had two hundred small shuttles and other light vessels that had been modified to work as fighters, but the only true fighters were the twenty five that had been captured during the first space battle with the Terran Navy. Kelem had flown one of the fighters and had decided that they were well designed and could fly in Mars' thin atmosphere quite well.

The following morning, with Kelem in command of the fighter wing, the attack was launched.

As soon as he and the others hit Mars' atmosphere, an intense barrage of rail gun fire issued from Latonga City. These were the same large caliber rail guns that had been installed in the Terran ships. As they approached the lower atmosphere, about fifty bright dots shot out from the MMC's launch site and the civilian space port. Within seconds, several plasma streams came out of the noses of the Terran fighters, fortunately the Kren shields repelled those fairly well. The Terran formation came at them and overshot the rebels.

Kelem smiled. These guys didn't have any experience flying in Mars' thin atmosphere! Their ships had been designed for the heavy air resistance of Earth's atmosphere.

"They don't have accurate control of their ships in our atmosphere. They're overcompensating. Let them come to you, and fire on them when they get within your gun's range." The pilots listened to Kelem's advice, and when the Terrans came back, the rebels opened with a well-aimed barrage and a dozen of the Terrans fighters were hit and fell down toward the planet in flames. The Terrans regrouped and split into pairs. The rebels did the same and the sky above Latonga City became a jumble of small dots firing plasma streams at each other in a dance of death.

The rebel frigates and destroyers were firing furiously at the gun positions on the ground. As the rebels began to decimate the rail guns, the telltale sign of missile launches lit up the buildings on the periphery of Latonga city. The missiles rose quickly and the rebels maneuvered to get out of their path. But these missiles were huge and were moving extremely fast. One hit a frigate and the ship was vaporized. Another came at one of the light cruisers and hit it square in the middle, sending it down to the surface in pieces.

Kelem ordered the bigger ships to retreat. These new missiles were too powerful for the Kren shields and had very accurate guidance systems. The rebel fighters were doing better than the frigates and cruisers, and were getting the upper hand over the Terran fighters. Soon, however, both the rebels and the Terrans had to leave the fight to refuel.

As soon as the Black Guard fighters retreated, the rail guns in Latonga city began shooting at the rebel fighters again. On their way back to the Man O' War, two ships in Kelem's squadron were hit and instantly destroyed.

The battle lasted all day and into dusk. Slowly, the Terran fighter attacks began to diminish by attrition. The rebels were better protected by their Kren shields, and by the end of the day they had eliminated more than half of the three hundred Terran fighters.

The following day, Kelem flew several missions to Gambert's Landing, Mars' main space port, where the rest of the rebel fighters were stationed. More of the same followed with the rebels overcoming the Terran fighters but also losing ships from gun fire and missile strikes.

By now, Kelem and the other pilots in the fleet were beginning to suffer from exhaustion after flying more than twenty sorties in less than twenty four hours. The Terran pilots were also in the same position and the outcome of the aerial battle over Mars' skies came down to which side could hold on the longest.

The Terrans were young and well trained but they had never been in real combat before, whereas the Martians had combat experience and were fighting for the liberation of their homeland.

By the start of the third day, all the Terran fighters had been downed and the Black Guards had run out of missiles. The rebel frigates and cruisers were then able to fire on the rail gun positions and destroy them all.

Finally and mercifully, at 10:17 AM on the morning of the 18th of May 2660, the few surviving Black Guards still alive in the cities and in Gambert's Landing surrendered, and the Battle for Mars came to an end.

The Martian landscape was littered with hundreds of wrecked ships from both sides. The rebels had lost more than two thousand pilots and crew. But the Black Guards and the Terran regulars had lost one hundred and sixty five thousand men.

The Martians now held fifty seven hundred Terran prisoners between the two prison ships in orbit around Mars, and thirty five thousand Black Guards left on the ground.

The number of dead civilians would be much, much higher.

CHAPTER 30

The Aftermath

May 18th, 2660 - 01:20 Pm

Kelem landed at the Mars Mining Company's launch site which had been severely damaged during the attack, but still capable of accommodating a few medium size ships. When he entered the main hangar, he was appalled to find one side of the structure filled with dead bodies lined up next to one another. Most of the bodies belonged to Black Guards, but a third of them were Martian civilians. The bodies had been there for less than a day and already the smell of decaying flesh was evident in the air.

Kelem covered his nose and followed the Helter Skelter who had met him and was to bring him to General Loeky, who was at Latonga City Hospital. "Why haven't these bodies been taken care of?" he asked the man.

The young lieutenant turned around and gave Kelem a funny look. "First of all, they're mostly Black Guards and second, the rest are MMC collaborators, so they can rot right down to the flesh as far as I'm concerned!" he stated with disdain.

Kelem thought of educating the man as to the truth about Billy Chong and the fact that many of MMC's employees were members of the resistance, but decided this was not the moment to correct misconceptions.

Kelem expected to be picked up by vehicle. Instead, the young lieutenant led him to Tunnel # 56-C. Tunnel 56-C, was the main thoroughfare that connected the MMC launch site with downtown Latonga. The center of town was three kilometers from here, and Kelem was already sweating inside his heavy pressure suit. "Wait… hold on!" he said, stopping the Helter Skelter who seemed to be in a hurry to reach the center of town. "I won't make it wearing this space rated suit. How come you couldn't get a vehicle to pick me up?"

The lieutenant looked at him with the same expression as before and Kelem recognized that this young man was in a state of shock. His mind was filled with images of carnage and horror, and he was walking fast, unconsciously running away from the ghosts that were chasing him. "I'm sorry, General, I should have explained. The few vehicles left in Latonga City are being used to ferry the injured to the hospitals."

"Oh, I see," Kelem replied as he got out of his suit. "Let's go back and see if we can find a pair of city suits for us, shall we?" Kelem suggested, realizing that the lieutenant wasn't wearing one either.

"You won't find any in there," he said pointing to the MMC's main pressure door. "I certainly won't take one from a dead body. Maybe when we get to downtown we might find some," he said, and then turned around and continued walking.

Kelem dropped his suit on the side of the tunnel and followed the lieutenant.

As they came within a few meters of downtown Latonga, Kelem's nose detected the smell of decaying flesh once again, this time mixed with acrid smoke. When the two of them reached the center of town, Kelem was shocked when his eyes beheld the scene in front of him.

There were bodies everywhere, some piled on top of one another in the streets. In certain places civilians and Black Guards were thrown together, now equal in death. Constitution Park was filled with even more bodies and many of the stores and businesses around the park were on fire or had burned down. A heavy cloud of smoke drifted above the park obscuring the upper floors of the business buildings that rose to meet the ceiling of the giant dome above downtown Latonga. The city's ventilation system had obviously been damaged or shut down. Constitution Avenue was so full of the dead that only a narrow lane of street pavement barely two meters wide was left to walk through it.

Kelem now began to understand the young lieutenant's state of mind. When he came to the corner of Constitution and Broadway, he found three Latonga City firemen sitting on the curb next to a fire hose connected to a fire hydrant. The hydrant's valve was open but the hose was dry. The men's faces were dirty with soot and sweat; their blood shot eyes barely noticing Kelem and the lieutenant as they passed by.

"The Black Guards sabotaged the air and water systems," the lieutenant said matter of fact, as he continued walking.

Kelem wanted to get some answers. "How did this come to be?" he asked himself. "Lieutenant, hold on!" Kelem shouted, and stopped the young man by grabbing his shoulder. The Helter Skelter spun around and slapped Kelem's hand away and then raised his pulse rifle and aimed it at Kelem's head.

Startled, Kelem jumped back. The young lieutenant's eyes blinked several times, then he dropped his weapon and collapsed on the floor sobbing and shaking. One of the firemen noticed what was going on and came over.

"I've seen a few like this one," he commented, himself showing the same distant look in his eyes that the lieutenant had. "He won't be able to do much of anything for a while I'm afraid. Me and my boys will look after him if you have to get somewhere," the man said, trying to be helpful.

Kelem read the Helter Skelter's mind and knew that the fireman was right. The lieutenant was in a catatonic state. His mind had finally snapped after witnessing so much death and destruction.

"Thank you, I'll send someone to pick him up later," Kelem told the fireman.

He crossed the park and headed north on Central Avenue, the large tunnel that ran the entire length of Latonga city. Here, there were more Black Guard bodies lying on the side of the road next to smoldering armored vehicles. Some of the bodies were horribly distorted and missing limbs. Kelem tried not to look at them, but he couldn't keep his eyes from taking in the scene and prevent his nose from smelling the scent of death.

When he reached Latonga City Hospital, he encountered yet another gory scene that horrified him and made him nauseous.

The sidewalks all along Central Avenue were covered with casualties. Among them were doctors and nurses tending to the injured and the dying. There was blood everywhere, and the murmur of people moaning in pain and begging for relief sounded like the background noise of hell.

Kelem knew that General Loeky and Nicolas had made light of the situation here on the ground, but this carnage and misery was beyond anything that he could have imagined. Then, he saw Nicolas up ahead standing over a patient wearing a surgical gown covered in blood stains. Nicolas looked exhausted.

Kelem ran to him. "Nicolas! Dear God, this is horrible!" Kelem uttered in disbelief. "Why are all these people on the street?"

"Thank God you're safe, my boy!" Nicolas said, embracing him. "We've run out of room in the hospital and we had no other choice than to start placing people in the street. We're using the Palm Beach Coffee House as a triage center. But now we're running out of pain medication, anesthesia… everything…" Nicolas said, his voice drifting as he perused the misery and pain that surrounded them.

"Where's Loeky?" Kelem asked.

"Over there," Nicolas said, pointing to a front store next to the coffee shop. "He's one of the casualties, but his injuries are not life threatening."

Kelem ran up to him and shook him gently to wake him up. The big man opened his eyes, and when he saw Kelem, he burst into tears. "Young pup! How are you?"

"I'm fine, general. I can't believe that you've been shot again. Are you all right?"

"Don't worry about me, I'll be up and around soon."

"General, right now I need to borrow your radio. Do you have it with you?"

Loeky grimaced with pain from the gun shot in his shoulder as he reached for his vest pocket and produced the device, handing it to Kelem.

"Man O' War, this is General Rogeston, come in please," Kelem said, hoping for a quick response.

"Come in, General," the com officer responded right away.

"Get me Admiral Valchek immediately. I don't care if she's asleep!" he said tensely.

"This is Valchek. How can I help you, General?" Veronica Valchek answered right away.

"Veronica, I need you to send down as many medics, doctors and medical supplies as you can spare. I know that we have our own wounded to care for up in the fleet. But that's nothing compared to the casualties here on the ground. You have no idea how many... how many have died and are injured, Veronica... It's horrible.... Please... you've got to help us," Kelem said, breaking down, unable to continue speaking.

"I will Kelem, I will..." Veronica Valchek replied, hearing how distraught Kelem was.

An hour and twenty minutes later, six rebel troops accompanied by fifteen medics and one doctor showed up at the hospital carrying several cases full of medical supplies. Kelem called Nicolas over and he instructed the new arrivals to follow him. He followed the group, and then spent the rest of the day and night assisting the doctors and medics wherever he could.

A medical team from Amazonis showed up the next day consisting of doctors, nurses and medics carrying two tons of supplies. By the end of the second day, Central Avenue was empty of casualties, and people had been moved to makeshift hospitals in converted building lobbies and stores.

The stench of dead bodies permeated the entire city of Latonga and something had to be done. In a desperate attempt to clean up the streets of corpses, it was decided that the sanitation department should pick up the bodies with their garbage trucks and bring them up to the surface until identification and burials could take place. The freezing temperature of Mars' exterior would preserve the bodies and keep them from stinking the city's air. The thought of laying Martian bodies out in the open was unpleasant, but the probability of disease being spread by decaying bodies was more dangerous.

Latonga City was finally cleared of all the dead by June 5th, and already a semblance of normality was returning to the capital of the red planet. The Martian people, ever so industrious, had turned out in great numbers to repair and rebuild their city.

Kelem took a few days off for a well-deserved rest. He retired to a small warren that belonged to a man who had perished in the struggle. The place reminded him a little of his Uncle Bernardo's warren, where Kelem grew up and lived until he turned eighteen. It was small but felt cozy and familiar.

He took to sleeping long hours and didn't leave the warren for many days. Even though the city had been cleaned up, Kelem couldn't bring himself to leave the warren and rejoin society. The images of so many men, women and children slaughtered so savagely haunted him day and night. Finally, a week later, Nicolas came by.

"Hello, Kelem. I hope that you've recovered from the ordeal that you went through, my boy," Nicolas said when he came in.

"I'm all right Nicolas. I just needed some time to pull myself together. What's going on? I haven't seen or heard from anyone since I came here," Kelem asked.

"Things are getting back to normal. Well…, as normal as can be expected under the circumstances, I suppose. Your presence is needed out there. Loeky and a few others have put together a provisional government. They're in the process of selecting people to serve as senators, representatives, and all necessary positions to run a government. Your name was mentioned, but I told them that I knew that you were not interested."

"Thanks, Nicolas. It would have been difficult for me to say no to them and have to deal with their disappointment."

"They want you to lead the Martian fleet when they go to Earth. And many are talking about occupation and retribution and executions without trials. People are angry and want revenge, Kelem. Some are even considering enslaving the Terrans to make them pay for what they did to us."

"Dear God! That doesn't sound like Martians talking," Kelem commented.

"When the rest of the rebel fleet came down to the city and saw what had happened, they became irate, horrified and suddenly bent on revenge. And who could blame them, Kelem! Many of them lost family and friends in the carnage."

"Yes, of course the Terrans should pay tributary penalties for sixteen years of occupation, but Nicolas, if we take revenge against the people of Earth and ruin their economy and make them our slaves, we'll be planting the seeds for the next war between them and us. Not to mention that we'll be no better than the Phalanx and the Black Guards!" Kelem exclaimed with concern.

"That's why you have to go and talk some sense into them before they end up making things worse!"

"I'm weary, Nicolas. Down to the bone weary and exhausted. I've done my bit. Let them go to Earth and dig themselves into a hole, because that's what they'll be doing if they go through with their vendetta!"

"Your <u>bit</u> here is not done, Kelem! You have to show them that they're wrong. Otherwise, all the pain and sorrow that you and I and all our dear friends, family and fellow Martians have gone through, will be for naught. If you leave for your precious Plantanimus now without finishing the job that you were destined to perform, Mars, the Earth and the Moon will never be free of war and strife."

Kelem rested his chin on his hands and sighed wearily. "Damn! I thought I was done, but you're right, Nicolas. At least I have to make an effort to make them understand that they'll be condemning themselves and Mars to centuries of military and political conflict."

"That's the Kelem I know and love!" Nicolas said, patting Kelem's shoulder. "How are you going to go about it?"

"I suppose I should meet with the provisional government and senior military officers and try to dissuade them from letting their passions rule their intellects," Kelem observed.

"They'll listen to you, Kelem. They love you and trust you. If anyone can set them right, you're the man to do it."

Two days later, Kelem stood on the Martian Senate's floor in front of the members of the provisional government, the entire senior staff of the rebel fleet, the Helter Skelters and the leaders of the many resistance cells on Mars.

"My fellow Martians, I've come here today in the hope that you will listen to my words of advice and choose the best course that we as a people should take in the rebuilding of our nation. There has been much talk about exacting retribution from the Terran people and of putting them through the same suffering and enslavement that we've endured for sixteen years."

"'We should destroy their cities and centers of industry and send them back to the Stone Age, some have said. Others would like the Terrans to become indentured servants to the Martian People and spend the rest of their lives in our service. Some want to incarcerate and execute the entire Terran government. A few would like nothing less than to eradicate the entire population of Earth and leave the planet in ruins."

A few "yeahs!" and cheers went up.

Kelem looked at those individuals and stared them down with reproach in his eyes.

"To those who feel and think that such actions are proper, I'd like to ask you a question," Kelem said, scanning the faces of the assembly. "Did sixteen years of occupation, starvation, torture, enslavement and the murder of thousands of innocent civilians, in any way, succeed in diminishing our desire for freedom, the will to resist and weaken our resolve to take our planet back by any means necessary?"

Shouts of, "No, of course not!", "We gave them hell!" and, "We showed them!" were said by many in the audience.

"All right! How then, do you think that the Terrans will react to our invading them, occupying their planet and enslaving them for several years?" Kelem proposed.

The group stirred and many looked uncomfortable.

"I see that you all suddenly became quiet as you contemplate being on the other side of the equation," Kelem commented. "It's a daunting prospect isn't it?" he asked with a wry smile. "How many of you see yourselves interrogating and torturing civilians in the depths of a Martian dungeon on Earth? Who among you will become the new Soltan Voltanieu? And how many of you think that you'll sleep well at night, knowing that you murdered innocent Terrans because you are filled with hatred for them and believe yourself to be a better human being than they are?" Kelem said vehemently, pushing hard with his mind to force them to think about the real consequences of such actions.

"It's one thing to kill a man in combat, fighting for your country. But to torture someone or pick up a weapon and murder an innocent human being who hasn't raised a finger against you, will kill your spirit and turn you into a monster."

"What the hell do you expect us to do about the Terrans, General? Should we go over there, kiss and make up like two lovers who had a romantic spat?" a colonel in the back said, causing some to laugh.

"Before I go any further, I should make clear my personal feelings regarding such matters. One, the Phalanx organization and Montenegro Industries should be dissolved and its leadership arrested, tried, and the guilty executed for crimes against humanity. Two, President Montenegro, his entire administration, most of the members of the senate and all the wealthy and influential rich men and women on Earth who supported the Martian occupation and profited from it, should also be arrested, tried and sentenced appropriately. Three, the Terran military should be dissolved for an undetermined period of time, leaving only local law enforcement and a Martian occupying force to keep and preserve the peace. And last, once a new Terran government is created, the Terran Nation should sign a peace treaty with Mars and agree to pay justifiable punitive damages to the Martian government for the pain and suffering inflicted on the people of Mars and its national economy."

The group applauded and many cheered after hearing Kelem's opinion on how Earth should compensate for the occupation.

"What about the Terran people?" They were all implicit in the occupation. How are they going to pay for their part in all the suffering and death that they inflicted on us?" another man asked in the crowd.

"Have you not been watching the news feeds from Earth in the past three weeks and missed the fact that there's a civil war raging over there?" Kelem asked with some sarcasm. "Our North and South American cousins, the British, the French, the Germans, the Spanish, the Benelux countries and the Italians have risen against their government and are demanding from the authorities, many of the same things that I just outlined before. Are we to enslave our ancestors? And what about our American cousins, the Canadians, all the people of Central and South America? They have been staunch supporters of Martian sovereignty from the very first day of the invasion. And have you thought about the Europeans? They're also calling for Montenegro's resignation and for the resumption of normal diplomatic relations with Mars. What are we to think of them?"

The group stayed silent as Kelem's words sank in.

"How many of you know a Terran personally, and by that I mean as a friend or colleague? Raise your hand if you do," Kelem asked, searching for people's hands in the air.

Only five people had their hands up, Kelem, Veronica Valchek, Rusty Deveraux, Nicolas Alfano and the exec officer of the Nation of

Love who served under Ndugu Nabole, the only member of the rebel fleet of Terran origin.

"Many of you know me and the folks who raised their hands. The five of us have one thing in common; we're all friends or colleagues of Ndugu Nabole. As you well know, Ndugu is a former Terran and Admiral Devereaux can testify to the fact that Ndugu has become a much beloved and appreciated member of the rebel fleet. And although all of us who know him personally, consider him to be a remarkable individual, he's not that different than most Terrans.

"I brought up this point to indicate that most Martians have never been in a position to become friends with a Terran. And before you say anything else, I also have to point out that, current evidence notwithstanding, the Phalanx goons and Black Guards are not typical examples of average Terran individuals. I spent time on Earth and, like you, I was of the belief that Terrans were stupid, lazy, violent and uncouth before I got there. But after spending a few weeks there, I learned that the average person on Earth is very much like us. The man on the street did not start the war nor did he want Mars to be enslaved by the Phalanx and the Terran military. The Phalanx and the government are responsible for that. When you go to Earth, you will find that my account of our fellow Terran humans is quite accurate. I dare say that many of you will come to befriend and, perhaps even love a Terran someday, as I and these other four people have come to know and love Ndugu.

"Please, don't go to Earth to exact revenge in the belief that such deeds will make things right for you and your fellow Martians. Nothing could be further from the truth.

"Six hundred and forty two years ago, a great war was fought on Earth in the early 20th century in the year 1914. That conflict was called World War One and it was started by Germany. It was the first international war fought on Earth and millions of people died, far more than have died on Mars during the last sixteen years. The war came to an end in 1918 and the countries that had allied against Germany demanded unduly harsh retribution from the Germans. The then President of the United States of America, Woodrow Wilson, wanted a more just and equitable settlement between the allies and Germany, but the United States was out voted and the treaty, named the

Treaty of Versailles, was signed, subjecting Germany to severe penalties. Woodrow Wilson warned that the unfair treaty would only serve to plant the seeds for another more violent and deadly war some twenty years hence. President Wilson died soon after, and fortunately didn't live to see his prophetic warning come true.

"Because of the treaty, Germany plunged into a financial depression that was partly responsible for a world-wide depression in 1928. These events gave rise to Nazism and brought Adolf Hitler to power. Twenty one years later, Germany initiated World War Two, a much more destructive and violent war than the previous one.

"My fellow Martians, our nation now faces the same exact choice that the allies faced in 1918. Should we do what the Europeans did then, and severely punish our defeated enemy? Or should we do what the United States wisely decided to do at the end of the second war; to assist Germany and the devastated countries of Europe to rebuild their infrastructure while making sure that the Nazi Party could never rise to power again, thus preventing a third world war?"

"This is the choice that has been placed on our shoulders. Exact harsh retribution from the Terrans and thus plant the seed for another war and then another and another and so on… Or follow the example of our North American cousins in 1945 and save the solar system and humanity at large from being condemned to fight consecutive wars which will surely be more deadly and violent than the one we just experienced.

"I will conclude my argument with these last words. Humankind now has the capability to travel to the stars. How long do you think it will be before we meet an alien species? And what will happen to us if that species is not friendly and would want to harm us or conquer us? How will we be able to preserve our race and our human culture if we're too weak to repel alien invaders because we're fractured and bickering amongst ourselves?"

"I ask of you… No! I beg of you, not to let your baser instincts prevail and lead us down a path that will only bring misery and ruin on the Martian people and our fellow human beings."

A vigorous applause broke out at the end of his speech. Kelem's words had stirred the hearts and minds of the majority present in the hall. Kelem nodded with appreciation, acknowledging their approval.

He read the crowd's mood and found to his relief that he'd hit the right note. Mars would manage the surrender of Earth with fairness and equanimity. Now he could leave Mars knowing in his heart and mind that he had done everything possible to leave a legacy of peace and prosperity for Mars and for the rest of humanity.

"Thank you for listening to me and for taking my message to heart. I must now perform the sad duty of announcing my decision to leave you as Commander of the Martian Rebel Forces. I hereby tender my resignation and wish that you elect Admiral Veronica Valchek to the leadership position. It has been a privilege and an honor to serve with you in the struggle to free our nation from bondage. Thank you very much and may god bless you all."

The senate chamber erupted in protest. Everyone rushed to the large central podium where Kelem was standing and assailed him with requests to stay and lead them to Earth. The outpouring of loyalty and appreciation from his fellow Martians and rebel comrades brought tears to Kelem's eyes. Their desire to keep him as leader tugged at his heart, but he knew that he'd come to the end of his time on Mars. He thanked them and left quickly to avoid having to feel their sadness and disappointment at his departure.

On the way back to Havana Flats, Kelem sighed with relief as he sat at the helm of the Solar Nations lander, thinking that he'd soon say goodbye to Nicolas and the others and then leave for Plantanimus. But he was wrong.

Destiny had one more fateful card to play for Kelem. The arc of the story of his life on Mars was about to come full circle with an unexpected event.

CHAPTER 31

The Sins of the Stepfather

June 25th, 2660

The lander was cruising leisurely over the Martian landscape. There was no need to push the ship now that everything had been resolved, at least in Kelem's mind. The Martian Fleet would depart for Earth in a week and Kelem was going to relax, visit Verena Chong, Billy's widow and reassure her that he didn't want to take back ownership of the Mars Mining Company. Wealth and power had ceased to be important to Kelem a long time ago. He had given up the MMC the day he left on the Solar Nations mission. Before leaving, he would visit the few friends and acquaintances that were still alive, say goodbye to the Brotherhood and then return to Plantanimus.

Now that he no longer needed to concentrate all his energy on freeing Mars, Plantanimus had once again taken first place in his mind. He was looking forward to communing with the Dreamers and seeing Anima once again. The voyage would take a year but Kelem planned to spend most of that time in Lectrosleep.

He leaned back in his pilot's chair and decided to take a snooze. The auto pilot would warn him when the lander came within three hundred kilometers of Havana Flats. He closed his eyes and let the monotone hum of the engines lull him to sleep. His body was relaxed, but his mind somehow was not. He wondered what could possibly be bothering him, and then he realized that the sense of worry and apprehension that he was feeling was not coming from him but from Nicolas.

He opened his eyes and saw Nicolas staring out of the lander's front window with a worried expression.

"All right Nicolas, out with it! I was trying to take a cat nap but the turmoil in your mind is keeping me up. What could possibly be worrying you, now that everything has been resolved?"

Nicolas turned and looked at him, his eyes full of conflict. He swiveled the co-pilot's chair to face him.

"I took it upon myself to keep a big secret from you, because I feared that if I told you earlier what I'm about to reveal now, the truth that I've been hiding might have prevented you from liberating Mars. I hope that when you find out what it is, you won't consider me selfish and meddlesome."

"For God's sake, Nicolas, what is it?" Kelem asked, sensing Nicolas' deep conflict and anxiety.

"Jude Voltanieu is your son," Nicolas blurted out nervously.

"What…? My son…? What do you mean, Nicolas? I don't understand," Kelem replied, his mind in utter confusion.

"I… I'm sorry my boy, I hope that you won't hate me for keeping this from you ever since you returned to Mars, so please let me explain."

Kelem nodded and leaned forward in his chair, his brain now fully awake. If this was true, it meant that Jude Voltanieu was his and Carlatta's son! "But how?" he wondered.

"During all the years that I spent in Stalag 47, I had many opportunities to read Soltan Voltanieu's mind during the endless interrogation sessions that he subjected me to. He never got anything out of me, but over time I was able to learn many of his deepest, most private secrets."

"The boy was conceived in Madrid, wasn't he?" Kelem half asked, half stated, now beginning to guess what had happened the last time that he and Carlatta had been together.

"Yes, but please let me tell you how and why all this happened without interruption."

Kelem leaned back and motioned for Nicolas to continue.

"This all started in November of 2635, right after Carlatta's father, Don Francisco Del Mar's Ambassador's Ball. That was the night you and Carlatta met and fell in love with each other. As you well know, the media had been there and the next day, pictures of you dancing with the ambassador's beautiful daughter were spread throughout the solar system."

"When the media reported a year later that you and Carlatta were engaged to be married, Soltan Voltanieu saw an opportunity that he could not help but take advantage of. You know that the Phalanx had been trying to recruit psychics into their ranks for years. And even though they found a few on Earth, none of those individuals could ever compete with Martian psychics. The closest they came were the two spies they sent to the Hawking Center and that poor woman Klia Sangrista. But as talented as Sangrista was, the Phalanx had to enhance her and the other two spies' abilities with bionic implants. But even with all that technology in their brains, they were no match for any of us in the Brotherhood, and they definitely were no match for someone like you.

"Voltanieu found out that you were the one who defeated the Phalanx plot to steal the *n'time* technology research data and knew then that you were the most powerful psychic in the solar system. He had to find a psychic who could help the Phalanx defeat the Brotherhood and eventually Mars, the place most hated, and at the same time desired by the Phalanx.

"Once Voltanieu learned that Carlatta and her mother were both named co-executors of the estate of Doña Anastasia's mother, the Duchess of Bourbon, he set his plan in motion. He had the duchess assassinated and made it look like she died of natural causes, the result of which was that both Doña Anastasia and her daughter had to return to Earth to settle Carlatta's grandmother's estate. Once they were both there, he had them abducted, knowing that it would bring you to Earth in an effort to rescue her and her mother and bring them back to Mars."

"But how... how did he know that I would even contemplate making such a foolish decision, even though I did ultimately go to Earth for that reason?" Kelem asked, knowing that Soltan Voltanieu's psychics were not good enough to predict future events or to have made such an accurate leap in logic.

"I know what you're thinking Kelem. How could he have known?" Nicolas said, raising his eyebrows. "Well, here's the ironic twist of all time! Soltan Voltanieu was the most powerful psychic on Earth! His abilities were almost as good as yours, Kelem! But, fortunately for all of us, he didn't know it! It was his own natural talent that somehow gave him the ability to predict what you would do if Carlatta was taken away from you. Thank God the man was ignorant of his power and never fathered his own children, believing that the only way to recruit a psychic with talents such as yours was to steal one. Otherwise, we could have been faced with multiple Jude Voltanieu's, in which case we might have failed to defeat the Terrans!"

Kelem shook his head, beginning to feel a rage deep inside for what had been done to him and Carlatta. Voltanieu had stolen their lives and that of their own child!

"Once Carlatta was abducted, he had her brainwashed, waited for you to come to Earth to rescue her and sent her to spend those last four days with you in Madrid. She had been programmed to have sex with you as many times as possible in the allotted time to ensure a pregnancy."

Kelem now realized how deftly and expertly he and Carlatta had been manipulated to produce an heir that he would never find out about. "So the information that I received from Patrick Bertrand, the Terran embassy's butler regarding Carlatta's location on Earth was all false? The whole thing was a setup?" he asked, beginning to realize how easily he had fallen into Soltan Voltanieu's trap.

"Yes, Kelem. However, Patrick Bertrand was an unwitting participant in the plot. The Phalanx cleverly made him believe that the information that he passed on to you was real. They knew that you could read minds so they let Patrick Bertrand believe that he had found Carlatta's possible locations on Earth by sheer luck, this way you would never doubt the veracity of the information."

"Please don't tell me that Ndugu was part of Voltanieu's plot!" Kelem said, hoping that it was not so.

"No, Kelem, Ndugu was a stroke of good luck, though his convincing you to go to Spain from South Africa instead of Paris in order to go back to Mars, almost cost both your lives," Nicolas informed him.

"How's that?" Kelem wondered.

"Voltanieu had Carlatta scheduled to be in Paris when you got ready to go back to Mars. If he couldn't have manipulated Carlatta to go to Madrid at the last minute instead, where she eventually found you, he would have been forced to abduct you and then he would have used some unpleasant means to inseminate her against your will. Afterwards, you and Ndugu would have been eliminated."

"Why didn't he get rid of me after I served my purpose anyway?" Kelem asked.

"Because to have done so, would have alerted the Martian government and the Brotherhood that something was wrong, and that could have eliminated or eventually ruined his plans to conquer Mars. It was better to let you and Ndugu go so that he could raise Jude and his possible siblings as his own son and use him as he did to discover a weak spot on our side. That weak spot turned out to be Solomon Vandecamp. So talented and powerful was your son at age two that young Jude was able to tell his step father that a Martian man named Solomon would do anything for wealth and power. That's how the Phalanx was so successful at seducing Solomon Vandecamp to come to Earth and betray his own nation."

"I was always leery of him but I never suspected that he could be so easily swayed to commit such treason!" Kelem remarked with anger.

"Voltanieu indoctrinated your son to become a Phalanx fanatic from the moment the boy could talk and understand conversation. Like his real father, young Jude was a child prodigy with an immeasurable intellect and the ability to read other people's thought's from millions of kilometers away. He grew up hating Mars and its people, and Voltanieu trained him to be cruel and soulless like himself. The boy never had a chance, Kelem! Voltanieu was able to control Jude with his own hidden psychic powers and filled him with evil and hatred and ruined him for life."

"What about… what about Carlatta, how… how did she die…?" Kelem asked dreading the answer.

"Voltanieu pumped her full of an experimental fertility drug that the Phalanx doctors had promised would produce quintuplets at the very least. He wanted to have an entire army of Kelem Rogestons trained by the Phalanx. Fortunately, the drug failed to produce multiple births. Unfortunately, its side effects were responsible for killing Carlatta during childbirth."

Kelem buried his face in his hands and cried with deep sadness for the cruel end of his beloved Carlatta who had been used as a mere breeder to produce a new generation of super-psychics. The pain and sorrow that he had once felt for her death and which he thought he had gotten over, now came back with full force, reopening the wound that had taken so long to heal.

"There's more…" Nicolas said, sharing Kelem's pain and tears. He had to tell him the rest of the facts and get this unpleasant conversation over and done with. Now he had to tell him the hardest part.

"Jude is still alive…"

Kelem stopped crying and raised his head. "I thought that he had died," he said, feeling a ray of hope that something of Carlatta had been passed onto the boy even though he had become as evil as his step-father.

"No, he's still alive, but he's very ill, Kelem. Marla and I have managed to stabilize him. I must tell you that he won't last much longer. After his crash and subsequent coma, he awoke a few weeks later suffering from permanent retrograde amnesia. The Terran doctors gave him several rounds of my nanites without first mapping his neural pathways. As a result, his brain was reconstituted successfully but any trace of who he was or of his psychic powers is gone forever, which in my opinion is a good thing. He is no longer the person that he once was. He could have lived a normal life, but Voltanieu in his ignorance and evil arrogance, put him through several torture sessions in his horrible machine, desperately hoping that Jude could regain his psychic ability, and as a result he damaged the boy's brain permanently."

"I want to see him, I don't care what shape he's in. He's my son!"

"He's in Havana Flats. He's been there for several weeks. That's why I asked you to go there now. But I wanted you to know about the whole story before we landed. If you never want to speak to me again, I'll understand. I kept you away from your own child and the only thing that you'll ever have from Carlatta," Nicolas concluded, feeling guilty.

Kelem shook his head and laughed, he could never be angry with Nicolas, who was the closest thing he ever had to a real father. He sat up straight, shut off the automatic pilot and pushed the engines to maximum.

Twenty minutes later they had touched down at the Fisher Madjal landing pad. Nicolas led him to one of the warehouse's lower levels where he and Marla had set up a very well equipped hospital room to care for young Jude.

On the elevator ride, Nicolas spoke. "I must warn you, he's in a very delicate condition. You might not be able to speak to him for long periods of time. He's in and out of consciousness."

"I'll take whatever I can get," Kelem replied, nervously anticipating meeting his and Carlatta's son for the first time. However, whoever or whatever he was.

Nicolas greeted the four Helter Skelters who were guarding the door to Jude's room and one of them opened the pressure door.

When Kelem walked in and saw Jude, his legs grew weak and he had to hold on to the side of the med-bed for a few seconds. There, lying with his eyes closed and sleeping peacefully, was a twenty year old young man who looked more like sixteen or younger. But what had stopped him in his tracks was the fact that his son's face was almost an exact replica of Carlatta Del Mar's face in male form.

He walked around the bed slowly, taking in Jude's tall and lanky body. His left arm and hand were out from under the covers and Kelem smiled when he saw how similar they were to his own arm and hand. He sat on the chair next to the med-bed and looked at Jude's eyelids which were moving in REM-sleep. He closed his eyes and tried to read his mind but was disappointed when all he could see was a jumble of fragmented thoughts, possibly the effect of Soltan Voltanieu's use of his hateful machine on the boy.

Then, suddenly, Jude woke up and opened his eyes, which were the same color as Kelem's, light blue. Kelem was taken aback, and for a moment panicked, not knowing what to do or say.

"Hello, who are you?" the boy asked him with a voice eerily similar to his own.

"Jude, this is the person that I was telling you about a few days ago, do you remember?" Nicolas said warmly.

"Oh yes, you said that there was a man who knew my mother. How are you sir," Jude said, extending his right hand to Kelem.

Kelem shook the boy's hand gently. It was very warm and soft. They were the hands of someone who hadn't done any manual work their entire life.

"Hello, Jude, my name is Kelem. How are you?"

"I'm fine, sir. Thank you for coming. I haven't met too many people since I've been sick. It's hard having to stay in this med-bed all the time, but I'm very weak so I can't get around by myself."

"You've been through a lot, I hear. You should stay put until your body is able to heal," Kelem replied, trying to control his emotions.

"I was doing better until the ugly man that claimed to be my father hurt me with a machine that he attached to my head. I hope he won't come back and hurt me again," Jude said with a trembling voice.

Kelem fought back the anger and sadness that was threatening to burst out in a flood of tears. "You don't have to worry about that horrible man anymore, Jude. He's dead and gone. He can't hurt anyone anymore. You're safe now. Besides, he wasn't your father."

"You said that you knew my mother. Please tell me about her."

Kelem swallowed hard and steeled himself to tell his own son, who would never know that he was talking to his own father, about his mother whom he had never met.

Your mother's name was Carlatta Del Mar. She was the daughter of Don Francisco and Doña Anastasia Del Mar. Your grandfather, Don Francisco, was the Terran Ambassador to Mars, one of the finest men that I've had the pleasure to meet in my life. Your grandmother, Doña Anastasia, was a lovely and vibrant woman who loved life and your mother with all her heart and soul. Your mother was one of the most beautiful women that I've ever seen." Then Kelem paused and brought up pictures of Carlatta Del Mar that were available through the net from her days as a professional dancer.

The boy looked at it with great interest. "She… she looks like me, I mean… I look like her," he added, fascinated by the physical similarities between mother and son. "She was very pretty, what happened to her?"

Kelem smiled and maintained his calm. "Your mother died during childbirth, Jude. If she had lived, she would have loved you very much and would have taken excellent care of you."

"And what about my father, did you know him too?" Jude asked innocently.

Kelem didn't know how to answer the question and he felt he was about to lose control and fall to the floor crying helplessly.

"Your father was a great man, Jude. His name was Kelem, just like

Kelem here," Nicolas said, pointing to the boy's real father. "He was lost during an expedition to the Eridanus system not long after your mother passed away," he added, feeling what Kelem was going through emotionally.

"So, I'm an orphan then," the boy said, looking downhearted.

"Yes, but that doesn't mean that others can't love you as much or even more that your parents," Kelem explained, reaching for Jude's left hand and holding it gently in his.

"Thank you, sir, maybe you could be my stepfather. There's something about you that feels familiar, as if I've known you before," Jude stated, sounding very young and child-like.

Kelem fought back the need to hug Jude and hold him in his arms and give him all the love that had been denied him during his short life. As he held his son's hand, he was finally able to read the boy and found that indeed, his former personality had been completely eradicated and what was left was the real person who was a sweet and gentle soul. Jude's level of intellect was in the order of someone half his age. The accident and subsequent abuse by his step-father had diminished Jude's intellectual capacity. Mentally, he was a little boy.

"I would be happy to be your stepfather, Jude. May I call you son then?" he asked, smiling.

Jude's handsome face lit up with an equally bright smile. "Yes! May I call you father?"

"Of course you can, Jude. Now, what else do you want to talk about?"

"I… I would like to see the outside. I want to see the sky and the land. Nicolas told me that the atmosphere is very thin and that means that there's no air to breathe, but I would like to see it anyway. Can you show it to me, father?"

Kelem looked at Nicolas for approval, but Nicolas shook his head slightly to indicate that Jude's condition was too fragile for him to be moved anywhere.

Kelem stood up. "Jude, Nicolas and I are going outside to talk for a minute. Will you excuse us?"

"Please don't leave, father! I'm so lonely here, stuck in this room for so long all by myself," the boy pleaded.

"Don't worry, son, I'll be right back," Kelem responded, leading Nicolas out by the arm.

Once in the hallway, Kelem asked Nicolas what risks were involved in transporting Jude and moving him to another location.

"He shouldn't be jostled about, particularly in a shuttle. His brain stem is very weak and the slightest jarring motion could kill him," Nicolas advised.

"But didn't you tell me that he was going to die anyway?"

"Yes, I did. But do you want to be the one that hastens the event?"

"The way I look at it is that if he's going to die anyway, it might as well be in my company while in the process of granting him one of his last wishes, which is to see the sky and the land," Kelem replied.

"Well, you're the best pilot on Mars. I suppose if we strap him securely in your lander and if you fly very, very carefully, we could take him up and he could see the 'outside' as he calls it," Nicolas suggested with a sad smile. "As a matter of fact, if he survives the flight, you could bring him up to your old apartment and stay there with him for as long as he holds on. The view of Latonga City from your old place is still as spectacular as it was, in spite of the battle damage to the city."

"My old apartment in Latonga City is available?" Kelem asked surprised.

"It was used by a Terran contractor who worked for the military. Major Loeky had it cleaned up and he and I furnished it the way it was before you left Mars. We did it in case you decided to hang around for a while. I didn't want you staying in that little warren on the north end of town anymore. I'm willing to come along with a nurse and stay there with you, looking after Jude's medical needs for however long it takes."

Kelem reached out and hugged Nicolas, weeping with gratefulness. The old man knew that Kelem needed this time with his son, however brief it might be.

Kelem went back to Jude's room and told him that he was going to take him someplace special. The boy was delighted and thanked his newly acquired 'step-father' for liberating him from his hospital room prison.

Early the next day, Kelem, Jude, Nicolas and a nurse flew to Latonga

City and brought the boy to Kelem's old apartment. The tower rose from the city's street level, past the giant dome of downtown Latonga and then continued twenty stories above the surface of Mars. Kelem's old penthouse was circular and it was surrounded with pressure proof windows.

They placed Jude's med-bed in the middle of the large living room where, in the past; Kelem had spent many hours with Jude's mother entertaining friends and family. Nicolas and General Loeky had gone to great lengths to furnish the place as closely as possible to the way Kelem had once had it. Jude was transfixed by the beauty of the Martian landscape and the towers and spires of the many industrial facilities that surrounded the capital of Mars.

Once there, Jude's condition improved and he became more energized and asked to be propped up to a sitting position so that he could enjoy looking out onto, what was for him, a wondrous new world.

Three days went by and both Kelem and Nicolas allowed themselves to believe that Jude might have a chance after all, and that Kelem's love and affection for the boy was miraculously healing his damaged brain. Kelem was already fantasizing about bringing Jude to Plantanimus with him.

On the third night, Kelem fell asleep holding on to Jude's hand next to his med-bed. And it was with great surprise and joy that sometime during the night he found himself on Plantanimus beneath Zeus' roots.

"HELLO, KELEM. WE HAVE MISSED YOU! YOU HAVE BEEN LOST IN DARKNESS AND PAIN FOR A LONG TIME. WE'RE HAPPY TO BE WITH YOU," Zeus' rumbling voice echoed in the forest.

Kelem looked around and saw Jude's body lying on the ground next to Zeus's roots. "My son is here with you, Zeus. Does that mean that you can heal him?" Kelem asked with excitement.

Zeus took a while to answer. "NO, DEAR KELEM, WE CANNOT HEAL HIM. HIS TIME IS ALMOST OVER. HE WILL MAKE THE TRANSITION ANY TIME NOW," the Dreamer answered.

"Why is he here then?" Kelem asked, disappointed that even the mighty Zeus and the Dreamers could not keep his son alive.

"HE'S HERE BECAUSE YOU BROUGHT HIM HERE," the Dreamer replied.

"I? I bought him here? I don't understand."

"THIS PLACE IS THE QUANTUM TIDE KELEM, OR DID YOU FORGET? THIS IS WHERE PAST, PRESENT AND FUTURE EXIST ALL AT ONCE. PERHAPS YOU'RE TRYING TO RESOLVE THE OUTCOME OF AN EVENT THAT AFFECTED YOUR SON'S LIFE THAT YOU WISH TO CHANGE," the dreamer suggested.

"Well, if I did, then it was foolish of me to try since you say that you can't help him anyway," Kelem replied, a little angry that Jude's fate could not be changed.

"WE THINK THAT YOU BROUGHT HIM HERE BECAUSE THERE MIGHT BE A WAY THAT YOU CAN HELP HIM YOURSELF," Zeus commented.

"How Zeus, what will bringing my son here do for him?"

"PERHAPS YOU'RE SEEKING HELP FOR YOURSELF AS WELL," Zeus suggested.

Kelem sat down on the floor of the virtual Dreamer's forest, feeling glum. It seemed that he sat there for a very long time until he felt his heart chakra begin to feel warm and then vibrate higher and higher until pure love and joy filled his entire being. Suddenly, Jude rose from the ground and walked up to where Kelem was sitting. Kelem stood up and looked at his son with wonder and happiness in his heart.

"You're standing, Jude! And you look healthy and strong, have the Dreamers healed you?" he asked with excitement, reaching for his son.

Jude backed away out of the reach of his father's arms. Kelem was hurt by his son pulling away and asked, "Why are you backing away from me, now that everything is all right?"

"Yes, everything's all right because you have healed me, father!" Jude said as his body began to glow with a soft golden light in the semidarkness of the forest. "You have healed me with your love and pure heart and I remember everything now. All that I did in this life, all the people I hurt and all the pain and misery that I caused because of the hatred that my stepfather forced on me. I must go away and spend a long time making up for what I did. But someday, father, we will meet again and we'll be able to be together in physical form and know one another."

Jude's body became brighter and then Kelem saw another figure, also bathed in light, approach him and Jude. As the figure came near, Kelem's heart jumped with joy when he recognized who it was.

"Carlatta!" he whispered with astonishment. "What does this mean?" he asked, but he already knew the answer in his heart.

"My darling, your love brought the three of us together, but it's only for a brief moment, I'm afraid. I'm here to help our son, my love. He needs to make the transition and you didn't want him to do it alone so you called me to guide him."

"Thank you, Father, thank you for loving me so unconditionally! I will be fine now that mother is here. Goodbye…," Jude said as he and Carlatta became brighter than two suns and then faded away.

The steady tone of Jude's heart monitor alarm awakened him, as Nicolas and the nurse ran out of their respective rooms to attend to the emergency. They reached Jude's med-bed and took out their equipment to revive the boy but Kelem stopped them.

"It's okay, he's all right, Nicolas. I was just talking to him and his mother, and she will help him where he's going," Kelem said with a peaceful smile, free of sadness and regret. He knew at that moment that Jude's spirit would go on and was absolutely convinced that they would meet again in another life.

The nurse looked at Kelem with pity, believing that his statement declaring that he'd been talking to his son and dead mother were the imaginings of a father grieving for the loss of his child.

But Nicolas knew better and as he read Kelem's thoughts, he felt the peace in his heart and knew that Kelem's time on Mars had truly come to an end.

CHAPTER 32

The Fleet Leaves for Earth

July 9th, 2660

Ndugu, Rusty, Veronica, Nicolas and Kelem sat together in the Captain's ready room of the Man O' War sharing a bottle of wine. The mood was light but the gathering had an undertone of sadness. Kelem was leaving Mars and the four knew that they would never see him again.

Ndugu and Nicolas would miss him more than the others because they had shared the most amount of time with him. Of the two, the most dissapointed was Ndugu, who had hoped against hope that Kelem would decide to stay on Mars after he reconnected with friends and family. But the Terran invasion had changed all the social conditions that might have convinced him to stay and forget about Plantanimus.

Nicolas at least had the knowledge that he and Kelem would communicate through the Quantum Tide. But his heart was aching as strongly as the others.

Rusty and Veronica would feel the absence of Kelem's leadership more than missing him on a personal level and both were a little insecure about filling his shoes. The two rebel leaders had come to love him and respect him like the rest of the fleet. Veronica more than Rusty, was concerned that Kelem's desire for Mars to treat the Terrans fairly might fall by the wayside in his absence.

For his part, Rusty was disappointed that Kelem couldn't take his son Louie under his wing to train him as a psychic, but Kelem had reassured him that the Brotherhood would be a much better choice for the boy.

Ndugu, Rusty and Veronica were aware of Kelem losing his son and even though Jude Voltanieu had been a monster and had killed and tortured many Martians, they were able to bypass their own prejudices against the Phalanx and support Kelem emotionally.

But now that the fleet was about to leave in less than a half hour, time was running out and there weren't enough words for all to express their inner feelings and say all the things that they wanted to say. Everyone knew that this truly was the final goodbye and that their dear friend would be gone forever.

Veronica looked at Kelem and smiled. "All right Kelem, I've asked Rusty where that big ball of a ship out there came from," she said, pointing at The Cricket parked above Mars, "and I can tell that he knows but doesn't want to talk about it. Ditto goes for Nicolas here," she added, pointing to the physician-psychiatrist with a smirk.

Kelem laughed and decided that he would tell Veronica a partial truth at least. "Yes, Veronica that is an alien ship, if that's what you were asking," Kelem replied calmly.

"I knew it!" she said, slapping her knee. "Where did it come from and who are the aliens?" she demanded.

"Unfortunately, I promised not to divulge their identities."

"But you told Rusty and Nicolas, and I know Ndugu knows because he returned with you from wherever the hell you two were all those years. And after you took five members of the rebel fleet up to that ship, we suddenly had shields and *n'time* radar. Believe me, I'm grateful that the aliens helped with those things but my curiosity is killing me!" she said begging for information.

"I'm sorry Veronica. I've already overstepped my agreement with the aliens by including Nicolas and Rusty and now you in on the secret. Suffice it to say, Admiral Valchek," Kelem said looking at her pointedly, "that the new Martian Navy should create a space exploration wing and begin traveling to the stars as soon as possible. Perhaps you can be the senior officer who will create that new department of the navy."

"Is that why you warned us about Mars not punishing the Terrans and for all humans to unite as a race for that future when we do meet aliens?"

"Partly, but mostly because it makes sense to be united, whether we as humans meet an alien species or not. Let this war be the last war that humans fight against one another," Kelem pleaded, reiterating his words from the speech he gave on the senate floor.

"What about the aliens on that ship? Why don't they reveal themselves?" Veronica asked, pointing to The Cricket.

"They feel that humanity at large is not mature enough to meet a different species just yet, particularly after witnessing a bloody war between ourselves."

Veronica Valchek shook her head feeling disappointed that humanity would have to wait for decades or perhaps hundreds of years before meeting an alien race. "Damn, I'm going to miss you!" Veronica said, her eyes turning a little red with moisture threatening to turn into tears.

"I will miss you all, but my destiny is elsewhere," Kelem announced, his throat tightening with emotion.

Rusty refilled everyone's glasses and proposed a toast. "To Kelem Rogeston, a true Martian hero, an exceptional man and someone who I feel proud to call a friend. We bid you goodbye and wish you luck wherever you're going. And we're a little jealous that you will make new friends and that we will be left without your company in the years to come. Salud and nastrovia!"

The five drank the wine in one gulp. Kelem made an attempt at humor.

"Jeez Rusty, I didn't know you had it in you!" he said, slapping the big Martian's shoulder, which had gained much of its original bulk from eating good food after fourteen years in exile.

Unexpectedly, Rusty put down his glass and embraced Kelem tightly with tears in his eyes. "I'm glad my arm's not broken this time!" Kelem said, trying to keep himself from breaking down but failing at it miserably.

Instinctively, the four surrounded Kelem and embraced him as a group. The ten minute bell for departure rang and everyone separated, drying their eyes before they went their separate ways.

Veronica Valchek reached for Kelem and kissed him sweetly on the cheek. "Goodbye, Kelem. I will miss you for the rest of my life." Then she left for her command station.

Rusty looked at Kelem with red eyes. "I have to go too. I have a dreadnaught full of Terrans itching to go back to their home planet! By the way, I changed the name of the ship from Stalag Deveraux to Man O' Peace! So long, Kelem. You saved us all, and even though we all want you to stay, I understand how much you've done for your people. You deserve your rest. God bless."

Rusty saluted him military style and then exited the room.

Nicolas, would you give me and Kelem a minute?" Ndugu asked.

"Of course, Ndugu, good luck on Earth, and I hope I get to see you sooner rather than later," Nicolas said, hugging him.

When the pressure door closed, Ndugu sat next to Kelem and was silent for a few seconds, then he spoke. "There is an old Nigerian proverb that goes like this: 'Not to know the good we have till time has stolen the cherished gift away, is cause of half the misery that we feel, and makes the world the wilderness it is.' You can be sure that Martians, Terrans and Lunarians will, from now on, think very carefully about the good we all have before we let it slip away again as we have in the past.

"By the same token, I will never forget the good you brought to my life and the gift of your precious friendship. I knew in my heart that you were going to return to Plantanimus one day and that eventually you were going to leave us all behind. I will miss you, and that's no lie, but I also love you like a brother and even though it's breaking my heart to see you go, I'm happy that you are going back to your paradise. No one more than you deserves that privilege, Kelem! Goodbye, my friend, think of me often as I will think of you throughout the rest of my life."

Ndugu got up, hugged Kelem with tears in his eyes and departed for his ship.

Kelem wiped his own tears and stepped outside where Nicolas was waiting for him.

The crew was making last minute arrangements, closing hatches and securing equipment before departure. Kelem and Nicolas hurried to leave the ship. They ran to the lander and exited the dreadnaught's hangar quickly. Kelem pulled a few hundred kilometers away from the fleet to watch the departure of so many *n'time* ships all at once for the last time in his life.

The skies above Mars began to glow purple as the Martian fleet engaged their *n'time* generators. The collective glow of all the ships grew in size and Kelem felt a lump in his throat realizing what a historic moment this was. The fate of humankind hung on the willingness of the Martian people to forgive the sins of their Terran brothers. Kelem could only hope that the Terrans would respond in kind. There was an entire galaxy out there waiting for humans to explore, and one day men and women from Earth, the Moon and Mars would encounter other sentient beings. Kelem hoped that humans would meet those aliens as one race, united in peace and harmony.

CHAPTER 33

Farewell to Mars

July 10th, 2660

Kelem had finally finished with the ordeal of saying goodbye to everyone and especially Nicolas, whose melancholy tears cut straight into Kelem's heart. The two separated with Kelem promising to reach out to him through the Quantum Tide as often as possible. Nicolas made a joke by asking Kelem to make sure that he visited often enough before he passed on from old age. Kelem assured him that he would live for many more years.

Now heading for the Kren ship, Kelem looked at Jude's ashes inside the sealed urn that the mortuary had provided for him. He had strapped it securely to the co-pilot's chair. Like his father, Jude had been a great pilot and Kelem fancied that his son's spirit was there next to him helping to guide the lander to The Cricket's cargo hold.

Exhausted and emotionally drained by everything that had happened to him since he'd returned to Mars, Kelem was looking forward to getting into the Lectrosleep chamber of the lander and slipping into unconsciousness for a very long time. Perhaps by the time Harriett revived him, his mind would be free of all the turmoil and drama of the last nine months.

One day in the future he might revisit in his mind, the events of this part of his life and remember fondly his adventures in the struggle to free Mars from the Phalanx, but not now. Tomorrow would not be soon enough for him to be on Plantanimus, holding Anima in his arms and climbing Mount Olympus to visit Zeus and the other Dreamers.

Before he knew it he was approaching The Cricket, floating in space above Mars looking like a miniature silver-clad moon. He felt a tug of emotion thinking about the Three Sisters, the three little moons of Plantanimus that Ndugu had so named, and the way that they illuminated the Dreamer forest once a year, when all three came within a few hundred thousand kilometers of one another, making it the brightest moonlit night in the Plantanimus year.

The door of the Kren cargo hold opened and Kelem brought the lander to a stop. He secured the ship, grabbed his duffle bag and Jude's ashes and left the chamber on his way to the rec-room. He knew Harriett would be there and he was looking forward to spending a couple of days in the company of the young Kren queen, enjoying her logical mind which would be a welcome change from the emotional roller coaster that he'd been on lately.

The door slid open and there was Harriett, leaning over a large basket-like object looking at something inside of it.

"How are you, what have you got there?" Kelem asked as he walked over to see what the Kren was doing.

"Hello Kelem, it is good to see you again," Harriett said, turning to look at him. "I missed your company these past few weeks. I have something to show you," Harriett said, pointing to the basket.

Kelem leaned over and was surprised to see several green gelatinous grubs about five centimeters long, wiggling in the bottom of the container. Inside the casing of each grub was a miniature Kren lying in what could only be described as a fetal position.

"Are those your…?"

"Yes, Kelem, these are my babies," the Kren said, answering his question.

Kelem was fascinated and repulsed at the same time but kept his reaction to himself.

"They're so tiny!" he remarked as he counted how many of them there were. The tally came to sixty.

"It's only my first birth. As I grow bigger, subsequent generations will be born larger in size and mature more quickly."

"How long will it take for these to become adults?" Kelem asked, wondering if when he came out of Lectrosleep he would have to be careful not to step on little Kren running amok.

"These will take a year to mature because they're still gestating."

Kelem realized suddenly that the sound of Harriett's voice issuing from the metal box around her neck sounded distinctly female and had inflections that sounded quite human.

"You voice… it sounds familiar, where have I heard it before?" he asked himself. "Oh, I know! It's Lola Irigoyen's voice… but how?"

"Lola and I became quite close and she grew tired of listening to my original monotone voice programming. So with her help, we sampled her voice in all possible moods and inflections and redesigned the speech translating software of my speech module."

"Harriett, not only do you sound human now, but you're using terms like, 'we became quite close' and 'it is good to see you again'. What's going on? Are you developing emotions?"

"In the time that we've spent apart, I've discovered a few facts about being a Kren Mother."

"Like what for instance?" Kelem wanted to know.

"Well for one thing, I realized a few weeks ago that all Kren queens have emotions. These emotions are not as complex as human emotions, but they are emotions nevertheless."

"How did this knowledge come to you? Are you hearing your mother in your head again?"

"In a way, yes. When Mother changed me, she imprinted many instructions in my brain in the form of memories which I now have access to whenever I need guidance. When I began to feel these new sensations which I now recognize as emotions, I consulted my implanted memories and understood for the first time that all Kren queens have emotions."

"Then, why aren't all Kren capable of feeling emotions like their hive mothers?" Kelem asked logically.

"Because, when we Kren changed ourselves from being a species that lived on planets to living in giant space faring colonies, the queens had to breed out emotions from their offspring. Otherwise, the drones would go insane from having to live so crowded next to one another."

"But why did the Kren change from a planet inhabiting species to living in crowded colony ships in the first place?"

"In ancient times, we Kren were more like humans when our species lived on our ancestral planet. And like you, we eventually suffered an environmental catastrophe that nearly decimated us due to over-industrializing our planet. The population had grown too numerous and we began to compete for resources. In those times, there were many colonies on our planet and they behaved much like countries do in human society today. Eventually, resources became scarce and colonies went to war against one another."

"So the Kren have a violent past after all," Kelem commented, shuddering to think what a frightening sight a warring army of Kren would be.

"Yes, and we nearly destroyed ourselves. So it was decided that in order to prevent our kind from becoming extinct, we had to develop the capability of space travel, and that led to space-faring hive ships. But when we finally were able to live in those hive-ships, colonies began to fall apart as individual Kren became psychotic due to overcrowding. So the queens began to breed out individuality and aggressive tendencies in order to keep the race from, once again, becoming extinct."

"And that resulted in Kren having no emotions?"

"Correct. The species would continue but at the cost of individuality."

"So, if the queens have emotions, how do they keep from going insane themselves, when their drone offspring have no personalities? Do they communicate with other queens through telepathy and have conversations with them to keep themselves entertained?" Kelem asked, wondering how Harriett would spend the rest of her five to six millennia length life.

"Kren queens inherit the memories of all the queens in their lineage, and those memories act like a kind of virtual presence of the minds of all the queens who have come before her. But in spite of that, Kren queens live, what you might call, 'lonely lives'."

"Thousands of years spent in lonely contemplation!" Kelem remarked, astounded by the knowledge that a sentient being with feelings and emotions could survive so long without becoming insane. The Kren were truly different!

"Yes, but your encounter with Mother changed that," Harriett commented.

"What! What do you mean?" Kelem asked, feeling responsible for having changed the fate of an entire species.

"When Mother communicated with you and learned that humans had developed the capability of traveling clear across the galaxy to the quadrant of space that the Kren thought was uninhabited, save for themselves, she knew at that moment that humans would eventually colonize the entire galaxy and within a few centuries, begin arriving in great numbers."

"I still don't understand how you running into us on Plantanimus affected the future of all Kren queens' future mental health."

"Not just the queens but all the Kren," Harriett replied.

"All the Kren? Please clarify," Kelem inquired with concern.

"Simple. Humans are emotional, complex creatures who live in large colonies made up of highly individualized members. To a Kren, that spells disaster because that is the one factor that nearly destroyed us. However, Mother also learned that your species survived your environmental holocaust which you call 'the Dark Period' and managed to flourish and continue your civilization in spite of your social complexities. No Kren queen before her had ever communicated telepathically with any other telepathic species until you showed up. Her contact with you changed her perception of reality and she had what you might call, an 'epiphany'."

"Crap! What the hell did I do?" Kelem remarked, feeling self-conscious.

"You made her realize that the Kren could have more fulfilling lives without being bred to be drones like I was. So, she changed me to a female and then implanted specific instructions in my mind on how to improve the future of the Kren species."

"So your babies will grow up with emotions and personalities like us humans?"

"Not exactly. No Kren can ever be as emotionally complex as you are, but my children will have their own minds and will be able to make decisions on their own, though they'll still belong to the hive and I will always be their queen mother. Mother wanted that because we will eventually interact with humans at large in the future, and Kren need to understand humans to prevent misunderstandings and conflicts."

"I don't know, Harriett - I fear that Mother may have made a mistake by modeling future Kren after an emotional and sometimes irrational species like us!"

"I don't agree, Kelem. After spending several months in the company of humans, I came to understand that it's your very individualistic nature that gives you the ability to be so creative and make leaps of logic that we Kren are incapable of. Mother said that without individuality, we Kren would eventually go extinct due to social stagnation."

"I hope Mother was right, because she opened a door that can't be closed by making you the progenitor of that new generation," Kelem commented.

"Indeed. Now, come my dear friend, I prepared you one of the human meals that Lola Irigoyen taught me how to cook, it's called spaghetti and meatballs."

Kelem laughed and followed Harriett to the chamber that she and the five humans had converted to a kitchen.

Kelem spent the next two days relaxing and winding down as The Cricket reached faster than light speed. Harriett's new personality and fascinating conversation had served to help Kelem put the events of the last nine months in perspective. He would always cherish in his heart the memories of the friends and loved ones that he had lost and of those he would never see again in this life. But overall, he was content with his lot. His destiny was on Plantanimus, and twelve months from now, he would return to the strange forest that he had seen in his dreams since the age of thirteen. That place had always been home for him.

The following evening, Kelem laid down on one of the lander's Lectrosleep chambers and bid Harriett goodnight as she closed the lid to the machine. Soon, Kelem felt the slight tickle of the machine's organic micro-tendrils penetrating his skin preparing him for months of unconsciousness.

As he began to drift into the blackness of Lectrosleep, he saw the image of Anima waiting for him by the meadow near their cottage at the foot of Mount Olympus. Then he heard the music of the Dreamers echoing in the forest.

CHAPTER 34

Perhaps Tomorrow...

October 5ᵗʰ, 2821

The very tall and very old, old man, stood near the edge of the cliff staring out into the sea several meters below. His right hand clung to a gnarled walking staff made of wood, supported his thin frame which swayed slightly to and fro to the rhythm of the winds that crept up the cliff's walls, and then continued up the flanks of the ancient volcano behind him. On his shoulders rested a long cape made of woven purple grass strands festooned with many flowers of bright iridescent colors.

The sun, now sitting low in the sky, cast an orange glow over the gentle waves of the Plantanimus Sea. Up forty five degrees from the horizon looking to the west, Luna, Metaluna, and Mezzaluna, the three sister moons of Plantanimus, were beginning to show their faces in the northern sky. For the next two weeks, the three little moons would line up next to each other as they always did once a year, and together, they would create the brightest moonlit nights of the Plantanimus year.

Their effect on the sea tides below would be minimal. The three moons were more than one hundred fifty nine thousand kilometers from the surface of the planet.

To the old man's left, erosion on the cliff had long ago uncovered a patch of black earth showing an array of shocked quartz, white quartz and large beautiful columns of purple Amethyst. The crystals were now shimmering brightly in the last rays of the setting sun.

Behind him to the west, the narrow thin trail that led to this part of the cliff gave way to the sub-tropical Plantanimus forest which continued all the way to the mouth of the old volcano. Long ago, the old man had named the place Mount Olympus.

At the edge of the forest, the youngest Dreamers who were normally barely visible through the thicket of wildly colored flora could now be seen plainly with the sun shining at a low angle on their tall, thick trunks. To a stranger not familiar with the way the sunlight played with the texture of the Dreamers' trunks, they would appear as beautiful twisted towers of pure gold peering through the thick canopy of the forest.

Farther up the mountain, the Dreamers became older and taller the higher one climbed toward its peak at five thousand meters. At the very top, sitting in the middle of the ancient caldera, Zeus, the oldest, rose majestically into the sky, its trunk one hundred meters tall and thirty one meters wide, its massive roots intertwined with the ruins of the ancient temple of the evil Tau priests who had brought about the cataclysm that almost destroyed Plantanimus more than ten thousand years before.

To the south, the semi-arid plains of Plantanimus stretched off into the distance, the only place on this world where there still lived a few original species of grasses and small critters that had somehow survived the near destruction of the planet.

In spite of his advanced age, the old man could still see that far into the distance. Even at this time of day with daylight fading, the ancient roads connecting the many cone shaped monoliths of the Tau priests could still be easily detected on the plains. The huge structures had once been painted black, made so to intimidate the people of this planet whose race had been called the Umhar. Even though the sun had bleached the towers white over the millennia, one could easily imagine the fear and trepidation that an Umhar would have felt just looking at those black monstrosities, even at a distance.

To the southeast, the ruins of the city that had once been the capital of this planet could now barely be seen as the mist from the ocean began its nightly trek inland.

The old man turned his eyes away from the south, for that part of Plantanimus held some very dark and unpleasant memories for him, and the one thing he didn't want to do now, was to bring up those memories. Although he had walked and explored that part of the continent in his younger days, he hadn't traveled there in nearly five decades. Now, aged one hundred and ninety two years (if one reckoned years in human terms), he hadn't traveled farther than five kilometers in as many decades.

He was sure that he was now the longest living human in recorded history. In Genesis, the Bible told of Adam and Eve's descendants living longer than he had up to now. But for him, now nearly two centuries old, the thought of living even another decade or two seemed ludicrous.

It wasn't so much the aches, pains and indignity of geriatric maladies that he minded so much. No, that wasn't what really bothered him. After all, physically, he looked and felt like a man perhaps in his eighties or nineties. He knew that back on Earth many people were now living past one hundred thanks to nano technology. In his case, the Dreamers had maintained his health all these past years using their own version of nano-tech.

He was sure that as far as the Dreamers were concerned, they expected him to hang around for a lot longer than he cared to think.

The oldest Dreamer, Zeus, was now over ten thousand years old, and it was obvious to the old man that Zeus and all the others didn't want to let him go.

After all, he was the one who had awakened them from their slumber of nearly ten millennia. And through him, the Dreamers had learned all about the universe that existed beyond the boundaries of Mount Olympus.

For all their incredible mental, spiritual and psychic abilities, the Dreamers were living sentient plants who were deaf, blind and most regrettably, stationary for their entire existence. The old man was their only connection to all the things that they could never experience on their own.

And although the Dreamers had always been able to communicate with each other, the old man was the only living being, besides his mate Anima who had ever linked with them telepathically.

The old man's problem was memories. Not the forgetting of them, for his mind was still as sharp as when he was young and he could recall almost any event that had transpired in his long life. The problem was too many memories. It seemed that the modern human brain had developed enough capacity to safely retain a lifetime's worth of memories, as long as that lifetime didn't exceed more than a hundred years or so.

If he weren't able to remember details of his early life, say, from age zero to his early twenties, the old man didn't think that that would be too bad. After all, he could go to the Dreamers and have them refresh his memory of a particular event and that would be fine. The Dreamers had recorded every single second of his life in their minds.

The main issue was that when he wanted to recall a particular event or person, several memories would crop up all at once, almost as if he had asked to see a particular page in a certain book, but the librarian had handed him several hundred pages without numbers, forcing him to read several dozen pages before he could find the one page that he had asked for originally.

When this problem had started a few years back, he had gone to Zeus and asked him for help. Zeus and the others, tried several therapies and they all worked to a certain extent, but eventually they were not able to render any significant remedy as the problem became more serious.

Worst of all, when he was linked with the Dreamers, they could not detect the information overload in the old man's head. Even when he was having a "memory overload event", the giant sentient plants somehow could not detect it.

So here he was, lucid as always. At least if madness ensued, he would perhaps forget the problem because of his madness! And still death would not come. He would never commit suicide, for it was against his principles, but a natural death with dignity would be most welcome at this point. The lone figure at the top of the cliff was tired of living.

With the sun now almost gone where sky and ocean met and with the darkness of night approaching, the old man's shoulders sunk as if under a heavy burden. As the sunlight faded, his legs seemed to lose strength with the setting sun, and moving backwards a bit he found a flat rock worn smooth by time and weather. He had sat on this rock many times over the years and it gave him some comfort to think of this chunk of igneous material as an old friend that had worked its way from the depths of the planet several million years ago for the express purpose of supporting his aging body these many years.

If he could talk to the rock and vice versa, what would he say to it if given the chance?

Would he say, "Old friend, how does it feel to be so old and do memories ever overwhelm you?"

And the rock might answer, "Old man, I'm just a rock, I do not feel and I have no memories, I just exist."

Now the old man spoke out loud to the wind. "How I envy you, rock, for I am a man and I have too many feelings and remembrances of so many things and I wish, oh so much, that I were like you, just a rock existing on this beautiful meadow by the sea."

The sun finally disappeared and the Three Sister Moons now cast a silver light on the old man's head whose long white hair seemed to glow in the night.

"Beloved, beloved, wake up!" whispered the green woman shaking the old man's shoulder gently.

He had fallen asleep holding on to his staff while sitting on the rock.

With her right hand she pulled the old man's head up gently and lovingly as she stroked his forehead with her left hand, clearing away several long strands of silver hair from his eyes.

The old man's blue eyes opened slowly at first, not knowing where he was. Then, as sleep left his head he smiled with recognition.

"My Anima, my sweet and gentle Anima," he said in a soft voice. "I was just dreaming about a rock, a talking rock at that!"

"A talking rock you say? That must have been an interesting dream. What did the rock say to you, my darling Kelem?"

The old man laughed softly and shook his head. "It told me what any good rock would say. It told me that it was just a rock and that rocks just lay there and are content to be rocks in the world."

"I've never spoken with a rock, but your account of the conversation rings true to me," replied the green woman as she placed the purple cape that had fallen off the old man, back on his shoulders.

"Indeed, Anima, I think rocks are probably some of the most logical and well-adjusted objects in the universe."

"That's probably true, my dearest. After all, the Dreamers are immobile and yet they are at peace with the universe."

The old man nodded in agreement and then turned to his left

looking at Anima's face just a few centimeters away from his. "My darling, in the moonlight your hair looks like beautiful strands of pearls."

"Ah yes!" she responded. "I was just swimming in the little lake by the cottage. I guess my hair is still wet."

"All these years and you're still so beautiful," the old man remarked with wonder, as he gazed at her beautiful features. "You haven't changed a bit, and here," he said, pointing to himself. "Look at me, a bent and wrinkled shadow of my former self."

"You shall always be my Kelem, the one for whom I was created."

"I'm not that man anymore," he whispered sadly.

"I've told you a million times, my beloved, your countenance is not what keeps me bonded to you," she said with a loving smile.

"I know. I know that what you say is true. But please forgive my human weakness Anima, the ego is a powerful beast to conquer. You have been with me for one hundred and sixty two years, and in all that time I've never had the slightest cause to doubt your unending love for me. And yet here I am feeling inadequate because of my old body."

"But darling, part of the reason why I'm so dedicated to you, is your humanity and all that it entails," she asserted with a sweet intensity in her voice. "You see, my beloved Kelem, when I came to be that night so many years ago, I didn't know anything about anything. And then you, patiently, over many months and then years, taught me how to be an individual and how to be human even though I'm not human."

She paused now, and then kneeled in front of the old man still sitting on the rock, head bent toward the ground. She held his hands in hers, her green eyes searching for his blue eyes in the soft moonlight.

"You see, Kelem, you've taught me how to live, and most of all, to know your love!"

"That may be true, my sweet Anima," the old man answered, his blue eyes filled with sadness, "but it seems that lately I've been forgetting how to live myself. I sense that my time has run out, that somehow I missed the appointment for my own passing."

"Please do not speak of this, beloved," replied Anima with concern in her voice. "I could not bear living without you. I know the Dreamers put me in Pralaya when you left Plantanimus for nearly three years, but being in Pralaya felt like a distant dream and it made me miss you more."

"My beautiful Anima, you must understand that no matter what you and the Dreamers want, I will die someday. Unlike you, my dear, my body ages and even though I've outlived every human that I've ever known, this body will eventually cease to work. A day will come when I will be no more."

"What a cruel thing death is!" Anima murmured softly. "Yet, I wish for it also if you are to die."

"Do not say that, Anima. You know that even after I'm gone there are others whose destiny is to come to Plantanimus. Both you and I and the Dreamers have seen this future and know it will come to pass," he said, pausing for a moment and then continued with an urgent tone in his voice. "Who then, will welcome these travelers and help them understand Plantanimus? Who will be left to teach them how to link with the Dreamers and tell them all about me and all that I did and learned while I was alive?"

"What a terrible burden you place on me, Kelem," she answered, feeling conflicted. "You want me to let you go and yet live with the emptiness of your absence."

"That's right, that's precisely what I want you to do. It's what you must do, sweet Anima, it's what humans have been doing for thousands of years!"

Now they both fell silent, lost in their own thoughts. After a while, Kelem spoke again.

"Do you remember how I treated you after we met?"

Anima nodded.

"I hated you. To me you were an artificial facsimile of someone I had loved and lost. The Dreamers, in their desire to heal my broken heart, created you to resemble, look and act like Carlatta, thinking that your presence would take away the pain of losing her."

She nodded once again, letting go of Kelem's hands. This was a painful memory for her. All that she knew back then was that her purpose was to be with Kelem and nothing else, yet all he did for a long time was to reject her.

"Thanks to Ndugu, I came to my senses and saw how my treatment of you was cruel. I was so selfishly involved in my own pain that I didn't see how much I was hurting you. Here you were, just a few months alive and all that you had learned from me was pain and rejection."

The old man's voice shook with emotion, remembering his cruelty.

"It wasn't until I let go of Carlatta in my heart and mind that I was able to know you, to respect you, and eventually come to love you."

Kelem reached for her hands and kissed them tenderly. "You see, my darling, if you don't learn to let go of me, you might suffer from the same cruel and selfish behavior that I inflicted upon you," he paused again, searching for words. "You know others are coming. You are the only one who can carry on."

A gust of wind from the sea came across the clearing and rustled the short grass covering the ground. Anima rose to her knees and embraced Kelem almost as if to protect him from the future that was to come.

Above, the stars were now twinkling fiercely in competition with the light of the Three Sisters. The two figures remained motionless for a long time, like a statue of two lovers embracing in the moonlight.

Next morning, Kelem woke up and found himself in his bed next to Anima's dirt mound where she slept every night. The sun was already up and its light could be seen flickering through the forest's canopy.

Outside, the sound of the waterfall near their cottage could be heard in its never ending dive into the lake's surface.

The smell of Martian stew drifted through the air into Kelem's nose from the kitchen outside. It was his favorite meal.

Excited, he began to get up from his bed but his body felt unusually heavy and stiff. With difficulty he struggled to his feet and put on his loin cloth. When he reached the door he saw Anima already setting the table, singing softly to herself.

"Good morning, my beloved," she said brightly as soon as she saw him by the door.

"How did I get back to my bed last night?" he asked, somewhat confused.

She put down the last piece of silverware and came around the table to hug him.

"My dearest, after we talked for a long time, you fell into a very deep sleep. I didn't have the heart to wake you up and have you walk up the mountain back to the cottage, so I simply carried you in my arms and put you to bed," she said with a smile, and then kissed him softly on the cheek.

Kelem wasn't surprised, knowing that Anima was stronger than ten men put together, but it bothered him that he had slumbered so deeply and not remembered being carried back to the cottage.

The smell of the stew soon replaced any questions about the night before and he gladly sat at the little picnic table that he and Ndugu Nabole had built so long ago by the shore of the small lake.

Besides the stew, Anima had made a salad of lettuce, carrots, onions and tomatoes from their garden behind the cottage. She had made the dressing from the juice of the fruit of the Kama tree, one of the many species of fruit trees that the Dreamers had created for Kelem.

Kelem was unusually hungry and he finished everything on the plate.

Anima sat and watched him eat with a smile on her face. Even though she didn't eat, she always enjoyed looking on as Kelem consumed her cooking with pleasure.

"What shall we do today, beloved?" she asked when he finished eating.

"I'm not sure. Today, Plantanimus' gravity seems to have an extra hold on me."

"I will carry you wherever you please, perhaps down to the river delta near the sea?" she suggested, knowing that Kelem loved going down there whenever possible.

"Perhaps some other time my darling," Kelem responded. "Maybe today I'll just sit on the hammock by the lakeshore and read one of my books."

Anima nodded and got up to clean the dirty dishes from the meal. Kelem smiled as she sang a melody from one of Earth's ancient songs accompanied by the sound of washing plates and silverware.

He got up from the table stiffly and went into the cottage to pick up a book to read. He scanned through the many reading tablets that he had rescued from the Solar Nations library before its orbit had decayed and crashed into the Plantanimus Sea.

He picked Sir Isaac Newton's Principia. He hadn't read that book since his days in college back on Mars. He looked forward to rediscovering the old classic containing the ideas and principles upon which all modern mathematics, physics and astronomy were based.

He went back outside, and as he headed toward the hammock suspended by two weeping willows, he suddenly felt dizzy and almost lost his balance. He stumbled as he reached one of the trees and leaned against it, feeling a little nauseous. He worried that Anima had seen him almost fall. He looked toward the kitchen but she was still tidying up, still singing her song.

Grateful that she hadn't seen him, he plopped down on the hammock and felt better lying down as the nausea went away.

Later, Anima brought out a pillow from the cottage and placed it behind Kellem's head so that he'd have a better angle to read.

"Now it's time for my breakfast," announced Anima. She ran to the lake and dove in making a big splash in the water.

Water and sunlight was what sustained her.

Kelem was proud of the fact that he had taught her to swim many years ago, but she soon surpassed the teacher. With her physical strength she could do things in the water that no human could ever accomplish. She also liked to climb to the top of the waterfall some ten meters above and dive in with the expertise of an Olympian athlete. After diving in from such a height, she would burst out of the water reminding Kelem of the power and grace of Dolphins back on Earth.

This morning she seemed particularly active and was performing some back flips and fancy dives such as he had never seen her do. He kept trying to start reading the Principia but her prowess and talent kept him so entertained, all he could do was to look in fascination.

He watched this wonderful water ballet performance with great joy for quite a while when suddenly, he felt a sharp pain on the right side of his head and the left side of his body went numb.

He knew immediately what was happening, and a curious mixture of fear and relief assailed him unexpectedly. He laid there for a while adjusting his mind to the fact that he might be dying. "What to do, what to do?" was all that he thought, repeating the words over and over for a while.

"Why you old fool," he thought to himself after a time. "There's nothing you can or should do. You're the one who's been hoping for this life to come to an end. Be like your friend the rock and lie there content with your lot."

If he had been able to laugh, seeing the black humor in this awkward situation he would have burst out with a guffaw to end all laughing fits.

His sight now began to fade as well and suddenly day turned into night.

After what seemed an eternity, he heard Anima's footsteps approaching and then there were water drops falling on his face.

"Kelem, Kelem!" she shouted, knowing that something was wrong. "Kelem, you look funny, your face is all twisted, what's wrong my beloved, what's wrong?"

His sight returned for a while and he saw the fear and dread in her eyes. His right arm and leg seemed to be working still and he realized that he was still holding on to the reading tablet.

He quickly raised the tablet to his chest and with great difficulty he managed to take out the stylus attached to the side of it and scribbled a message on it.

"HAVING A STTROK, PROBALYB DYYIN', I LOV U."

She took the tablet from his hand and a look of horror came over her face.

"No, you can't, I won't let it happen!" she said more to herself than to him.

She stood up and looked at Kelem, her mind filled with turmoil. She looked at the reading tablet and read it over and over as if somehow the message would magically disappear and all would return to normal.

Kelem's heart was breaking. He didn't care that he was dying, but the pain of seeing her so grief stricken and desperate, filled him with sadness beyond description.

A tear fell from Kelem's right eye running down his cheek and then he felt himself falling and everything went dark and silent.

Sometime later he came to again and wondered why everything was shaking so much. In his right ear he could hear Anima's heavy breathing as she ran mightily up the mountain while carrying him. He realized that she was bringing him to Zeus. He tried to speak and move but his whole body felt cold and numb now. His eyesight came back to him now and again and all he saw around him each time he opened his eyes, were the large trunks of the oldest Dreamers rushing by quickly as Anima climbed Mount Olympus.

Above the canopy covering the mountain, the light of the sun was beginning to fade. As night fell, the light of the Three Sisters pierced through the foliage here and there creating thin shafts of silvery moonlight giving the forest a ghostly shimmer.

Anima's lungs were burning as she fought for every breath of air, trying to get as much oxygen into her body as possible. She had somehow managed to climb to the top of Mount Olympus in less than eight hours. With the last ounce of strength from her formidable struggle, she staggered for the last few meters to place Kelem at the foot of Zeus' massive trunk, the oldest of the Dreamers.

Carefully and tenderly, she laid Kelem on the ground as her arms and legs trembled from the mighty effort of having carried him so far.

She covered his body with the purple cape and then collapsed in a heap next to him breathing heavily.

After a few minutes had passed, the ground began to vibrate as the Dreamers began to synchronize their minds in preparation for a link.

Anima's exhaustion went away as the vibrations climbed higher and higher in pitch and intensity, filling her body with renewed energy.

Soon the entire forest of Dreamers was pulsating, creating a symphony of harmonic pitches that would have drowned the senses of most humans.

But to Anima, this was the music of spirit come to life. Communing with the Dreamers was like drinking from the fountain of universal life.

Anima raised herself from the forest floor and walked underneath Zeus' roots. She glanced at Kelem once more, hoping that the vibrations had healed him and he would get up on his own. But he just laid there immobile, his face ashen under the light of the three moons and the stars.

She put her palms on Zeus' roots and closed her eyes.

After a while she heard the Dreamers' voices inside her head.

"DAUGHTER, YOUR MIND IS IN CHAOS. WHAT TROUBLES YOU?"

"Wise ones, makers of my life, my beloved Kelem lies at your feet. He's very sick and needs your help."

The mountain shook and trembled as the Dreamers digested the meaning of Anima's thoughts.

"IS HE WITH YOU?' asked Zeus by himself this time. "I DO NOT SENSE HIM NEAR US."

"He is at your feet. I am looking at him as we speak."

After a while as the Dreamers looked through Anima's eyes, they understood.

"THIS IS GRAVE NEWS INDEED, DAUGHTER, WE ARE ALARMED BEYOND THOUGHT."

Anima waited impatiently for the next thought from the Dreamers. She knew that all of them had to process an idea together before they could communicate with her. "DAUGHTER, WE NEED YOUR ASSISTANCE TO HELP HIM. PLEASE REMOVE ALL CLOTHING FROM HIS BODY."

Anima let go of Zeus' roots and jumped over to where Kelem was lying and quickly removed his cape and loin cloth revealing his thin and aged pale body.

She stood there and watched with fascination as thin white tendrils emerged from the ground and gently covered Kellem's entire body, leaving openings for breathing through his mouth and nose.

The dreamers vibrations raised in pitch and intensity so much so that the dew on their bodies began to vaporize, creating a bluish haze lit by the moonlight above the forest.

Through the haze, the ghost like image of Kelem appeared standing next to his prostrate body. He appeared to be looking at Anima and Zeus. His mouth was moving but she could not hear the words.

She yelled out loud trying to be heard above the sound of the Dreamers' music.

"What is he saying, what is he trying to say?"

"LET ME GO, LET ME GO, IS WHAT HE'S SAYING, DAUGHTER. HE DOES NOT WANT TO REMAIN."

"No, no, please don't let him go, wise ones!" she screamed at the top of her lungs. "Givers of my life, he is the one for me and I'm the one for him. You made me for him, my life is for him!"

Anima fell to the ground on her knees, pounding the forest's floor in deep anguish.

"YOUR SADNESS OVERWHELMS US, DAUGHTER. WE ARE GRIEVING FOR HIM AS WELL, BUT THERE IS NOTHING MORE WE CAN DO. GO NOW TO HIM, CHILD,

AND COMFORT HIM IN HIS LAST MOMENTS OF LIFE. HOLD HIM AND CARESS HIM AND TELL HIM OF THE LOVE AND APPRECIATION THAT WE ALL HAVE FOR HIM. TELL HIM HOW GRATEFUL WE ARE THAT HE AWOKE US FROM OUR SLUMBER. TELL HIM HOW HE GAVE US EYES AND EARS AND SHOWED US THE WORLD OUTSIDE THIS FOREST. A PART OF US DIES WITH HIM THIS NIGHT."

The tendrils covering Kelem's body returned to the ground and the symphony came to a soft end as the Dreamers' music faded away.

Now, only the sound of the wind rustling the leaves on the canopy above could be heard.

With weariness such as she had never felt before, she crawled to where Kelem lay and covered him with his cape. She sat next to him and pulled him to her bosom, embracing him with her arms.

Like a mother comforting a sick child, Anima rocked Kelem back and forth. She spoke softly to him, telling him all the things that the Dreamers had asked her to say and more. She sang to him all the children's lullabies and songs that Ndugu and Kelem had taught her and, for the first time in her life, she cried tears of mourning, and her tears fell gently on Kelem's face as his life ebbed away by the roots of Zeus' trunk.

Near midnight, Kelem's eyes opened wide and his back stiffened for a second as he took his last breath and then he was gone.

Anima had never seen anyone die, but she knew instinctively that Kellem's spirit had left his body.

She held him for a long time after that, kissing him and caressing his brow, fixing his hair and stroking his beard as she had done so many times in the past.

His face looked so peaceful under the glow of the Three Sisters now giving way to the coming light of the morning sun.

She put him down gently on the ground and began to dig a grave with her bare hands for her beloved Kelem. She knew that it didn't need to be very deep. Zeus and the others would use his body to sustain them and add his essence to theirs.

In the early light of dawn, Anima stood over the shallow grave and said a final goodbye to the only being she had loved her entire life.

She turned around and began walking down Mount Olympus

carrying Kelem's cape in her arm. The cape felt warm and soft to her, almost as if his body was still inside of it. Tomorrow she would put new flowers on it to replace the ones that had faded away.

Her sadness was deep, but Kelem's words from barely a day ago rang in her ears giving her comfort and courage to move on. "You know others are coming, you are the only one who can carry on."

She would carry Kelem's love and legacy in her heart and tell others of his remarkable life and accomplishments, and help the next generation of visitors learn all about the wonders of Plantanimus.

She reached the cottage and after spreading Kellem's cape neatly on his bed, she ran down to the meadow on the cliff by the sea.

When she got there, she stood atop the old rock worn down by time and weather, and with her hand shielding her eyes from the bright morning sun, she scanned the sky for the tell-tale sign of a ship entering the planet's atmosphere.

She realized that it might be a while before this would come to pass.

Perhaps tomorrow.......

THE END

Epilog

The years after the war

The Martian fleet arrived on Earth and demanded the unconditional surrender of the Terran government. Earth surrendered immediately, and when Martian troops landed on the planet they were surprised to be welcomed by the average Terran citizen as liberators instead of invaders.

President Sylvan Montenegro was arrested along with his entire administration, several senators and members of congress, all the top ranking members of the Phalanx and a number of their underlings. Also arrested were a number of wealthy industrialists and financial investors who had supported the occupation of Mars and had profited from it.

An international tribunal was formed, comprised of Terrans, Lunarians and Martians. The guilty were tried and sentenced. A significant number of them were executed for crimes against humanity.

The Terran military was disbanded and the Phalanx was dissolved, never to exist again.

Former Martian President Solomon Vandecamp was arrested and brought to Mars to stand trial for committing treason by giving the Terrans the intelligence that led to the invasion and subsequent occupation of Mars. He was found guilty and sentenced to death. On Mars, the surname Vandecamp became synonymous with treachery and evil.

Admiral Veronica Valchek remained in charge of the Martian fleet for three years, and was relieved of its command and then put in charge of re-organizing the Martian Space Navy. She created the Space Exploration wing of the navy and was instrumental in preparing humanity for interstellar travel. She retired at age seventy six and lived to the ripe old age of ninety seven with her husband, former Navy Captain Ron Hugh.

Admiral Rusty Deveraux took charge of the Martian fleet when Admiral Valchek left and remained as its commanding officer until 2670 when the fleet's mission was completed and recalled back to Mars. He resigned his commission and he and his wife decided to remain on Earth. His daughter Anna had grown up there and did not want to relocate to Mars. Anna Deveraux married a Terran young man and became a naturalized citizen. Louie Deveraux returned to Mars and was trained by the Brotherhood of the Light and became a powerful psychic. He graduated from the Amazonis College of Medicine and became one of the most respected diagnosticians in the solar system. Rusty and Danielle Deveraux lived into their late nineties and were buried on Earth. Admiral Deveraux was celebrated by both Terrans and Martians as a hero.

Nicolas Alfano was chosen as the Martian Ambassador to Earth and served in that post into his late eighties. He became respected and admired for helping mend the wound that had separated Martians and Terrans for more than two centuries. He returned to Mars and lived to see his great-great grandchildren graduate from college.

General Greg Loeky, a hero of the Martian revolution, became the 47th Martian President and ran for two consecutive terms. He left behind a legacy of progressive policies and was responsible for creating a strong Martian Military.

Admiral Ndugu Nabole served for one year as a senior officer of the Martian Fleet on Earth, then resigned his commission and became an advocate for the African territory. His efforts helped restore that continent to its former glory. Africa was the last area of Earth to fully recover from the effects of the "Dark Period" (Earth's environmental disaster of the late 21st century). He remained on Earth for twelve years working in that capacity. He married a Terran woman of Chinese origin named Guan-yin and together they raised four children, Kiku, Kelem, Zeus and Anima. Ndugu and his family returned to Mars and he became a Martian senator serving six terms. He died at the amazing age of one hundred and seventeen surrounded by his children, grand-children and great-great grandchildren. He wrote one of the best biographies of his beloved friend, Kelem Rogeston.

Billy Chong's widow, Verena Chong and her two sons, Kelem and Bernardo Chong, ran the Mars Mining Company successfully well into the next century. The MMC opened headquarters on Earth as well as the Moon and shared the asteroid mining technology that had been a well-guarded Martian secret for over two hundred and seventy years. Sarah Chong, Bernardos' daughter became the 54th president of Mars.

Captain Magrut Belichek, the Black Guard captain who helped the Martian resistance during the revolution, remained on Mars and was granted citizenship. He married a Martian woman and raised three children. One hundred other former Black Guards who also helped the Martian resistance remained on Mars and settled there for the rest of their lives.

Soltan Voltanieu and his son Jude Voltanieu became infamous for their horrible crimes against humanity and remained as hated figures in history books for all time.

Sister Ornata Marchant, who later changed her name to Sister Ornata Rogeston, remained as the head of the Church of the Universal Mind God until her death at the age of one hundred and five. The church would later be known as the Church of St. Kelem, and would grow to become one of the largest religious organizations in the solar system.

The Brotherhood of the Light recovered from the effects of the Terran occupation and continued with its original purpose of recruiting and training talented Martian psychics. The organization came to the decision that the Brotherhood should remain secret because mankind was not ready to accept the existence of individuals with such powers and abilities. Public knowledge of the Brotherhood faded into the fog of time, though it continued serving mankind for many centuries.

Kelem Rogeston became one of the most famous and lauded historical figures in human history. The story of his life and accomplishments, and his legendary adventures during the Martian Revolution were the inspiration for thousands of drama-vids, biographies, theatre plays, fictional books, children's stories and the subject of numerous rumors and theories regarding his abilities. Many believed that he had brought an alien with him when he returned to the solar system and that this alien had given him super-human powers. The alien was named Harry and he was a monstrous spider with venomous fangs that liked to eat members of the Phalanx for breakfast. The surname Rogeston became very popular and many Martians changed their last names legally. The fad also took hold on the Moon and even on Earth. By the end of the 27th century, hundreds of thousands of babies carried the Rogeston surname legally. In the centuries to come, many claimed to be direct descendants of the man. Statues of Kelem Rogeston typically holding a model of the *n'time* generator in one hand and a pulse rifle in the other, could be found throughout Mars, the Moon and Earth. To the members of the Church of St. Kelem, he was worshiped as a messiah sent to Mars by God to liberate its people from their bondage to Earth.

By the year 2722, the distinction between Terrans, Lunarians and Martians had blurred to the point that passports and visas became unnecessary to travel between planets. In the year 2751, the three sovereign solar Nations voted to enact a unified Solar System Government. From that point on, all humans became a homogeneous social group having a single national identity. The second Martian War of Independence was the last war fought between humans.

In the year 2794, one hundred and twenty eight years after the end of that war, a human space ship the "Solar Nations II", made contact with a humanoid species called the Tarsians.

NEXT, IN THE LAST BOOK OF THE TRILOGY,

The Gulax War

The encounter with the Tarsians begins a new era in human history. Within a short time, humans and Tarsians are trading goods between their two worlds. The Tarsians are not as advanced as humans, though they have space travel technology. The Tarsian Empire, ruled by a constitutional monarchy, is a conglomeration of over thirty planets located nine hundred light years from Earth.

The Tarsians are excellent craftsmen and their art and luxury items are like nothing humans have ever seen. In turn, the Tarsians are amazed by _n'time_ technology and all the other scientific advances that humanity has made. Fortunes are quickly made from the import and export of goods and technology, and the two civilizations soon become dependent on each other's economies.

But in 2804, the Tarsians are invaded by an unknown species called the Gulax. The Gulax are a reptilian warrior race bent on conquering the galaxy and they begin invading Tarsian worlds one after the other.

The Solar System Government decides to come to the aid of the Tarsians to protect the economy of both civilizations and to prevent being conquered by the Gulax in the future. At first, the humans and the Tarsians succeed in repelling the Gulax. But the Gulax eventually strike back and retake even more territory. Now, in the year 2834 the War has been going on for thirty years, and the alliance is losing to the Gulax.

Alexei Rogeston, a possible relative of Kelem Rogeston, is a career officer in the human military forces. He and other members of the military uncover a plot to bring an end of the war in favor of the Gulax. Some of the conspirators appear to be human and Tarsian.

Alexei becomes the target of assassination when the conspirators find out that he's learned of their plot. In his struggle to stay alive and save the alliance from defeat, he becomes involved with the beautiful and exotic Princess Kani, daughter of the King of Tarsia. Together, they fight against spies, betrayal and inter-species prejudice and discover the surprising origin of the Gulax and the hidden forces behind the plot to defeat the alliance.

The Gulax War, due out in 2013

About the Author

A resident of Los Angeles, California, Joseph M. Armillas is an author, actor and musician. Born in South America to show business parents and raised in the USA, Joseph has traveled extensively throughout the world and speaks three languages. In 1964, Joseph joined the US Army and served honorably until 1967. A science fiction fan since childhood, Joseph began writing short sci-fi stories while in grammar school. His love of the genre inspired him to write the Plantanimus Trilogy of which "Return to Mars" is the second book. He's currently working on "Reunion," the sequel to the trilogy.